For Dylan, Murray, and John,
with all my love

Prologue

Star Bluestone had talked to bees all her life. She talked to her flowers too, murmuring to the rare yellow poppies she'd nurtured from seeds gathered in the old Italianate garden thirty miles away across the Wicklow hills. She and the young Kiwi gardener there had such great chats, he walking her through the orchard and reaching up to cradle a baby apple bud the way another man might touch a woman.

He understood that people who loved the soil talked to their plants and to the bees whose careful industry made their flowers bloom. Even though he was only thirty to Star's sixty years, he didn't think she was an eccentric old lady. Rather, he was impressed by Star's encyclopedic knowledge of plant life. His earnest, handsome face became animated when they talked.

When she watched this kind boy, Star always remembered fondly that good gardeners make good lovers. Nobody capable of the tenderness required to separate delicate fronds of fern for replanting would ever be heavy-handed with another person's body.

It had been a few years since Star had lain in a man's arms. She'd had many lovers, but the one she would remember for the rest of her life, the one whose memory was imprinted upon her skin, hadn't been a gardener. He'd been a poet, although that wasn't how most people knew him. To the world, he'd been a conventional man, handsome, certainly, with beautiful manners and an important job waiting for him. To her, he'd been the man who sat with her under the stars and recited poetry as he traced his fingers along her face and talked about their future.

That had been more than thirty-five years ago. Star had talked to flowers and her beloved bees in their white hives back then, too.

When she was growing up, her school friends hadn't understood why Star did this, but they didn't question it. After all, Star was different in most things. So was her mother. Her friends' mothers didn't grow herbs with such skill or know how to brew potions of feverfew and chamomile to soothe menstrual cramps, nor did they stand gazing up at the midsummer moon.

Eliza Bluestone did, and that it picked her out from all the other mothers in the small town of Ardagh south of Dublin was both a blessing and a curse to Star. The blessing was the knowledge her mother gave her. The curse was that knowing so much separated her from all her friends.

Eliza mightn't have *told* her daughter all the wisdom in her huge, midnight-dark eyes, but that knowledge somehow transferred itself to Star anyhow.

When she was a lithe young girl of twenty and wanted to dance with her friends and flirt with young men, being wise was an impediment. She just *knew* that few people would be lucky enough to meet their soul mates in a pub ten miles from home. Finding the right man to be her husband was going to be hard because the Bluestone family—which meant Star and her mother—was hardly conventional, and it would take a strong man to love them. In the same way, she knew that her friends would not all have the joy and happiness they expected in their lives, because not everybody could. It was obvious. To imagine anything else was folly.

Though Star, like her mother, couldn't actually predict what would happen in the world, she had enough wisdom to understand the rules of the universe. While her friends threw themselves blindly into everything and were surprised when the men they'd met at the club hadn't called, or shocked that other people could be bitchy, Star was never surprised by anything.

As she grew older, Star's ability with her flowers and her garden grew. Talking to her plants wasn't the whole trick; caring for them with reverence was, and Star did that, plucking weeds from around the orange-petaled Fire Dragon so it could breathe again, moving the old red currant bush away from the dry soil beside the shed, pausing occasionally in her labors to listen. For

Star loved music. She never grew tired of hearing the distant singing of the church choir, even though she had never set foot in the building—another thing that set her apart from her friends. Star's church was the trees and the mountains and the mighty roar of the sea. And although she loved church music, she loved the music of nature better. The song of the bees was, her mother had taught her, the earth's song. Melodic and magnetic, with the bees moving to some ancient dance they'd moved to long before man came calling. And was there anything more uplifting than the sound of pigeons under the eaves, skittering about and squabbling as they sheltered from the rain?

It was raining now. As Star lay in bed, she could hear the raindrops bouncing off the windowpanes. As usual, she had woken at 6 a.m.; in summer, she would have risen immediately to make the most of the golden sunrise, but on this cold February morning, dawn was at least two hours away—and it promised to be a murky one.

Danu and Bridget, her two cats, stretched on the bed beside her, making their morning noises. Bridget was a showy white ball of fluff, her magnificent fur requiring lots of brushing. Danu, the smaller of the two, was a rescued tabby who'd been given to Star the year before, the moment exactly right because Moppy, Bridget's sister, had just died. Life had an odd way of doing that, Star knew: giving you what you needed when you needed it. Not *wanted*—your want didn't come into it. Want and need were very different things.

Star lay in bed for a while, stroking the two cats and staring out her window at the dark shapes of the trees and shrubs in her garden. She could see the red maple tree she'd planted when she was twenty and lost in love.

"Plant something to remind you of this," her mother had said, and Star had been surprised.

"I'll always remember," she'd said simply.

Everyone said she was at the peak of her beauty then, lush like her mother's precious peonies, full-lipped, and with hair of spun gold—the Bluestone women always had golden hair, no matter

what their fathers looked like—that fell about her slender waist.
She'd secretly picked out her wedding dress with her best friend,
Trish, and she knew that Danny and she would be so happy if
they rented the house on the hill road. From there they could see
the town and the sea, and he could be at his father's garage, where
he was one of the mechanics, in five minutes.

Still, she had liked the idea of a tree for them both and planted
the red maple.

But, "I'm too young to settle down," Danny had told her not
long after the tree was planted, when its roots had barely had time
to unfurl into the earth and Star was still patting it each morning
with joy at all it represented.

"That's not what you said before," Star replied, knowing in a
painful instant that the wedding dress, a jewel she'd mistakenly
thought was meant for her, would remain on the rack in Brenda's
Boutique.

"It's my mother," Danny said reluctantly. "It's about the business, too. She said—"

"She said you need a better wife if you want to expand the
garage. She said she didn't want you marrying one of those athe-
ist Bluestone women with their strange herbs and their unnatural
hair."

Star wasn't bitter toward Danny. It wasn't his fault. She should
have known that he wasn't strong enough to withstand the tide
of public opinion. Even in the midseventies, when the rest of the
Western world seemed to be enjoying free love and the pill, the
more conservative parts of Ardagh ate fish on Fridays, blessed
themselves when they passed the church, and looked askance at
the Bluestones.

Old Father Hely, the parish priest, and Sister Anne, head-
mistress of the Immaculate Mother of God Convent, had both
been remarkably understanding about Eliza's preference that her
daughter not practice the Catholic traditions. Learn them, yes.
Eliza was all for learning and tolerance. She was fascinated by all
religions: Catholicism, Protestantism, Hinduism, Buddhism, everything out there. But not practice them. Eliza saw the central truth

in the world around her, a world that had been there longer than any man-made religion.

"We'll take care of Star in school," Sister Anne said firmly. "You might not come to our church, but you understand Christianity, Eliza. I know how kind you are to those who need it. There are plenty here in town who trot along to Mass every day and still don't love their neighbor," she added grimly.

"Indeed, you're right, Sister Anne. Nobody in this parish will ever hear me say a word against you, Eliza," agreed Father Hely, who'd studied too much Christian history, from the Crusades to the Inquisition, to be doctrinaire when it came to unusual Eliza Bluestone with her earthy wisdom and her homemade elderflower wine.

However, not everyone in Ardagh agreed with Father Hely and Sister Anne, and many of the people who went to Sunday Mass and hung holy-water fonts inside their front doors disliked the Bluestones because they were different. Clearly, Danny's mother fell into this category. Star hadn't realized before quite how strong this dislike was. She herself didn't care what or whom anyone worshipped and was astonished that other people could object to her views.

"You'll always have your tree," Eliza told Star the night Danny broke the news there would be no wedding. Mother and daughter sat in the hand-hewn walnut love seat in their garden overlooking the sea and sipped rose-hip tea.

Star gazed gloomily at the tree. And then looked around at all the other trees on the five-acre plot. The house, a higgledy-piggledy concoction of white clapboard with slanting roofs and an oriel window, was surrounded by trees: smooth-skinned, tall ashes, swooping willows, a graceful plane tree, a crowd of copper beeches by the vegetable garden, and another sharp-leafed maple that turned bloodred in the autumn.

"We have lots of trees," she said, suddenly understanding. She got up to touch the other maple. "You once said this was my dad's tree?"

Star's father had been the sort of man who preferred traveling to settling down. India was his favorite place in the whole world, especially the beaches of Goa, where a man could lie in the sun and not have to think about anything except what the human race was *for* and other philosophical questions.

"I loved your father," Eliza said.

"But he left?"

"I planted the tree when we were in love," Eliza answered.

"Then he left." Star got it. "What about the other trees?" she asked, wondering how they'd never discussed this before. But then, her mother was a gentle and slow teacher: the lesson came when the lesson came; it would never be forced.

"Two more I planted, both before you were born, before I met your father."

Three loves.

"And all these other trees?" Star gestured.

"My mother's, her mother's—all the Bluestone women have planted trees for as long as we've lived here."

Star laughed then and ran around the garden, touching the bark of each of the precious trees. She loved this link with her female ancestors. It was like holding hands with all of them, listening to them laugh and talk, strong women who'd seen so much.

The trees, plants, and flowers of her wild garden that gave such comfort to Star eventually provided the raw material for her livelihood. She designed and made tapestries embroidered and appliquéd with wools and silks hand colored from natural dyes. Star's eye for nature meant her pictures were landscapes of hills and woodland glades, sometimes with a brightly plumaged bird peering out from the undergrowth, or a blossoming creamy magnolia positioned against a backdrop of verdant green, even the misty shape of a unicorn in the distance. For many years, she had sold her work in a tiny craft shop on the outskirts of Wicklow town and just about made a living out of it. Then someone had brought one of her tapestries to the attention of a buyer in Kenny's department store in Ardagh.

Kenny's was always on the lookout for new talent, the woman said, and Star's exquisite artisan works would complement the homes department perfectly. The store didn't deal in paintings—too complicated and time-consuming—but the Bluestone tapestries were exactly what they were looking for. Within six months, Star's tiny business had become a thriving cottage industry. That was five years ago. She had three employees now, and they'd been working flat-out to complete their latest order for Kenny's, which was where Star was bound that morning.

There were twenty hangings of all sizes ready in their moss green tissue paper. She was dying to see what Lena, the buyer and one of the store's directors, would think of her new departure, a large mermaid tapestry. Star hadn't worked on many sea pictures before: the pigments were hard to make. It was easy to mix up rich loden greens and dusty ochers, but the pure blues and aquas for marine scenes were more difficult. When she'd got into sea tapestries, she'd finally begun using handmade dyes bought from artisans, although she still used the heads of pure blue hydrangeas to make rich blues, and her blackberries summoned up an inky purple that spoke of the ocean depths. Star had been of two minds about selling the mermaid tapestry at all. It would have looked perfect on the wall in the kitchen, under the rail where the copper pots hung. But she'd hardened her heart and packed it up. The mermaid, with her foamy sea green eyes and skeins of pale hair, needed to be out spinning her magic on someone else's wall.

Star fed the cats, then made herself a breakfast of fruit and yogurt and brewed a cup of mint tea, which she drank in the tiny conservatory. Breakfast over, she dressed. Her toilette never took long: she would shower, brush hair that was still as blond as ever, albeit with many strands of white, and apply a little kohl around her dark eyes. It was an unusual combination: pale hair, olive skin, and dark eyes. Her old friend Trish, whom she sometimes bumped into in the supermarket, had grown round and always wanted to know how Star remained as slim as ever.

"It's nothing I'm doing," Star would say. "My mother was the same, you remember."

Trish would nod, remembering. And Star could almost read Trish's next thought, which was that three children made a person put on weight, and Star, after all, had no children and no grand-children, and what was the point of being slim and sixty if you hadn't the pleasure of a family?

Star would have loved to have children, to feel a small, trust-ing hand in hers, to have a little girl of her own to sit with in the walnut love seat and teach to plant trees. But that hadn't been her path. She'd been given the gift of creating works of beauty, and the gift of making plants grow. Once, it might not have been enough. Now it was.

Besides, the women she'd helped in her life were almost like children to her. Star's talent for collecting lost souls had given her mothering instinct a powerful outlet.

She dressed with speed. Her clothes often matched the colors of the garden she loved: pastels in spring, warm rosy hues in sum-mer, golds when the leaves were turning in autumn, and the cool shades of a snowy landscape in winter. Today, it being February, she donned a cream woolen dress with a gray fitted coat and black high boots. She swept her hair off her face and fastened it in a low knot at the base of her neck. Her everyday uniform was very dif-ferent, a loose skirt or jeans and a T-shirt; but today she needed to appear the smart businesswoman.

Kenny's department store was an institution. The word had become a cliché, but Kenny's truly was one. Established in 1924, when Europe was recovering from the Great War and Ireland was emerging onto the world stage after the ravages of its own civil war, Kenny's became the local byword for style. It was the place where all were welcomed, the moneyed classes and those who hoped one day to belong to the moneyed classes. Old Mr. Kenny's dictum was that every customer was to be treated with courtesy, workingman and titled lady alike. Its combination of elegance and egalitarianism contributed to its success.

Over the years, so much of Ardagh had changed; entire streets had been transformed as old family businesses made way for chains and big conglomerates. The Classic Cinema, where Star and her friends had eaten popcorn and screamed their way through *Jaws*, was now a car park, and the Soda Pop, where they'd drunk cheap coffee and occasionally had enough money to indulge in the house specialty—a banana split—had been demolished to make way for a supermarket.

But Kenny's never changed. It had been updated, with plenty of money spent, but the place looked and felt essentially the same: a graceful old-style Edwardian shop front that took up an entire block, with glossy small-paned windows and swing doors ornamented with shiny brass fittings. A curlicued sign hung over every door: *Kenny's—Established 1924.*

Star left her car in the car park behind Kenny's, walked around to the delivery door at the back, and pressed the bell. It was more than an hour to opening and most of the staff wouldn't have arrived yet, but Lena had promised to be at the delivery door at eight. The door buzzed and Star pushed it open, pulling the small wheelie cart with its precious cargo of tapestries behind her. The place was dark and there was nobody visible, so Star wasn't sure who'd buzzed her in, but she walked in the direction of the back stairs to the offices, looking around for signs of life. The doors to the stairs were locked when she tried them. The only bit of light was coming from the double doors that led to the shop floor. Perhaps that's where Lena was.

Star pushed open the doors and breathed in the magical scent of Kenny's.

After the gloom of the delivery area, it was like entering a beautifully lit jewel box. In the distance, she could hear the faint drone of a vacuum cleaner. All the lights were on in the shop, and the scents of perfume mingled with the smell of furniture polish and a faint hint of warm pastries wafting down from the café upstairs. She left her cart against a wall and began to walk through this paradise, enjoying the sensation of being there all on her own.

Lena often chatted about the various departments. How David Kenny, the current owner, had said he wanted a very distinctive jewelry area, with unusual pieces from local craftspeople as well as the big brands. It was the same in the fashion department: there was a small section where young, just-out-of-college designers could display their clothes. The perfume and cosmetics halls, the most valuable space per-square-meter in any department store, were filled with all the usual brands, but pride of place went to Organic Belle, a line of skin products made entirely in a small village in West Cork.

"David has a great eye for the next big thing," Lena had confided. "Nobody had heard of Organic Belle when he brought it in two years ago; now it's big in Los Angeles and some famous hotel chain wants the line in all its spas. It's going to be huge. You should try the products. We've a lovely woman who works at the Organic Belle counters, Charlie Fallon. She could help you."

Star sensed that Lena thought she was the epitome of an eccentric artist, partly because she lived in such a remote spot, and partly because Star had said she rarely visited Kenny's. Lena, who lived and breathed the store and didn't see how anyone else could fail to adore the place, had been shocked.

"You mean, you don't shop there?"

"I was there twice last year," Star pointed out.

"But that was to see me," Lena said.

Consequently, she did her best to sell the notion of Kenny's to Star, highlighting bits she thought Star might like, which included anything vaguely natural.

Passing the Organic Belle counters, Star inhaled the subtle scent of the brand's best-selling balm, an instantly relaxing combination of lemongrass and lavender.

Star had seen Charlie, the woman Lena had spoken of, on one of her earlier visits. Although she didn't exactly resemble her mother, Star was pretty sure that Charlie was the younger daughter of Kitty Nelson, a stalwart of the feminist movement in the seventies and someone Star had known many years ago. It was the eyes, shaped ever so slightly like a cat's. But while Kitty's eyes had been feline in every respect, particularly when it came to men, Charlie's were soft and gentle. She would be a very different sort of woman from her feisty, femme-fatale mother, Star instinctively felt.

Beyond the Organic Belle counters lay the entrance to the food hall, and even though all the sweets and cookies were packed away, the lingering aroma of caramel and butter filled the air.

"I love the food hall," Lena had explained, determined to convert Star into a Kenny's fan. "We sell proper food there. David realized there was a vast market for ready-to-eat gourmet food, and since we've started selling the locally produced I Made It Myself, Honest line, sales have been enormous." People loved the food, Lena went on, simple produce expertly cooked with zero additives.

On her previous visits, Star had been into the homes department, which sold Irish pottery and glass. Star could never resist pottery, but she hadn't visited the lingerie department, despite Lena's enthusiasm for its biggest seller: a line designed by a former home-economics teacher from Dublin who was fed up with trying to find comfortable suck-it-all-in underwear for plus-size women.

"Fabulous idea," said Lena. "She made it all on her sewing machine, but when she went round the shops trying to get business, David was the only one to bite. And now look at it. We can't keep it on the shelves, and all the big stores in London want it too. What other man would see that there was a need for that?"

Star smiled. Lena would have died of embarrassment if she'd thought she was implying that slender Star needed control pants.

"And it's not as if he has any experience with a wife at home looking for control pants every time she needs to dress up," Lena went on. "He's married to Ingrid Fitzgerald, for heaven's sake—she has an incredible figure. So it's pure business sense on his part. You have to admire that, don't you?"

Star rarely watched television. She *had* one, but it was ancient and she really only turned it on for the news. Even so, she knew who Ingrid Fitzgerald was. In a world where many political television journalists were male, Ingrid stood out as the best of them all: highly intelligent, poised, and adept at getting answers to the hard questions. And beautiful, too. Not the fleeting type of beauty that came from fluffed-up hair and a carapace of makeup, but a real, deep-down kind—lovely bone structure, intelligent eyes, and an expressive, warm face.

And the thing was, Ingrid looked as if she was as lovely inside as she was out. Star had always been a very good judge of that. They were similar in age, too, although Ingrid might be younger, Star thought. In another world, they might have been friends. Ingrid had two children, grown-up now, and her daughter, Molly, shared a flat with a girl Star had known when she was just a baby. Natalie was twenty-three now; Star kept count.

Natalie had nearly been born in Star's house, and Star would never forget the frantic dash to the hospital with Des, while Dara lay on the backseat howling in pain. Star had been one of the first people to hold the tiny baby with the head of curly dark hair, and she'd felt what she always felt when she held a newborn—that they knew all the wisdom of the world.

Star had been part of Natalie's world for little more than three years before Dara had died. Star, like everyone else in Dara's circle of friends, had sworn to abide by Dara's rules about her little daughter.

"Let me go, don't try to hold on to the past," Dara had insisted, fearing that the memory of her dead mother would darken Natalie's future.

"She deserves to know who you are," Star had pleaded. "*Were,*" she amended sadly.

Dara had shaken her head fiercely. "It's better this way," she said. The past could destroy people, and she didn't want that for Natalie. What she wanted for her daughter was a new life with her father. "Des is wonderful; he'll bring her up so well. Perhaps he'll marry again, and they'll be much happier without me like a specter in the background."

And so everyone who loved Dara had promised her that they wouldn't be a part of little Natalie's world, telling her how like her mother she was or recounting tales of the days before she was born. Though Star had only known Dara a few years—since that rainy day she'd found her lying in utter despair on the coast road— she was one of the few people who'd heard the heartbreaking story of Dara's earlier life.

"The past hurts," said Dara, determined to spare her beloved daughter the pain.

"But knowing can bring about healing," Star replied. "One can transcend the misery—you have."

But Dara was firm. For Star, who lived by instinct, staying out of Natalie's life as she grew up had been one of the hardest vows she'd ever kept.

Her thoughts were interrupted by the sound of the double doors from the street swinging shut. A blast of icy February air whirled in, along with a man in a long gray overcoat, the collar turned up. He was tall and broad-shouldered, and he walked with speed, as if there wasn't enough time to do all he wanted in life.

From her position beside a display of jeweled pins and silk-flower hair clips, Star watched David Kenny pass through his department store. He didn't survey his surroundings the way she imagined he normally did, those clever eyes noting every detail and marking it down in his memory if something needed to be changed. His eyes were focused on something else entirely, something inward. The closer he got, the more she could see the tension in his face. His hair was graying, salt and pepper around the temples. *Distinguished*, Star thought; that was the word for it. He reached the stationary escalator in the center of the store and, instead of climbing up, showing how fit he undoubtedly was, he jabbed a red button. The escalator hummed to life, and he stood in perfect stillness as it bore him up to the next floor.

Star had heard that David Kenny, like his father before him, made a practice of walking through his beloved store every day, making sure all was well. All might have been well in the store this morning, but watching him now, Star was certain that all was not well with David Kenny.

Most people wouldn't have noticed. Only someone who knew him well could detect the strain on his carefully composed face. Once, she'd known David Kenny better than she'd known any other human being. Now the closest she got to him was when she reached out a hand in her garden and touched his tree, a rowan that had grown tall and strong in the thirty-five years since she'd planted it. She hadn't talked to him since then, though she was sure he was well aware that she was Bluestone tapestries. Lena's initial attempt to arrange an introduction had been gently brushed away, with Star explaining that she "didn't do corporate stuff."

"Oh, but David meets *everyone*," Lena had said.

"Not me," Star replied, smiling to show that she was happier that way. And she was grateful that David appeared to accept this, for he had made no attempt to meet her.

It wasn't that she was angry with David. No. It hadn't ended that way at all. It just wasn't meant to be for her and the passionate young poet who'd written verses to her beauty and made love to her as if he'd found his life's meaning when their bodies were together. No, she wasn't angry with him. Her life had worked out in its own way. Until now, she'd imagined David's had too.

But seeing how tense he looked, she wasn't so sure.

An old saying of her mother's came to mind: "What's meant for you will find you." Many people took that to mean good things, but Star was enough of a student of the universe to know that it could mean bad things too.

Whatever terrible sadness was touching David, Star hoped he was able to deal with it.

One

Be kind to other women. It really works—most of the time. And even on those days when it doesn't, it'll make you feel better inside.

That night, Ingrid sat at the beautifully laid dinner table in a grand old house with her husband, David, and eleven other elegantly dressed couples, and wished with all her heart that she weren't there. The scent of the freesias in the crystal bowl in the center of the table fought valiantly with the women's perfumes, which were predominantly musky with the odd note of sharp florals. Ingrid loved scent, but she hated the heavy, cloying perfumes so many women wore at night, as if they were using pheromones to attract cavemen rather than attending a civilized dinner party with their husbands.

She reached across the snowy white tablecloth and pulled the bowl closer, leaning forward to smell the pure, clean flowers. Instantly, she was transported to her terrace on a late spring day, where she would sit reveling in the seclusion as she read the morning papers. Pity she wasn't there now. *Stop,* she told herself. The evening wasn't going to grow magically shorter by wishing it was over.

The problem was that these people were David's friends. Odd how a couple could be married for thirty years and still have such disparate friends. They shared some, people they'd known all their married life, but their careers had brought them a collection of acquaintances from two completely different worlds.

Tonight was a night for David's people, in particular their host, the owner of a large transport company useful to Kenny's.

Three other businessmen whom David knew were also present: wealthy men with glamorous wives who had beautiful hair and nails and wore diamonds of every possible cut.

Looking around the table, Ingrid decided that the dinner party was entirely made up of successful men and their wives. There were no businesswomen; Ingrid could spot them from fifty paces, for no matter how successful they were, they were never quite as polished as the wives of alpha men. Years of interviewing the great and the good on *Politics Tonight* had taught her that it was rare for an alpha man to form a lasting relationship with a woman who had as much power as he did. People were probably amazed that she and David had stuck together; most men would have been uncomfortable sharing the limelight with a woman who made her living grilling politicians on live TV. But then, David wasn't most men. He was, Ingrid thought, smiling across the table at him, special.

He caught her eye and smiled back, and she thought how well he looked in his gray suit and pale pink shirt. She knew he was tired because of the lines around his eyes, but nobody else would pick up on that. They'd see the usual handsome, charming David Kenny, the man who'd inherited the family firm and taken it to a whole new level. In the same way, nobody looking at Ingrid would see a woman with a mild headache who didn't want to be here. They'd see what she wanted them to see: a woman who'd pulled out all the stops with hair and makeup, yet remained modest in the diamond department. Ingrid felt that knuckle-duster rings were like push-up bras: you either liked them or you didn't.

The only interesting thing about nights out schmoozing David's business acquaintances was that Ingrid ceased to be Ingrid Fitzgerald, the television personality who'd kept her maiden name from her days as a radio producer; she was Ingrid Kenny, David's wife. And sometimes, just sometimes, that made her deliciously invisible. Like now.

The man seated on her left turned to talk to her.

"You're Mrs. Kenny, aren't you?" he said. He was sixtysomething, balding, with a weathered complexion that spoke of many hours spent outdoors, probably on the sea, Ingrid decided. His outfit, a blue blazer with gold buttons, had a hint of Commodore of the Yacht Club about it.

"Yes," said Ingrid gently, sensing that he had no idea who she was professionally. "I'm Ingrid, David's wife."

"Marvelous business," the commodore said, grabbing his glass of red wine. "Kenny's—what a store. I don't suppose you have time to be involved yourself, do you? I know what you ladies are like; so many other things to do, charities, committees. . . ." He smiled at her benignly. "My wife, Elizabeth—that's her over there in the red—she's on four committees. I don't know where she finds the time."

Elizabeth was a steely-eyed brunette who was expertly made up and wore an exotic beaded creation. She was watching Ingrid and her husband with interest. Ingrid reckoned that Elizabeth recognized her from television and was just as sure that Elizabeth knew the poor old commodore wouldn't.

"Well, I am involved in some charities," Ingrid said to her neighbor. She was a patron of an AIDS charity, served on the board of a domestic abuse organization, and regularly hosted charity balls. "But I don't have that much time, because I work too."

"Oh, really," said her neighbor airily, as if the notion of a woman working were highly eccentric and would never catch on. "And what is it you do?"

It was moments like these that Ingrid stored up to tell her friend Marcella whenever Marcella claimed that everyone and their lawyer knew who Ingrid was.

"You've such a recognizable face," Marcella insisted.

"It doesn't work that way," Ingrid replied. "Famous is for film stars and singers, not people like me. People recognize me, they just don't know where from. They think they must have seen me in the supermarket or something."

The downside of her being on television was going into Marks and Spencer and nipping up to the underwear department to find several people watching her with fascination as she searched among the briefs, trying to find a five-pack of knickers that suited her.

Anyway, here was this sweet man who clearly had no idea who she was, and it was quite nice, although difficult to explain what she did without making herself sound bigheaded about it. Another woman in her position might have fixed him with a grim glare and told him she was one of the highest-paid broadcasters in the country and could make politicians whimper for their mummies. But Ingrid preferred a low-key approach.

"I work in television," she said simply.

"Oh, really! Interesting. My daughter worked in television for a while, researching stuff. It was a terrible job, awful pay, and, goodness, there was no hope of really climbing the ladder. Only a few seem to make it," he went on.

"Yes," echoed Ingrid, "only a few do seem to make it."

Ingrid thought of her years climbing the television ladder. It had been challenging at times, but she hadn't had to stiletto anyone in the groin to make it to the top—a fact that many people inter-viewing her these days for newspaper profiles found incredible.

"It must be so much tougher for a woman," they said, eager to hear about glass ceilings, male-dominated power structures, and male broadcasters bitching about her as they got subtly patted with MAC Face and Body in makeup.

"The media—this part of it, anyway—is one of the few areas where women can do well easily," Ingrid would explain. But no-body appeared to believe that her own calm self-confidence and native intelligence had made it work.

"What about you," she said politely to the commodore, "what do you do?"

It was all the encouragement the commodore needed. He was soon explaining the difference between a yacht and a boat, and Ingrid let her attention wander. Across the table, her husband seemed to be enjoying himself talking to a lovely woman who'd been introduced to her earlier as Laura.

She liked watching David. He was charming to everyone, not

in a false way but in a way that said he was interested in other people. His father had been the same, always ready to talk to everyone in the store, from the cleaners to the general manager.

Okay? David mouthed at her across the table.

Ingrid nodded imperceptibly. She was fine.

"Sorry you got stuck with Erskine," he said three hours later in the back of the taxi on their way home. He put his hand in hers and held it tightly as they both sat back after what had turned out to be an incredibly heavy meal. Double cream with everything. Ingrid's insides yearned for Pepto-Bismol.

"Oh, don't worry," Ingrid said. "He was quite nice really, but I'm now an expert on boats, and if I ever need to interview anyone on the subject, Erskine is the man I will ask."

David laughed. He had a great laugh, rich and deep, the sort that made everyone else want to join in. Out of the corner of her eye, Ingrid could see the taxi driver grin as well. They were undoubtedly the sort of customers the driver liked: polite, sedate, middle-aged people being picked up from one beautiful suburban house and whisked off to another, with no chance of anyone throwing up in the back of the cab or not having the money to pay him.

"Erskine probably didn't have a clue who you were, did he?" David asked perceptively.

"Not the foggiest," Ingrid said. "I may have left him with the impression that I made the tea in the television studios."

"Oh, you shouldn't have done that!" David laughed. "That's cruel. I bet his wife knew, all right. She's probably telling him the truth right now."

"No, it's not cruel," Ingrid said. "He was terribly sweet and everything, but you know, he does live on this planet, he should be interested in politics."

"I'm quite sure he is interested in politics, darling," David replied mildly, "but not everyone watches television."

It was an idea that Ingrid had heard many times before, but one that she could never quite grasp. She was of the opinion that people should know what was going on in the world, and television news and debate was an inherent part of that.

"I'd say old Erskine sits at home reading copies of *Yachting Man* and books about naval battles from three hundred years ago," said David. "Happy in his own world. And why not?"

Ingrid shrugged. She and David would never agree on this one. He was able to forgive people for not wanting to read four newspapers a day; she wasn't.

"You were lucky," she said, "sitting beside that gorgeous Laura person."

"She was a sweetheart," David said. "Although she did spend a fair proportion of the evening telling me about her daughter, who'd love to get some experience in the store and has lots of marvelous ideas for fashion design."

"God, no," groaned Ingrid, "not another one of those."

When she went to media parties, she was forever being cornered by people desperately pitching their CVs or their son's or daughter's CVs in the hope of breaking into television via a personal introduction from the powerful and famous Ingrid Fitzgerald. When David went to parties, people told him about sons and daughters who were clothes designers or who had created a line of pottery that Kenny's couldn't afford to be without.

"Did the girl sound okay?" Ingrid asked.

"She sounded very promising," David said. "I told Laura to send the CV to Stacey."

Stacey O'Shaughnessy was his executive assistant, a wonderfully kind person who ran his office life as expertly as Ingrid ran his home life.

"You're a terrible old softie, do you know that, David Kenny?" Ingrid said.

"Right back at you," he said. "You could have flattened poor old Erskine by telling him exactly who you were, but you didn't, did you?"

"No," Ingrid said. "I wouldn't be able to sleep at night if I was mean to the Erskines of this world, even though I disapprove of their ignorance."

"I'll tell that to the minister for defense," murmured David.

"Erskine is an old duffer who obviously inherited money and

never had to do more than put on an old school tie to get on in the world. The minister for defense is a highly paid public representative who should know better than to write character references for a man on trial for rape, just because the accused's parents happen to live in his constituency. There's a difference," Ingrid said. She could feel herself getting heated again, the way she had before the program in question. Ingrid never lost it on the show; then, she was coolness personified. She used her passion for her preparation, when she worked out how to phrase her questions in such a way so that her subject couldn't avoid answering.

"True. You were right to nail him," David said. "He deserved it."

"Yes, he did." Ingrid sighed, the flare of anger gone. At least David understood why she did what she did. She couldn't bear injustice. The idea that a government minister's character reference could hinder the conviction of a rapist incensed her. David knew her so well, he understood her crusading spirit.

"Just here is fine, beside those big gates," David said to the taxi driver.

They got out and Ingrid found her keys in her handbag while David paid the driver. She was delighted to be home on the early side. It wasn't even twelve yet. With luck, she'd be asleep before one and get up late the following morning; maybe the two of them could sit in the conservatory with some coffee, reading the Saturday papers. She had just keyed the security number into the side gate when David joined her.

"Lie-in tomorrow?" she asked as they walked up the path to the house.

"Sorry, afraid not," he said. "I have to go into the office for a couple of hours. I've an absolute ton of work on."

"Oh, David," she said, "you live in the bloody place." The words were out before she could stop them. Ingrid hated sounding whingey. Her own job could be all-consuming at times, and if anyone understood how work could claim a person, she did.

"Just for a few hours," he said, "all right? I'll be back by two, three at the latest."

"Okay," she said, and squeezed his hand. "Sunday morning lie-in?"

"Promise," he replied.

"I'm holding you to that. I have my needs, you know," she added in a teasing voice.

"I know all your needs, Ingrid Kenny," he said, "and wouldn't the public love to, too!" His voice trailed off mischievously.

The dogs greeted them as they opened the front door. While David went to switch off the alarm, Ingrid got down on her knees to pet them. "Hello, darlings," she said. "Sorry we were out, but we're back now."

Somewhere in the back of her mind was the awareness that David hadn't reacted as he normally did to her flirtatious reference to needs: instead of grabbing her by the hand and taking her upstairs to bed, he'd made a joke about it.

He was tired, she told herself. She was, too. She was so used to reading nuance into every sentence at work; it wasn't fair to do it to poor David.

The duty dinner done, the weekend stretched ahead of her. She had no work, no functions to attend, no charity events; it would be one long, glorious rest, and she was looking forward to it. Molly, their daughter, was coming for lunch on Sunday, which would be wonderful. If only Ethan were coming too. . . . Ingrid felt the magnetic pull of her laptop in the study. She could just nip in and see if Ethan had e-mailed her from Vietnam, which was where he and the gang were now. But if he hadn't e-mailed, that would make it four days since his last contact, and Ingrid found that after three days she went into a kind of slow panic if she hadn't heard anything. No, she'd go to bed. If he hadn't e-mailed, she wouldn't sleep for worrying. Though even if he hadn't e-mailed, it didn't mean anything bad had happened, did it?

Ingrid woke alone the following morning, starfished in their huge bed. Her hand reached over to David's pillow and found nothing. He must have gone to the store, she thought drowsily, and wriggled farther under the covers to doze again. The sheets felt warm; the bed was soft. She felt *in* the bed, her limbs a part of it. If she kept her eyes closed and allowed her mind to drift, she'd be asleep again.

After about five minutes, she knew that wasn't going to happen. Her mental database had started up. Ingrid often wished there were some system whereby she could plug a USB cable into her head and connect it directly to the computer, so that all the stuff that rattled around in her mind could be magically transferred to her laptop hard drive instead. She could compose entire e-mails in her head, write letters, draft speeches, work out exactly what she'd say to the opposition health spokesperson on the program that night, all while lying in bed at five o'clock in the morning. Some of her best work was done in that perfect predawn stillness. She'd once been asked to take part in a magazine feature about career women's hints for success. She'd said the normal stuff everyone else did about making lists and trying to be organized, doing grocery shopping online, catching up on phone calls on her phone headset in traffic. She *did* all those things—but she'd never mentioned the early-morning mental download. It sounded too manic, as if she was constantly switched on. But then, she was—her mind racing, scanning ideas, deleting them, speeding on to the next one. Like now.

Fighting it never worked. It was better to go with the flow. She needed to take the cream dress with the caramel beading on it to the dry cleaner, because she would need it for the Domestic Abuse Association's dinner at which she was the guest speaker on Thursday night. It was a good dress, always worked; it didn't matter whether she had put on a few pounds or not. Which reminded her, she hadn't been to the gym all week, and she needed two workouts and a swim to keep that awful middle-aged spread at bay. Ethan might have e-mailed. She sent a silent prayer that he had. Please, God, please keep him safe.

She had to reply to the latest batch of e-mails from people looking for a start in the TV industry. She loved helping people, but sometimes she got so many e-mails that it was impossible to deal with them all. She liked to answer those herself; they weren't something she could hand over to her personal assistant, Gloria. Gloria was wonderfully efficient—she handled Ingrid's diary and organized all the reams of research she needed for her job—but Ingrid preferred writing a lot of her letters herself. No journalist could let someone else write for her. Hell, that was another thing—she'd been asked to be a patron of a journalism course.

Ingrid had never attended a journalism course. She had come into the business by a rather circuitous route: after her politics degree, she got her start in radio, working behind the scenes as a researcher and then producing, before moving into television news and, from there, taking the totally unexpected giant leap into presenting. She approved of journalism courses and approved of helping people, but there really wasn't enough time. Her schedule was always hectic, too hectic for all the causes she wanted to support. And even though the children were grown up, she still needed to make time for her family.

Tomorrow, Molly was coming for Sunday dinner. As she lay in bed with her eyes closed, Ingrid smiled. Her darling daughter was the reason the beautiful cream dress needed a trip to the cleaners. Molly had borrowed it for a formal event two months before.

"Mom, I'm really sorry, I meant to get it dry-cleaned," she said, "only I knew I'd forget about it and it'd get left there, so I thought I better drop it back to you first and—"

"It's fine," Ingrid had interrupted. "Honestly."

And she meant it. Kind, wonderful Molly was twenty-three and hopeless at things like dry cleaning and having milk in the fridge, but she was a one-woman powerhouse when it came to campaigns to help other human beings. Molly's ethical work made Ingrid feel like a capitalist pig. Molly was involved in so many causes that it was a miracle she found time to do anything. By day, she was press officer for Fight Poverty, an organization that worked with disadvantaged children. At night and on weekends, she solicited donations for an animal shelter and donated her services to a charity that funded a small school in Kenya and hoped to fund two more. She cared about her carbon footprint, cycled everywhere, and owned two rescue cats. She didn't care much about ironing her clothes or eating food by its best-before date. Her mother was endlessly grateful that Molly lived with Natalie, her best friend and a person with organizational skills to rival Madonna's; otherwise Molly and the cats would all be in their respective hospitals with food poisoning.

If only Ethan, twenty-one and currently on a yearlong trip around the world with a group of friends, had one person in his entourage to match Natalie, then Ingrid would sleep so much better at night.

Ethan was usually quite good at e-mailing home, although most of the time his missives were frustratingly short.

Hi, Ma and Pa—Having a brilliant time, weather not great but the people are. Don't worry, we're all fine. Love Ethan.

Ingrid, who looked at everything in the paper and had the news on practically twenty-four hours a day, could hardly bear to look at any story about twentysomething world travelers anymore. When she came across stories about Vietnam and Thailand, she was terrified that she might see something that would spell impending disaster for Ethan. He was traveling with five friends, all big, strong lads, and clever too, but that didn't stop her worrying. At twenty-one, they were innocents abroad, a bunch of friendly Irishmen who thought the best of people and had a smile for anyone. All it would take was for them to turn up in the wrong place at the wrong time, and who knew what might happen. No matter how hard she had tried to teach her children a little of her own cynicism, it hadn't worked. Ingrid could imagine Ethan smilingly helping some sweet girl get on the plane, holding her rucksack to be kind—and he'd be the one caught with whatever drugs she was trying to smuggle. Nobody would believe Ingrid if she told them that her son didn't do drugs, that he was a good kid, that he'd clearly been duped. She'd be like every other mother who protested her son's innocence. And they'd say: "Of course she believes him, but we know he's guilty."

She couldn't bear it. She had to get up and stop thinking like this.

Even if David had been there, Ingrid wouldn't have told him about her anxiety. David simply didn't understand it.

"Ethan will be fine, you know," he'd say when she let herself go with a stream-of-consciousness rant about what could happen to six hopelessly naïve young guys. No, even worse, what was it David had said the last time?

"You have to let him go, Ingrid. He's an adult, not a little boy."

She felt the rip of rage again, the combination of anger and helplessness at knowing that she couldn't give her son a quick hug. That's all she wanted: to jump on a plane to see him, to touch him for five minutes; then she'd get back on the plane happy, because she'd know he was okay.

"I have let him go," she'd hissed at David. "But he's my son. I love him and he'll always be a part of me, so I'm frightened."

Then the analytical Ingrid Fitzgerald had taken over, the woman who had interviewed thousands of spin doctors and psychologists over the years, who knew how to skewer an interviewee but who never normally brought her interviewing skills home. "Letting go is not what I'm talking about," she said coolly. "You can let somebody go and still worry about them. I need to be able to share that with you, because if I can't . . . well, we shouldn't be together, should we?"

David had sat up straight then. He'd been lolling on the couch with an after-dinner brandy, idling through one of the many newspapers they had delivered to the house every morning. The sharpness of her words had hit him hard. Something flickered in his eyes: fear, Ingrid thought, and she was glad she'd hurt him, glad she'd given him a kick to remind him that he had to work at this relationship too. Then she'd done something she almost never did: she walked out of the room, because she didn't want to talk to him anymore. She loved David, absolutely. After thirty years of marriage, she still loved him, but she adored her kids. Children were the third point in the eternal love triangle. It was a pity David didn't understand that.

He'd apologized, and she'd forgiven him, almost. Ingrid didn't believe in nursing grievances or in letting old arguments take root, but it had been very hard to accept David's apology without screaming at him that he didn't understand her at all.

Molly and Ethan might be grown-ups, but they would always be her children, and when it came to protecting them she would kill with her bare hands, if it came to that.

She turned the shower off, wrapped herself in a towel, and faced herself in the mirror. She looked tired today, every one of her fifty-seven years. It took longer in the makeup chair at the studio now to make her look like Ingrid Fitzgerald, longer to make those shrewd gray eyes appear open and alert, especially with that drooping skin above her eyelids. She'd had her skin lasered to reduce fine lines, but the next step was an eye lift, something she was putting off. She'd seen too many women who were preternaturally young; and while photographic retouching could make surgery look good in photos of movie stars, in real life women could appear strangely wrong, as though their faces were denying the wisdom of the lines they'd earned. Only the best surgeons were able to make people look like themselves but better. Ingrid knew such a surgeon, but she was still scared. Regular Botox was an occupational imperative. She was fundamentally opposed to the very notion of it. But she was also a realist who liked her job. Youth had such power. She was lucky—and, yes, she knew there was some luck in there—that in current affairs, age was less important than in other television arenas. If her job had been presenting a chat show, she'd have been fired about the time she turned forty-three. But in her field, age and gravitas were valued among men *and* women. Yet who knew when that might change? Ingrid accepted that one day, her face would be judged too old for television. All it would take was some focus group led by a twenty-one-year-old hotshot pronouncing that young viewers switched off in droves at the sight of a postmenopausal woman, and that would be it. Ingrid Fitzgerald's television career would be summarily over, except for voice-overs on history compilations or an occasional documentary. She was far too shrewd not to know that one day this would happen.

Still, there was nobody here to see her or her wrinkles today. God knew when David would be back. Off with his mistress, she thought with a hint of bitterness: the store.

Down below, the dogs began to howl. They weren't allowed upstairs, but when they sensed someone was up and wasn't rushing down to play with them, they began to whine pitifully.

"Be down in a minute," roared Ingrid. It was nearly ten, so it had been a lie-in after all.

When she was ready, she hurried down and sat on the bottom step as the dogs nuzzled into her with frantic delight. "Don't pretend that David didn't let you out earlier, you little scamp," she said affectionately as Lucinda, a golden cocker spaniel, started her desperate-for-a-pee dance. Then Sybil, a black-and-white mutt they'd got from Molly's dog shelter, began to do the dance too.

Ingrid opened the kitchen's double doors into the garden, and both dogs barely made it out before they sank to their haunches in prolonged peeing sessions.

Ingrid stared, puzzled. They clearly hadn't been out. The only explanation was that David, up at the crack of dawn, had left without going into the kitchen for breakfast and the dogs hadn't heard him. Occasionally, if Ingrid woke early, she found the dogs snoring peacefully in their baskets and had the pleasure of seeing them wake and sleepily wag their tails. They were both old and their hearing wasn't as good as it had once been, rendering them pretty hopeless as guard dogs.

What was David doing, racing off so early on a Saturday that he hadn't even had time for coffee or to let the dogs out?

A flutter of disquiet beat in her heart. True, he'd always been obsessed with the store, even more so in the past five years since the expansion.

"When you borrow that much money, you need to spend more time at work," David had told her in the months after the store reopened following its twelve-million-euro revamp, and he was there morning, noon, and night. "Nobody else can do it but me, Ingrid. I have to be there. You know that."

Ingrid, who normally felt a certain relief that David was the main shareholder of Kenny's because she knew of other family-run businesses where there were constant arguments over each mug bought out of petty cash, wished for the first time that he had brothers or sisters to help him.

Money wasn't the issue. She got a good salary: without a penny of David's money, they'd have been able to live comfortably. Ingrid had no desire for massive wealth. Lord only knew why, most of the people with vast sums of money seemed to double their problems with every year. For every rich person donating money to AIDS research, there were fifty more with kids who refused to work and wanted to do nothing more energetic every day than use cocaine and wrap their Lamborghinis around lampposts.

Who needed huge wealth? They didn't.

Surely they were at the point in their life when they could slow down a little, take more time off. She was doing less work these days; why couldn't David do the same?

With the same disquiet, Ingrid let the dogs back in, fed them their breakfast, and took out the coffee to make hers. She felt like phoning David and asking what was so bloody important that he'd had to rush off at dawn. But that type of conversation never worked. Being a skilled interviewer had taught her that there was never going to be a civil answer to a question couched in such terms.

"What do you mean, 'what was so bloody important' . . ." he'd respond, and they'd be off arguing.

No, far better to say nothing until later and then remark kindly that he must be tired after getting up so early, and that they could postpone their dinner out that night so he could go to bed early. And then he'd explain why he'd been up early, and they'd be having a conversation instead of a hostile interrogation. If there was a problem, he'd tell her then. And Ingrid had the strangest feeling in her gut that there *was* a problem.

She had breakfast watching satellite news, the dogs at her feet hoping for scraps of wholemeal toast and honey.

"I promise we'll go for a walk soon," she told them.

She normally loved Saturdays when she had no specific place to be; the luxury of knowing that her time was completely her own thrilled her. But today she felt unsettled and couldn't put her finger on exactly why. Keeping herself busy, that was the trick.

When she'd walked the dogs, she tidied the kitchen with her usual energy, then went into her small study to make a list of e-mails and letters she had to write. Nothing from Ethan. She did her best to calm the anxiety she felt at no word from him. She worked methodically for an hour, then powered down the computer, ran upstairs, and collected everything that needed to be dry-cleaned. Finding a jacket of David's, she sat down for a moment, thinking about him. Between him and Ethan, all she did was worry. No, she must be positive. Ethan was probably having the time of his life. And as for David . . . Marcella—that was it, she'd ring her best friend, Marcella.

She went down to the hall phone, the one with the programmed numbers on it, and brought up Marcella's.

It was an unlikely friendship—Ingrid Fitzgerald, whose interviewing technique exposed the inadequacies of the great and the good, and Marcella Schmidt, image guru, whose job was keeping those inadequacies from the public view. Marcella ran her own spin-doctoring company and taught politicians and captains of industry how to talk to the media. If a formerly babbling, foot-in-mouth minister showed up talking sense and wearing a decent suit instead of a shiny one, odds were he'd been given the Schmidt treatment. And if a big company boss found himself on an industry advisory panel that covered him with glory and made people forget that he'd been caught coming out of a lap-dancing club three sheets to the wind with his arms round two lithe dancers, he'd been Schmidted too. Marcella was brilliant at her job and she loved it. That was why the two women had hit it off, Ingrid knew: shared passion. So what if Ingrid's job was to find the cracks in the politicians Marcella had Teflon-coated? They worked in the same lions' den.

Ingrid knew that if she were photographed in flagrante in a hotel room with some glamorous captain of industry, Marcella would be the one she'd turn to. Not that such a thing would ever happen, but still. If shit ever hit Ingrid's fan, she'd speed-dial Marcella Schmidt.

"Hi, Marcella, it's Ingrid," she said now when her friend picked up the phone. "How's the luscious Ken Devlin?" It was their running joke. Latin-looking god Devlin was television's hottest young talk-show host and one of Marcella's big successes.

"Can't get enough of me." Marcella sighed as if she were worn out from his amorous attentions.

"Still?"

"Still. Wants to have wild sex with me into the middle of next week."

"Only next week? What about the week after?"

"He doesn't have the stamina for the week after," Marcella said with a grin in her voice. "Young men—can't keep up with older women. That would be an interesting opinion piece for the papers: 'When Your Sexual Peak and His Don't Match.'"

"Only if you want to be humiliated forever for being a forty-something woman writing about having sex with a younger man," said Ingrid. She realized that Marcella was kidding. "You know the rules. Male silver fox and younger woman? Totally acceptable, and man gets slapped on the back by all his envious friends. Female silver fox and young man? Collective 'yech,' and everyone thinks either she's paying him or he has an Oedipus complex."

"Pity," sighed Marcella. "I need an op-ed idea for the *Courier Mail*."

"Personal never works," Ingrid said. "You should know—you tell people that often enough. Anyway, when did you bonk a much younger man? How did that slip past my radar?"

"Nothing slips past your radar," Marcella retorted. "Oh, it was years ago. Technically, it probably doesn't count, since I was only thirty-seven and he was thirty-one, and the age issue only counts when you hit forty. Before forty, you have a permit to screw anything you like. After forty, it needs an act of parliament. Besides, it was before I knew you. Just after I divorced Harry."

The big difference in their lives was personal: Marcella had been married twice in her youth and divorced both times. The first husband was rarely mentioned, but she was still friends with her second. Harry was often around; he was funny, kind, handsome in a rumpled-professor sort of way. Ingrid adored him and was curious as to why he and her best friend had divorced, but because it had all happened before she'd met Marcella, it had never been discussed on a forensic level. Marcella merely talked about how she and Harry were too similar for comfortable living conditions. Clever, opinionated men who were used to being in control were great as friends but very annoying as actual husbands.

When Ingrid saw the two of them together at a party, arguing happily over everything from politics to the merits of the latest movies, she wondered if it would have been different if they'd had children. Kids rubbed off rough edges very quickly. But that had never happened. After Harry, a suitable settling-down man had never come along. Marcella had looked for him, that was for sure. She'd gone to parties, met men at friends' dinner parties, taken scuba-diving holidays with a lone-travelers group, trekked Peru and made fabulous friends with two men—a gay couple who ran a successful restaurant in Donegal. But the man of her dreams eluded her. Without him, there were no babies with Marcella's laughing dark eyes and sallow skin. At forty-nine, Marcella fitted so seamlessly into the role of aunt-by-proxy that nobody would ever guess she'd longed for her own children.

Occasionally, the subject came up. Like the time a journalist phoned Marcella with a blithe request for an interview for a piece called "Childless by Choice."

"Childless by choice?" Marcella had hissed that night as she sat in Ingrid's kitchen and sank a glass of Stellenbosch red, even though it was a weeknight. "Who is childless by choice? Very bloody few people, that's who. And if they are, good luck to them. Let *them* talk to journalists about their decision and how they prefer not to add to the world's population or how they know parenting's not for them and decided to be grown-up about it. Good luck to them." She was hoarse with anger. "But most of us aren't childless by choice. We're childless by mistake, childless by never finding the right bloody man, and if we do, he's putting off being a father till he's made his money and he's not interested now, honey, and *'let's just have fun! Have you thought about Capri for a holiday?'*"

"She's totally insensitive, that reporter," Ingrid said, trying to lessen the blow. "When we were doing the general election program, she did an interview with me and asked was it depressing at my age to work in an industry where women in their fifties were sidelined because their looks had disappeared."

David, who was cooking at the stove, exploded with laughter. "What did you tell her?" he asked his wife.

"I gave her my very intense interviewing stare," Ingrid replied with a grin, "and said it was sad that women were still judged on their appearance, and that the glory of being older and wiser was not worrying so much about the outward face but rather about the person inside."

Marcella looked up miserably from her glass of wine. "So you *didn't* tell her we spend ages discussing plastic surgery and that we'd be having face-lifts like a shot if only we weren't so photographed that people would instantly know we'd gone under the knife?"

David laughed uproariously again.

Ingrid joined in, then sighed. "I get so sad thinking that I have to have a face-lift," she said. "Botox is one thing." Her hand stroked her smooth forehead. "But a face-lift is so radical. Yes, I know I work in television, but it goes against all the things we believe in, Marcella: that women are brilliant and a few lines on your face shouldn't make you any less brilliant."

"I don't know what I believe in anymore." Marcella sighed. "I used to believe there was someone out there for me, and there isn't. Just me, my job, and people asking me how it feels to be a sour old spinster who's childless by choice."

"Believe in that wine," David said, refilling her glass.

"You're such a lovely man," Marcella said. "Why don't you have a brother for me, David? Why didn't I ever find someone as nice as you?"

Ingrid and David exchanged worried looks. Marcella didn't get down very often, but when she did, her emotional elevator went down to the basement at warp speed.

"I'm not as lovely as you think, Marcella," David said kindly. "I'd drive you mad, wouldn't I, Ingrid?"

"Stone mad," Ingrid had agreed.

Ingrid wondered now what Marcella would say if she blurted out her concerns about David, that he'd rushed off to work at first light on a Saturday morning leaving her with the feeling that something was wrong, that David was keeping something from her.

Marcella was lightning quick. "Is there trouble with the store?" she'd ask, which was exactly the question rippling through In-grid's mind. She decided not to mention her anxiety to her friend. If there was something wrong, David would tell her. It was dis-loyal to mention her fears before she had anything concrete to be worried about. Perhaps tonight they'd have a chance to talk.

"What are you up to today?" Marcella asked.

"I was about to ask you that," Ingrid replied lightly. "I'm here on my lonesome, as David has rushed off to Kenny's to make sure it doesn't all blow up in his absence."

"Men, huh?" Marcella laughed. "Can't live with them, can't run them over with a truck."

Ingrid relaxed. Her lightness had worked. Normally, Marcella was so attuned to people's tone of voice that she could gauge any-one's mental state from a five-second conversation.

"Do you want to have lunch with me?" Ingrid asked. "I keep hearing about this new brasserie in Dun Laoghaire near the pier. Want to try it?"

"Beside the fish place? Tonio's or Tomasio's or something? Count me in. Meet you in Dún Laoghaire at one?" Marcella said.

"Perfect."

Ingrid dropped off the dry cleaning and arrived at the restau-rant at exactly the same time as Marcella. Lunch was hugely en-joyable. They generally tried not to talk too much shop. It would have been wrong to discuss which client Marcella was working with because chances were, sooner or later, he or she would end up on one of the navy leather chairs on Ingrid's set with Ingrid as high inquisitor. They talked about politics, policy, and people.

It wasn't gossip, Marcella always pointed out. Gossip implied a certain nastiness, and there was never nastiness in their talks. They were interested in human nature, that was all. And they met every aspect of human nature in their work. In the middle of all the policy talks, business meetings, and sound bites were people who worked hard, got passionate about their jobs, made mistakes, made deals, fell in and out of love.

Marcella and Ingrid were fascinated by the people behind the public façades: who had to make a speech in the Dáil chamber after being up all night with a colicky baby but would never mention it, and who'd use every nugget from their personal life for their own gain while not really caring about their family at all. It was no surprise that they both loved *The West Wing*; but wonderfully, they also both loved Neil Diamond, dancing, and clothes.

Marcella had the knack of wearing layers well. Expensive layers. It never worked when they were cheap layers, Marcella explained, because two cheap T-shirts and a little top worn at the same time looked bulky on anybody. Only the flimsiest fine layers that cost the earth and looked as if they'd been boiled for years in a washing machine hung with the right sort of casual elegance.

Ingrid, who had a more formal style for television and was used to fitted suits for work and elegantly cut jeans and jackets for weekends, envied Marcella's exquisite wardrobe.

"It all looks like you just threw it on effortlessly, yet you look fabulous," she said in exasperation.

"Effortless is very hard," Marcella responded, looking down at her layered sleeveless tops, wrap top, and long, slender skirt in varying shades of silver gray. "And expensive. Have you any idea how much these little vest-top things cost? I could buy a Fendi handbag with the cash I spent on this outfit."

"That's obscenely expensive," said Ingrid, shocked.

Marcella laughed. "You sound just like Molly when she was going through her secondhand stage."

"She still is. Mind you, it's better than spending millions on clothes."

"You old lefty! You've only yourself to blame. You and David gave her a social conscience so she wouldn't be another spoiled-brat celebrity child. It's nice that she prefers to give money to developing countries rather than spend it on clothes."

"You're right," Ingrid said proudly. "There aren't many people as kind as Molly out there. Although I'd love her to come round to the idea that you can feed the world *and* wear nice things. Still, she borrowed a dress of mine for a wedding, so perhaps she's moving out of the all-secondhand stage."

"There must be a man on the scene."

"No." Ingrid was thoughtful. She rather wished there were. Not that she desired her daughter to be married off for any reasons of propriety, but she wanted to think Molly was happy being loved in the same way that Ingrid and David loved each other. Love and honest partnership with someone you cared for and respected: what a joy that was.

It would be Ingrid and David's thirty-year anniversary later that year, and they'd talked idly about a party and a cruise in the Indian Ocean. They were so lucky, Ingrid thought every time she heard of another marriage going belly-up. And luck was involved, no doubt about it. They worked at their marriage, for sure; but it had been luck that brought them together in the first place, two people so instantly compatible.

Lots of breakups came as no surprise to Ingrid. As a person wildly interested in human behavior, she couldn't be shocked when Laurence and Gillian, old friends of hers from college and married twenty-seven years, separated abruptly. The only surprise was that they'd stuck with each other for so long. Laurence was at his happiest sitting in his garden doing the crossword and planning, someday, to mow the lawn. Gillian played badminton competitively, worked full-time, and was never home.

She and David, on the other hand, were very different in many ways, but they complemented each other. She felt a rush of love for him and wished he'd confide in her about whatever was wrong. He might not understand the fierce, feral passion of a mother's love, but then, could any man? And she loved him with all her heart, no doubt about it.

When she got home at three o'clock, David was back and with a small gift: a tub of goose fat from Kenny's exquisite food hall.

"For me?" she asked in amusement, turning it over in her hands. "Am I supposed to rub myself in it?"

"It's for the potatoes tomorrow," David said, planting a kiss on her cheek. "I know, a tub of bath oil would be better, but Molly's coming for Sunday lunch and you know what she's like about roast spuds. This is a present for all of us, not just you. Although"—he was smiling—"you can rub yourself with it if you'd like to."

He seemed in such good humor that Ingrid knew she must have been entirely mistaken to worry about him earlier. She put her present down, grinning. Many women would have thrown the tub at him, but Ingrid had always been realistic about romance. David, despite working in a store overflowing with feminine gifts, had never been the sort of man who came home every week with perfume and flowers. And Ingrid could cope with that; if she wanted flowers, she bought them herself.

"There's nothing like goose fat for proper roast potatoes," he went on, opening the fridge and poking in it for a snack.

"Did you not have lunch?" Ingrid asked.

"I had brunch," he said from the depths of the fridge. "I woke up very early and thought I might as well go to work and get it over with, and then Stanley came in with a BLT and it smelled so good, we all had them. From O'Brien's Deli—the place is booming since they got that new cook."

Ingrid relaxed some more. She knew there was an explanation for his early start. She was right not to have said anything to Marcella.

"You must be tired, darling," she said. "We can skip dinner out tonight, if you want."

They'd planned on a pizza out, just the two of them in the place down the road.

"Well . . ." he said, looking a bit shamefaced. "We can't. Jim Fitzgibbon is over from London, he was on to me this morning, and I'd forgotten I'd promised him dinner next time, and he insists it was tonight we set it up for—"

"Dinner with Jim and Fiona?" Ingrid gulped. Fiona was a sweetheart, but Jim, one of David's oldest friends, was a property-obsessed bore.

"Not Fiona, no," said David reluctantly. "He and Fiona are going through a bad patch. It's someone else."

"Someone else? Are they getting divorced?"

"I think that might be in the cards. They've separated. He's very cut up about it. Sorry, love, I know it'll be a pain for you, but I can't let him down. You don't have to come if you don't want to. I can say you're not well or—"

"I'll come."

Solidarity was another vital ingredient in a marriage, Ingrid thought. Women's magazines from years ago used to go on about how romantic gestures were the be-all and end-all of a relationship, but Ingrid, recipient of a lovely tub of goose grease, knew there was a lot more to it than that. If David wanted to comfort his old friend about the breakdown of his marriage, she'd be there too. She made a mental note to contact Fiona on Monday. There were few things Ingrid hated more than people who cut off half of a couple after a split.

"Who's this woman he's bringing tonight?" she asked David in the car on the way to the restaurant in Dublin.

"Don't know," he said simply.

"You're hopeless," she said in exasperation. "That's the sort of thing I like to know."

"Ah, that's only people like you and Marcella," David replied, "people who are obsessed with the world's private business. The rest of us are quite happy to meander along."

"Are we obsessed?"

"Totally," he replied.

Ingrid was wary of what was waiting for them in the restaurant. Jim was bad enough with the lovely Fiona to offset his awfulness, but God alone knew what sort of woman he'd come up with now. Fiona dated back to the time before he had loads of money.

Ingrid loved eating out. She always reckoned that the people who ran restaurants were the people who really knew what was happening in a city. Renaldo's was one of the country's premier spots, with a Michelin star to its name and a twenty-year reputation for fabulous food and wonderful service.

But tonight she wasn't in the mood. Two nights with people she didn't know was two nights too many. At least Molly was coming to lunch the next day, something to keep her sane.

The dinner was interminable. Jim, florid in a red striped shirt and cream jacket, was in show-off mode, and Ingrid didn't know whether he was showing off to his new amour or just showing off in general.

He was back in Dublin for the opening of an apartment complex, and within the first ten minutes the entire restaurant must have heard how they'd "cleaned up, totally cleaned up. Cost us fifteen million yoyos, and now we're on the pig's back. Sold fifty apartments off the plans. On the pig's back, David, I tell you! Yeah, waiter! We're ready to order the wine. Let's have some of that Cloudy Bay, the '99, I think, and a bottle of Dom Perignon to start. That'll get the party going!"

Jim's new woman was a showy brunette named Carmel, an unusually normal name for someone who looked as if she'd prefer to be called something exotic like Kiki or Scheherazade. Carmel was in her late thirties, had clearly been Botoxed and Restylaned to within an inch of her life if her relentlessly smooth forehead and big lips were anything to go by, and was heavily spray-tanned from the roots of her sculpted dark hair down to her pedicured designer-sandal-clad feet. She wore vinyl-red lip gloss and a very expensive dress, and spoke in a faux low voice about herself all night.

"I'd love to work in television," she said.

Ingrid tried to smile. Those words had been the death knell for many an evening.

"I'm very intuitive, you see," insisted Carmel, and then embarked on a monologue that showed her to be far too fascinated by herself to ask even a single question about anyone else.

Ingrid, who was forever finding herself seated alongside dinner guests with narcissistic tendencies, zoned out and merely nodded or murmured yes from time to time. Experience had taught her that it was fatal to attempt any real conversation. People who liked talking about themselves never had any. Easier by far to smile and acquiesce.

Carmel also made several trips to the ladies' and returned slightly more animated each time, which convinced Ingrid that her other interest—apart from newly separated millionaires and being intuitive—was cocaine.

Hell wasn't other people; it was coked-up other people.

By eleven, they'd just finished the cheese and Jim was waving his arm to urge the waiter with the liqueurs trolley to take another turn in their direction. Ingrid thought she might get up and stab Jim with her knife. Or even a spoon. It would be possible, she was sure, if she used enough force. She looked longingly at her husband, but he was avoiding her anguished gaze.

What was wrong with David? He'd been talking in a low voice to Jim all night. Even though he knew she was being bored rigid by Carmel, he hadn't tried to include the two women in their conversation or even to drop the "we can't stay late because we have to go home and let the dogs out" excuse.

Ingrid tried to kick him under the table, since she was too far away to grab him with a clawed hand and scratch "help" on his thigh. But she couldn't reach to kick. She glared at him. He knew her signals by now.

"Another cognac, David? Ah, you will. Sure, it's Sunday tomorrow. You don't have to get up or anything. Herself can bring you the breakfast in bed." This was accompanied by a nudge and a wink.

Ingrid folded her napkin and put it firmly on the table. "Jim, Carmel, what a lovely evening," she said crisply, reaching down for her small clutch bag. "But we'll have to pass on another drink.

I'm exhausted, and I know David is too. Thank you so much." She got to her feet, slipped her wrap from the back of the chair, and put it round her shoulders.

Jim and Carmel stared up at her, but David, who'd seen Ingrid utilize her emergency departure trick before, merely smiled and got to his feet. Action was important, a legendary Irish actress had once told Ingrid.

"If they're bores, they're going to want to continue to be bores, and no matter how much champagne you drink, that won't improve. Get up gracefully, move back from your chair, gather your things, and say good-bye firmly. There's no way back from that."

"Might they not think you're rude?" Ingrid wondered.

"You do it with style and speed," the actress went on. "Imbue yourself with the glamour and power you've worked for, my dear. You're a star and, though you might not like to turn it on, you can when you need it. Flick that switch, become the TV star, and state that it's time for you to go. Never fails."

It didn't fail now either.

Jim blustered a little bit. "You don't have to go yet—"

"Thank you for a lovely evening," Ingrid repeated. Really, there were things in her fridge that were smarter than Jim.

"Good night, Carmel." Ingrid held out her hand. She couldn't face the hypocrisy of kissing this woman good-bye.

They didn't speak in the taxi on the way home. If David had wanted to ensure that they didn't have any civil conversation that night, he'd done a good job, Ingrid thought as she lay in bed, too annoyed by the whole evening to sleep.

He was dozing already, and Ingrid sighed and picked up her book.

Ingrid enjoyed Sundays; they were family days, and she prided herself on cooking Sunday lunch. She liked cooking. Nothing fussy, just good simple food with no pretensions. Everyone had their favorites. Molly adored grilled fish, salad, and roast potatoes followed by Ingrid's homemade caramel meringue. Ethan loved roast beef with Yorkshire pudding and something sinful in the chocolate department for dessert. David's favorite was garlicky chicken with stuffing and smelly cheese to follow.

Ingrid's own favorite was nothing to do with food: it was having them all there.

Today, she had the radio set to her favorite Sunday news chat show; the double doors into the garden were ajar to let a little air in, and the dogs were arranged bonelessly on the tiled floor, worn out after a fast four-mile walk. Ingrid had woken early again and found she couldn't sleep, except this time David was fast asleep beside her, looking gray with tiredness. She'd slipped out of bed quietly and taken the dogs out for their walk before buying the papers and sitting down to read them with a pot of coffee beside her. He'd finally emerged at nearly one, unshaven and unshowered.

"Coffee?" Ingrid had asked. It was unlike him to sleep so late, and now he looked wretched. "You look terrible, David," she added. "Didn't you sleep?"

"No," he said, and it was almost a growl of exhaustion. "I'm overtired." He sank into one of the kitchen chairs.

"You don't have any pain in your arm or anything?" she asked, trying to stay calm but feeling terrified because he looked so unwell. He could be having a heart attack and he mightn't know it. It would be just like him to sit there and say, "Yes, darling, phone for an ambulance if you have a moment."

"Don't fuss, Ingrid," he said sharply. "I'm fine, really. I've a pain in my head, not my arm, and coffee would be great. Please," he added after a pause.

She nodded, feeling weak with shock. And then anger. There was no need to speak to her like that. She'd only been asking—

"Surprise!" said a voice.

"Molly!"

Their daughter stood in the kitchen, arms full of bags. "You're all getting deaf," she said, putting down her stuff and then petting the dogs. "I yelled hello when I came in."

Ingrid shot her daughter a look that Molly could interpret easily after twenty-three years. It was the "don't bother your dad" look.

Molly nodded imperceptibly and hugged her father gently. Ingrid could see his face relax.

"How are you, pumpkin?"

"Fine, Dad." Molly planted a kiss on his forehead. "Late night?"

"A bit," David admitted ruefully. "Jim Fitzgibbon was pouring wine into me."

Molly chuckled, and left her father to give her mother a hello kiss. "Since when has anyone had to pour wine into you, Dad?" she teased, and just like that, the tension went out of the room.

"Are you calling me a boozer, you brat?"

Both women laughed.

"If the cap fits . . ." said Molly. "Only kidding. Where were you, anyway?"

"Renaldo's," said Ingrid, getting out another cup for her daughter. She poured more coffee and sat down at the table beside her family.

"How's Fiona?" asked Molly.

"That's the problem." Ingrid sighed. "Jim and Fiona have split up, so we had to meet his new woman. I don't think she was your cup of tea either, love?"

Ingrid smiled at her husband, a peacemaking smile to say she was sorry she'd been so angry about having to endure the evening, and could he be sorry for being such a grouch?

"No," David agreed. "Sorry about that. On the phone, Jim made her sound like a cross between Mother Teresa and Angelina Jolie."

Molly's eyes widened. "And was she?"

David's smile to Ingrid reached his eyes. "Not really. She looked fine—"

"—a bit obvious," Ingrid interrupted. "A spray-on Gucci mini-dress and pole-dancing sandals isn't exactly the right outfit for a first-time dinner with your new partner's oldest friend."

"It was the conversation that was the problem," David went on. "She wants to be in television."

"You were listening?"

He grinned. "Sorry, I know you thought I wasn't rescuing you. Despite all his boasting, Jim's business is in trouble, and he wanted to bend my ear about it. I couldn't interrupt him, but I heard the bit about television."

"One of those." Molly groaned.

"How's Natalie? When's Lizzie's wedding?"

"The fourteenth. Apparently Lizzie's always had a thing about being married on Valentine's Day. The hen night's next weekend, and the flat's full of mad stuff, pink fluffy ears and things."

Ingrid smiled. Her pre-wedding party had been a very sedate affair compared to the ones girls had now. "Are you going to the hen night?"

"Not so far. Natalie wants me to, but I'm trying to get out of it. Lizzie's great, but I'm not one of her longtime friends and everyone else at the hen night is. She's known them for years."

Ingrid nodded, but she felt the catch in her throat she so often felt about her older child. Molly had always been shy, although she hid it well enough. She was friendly and charming, well brought up enough to be polite, so few people realized how shy she was. She'd never been one of those children comfortable in the middle of a group; for the first year of school, she'd cried every single morning when Ingrid left her.

"Oh, hen parties are all a bit mad now," Ingrid said nonchalantly. "It'll probably be wild," she added, wishing that, for once, Molly would want to join in. Ingrid knew that you couldn't make a person behave in a certain way, but how could two such outgoing people as herself and David have a daughter who was the opposite?

At school, there had never been any special friend, never any one little girl Molly adored and brought home to play. Molly was at her happiest in her own company, reading or talking to the pets—back then, the family had a mad collie with one ear and a minxy cat who collected small cuddly toys and brought them into Molly's bed at night.

Molly loved to curl up on her bed and read, with one or both of the animals snuggled beside her. Accepting that her daughter was a solitary little person had been one of the toughest lessons Ingrid had ever had to learn.

Ingrid was thrilled that her darling Molly shared a flat with Natalie. They'd met at college and, for the first time in her life, Molly had found a close friend.

Both were serious in their own ways: Molly with her charity work, and Natalie with her absolute dedication to jewelry design. Natalie had put herself through college and was working part-time in the café in Kenny's to raise funds to set up her own business. She had lots of drive and ambition, yet there was a vulnerable side to her, Ingrid felt.

Trust Molly to have held out until she found a friend with integrity.

When Molly had gone, Ingrid walked around tidying up. She loved their house. Guests were surprised to see that it was the antithesis of Kenny's Edwardian charm. Instead, Ingrid and David's home was coolly modern, with large open-plan spaces and swaths of pale wall. The floors were bleached wood, except in the kitchen, where the restaurant-style stainless steel was offset by polished poured-concrete slabs. Ingrid's love of white was reflected in couches and chairs upholstered in warm white loose covers, with color coming from the artwork on the walls, including many works by the emerging artists whom David loved to support. The large burst of color in the hall came from a giant tapestry from Kenny's, one of the unusual Bluestone tapestries. It depicted a wooden house nestled in a glade of trees, all of which was partly obscured by banks of peonies in the foreground.

The nine o'clock news began, and David was already yawning. Ingrid watched him affectionately and thought of the joke when they were younger about being "in bed before the news." Of course, back then they went to bed to make love. These days, that happened somewhat less. Tiredness, Ingrid knew, was a major reason. And although it was a subject they were careful to talk about, it took longer for both of them to get in the mood than it had when they were younger. The wham-bam-thank-you-ma'am days were over. Ingrid had never liked speedy sex anyway, even though it was flattering to think that David couldn't wait for her, needed to be inside her. But she rarely orgasmed that way: she needed time and gentleness, and now their lovemaking took time. It suited her, working up to heat instead of exploding into a fireball straight off.

"Let's go to bed," she said softly.

David looked up from the news, his clever gray eyes intense as they stared at her. Unreadable, she would have said, had it been anyone else. But she knew him and all his moods. She could see desire there.

He flicked off the television with the remote control, stretched long legs out slowly, then got to his feet. He held out his hand. "Come on," he said.

Their bedroom was one of the few carpeted rooms in the house, and as soon as they reached it, Ingrid took off her shoes and let her bare feet luxuriate in the soft wool. She switched on the lamps, letting light warm the room, creating a burnished glow on the expanse of bed covered by a king-size silk throw in muted jade.

"Are you too tired?" she asked David as she sat on the edge of the bed and began unbuttoning her crisp white shirt.

He shook his head, then joined her.

Ingrid hadn't been a virgin when she'd met David. She'd had three lovers, which, she knew, was quite average. He'd had more, and they'd promised never to become jealous of people long gone in the way some couples did.

All Ingrid knew was that her other lovers had never been able to make her feel as if this was the only way to make love, as if now was the most perfect moment. She had no idea how many times they'd gone to bed together over the course of their marriage, but as soon as David's hand wound its way around and pulled her closer so he could kiss her, she felt that familiar stirring inside.

Tonight, there was an urgency in his kisses, and he cradled her skull in both hands as their mouths merged. When he gently pulled her shirt away from her body and curved his fingers over her breasts, it was as if he'd never done it before. Ingrid let herself melt into this fresh passion. This was his apology, she knew. He was saying sorry for his distance in the only way he could: by making love to her.

When he finally entered her, his familiar face above hers, Ingrid felt a surge of pure happiness. This was love, she thought, raising her head to nuzzle his shoulder. Sharing everything with another human being. She knew his body as well as she knew her own, knew when he was close to orgasm, knew that if she concentrated on the fierce heat and if his fingers reached into her wetness, she'd explode at the same time he did. And then it came: fireworks inside her, a single explosion searing into thousands of exquisite ripples that made her cry out.

He fell onto his side of the bed with a groan afterward, and Ingrid kept the contact between them by stretching one bare leg over his. She lay there quietly and happily, listening to his breathing slow until she was sure he was asleep.

"Good night, darling David," she murmured, kissing him.

In reply, he muttered something she didn't quite hear.

With one last gentle pat, she drew the sheet up around his waist, then got out of bed to go through her nighttime routine. Cleanse, moisturize, brush teeth. As she stood in the bathroom and carefully creamed her skin with body lotion, she reflected again on how no cosmetic could make a person feel beautiful in the way being loved did.

Two

Be true to yourself. Sounds mad, doesn't it? I mean, what's true? But you'll know when you get there, trust me on this.

The following Saturday night, Natalie Flynn sat on a bar-stool in Club Laguna, letting the music and noise flow around her, and thought idly of her word for the day. *Lodestone.* A person or a thing regarded as a focus. *Lodestone.* Natalie rolled it around in her mouth. She looked up a new word in her dictionary every day. People with dyslexia were liable to have diminished vocabularies, and Natalie knew she was one of them, so she'd bought a dictionary when she left school. Each day, she closed her eyes, opened to a page, and pointed.

When she was a kid, a boy in her school named Ben had dys-praxia. Natalie asked him what it meant.

"I fall over things. Clumsy, they say."

"You're not clumsy, you're just a big person and the world is too small for you," she'd said. Ben was massive, with hands like giant hams. "They said *I* was stupid. Not my family, other people did. And it turned out I'm not; I'm dyslexic, that's all."

"All the *dy-* words are bad," Ben said gloomily. At the time, they were sitting outside Miss Evans's room. Miss Evans taught special education classes. People who didn't have to go to special ed made hunchback of Notre Dame faces and mouthed "special" as if they had speech defects at people who did. Ben and Natalie were used to it. Natalie sometimes stuck her tongue out at the people involved, but not all the time.

She'd finally worked out that the people who teased about special education were the very ones in need of it themselves.

Ben and Natalie considered the *dys-* words.

Dyspraxia—called "clumsiness" by stupid people.

Dyslexia—"word blindness" was how Natalie liked to describe it.

"Dysfunctional," added Joanne, who was in her final year in school, and who went to special ed because she kept missing classes. Joanne's father was unreliable, which Natalie realized was some sort of adult code for "crazy." During his unreliable periods, Joanne didn't turn up for school much, which meant she would not be doing her Leaving Certificate exams with everyone else in her class.

Natalie sometimes wondered what Joanne was doing now. Joanne had seemed so grown-up then, yet she was only four years older than Natalie. She'd be twenty-seven now.

Yesterday's word had been *opaque.* Natalie had loved that. It was a word you could touch. Back on her father's farm in the small shed that she used as a studio, she had sifted the semiprecious stones through her fingers, working out which ones were opaque. Some tiger's-eye, lots of the misty, smoky quartzes. *Lodestone* was a good word, too. She wondered how she'd never heard it before. That's what she did as a jeweler: work with metals and stones to make talismans that hung around people's necks or on their wrists, stones that meant something to them.

Lodestone. It could mean a person who was the focus of attention, too, not just a thing. Sitting quietly on her barstool, a little apart from the other girls at Lizzie's hen night, Natalie gazed around and tried to apply her new word to her surroundings.

When they were alone or uncomfortable, other people read magazines or texted their friends. Because of her dyslexia, Natalie did neither. She hated text-speak; the strange jumble of letters seemed utterly wrong to her even when the predictive-text gizmo claimed it was right.

"You're like my mother," Molly, her flatmate, had said. "She hates texting."

Natalie smiled at the thought of being compared to the erudite Ingrid Fitzgerald, who'd probably read the entire dictionary cover to cover and committed it to memory. Molly's mother was the sort of person who should have made Natalie feel insecure, yet she didn't. Ingrid wore her intelligence lightly, treating everyone with the same level of respect. Natalie never felt like an idiot in her presence.

"Your mother only hates texting because it stops people from being able to spell properly. I've never been able to spell in the first place."

"You spell just fine. You're clever where it counts," Molly said. "Look at all the people we know who have degrees coming out of their ears and are still clueless."

They'd met at college, while Natalie had been painfully trying to negotiate the written part of the foundation art course. Give her clay to mold, and she could spin poetry. But hand her a pen, and she was like a small child wielding a crayon and trying to work out the difference between the number six and the number nine. It was why she'd hated school.

She wished Molly were here tonight for the hen-night extravaganza, but her flatmate, not being much of a party person, had elected to stay home with the cats. Hopeless at small talk with humans, Molly talked to her beloved Bambi and Loopy as though they were her babies, all three of them curled up together on the couch watching TV. The cats liked programs with fish in them best.

"I love them too, but an hour of National Geographic just for them?" Natalie had said before she left the house, toting a sports bag jammed with hen-night paraphernalia, the pièces de résistance being fake zebra-skin cowboy hats.

"We're only watching till the end of this show," Molly said seriously, "and then we're switching to the salsa program."

Natalie nodded. "When the men in the white coats arrive, shall I make them tea or coffee?"

Molly beamed a wide smile that lit up her small round face and made her eyes dance. Apart from her eyes, she looked nothing like her famous mother. Short and adolescently skinny, she had reddish-brown curly hair that she liked to wear in a ponytail. Even when dressed for work and presiding over weighty reports on poverty, she looked about sixteen instead of twenty-three.

"The men in the white coats had tea the last time," she said. "They might have coffee this time. I know I'm mad, but I like the fish programs too," she added. "Fish are very soothing. And there's nothing else on TV tonight. I'm fed up with forensic science shows, they give me nightmares. There's a good film on later."

Something romantic, Natalie guessed fondly. Molly might work at the squalid end of society, but for relaxation, she devoured romantic novels and movies. The only thing that might get her off the couch was a real-life Johnny Depp type in Regency costume with the desire to crush Molly to his manly bosom.

"I got you a hat, just in case you wanted to come. . . ." Natalie plonked a faux-zebra cowboy hat on her friend's head.

"I love it!" Molly sat up to adjust the hat, then wriggled back down into the couch. "I'm happier here, Nat, honestly. I'm no good at that party thing. I'd prefer watching it to being in the middle of it, but if you watch, everyone thinks you're a weirdo. Besides, we haven't organized a cat-sitter."

"See you later, crazy lady," said Natalie, leaving.

Lizzie always said that Natalie and Molly were bad for each other because they liked being home so much. Her idea of a good time didn't involve cats, TV, or books. But then, Lizzie didn't appreciate that Natalie stayed in at night slaving away on her designs because she was determined to succeed as a jewelry designer. She couldn't do that and be in clubs and pubs every night of the week like Lizzie. Natalie enjoyed going out when the mood took her. Though tonight, strangely, she wasn't in the mood. Instead, she was worried.

There had been such an emotional buildup to the hen night and Lizzie was so fiercely determined to have a good time, determined to have one last wild party before she tied the knot, that Natalie feared the evening wouldn't end well.

Club Laguna itself was opaque, from the all-subdued lighting that made you think you were wearing your sunglasses indoors. Even the mirrors behind the bar added to the effect: opaque glass, and the lodestone was . . . Lizzie. Which was only fair; it was Lizzie's hen night, after all.

Ten women from Lizzie's life had been hauled together for this momentous party: Natalie and Anna from school, Lizzie's two mad cousins from Donegal who'd rolled up looking like off-duty supermodels, a couple of girls from college, and three from Lizzie's office. The party had started three hours earlier in Lizzie's flat, and Lizzie clearly wanted it to go on all night. As the person charged with organizing the whole thing, Natalie would have to stay to the bitter end. But she was tired. Working in the café in Kenny's by day and designing her jewelry by night meant she had very little energy. Certainly not the energy Lizzie and the other hens seemed to have, squealing as they admired dresses, shoes, and passing men. Wearing their zebra cowboy hats—"Nat, you *genius*! I love them!"—the hens were attracting plenty of attention from several predatory men. So far, all boarders had been repelled, although one guy—in a denim shirt that displayed his fabulous muscles and with a tiny skull-and-crossbones earring in one ear that showed off how cool he was—was watching from the side-lines, clearly pretty keen on Lizzie. He'd get bored, Natalie hoped.

She watched the barman diligently mix the cocktails. Swirl some crimson liquid into the shaker, do a little smooth move to impress the ladies, add something clear from a modern frosted-glass bottle, crash in some ice, then shake.

The women clustered round the art deco glass bar murmured approval.

"More vodka," shrieked Lizzie, a tousled brunette who was kneeling on the barstool so she could see all the action, though she'd definitely had enough vodka already. Four vodka tonics and a white wine spritzer, and now she'd ordered the bar's specialty: the Laguna Beach, a concoction that came complete with a voucher for the Betty Ford Clinic. Earlier she'd decided she wasn't wearing enough makeup and had clumsily added another layer of eyeliner in the gloom of the ladies', where you needed a flashlight to find the flush button on the loo. The dark and the drink combined had not resulted in a classy makeup look.

Natalie thought there was a business opportunity for anyone who patented a line of makeup bags with Breathalyzer gadgets fitted to their zips: once you were drunk, you couldn't open the bag and start applying drag-queen levels of cosmetics.

She'd done it herself and had the photos to prove it—Marilyn Manson meets Picasso with a dash of vampire chic thrown in. It wasn't a good look, given that she could pass for a gothic heroine easily enough anyway. Depending on what she wore, Natalie's look could go either way: young and interesting or consumptively strange. She was pale-skinned, prone to purple shadows under her heliotrope eyes, and with long ebony hair that never looked entirely brushed. In jeans and a T-shirt, her lean legginess and youthful skin gave her the look of a student, even though she was twenty-three and out of college. In tonight's party outfit of sapphire slip dress, she was working the girl-next-door-with-a-hint-of-edginess look.

"Hot and sexy," Molly had decreed earlier when Natalie was getting ready. "But in control; not 'I'm available, big boy' sexy, more 'You can look, but don't touch' sexy."

Part of their routine was outfit grading before they left the flat. Despite her own charity-shop look, Molly was brilliant at gauging outfits and their suitability for events. Natalie could do it with jewelry, but it was so easy to get clothes wrong.

"That's good. Don't want to be too hot and sexy," Natalie had said, pulling the dress down, wishing it were longer and covered more leg. "It'll be mad enough tonight as it is."

"More juice!" she heard Anna yell to the Club Laguna barman, who winked at her as he wielded his shaker. Anna wasn't much of a drinker. "I can't stand feeling woozy."

That statement was like a red flag to most men. In the many years the three girls had been friends—ever since bonding as five-year-olds in the school yard—Natalie had lost count of the number of guys who'd tried to get Anna to lose control, hoping that a few more sips of chardonnay would make her unfurl her sweetly prim manner like a secretary in a cheesy movie letting down her hair. Lizzie, who was permanently unfurled and smiled at men like an eager puppy, was generally ignored in the rush to Anna.

"It's not fair," Lizzie used to say without bitterness. She adored Anna, even if her friend was a man magnet while she herself appeared to repel them.

"It's the hair," Anna said apologetically. "There's some evolutionary thing about natural redheads; men love the hair. They're programmed to want to mate with it. It's nothing to do with me."

"It's more than the hair," Lizzie would sigh. Anna was so perfect: tiny, perfectly proportioned, and with those dancing pale blue eyes. Men loved how big she made them feel. Her wrists were as delicate as a porcelain doll's.

And then Steve had come along. Without giving Anna a second look, he'd been instantly besotted with Lizzie.

Natalie wondered how Steve's stag night was going. There had been talk of the men going to a lap-dancing club with Steve's old college friend who was over from San Diego, but Lizzie had been outraged.

"It's supposed to be your last night out before marrying the girl you love, not an excuse to drool over naked women with figures like Barbie's!" she'd exclaimed.

It wasn't the latent sexuality she had a problem with, Natalie knew, more that Lizzie wished she were a Barbie look-alike herself. The pre-wedding diet hadn't been as successful as hoped. She was still eight pounds over her target weight and complained of appearing heiferlike.

"I'll look huge in the photos standing between you two," Lizzie had grumbled earlier as they donned their party gear. She was wearing a silky slip dress with long trailing skirts and a tiny camisole bodice that was doing a mediocre job of holding her breasts in. She was not wearing a bra. Neither was Natalie, but then she was a 32A and Lizzie was a healthy 36D.

"Oh, Lizzie, get down off the cross," muttered Natalie. "Somebody else needs the wood. We have three different looks, that's all," she added, relenting. Lizzie's figure anxiety was a barometer of her mood. In times of stress, it became more pronounced and she needed more reassurance. "Anna works the cute look, you do curvy and hot." Lizzie grinned despite herself. "And I'm the lanky one. I wish I had curves like yours."

A lie, but a white one to make Lizzie feel better. Natalie's step-mother, Bess, was a seamstress who made a lot of wedding dresses, and Natalie had grown up hearing about bridal anxiety.

"No, you don't," Lizzie replied, but she was smiling as she put on her hen-night regalia.

As part of her preparations for the evening, Natalie had dutifully bought pink fluffy horns and T-shirts emblazoned with BRIDE ON TOUR and had booked a booth in Laguna, a happening club where the karaoke machine got turned on at eleven and poles were put up onstage for anyone wanting to try pole dancing and willing to sign the insurance waiver first.

It was ten to eleven now. Natalie knew there was still a long night ahead.

She was thrilled that her friend was happy. Steve was such a nice guy: kind, polite, decent. But Natalie couldn't help recalling how, when they were younger, the three of them had had such dreams about conquering the world. And now they were twenty-three and suddenly it seemed the world had shrunk. Anna was dating a guy who was perfect on paper but slightly dull in real life. Gavin worked in a bank, owned his own flat, played rugby with his old school friends at the weekend, and wore rugby jerseys with the collars turned up. Give him another ten years and he'd have a golf club membership and a rowing machine with clothes thrown over it in the bedroom. They used to *laugh* at guys like him, the safe guys, and now Anna was enraptured.

Lizzie was getting married in a week to the sweet and kind Steve—and she wouldn't be wearing bright red, the way she'd always promised: "I'll never go down the aisle in white—the roof of the church would fall in!"

Instead, her dress was creamy lace with a bustier top to make the most of her assets; her dark curls would be covered by a demure veil, and the guest list included all the various horrors of relations whom she'd sworn blind would never get invited.

"You *have* to ask them," she'd said when Natalie dropped by and found her fretting over the seating plan. Great-Aunt Mona couldn't sit with Uncle Tom or they'd kill each other. They hadn't met without fighting in fifty years, and it was unlikely they were about to stop now.

"Why do you have to ask them?"

"*Because*, that's why."

"You never see any of them, except at other people's weddings and funerals. I thought this day was supposed to be about you and Steve, not the usual outdated cliché of a wedding with ninety awful second-cousins-once-removed."

Lizzie grimaced at having her words quoted back at her. "My mother would die if we didn't have a big wedding," she said. "You know what she's like, Natalie. Anyway . . ." Lizzie paused. "I know it sounds strange, but I like the idea of having them there. It makes it *real* when all the cousins and aunties show up. Like we wouldn't be properly married if we did it on a beach somewhere without them all clucking over the waste of money spent on the flowers or complaining about the bones in the fish."

Natalie laughed. "Point taken. But when they're all squabbling because you've sat them too far from the top table, don't say I didn't warn you."

"Mum will sort them out," said Lizzie, chuckling.

Once, thinking of Lizzie's mum might have upset Natalie. When she was a child, she'd felt different because she didn't have a mum. She wasn't the only kid in her class to have an unusual family setup. There were two kids whose dads lived elsewhere, and one boy who had two families: his mother and stepfather, and his dad and stepmother, plus assorted brothers and sisters. And there was Eileen, a quiet mouse of a girl with long strawberry-blond hair she wore like a curtain hiding her eyes. She lived on her own with her mother and went mute whenever any event came up that involved dads.

Eileen might not have had a dad, but she had a mother. Even when Natalie was seven and her mind was gently exploring such things, even when Eileen was by far the strangest kid in the class, even then Natalie knew that Eileen had something she didn't: a real mother.

Dads sometimes got involved in other things or worked all hours, but mums didn't. Mums were there. Except for Natalie Flynn's. Her mum was dead. She had Bess instead, her stepmum, who was wonderful and so kind, but still wasn't her real mum. She'd said Natalie didn't have to call her Mum, so Natalie hadn't; and that simple thing, that name, had strangely made all the difference. Other kids had mums and dads; Natalie had Dad and Bess. And Bess, no matter how wonderful, wasn't Mum.

Natalie forgot loads of things—the sheer pain of writing her thesis had burned off so many brain cells—but she'd never forget the first time she was asked: "What's it like not to have a mum?"

Toby—now grown-up and cute, and always friendly whenever she went to the garage he ran—had been a teacher's nightmare at the age of seven: hyperactive and overfond of the word "why?" "Why does the sun go down at night?" "Why are the people on the television so small?" "Why do we have to go to school?" "Why did your mum die? Are you still sad about her being dead?"

Natalie could see her seven-year-old self: a skinny little thing with those matchstick legs poking out of the gray-and-white school uniform and her dark hair tangled and escaping its ponytail no matter how carefully Bess did it before she went to school.

"I'm not sad," she'd said defiantly. Toby obviously wanted her to say she was sad, so it was important to say she wasn't. Toby said girls couldn't climb trees, and she'd shown him he was wrong. She'd skinned her knees in the process, but she'd shown him. "I'm never sad."

Had she stuck her tongue out at him then? That she couldn't remember. Probably. Sticking out her tongue was a vital way of winning arguments when she was seven, akin to pulling wimpy girls' hair and jumping onto any bit of wall to dance along it.

She'd gone home and told Dad and Bess what Toby had said, and they'd exchanged that *look* that grown-ups did when they didn't want to answer a question.

She had no memory of what her father had said, although she could remember subsequent conversations: "God takes people sometimes, we don't know why."

God's responsibility had shifted vastly when ten-year-old Natalie had said: "I hate God."

Bess hadn't missed a beat. "We don't always understand what God does. We just have to accept it."

Natalie had never accepted it.

There were so many pluses in her life: a lovely family with Bess as the centerpiece, Dad being sweet and just a little bit not-of-this-planet, her half brothers, Ted and Joe, and good friends like Molly. She had so much, particularly when she looked at the disadvantaged kids with whom Molly worked. Compared to them, she was rich in every way. Yet Natalie felt as if there was a part of her missing.

Lizzie and Anna seemed to think that any missing bit could be fixed with the right man. Natalie felt it was more than that. But what exactly?

"Hi, beautiful, can I buy you a drink?" she heard the guy with the skull-and-crossbones earring ask Lizzie.

Natalie could see him reflected in the bar mirror. He was tall and good-looking enough for one of Lizzie's model cousins to be giving him a hard, appreciative stare. Natalie took in the tousled fair hair and the honed body. She also saw Lizzie's lustful look.

"No thanks," Natalie broke in as politely as she could. "It's a hen night. No men allowed."

"Spoilsport," murmured Lizzie, leaning on Natalie and smiling up at the guy.

"No, really, no guys allowed," Anna said firmly, hauling Lizzie away.

He shrugged and walked off.

"He's cute," Lizzie sighed. "I could take him for a test-drive. . . ."

Anna and Natalie exchanged a look. It was indeed going to be a long night.

* * *

It was nearly two when Anna and Natalie realized that Lizzie was missing. The group had been dancing nonstop, so each time Natalie came back to their booth and didn't see Lizzie, she assumed her friend was dancing with the other girls.

"I thought the same," said Anna, shouting so they could hear each other over the music.

Nobody else had seen her for an hour.

Natalie found Lizzie first. At the very back of the club, in a dimly lit spot beside the fire exit, she was perched on a man's lap with her arms wrapped around his body and her mouth clamped to his as if they were giving each other mouth-to-mouth resuscitation. One of his hands was tangled in Lizzie's dark hair and the other was burrowing up under her flirty dress, so that her thigh was totally bare.

Natalie's first thought was that her friend must be comatose to be behaving like this, but then she looked again. Lizzie was as ardent as the guy; she was writhing around on his lap, plunging her tongue into his mouth. It was the same guy who'd made a move on Lizzie earlier, the one in the denim shirt and the skull-and-crossbones earring. Lizzie had wanted this, Natalie realized; she was a willing partner.

"Lizzie!" shouted Natalie, trying to be heard over the throbbing bass notes of the music.

"Lizzie!"

She shook her friend's arm and Lizzie turned round, the crimson lipstick almost gone but for a giant red Munch-like scream smeared around her mouth from kissing. She smiled lazily at her friend and snuggled close to the man's chest. Her eyes glittered with raw excitement.

It was the smile that hurt Natalie the most: a knowing, satisfied, mocking smile.

"Lizzie, we've got to go," Natalie said, trying to stay calm in the face of this unrecognizable Lizzie.

"Not yet," said Lizzie, still with that smile plastered across her face. She nuzzled into the man's neck. "We're having fun."

Natalie decided she'd have to try another approach.

"This is her hen night," Natalie explained to the guy. "She's getting married in a week. Her fiancé's a cop. He's on the drugs squad." This was, of course, entirely untrue, but she guessed it might be a deal-breaker.

Sure enough, alarm flickered in the man's face and he got up at speed, letting Lizzie fall unceremoniously to the floor.

"Ouch!" she roared.

Natalie and the guy ignored her.

"For real?" he asked. He meant about the drugs squad.

Natalie nodded grimly. "For real."

Without a backward glance, he shoved the bar of the emergency exit and opened it. Cold wind and a gush of rain blasted in as he vanished out into the dark. Natalie shivered.

She glanced at Lizzie on the floor. Lizzie looked sulky now. She had a big tear on one side of her bodice where her admirer apparently had been trying overenthusiastically to access her boobs.

"Home," Natalie said.

"You ruined it all, Natalie!" shrieked Lizzie.

"Yes," Natalie agreed, "I ruined it all. Come on, let's go. Where's your stuff?"

When Natalie hauled her back to their booth, there was no sign of her bag or coat there.

"Is she okay?" asked Anna.

"Oh, fine," Natalie said brightly. No point in telling Anna what Lizzie had really been doing. "She's tired and emotional."

"Me too," sighed Anna. "And I'm exhausted. Can we go home now?"

"Sure. I need to find Lizzie's things."

Lizzie's coat was found in a heap on the floor under the table, but her bag was nowhere to be seen.

Lizzie was too out of it to be the slightest bit worried about this. "Cheap bag!" she kept saying loudly. "Cheap bag."

"What's inside it is what counts," Natalie said, "your wallet, keys, and phone."

"Cheap, cheap—"

Finally, Natalie gave up looking. The club was heaving by now and she was tired. "Home," she said to Lizzie, then realized she couldn't send Lizzie back to the flat she shared with Steve in that condition. "You'd better come with me."

The next morning, Lizzie woke first and ran to the bathroom. Natalie could hear retching, and the bedroom reeked of stale alcohol. Even the bed smelled of boozy sweat. Natalie got up and began stripping off the sheets. She couldn't wait to wash them, to get rid of the memory of last night. There had been something disturbing about seeing her friend in such a terrible state. Lizzie had been more than drunk; she was out of control. The pillowcase from her side of the bed was striped with makeup. Skin cleansing hadn't been high on the agenda when Natalie had finally got her back to the flat. She'd had enough trouble getting Lizzie into bed at all. It had taken a lot of cajoling. And then Lizzie had shouted how nobody understood her and how horrible Natalie was being, when all she wanted was to have some fun. Then, suddenly, she'd lain down on the bed and fallen asleep in an instant.

"Don't do the bed," moaned Lizzie, staggering back into the bedroom looking like a representative of the undead. "I need to lie down, pleeease."

"You can lie down on the couch," Natalie said shortly. "This place stinks and I need to wash the sheets."

"Oh, nooo." Lizzie lay down on the pile of dirty sheets and curled up into a ball. "I can lie here. I'll wash them later."

"Later, if you remember," Natalie reminded her tartly, "you're meeting Steve's friend from San Diego. The one who went with them for the stag night—the wild one, remember? The one you were scared was going to take Steve to all manner of unsuitable clubs to meet unsuitable women."

Lizzie was chalk white as it was, but at the mention of her fiancé, her face looked even more ghostly. "Shit."

"You can say that again," Natalie said.

"Don't, please don't," begged Lizzie.

"Don't what? Remind you about last night?" Natalie thought

of how she'd hauled Lizzie out of the club after giving up on her handbag, and of the people Lizzie had drunkenly careened into on the way, threatening to start a fight over it even though she was the one who'd bumped into them. Lizzie! Funny, normally gentle Lizzie.

It had been a nightmare. And the guy, the man Lizzie had been with, while she'd totally forgotten poor Steve. That was the worst.

"What do you remember?" Natalie demanded.

Lizzie covered her eyes with her hands. "Lots of it. Too much. I had far too much to drink—"

"That's not what I'm talking about."

"The guy at the bar, I kissed him—"

"Kissed him! I thought you were going to devour him, Lizzie. You were glued to him, and I had to practically drag you off. If anyone else had seen you and told Steve, can you imagine that?" Natalie shook her head in disgust. "There's drunk, Lizzie, and there's crazy—and you were crazy."

"I know," Lizzie said brokenly. "It's awful, I'm awful. And I promised I'd never, not after the last time—" She stopped abruptly.

Startled, Natalie stared at her. "What last time?"

Lizzie hesitated before whispering: "The Christmas party at work. It was work people only, no partners, and there was this big joint being passed around and—oh, Natalie, you don't want to know."

"You slept with someone else?" Natalie knew she sounded like the mother superior of a convent, but she couldn't help it.

Lizzie didn't reply, and that made Natalie absolutely furious.

"You did! You actually slept with someone because you were stoned, Lizzie, and that didn't shock you enough, so you still went out on your hen night and got absolutely plastered. If I hadn't found you, where would you be now? I'll tell you: you'd be waking up in that guy's bed—I doubt if you even know his name—and we'd have phoned the police because we thought you were in trouble, and everyone, *including your fiancé*, would be searching for you now, while you'd be holed up in bed with a hangover with a bloody stranger. That would wreck the Valentine's Day wedding, for sure. Why would you do that? You don't need to sleep around with strangers—you've got a man who loves you."

"Oh, shut up! I hate myself enough, I don't need you hating me too!" Lizzie screamed. She clambered to her feet, still bleary-eyed, clutching the sheets to her. "Why are you so bloody judgmental, anyway? It's none of your business; I didn't kiss your bloody boy-friend, did I? It's only my life I'm fucking up!"

Suddenly, Natalie felt sorry for what she'd said. Lizzie was right; she was being judgmental and she didn't know why, because lots of people went out and got terribly drunk on their hen nights. It was almost a rite of passage, wasn't it? But this had been some-thing worse. Natalie had never seen anyone she loved change so much under the influence of alcohol. Her father barely drank, Bess was the same, and even the boys didn't drink to the extent that Lizzie had, although she knew many guys their age who did.

It had been part of the family ethos when they'd been growing up: treat alcohol with respect.

But it seemed that Lizzie's family hadn't given her the same message. Last night, Lizzie had been like another person, someone Natalie didn't know and certainly didn't like.

"Sorry," Natalie said, and sat down on the mattress. She felt weary after so few hours in bed. "I am your friend, Lizzie, but I wouldn't be a proper friend if I pretended last night was normal or good. I'm not trying to take the moral high ground. You can sleep with who you like, but I can't stand by and be your brides-maid if you really don't want to marry Steve. Why marry him if you want to sleep with other men?"

"I do want to marry him!" protested Lizzie. "I was drunk, it was a blip. Really."

"But—"

"But nothing. I love Steve. Last night was stupid, that's all. And he doesn't need to know, does he?"

"I suppose not." Natalie opened the drawer where she kept clean sheets. She couldn't believe she was having this conversation with Lizzie, discovering a totally different side to one of her old-est friends. She'd had no idea that Lizzie was capable of having a one-night stand before her wedding and then convincing herself it was all fine, as long as nobody found out. Natalie had found Lizzie's drunken aggression frightening, but her cool "it doesn't matter as long as nobody knows" theory was even worse. Lizzie would be devastated if Steve slept with someone else. It wasn't right not to care that she'd done exactly that.

"Where's my handbag?" asked Lizzie, looking around the room.

"You lost it," Natalie reminded her. "We looked everywhere but couldn't find it. You should cancel your credit cards, actually."

"Oh, shit, that's my phone, my cards, *everything*!" wailed Lizzie. "What am I going to tell Steve?"

Natalie stared blankly at her clean sheets. She liked the violet-sprigged ones best, and her fingers ran absently over the smooth percale. "I'm not sure what you should tell him," she said slowly.

"I know." Lizzie sounded confident. "We'll say you and I got totally plastered. We came back here and, even though I'd meant to go home in a taxi, I decided to stay because it was so late. Okay?"

No, not okay at all, Natalie thought. But then, it wasn't her job to fix Lizzie's relationship or be her moral guardian. "Okay," she said. But her insides felt like lead.

Three

Learn how to say no. Practice. Say it at least once every day, and you know what? You'll get better at it.

*C*harlie sat down with a sigh and eased off her shoes. Blissfully cool air enveloped her toes and she wriggled them. The Hatbox Café on Kenny's second floor wasn't too busy. The lunchtime rush was over and the afternoon tea people hadn't yet started wandering in looking for the café's specialty: pink cupcakes with quirky shoe designs in multicolored icing.

The Hatbox had retained its traditional appearance. Old Mr. Kenny, who set up the store all those years ago, would have been right at home here. The fittings were still cherry wood and brass, the wallpaper a riot of bosomy Belle Époque girls spilling out of Grecian gowns, and the chairs were still upholstered in ruby velvet. But the staff no longer wore black and white with frilled caps for the women, having long since moved into chic navy trousers and tops with waiters' white aprons. The menu was similarly up-to-date.

Charlie's lunch was a bottle of water and a brown-bread sandwich. She'd brought a magazine borrowed from the staff room. The magazine was a cover. Once she realized nobody wanted to join her for lunch and that she'd have privacy, she took out her little notebook and pen and furtively began to write.

My mother's a travel agent for guilt trips.
You think that's a joke? Wrong.
She phoned me at ten to eight this morning.
"Charlie, I'm in bed with the flu. Can you pick up my dry cleaning

on your way to work? I left my good jackets in, the tweed ones, and my baby-blue coat, and I need them."

You wouldn't think that two fake Chanel jackets and a baby-blue woolen coat circa 1963 could make a grown woman want to kill someone with her bare hands, but they can. Dry cleaning can be a powerful tool in the hands of a master.

"I don't really have the time. I'm leaving in a few minutes and I have to drop Mikey at school. Can't you phone Iseult and ask her to do it?"

Pause. The phrase "red rag to a bull" comes to mind. I knew I shouldn't have said no, but I had to. I mean, I'm the supervisor of the Organic Belle department in Kenny's, which is not the sort of place where you can be late. Plus, I have a thirteen-year-old son who views arriving a moment late to school with the horror of a Japanese train scheduler facing a leaf-on-the-line crisis, so we don't have time for either morning phone calls or emergency dry-cleaning stops.

The pause ended abruptly.

"No, that's fine," snapped my mother. Think Lady Bracknell on crystal meth. "I'll do it myself. I couldn't sleep last night, you know. My cough's worse. I don't know if I'll last the winter. . . ."

This is where I think that if only she gave up her bloody thirty-a-day smoking habit, the cough wouldn't get worse, but I don't say it. There's only so much reckless abandon I can manage of a morning.

"I'll pick up your dry cleaning," I say.

"No, you're too busy. I'll do it—"

"Really, I'll fit it in."

"No, I can look after myself, thank you very much. Nobody needs to fit me into her life."

Sound of phone slamming down. My mother has broken many phones in her life and refuses to have a portable one because there's no satisfying slamming down involved.

Not having a portable means she often doesn't get to the phone in time when I ring, and I then panic, imagining her unconscious at the bottom of the stairs or falling asleep in the bath thanks to an enormous martini (triple measure of gin with the vermouth bottle sort of waved about in the vicinity), and I have to keep redialing until she answers with an inevitable growl: "What is it? Can't a girl go to the bathroom in peace?"

My mother likes describing herself as a girl. She waxes lyrical about how she and her friends from the sixties and seventies fought the tyranny of State and Church to bring the pill and women's rights into Ireland, all the time referring to "this wonderful girl" or "that darling girl" who faced furious right-wingers waving crucifixes. And that's all wonderful, really. My mother was part of something incredibly important at a time when women couldn't control their fertility and were prevented from achieving all that they should, and so on and so forth, but — I can't believe I'm admitting this finally, even if it is only on paper — I find it insanely irritating. I HATE IT! Because "girl" implies sweetness, innocence, and a hint of gentleness. My mother is about as girlish as a Hell's Angel.

She is tough — had to be tough. So stop with the "girls" thing, please. Let everyone else see the gritty person underneath and stop saving it just for me.

She can do the girlish thing, all right. This involves smiling at people (mainly men) and fluttering her eyelashes — she was never one of the bra-burning feminists. She's the more modern variety, the kind who want red lipstick and push-up bosoms to go with their financial equality in the workplace.

With me, Number Two Daughter, she gives the smiling and fluttering a miss. I get instructions on where I'm going wrong in life: not wearing my hair the correct way, having middle-aged spread ("So aging, Charlotte," she murmurs), and doing what she considers a menial job are chief on the list. Ideally, I should be ruthlessly running my own company instead of standing at a counter in a department store selling hope in pretty bottles to women. The ideal me would also credit my mother with all my success, along the lines of "She taught me everything I know."

Iseult, my older sister and Number One Daughter, who is beautiful, clever, and successful, does not get instructions on where she's going wrong. She gets compliments and her newspaper clippings kept. Iseult is a playwright. She's written three plays, two of which were wonderfully received, and there's talk of one of them going to Broadway. Iseult's *plays are her work-in-progress. My mother considers Iseult to be her best work and has a folder of Iseult's triumphs since her first play was performed; her favorite is the article in a Galway paper where a famous person and their mother talk about their relationship and Iseult said, along with the obligatory "my mother taught me everything I know," that our mother was always so glamorous that our boyfriends fancied her more than either of us.*

I can't quite remember this myself, but my mother has taken the story and run with it. Not only was she personally responsible for female emancipation in our historically embattled country, she sees herself as a dead ringer for Mrs. Robinson in The Graduate.

Now, that sounds like carping. It's not poor Iseult's fault, don't get me wrong, God, no. It's just the way things are in our family, and families are weird, aren't they? Ours is no weirder than anybody else's probably—I'm just bad at dealing with it all. I should know better at my age. I'm nearly forty, have a wonderful son and a wonderful hus-band, can't complain about any of that. It's just my mother: she drives me nuts. And that's not normal, is it?

Charlie had never kept a diary before; she'd simply never had the inclination. Iseult was the writer in the family, and Charlie liked keeping her own thoughts to herself. But a gratitude jour-nal—now, that was a different proposition. She'd heard a woman on the radio talking about a gratitude journal, where you wrote down all the things you were thankful for. Eventually, some al-chemy was supposed to take place and the act of writing about being grateful somehow made you actually grateful. That's how she'd started out at Christmas.

I'm grateful for today when I watched Mikey at soccer practice and he was so happy, joyful. . . .

. . . Brendan took me to dinner last night at the Chinese place on the hill, and it was wonderful. There was no special occasion; he just thought it would be nice to do something on the spur of the moment. It was. It's silly how something that simple makes me happy, but it does.

. . . Sales are up, and David Kenny, the big boss, came down to

congratulate us and we had champagne—Laurent-Perrier, no cheap muck for David—and a bit of a party. Shotsy and I sat in a corner and decided that the bonuses would be up, too, which is brilliant because Brendan and I are still paying for the garage conversion and Shotsy has her eye on a little red MG.

Two days before Christmas and a week into pure gratitude, the day came when she was so irritated with her mother that attempting gratitude was a waste of time.

Mother is NOT coming to us for Christmas, even though it was our year to have her and we'd had to say no to going to Wales with Brendan's family. No, she's just blithely told me she's going to Biarritz with Iseult, and who cares if I've spent a week getting the place ready for her to stay and buying her favorite food! We can't go to Wales because Brendan's sister is now going and there won't be room for us. And we'd love to have gone, would have loved it. I am so angry I could scream.

Bizarrely, it had worked. Charlie, who hadn't written an essay since she left college many years before, filled seven pages.

Instead of burning rage, she felt an unusual sense of calm when she was finished. The anger was no longer in her head; it was on paper. Writing words down had a magical quality. It was absolutely alchemy. Anger in her head throbbed relentlessly, but anger on paper was flat and had no power over her. The diary itself still made her feel guilty—treasonous, even. Writing down things that annoyed her was one thing, but the person who annoyed her constantly was her mother, and that couldn't be right. Everyone else adored her mother.

"She's fabulous, such a raconteur," everyone said.

"She must have been so beautiful when she was younger." Charlie always hoped Kitty never heard that one: the implication was that the beauty was very much a thing of the past, and Kitty Nelson didn't care to be an ex-beauty. She wanted to be a still-beautiful-for-her-age.

I wish I handled her better, she wrote now. *That she didn't make me so angry all the time. Or, as Brendan says, that I could learn not to get upset. But she has that knack of saying exactly the thing to upset me.*

"The reason your mother can push all your buttons is because she installed them," he says to me.

I think he read it on a postcard. Isn't it annoying that postcards nowadays all come with the wisdom of Nietzsche?

"Detach with love" is what Shotsy says to me. If she explains what that means, I'd like to try it, but I have absolutely no idea —

"Charlie?"

Charlie jumped and her pen leapt across the page with an inky scrawl and fell to the café floor. She actually felt guilty every time she took the notebook out of its hiding place in the ripped bit of lining of her black handbag. No matter how good it felt to write down her feelings, she'd die if anyone actually saw any of it.

"You writing love letters?" said a teasing voice. Dolores, who'd worked at Kenny's since she was in her teens and was now nearing retirement, plonked a tray onto the table beside Charlie's untouched sandwich.

"No," answered Charlie cheerily, closing the notebook and stuffing it into her handbag. She leaned down to retrieve her pen. "Lists, you know," she added vaguely.

She loved lists. The trick, according to the experts, was not to have too many items. Then you could realistically achieve them.

"I hate lists," Dolores said, stirring sugar into her coffee. "I found one the other day and it was years old, from my fortieth, and it was all the stuff I wanted in my life by the time I turned forty-one."

"Like what?"

"A new car—not a secondhand one, but new. To have lost thirty pounds. To have found the man of my dreams. . . ." She sighed and began opening her salad dressing. "None of it has happened. So much for bloody cosmic ordering."

"Does it work like that?" Charlie was instantly terribly sorry she'd asked. Dolores's ill-fated love life had monopolized many a lunchtime among the Kenny's staff; and while Charlie wished her love, happiness, and a double portion of George Clooney with cream on top, she wasn't emotionally up to another session of There Are No Decent Men Left.

"Clearly not," Dolores said gloomily. "Unless it's cumulative, like compound interest. If you do enough lists, eventually you get some of what you asked for. Perhaps the fact that you stuck at the whole thing counts for something."

"Stuck at what? Marriage? Life? Working here?" Shotsy, bird-like, brown as a walnut, and with a whirl of platinum-blond hair, placed a cup on the table. Charlie didn't have to look to know what was in it: a triple espresso. Shotsy ran the handbag and ac-cessories department, lived for fashion, and was only ever seen putting two things in her mouth: strong cigarettes and black coffee.

"Here's not so bad," said Charlie, smiling at Shotsy.

"Speak for yourself," muttered Dolores, going to get more milk for her coffee.

"Have news for you," Shotsy whispered to Charlie.

"What?" Charlie could tell from Shotsy's frown that it wasn't good news.

"Later," mouthed Shotsy.

Shotsy waited until Dolores—not known for discretion—had gone before spilling the beans.

"Don't tell anyone," Shotsy whispered, "but I've heard that David met with Stanley DeVere last week."

Charlie gasped out loud. "You sure?"

DeVere's was the country's premier department store, a high-end chain with branches in five Irish cities and three of the big-gest shopping centers. It stood for money. Big money. Stanley DeVere was the complete opposite of David Kenny: a wearer of loud stripey suits, he thought that waving an unlit cigar around somehow enhanced his image as a bon viveur. Charlie had only ever seen him on television, and she'd disliked him on sight. It was no secret that DeVere's would love to have another store on the high-density east coast, and buying out Kenny's, with its fabu-lous location near Dublin and its reputation as the country's only bijou department store, would be a real coup. It was also no secret that David disliked Stanley DeVere and had vowed that he would never sell Kenny's.

Meeting with Stanley undermined that vow.

"Why? I thought Kenny's was doing well," Charlie said.

"Margins, I expect," said Shotsy sadly. "It's all about margins. We can't compete with the likes of DeVere's on price. They're buying ten times as much stock as we are, so they get much better deals from retailers. And the supermarkets, the big chemist chains, and the home-furnishing outlets are hurting us too. We can't match anyone on price anymore. Our saving grace is that we're a niche store. Take Organic Belle, for example. They're after exclusivity, it helps them with their brand, but one day some huge conglomerate like L'Oréal will buy them out, and then they'll go global—world domination in every store. When that happens, we're in trouble. So, we're not doing well, and the global downturn hasn't helped. Who has money for luxury nowadays?"

"This is awful," said Charlie.

"At least we heard about it. Forewarned is forearmed," Shotsy said grimly. "DeVere's has its own handbag buyers, and they won't want to hire me. Too many cooks and all that."

"You're brilliant at what you do, Shotsy," protested Charlie.

"Brilliant means nothing. This is hostile takeover time, and no matter what sort of flannel they give us about merging the two companies and how the staff will join up seamlessly, it won't happen—not when DeVere's and Kenny's have such different cultures. People like me will be made redundant. End of story, kaput. I wish we could still smoke inside."

Charlie stood up, got two empty takeaway cups, and put one in front of Shotsy. "Decant your coffee and come out onto the roof. You can smoke and we can talk."

"Thought your mother had put you off nicotine for life?" said Shotsy, pouring her espresso into the takeaway cup.

Shotsy was one of the few people who seemed to understand that Charlie's mother wasn't quite the lovable revolutionary glamourpuss she pretended to be.

"Tough growing up with a mother like that," she'd said shrewdly on first meeting Kitty, an event in the shop. "She has very strong opinions on everything, your mother."

Charlie had sent her a grateful look. Shotsy wasn't a member of the Kitty Nelson fan club, won over by the purred "dahling"s and the war cry that she'd let her daughters live their lives their own way because it was wrong to inflict archaic moral codes upon them.

"I can't stand the smell of smoke," said Charlie now, "but I need to hear everything and you need cigarettes to get your brain working."

The roof terrace was far less glamorous than it sounded—a flat area of the store's roof, surrounded on all sides by slanting mountains of tile. To get there, the women had to climb the back stairs that led past accounts and credit control.

Finally, Charlie pushed the old metal door open and they emerged, panting, into the cool February sunlight. Charlie shivered without a jacket, but waited until Shotsy had a couple of decent drags on her cigarette before asking, "What do we do?"

"Keep our eyes and ears open, and wait," said Shotsy.

"That's it? Wait?"

"Nothing else we can do. We're just the worker bees."

Charlie wrapped her arms around herself to ward off the cold. "If DeVere's buys us, they mightn't make radical changes," she said hopefully. "If it's not broken, don't fix it, right?" She loved her job; and she was good at it, too. Shotsy was brilliant as an accessories buyer; she understood that women who could never afford to dress head to toe in designer clothes still loved having the designer glamour that went with an expensive handbag or a pair of designer sunglasses. How could DeVere's belittle what the Kenny's staff had to offer?

"It mightn't be broken," Shotsy said, stabbing out her cigarette, "but they'll still want to fix it so that Kenny's isn't Kenny's anymore. It will become DeVere's. Branding," she added in a low voice, "that's what it's all about now. People like me are part of the Kenny's brand, and we just wouldn't fit the DeVere's brand. There's no reason they won't keep you, though, Charlie."

"Except for one thing," Charlie pointed out. A horrible idea had just occurred to her. "DeVere's doesn't stock Organic Belle. It's like you said a moment ago: Organic Belle wanted to keep its brand exclusive, so Kenny's is the only retailer on the east coast. There's us and Pathologie in Galway, and then the three Organic Belle shops in Cork and Kerry. And now Harrods. That's it. I'm sure DeVere's was furious not to get it. What if they decide not to stock it out of pique, just to make a point? Or if the Organic Belle people pull out? What then? I'm out of a job."

"There's making a point and there's doing business," Shotsy said. "They're not stupid."

"Getting rid of you would be stupid, but you're sure they'd do it," Charlie retorted.

"Let's hold off worrying until we know what's happening." Shotsy rearranged her platinum hair and opened the door to the fifth floor. "Just keep your eyes and ears peeled. After all, David's a good man. He wouldn't sell out without looking after all of us, would he?"

She didn't say it with conviction, Charlie thought. David Kenny was a good man, and he did look after his staff. But if he needed to sell the department store for some reason, perhaps he mightn't be able to look after them quite as well as he had in the past.

The rest of the afternoon on the cosmetics floor was mercifully busy, so Charlie didn't have a moment to brood. There were three women who worked in the Organic Belle department, and Charlie was always the most popular both with newcomers to the product line and with long-standing customers coming back for more. She had a kind of empathy that allowed her to understand how someone could feel nervous walking into an elegant department store and facing the beautifully made-up women behind the counters.

Part of her appeal was that she didn't fit the traditional vision of stunning beauty usually found staffing the counters in cosmetics departments. Yes, her subtle makeup was beautifully applied, thanks to the courses she'd taken when she signed up to handle

Organic Belle, but she chose never to look too glamorous or inaccessible.

Charlie was petite with a curvy figure, shiny chestnut hair that she wore in a groomed ponytail, a round, smiling face with neat features, and slightly feline eyes inherited from her mother. However, she didn't have her mother's fine-boned face or the fabulous lips that Kitty Nelson painted various shades of red: pillar-box, fire engine, crimson. And she'd missed out on the long, elegant legs her mother and sister liked to show off with their high heels, sheer stockings, and lashings of attitude.

What she did have was a friendliness that drew people to her.

Her husband was constantly trying to make her understand how important that was, and how long legs, sultry lips, and a hand-span waist couldn't hold a candle to innate kindness.

"You light up a room when you smile, do you know that?" he would say to her.

"Stop it, Brendan!" Charlie would laugh and kiss him. But she loved him saying it. She hadn't known such kindness since her father left.

Growing up with her mother and sister, two fiercely strong personalities, Charlie had often felt like a plump little mouse who'd sneaked into the lions' cage. The lions ensnared people with their glamour and ferocity, and nobody could quite believe that Charlie, who listened far more than she talked, could possibly be related to Kitty and Iseult.

Her champion had been her father, who was just as capable of being the egotistical big cat as his wife and older daughter, but who adored his little Charlotte.

And then one terrible day, when Charlie was fifteen and Iseult was eighteen, he'd packed his bags and left.

"I'm not leaving *you*, Charlotte," Anthony Nelson had told her, extracting tissue after tissue from the box to wipe away Charlie's tears. "I love you, remember that."

"But you *are* leaving," Charlie had sobbed.

"I can't live with your mother anymore, that's all, Charlotte. I can't. Lord knows, I've tried, but she's destroying me—" He collected himself. "Grown-ups sometimes leave each other, but that doesn't mean they leave their children. I love you and Iseult. That will never change."

"Can I come with you?"

He looked shocked. "Kids don't live with their fathers, Charlotte. They live with their mothers, you know that."

"Do they have to?" she whispered. If her mother heard, she'd explode with anger. The volume of screaming in the house had already been dangerously high for the past hour. It was only quiet now because Kitty had slammed the door to the sitting room and was in there with "It's Too Late" playing over and over on the stereo, almost drowning out the clinking of the gin bottle. But if she'd crept out and was secretly listening to what Charlie had said, she'd be furious. . . .

"I will never say anything bad about your mother to you, Charlotte," her father said urgently, holding her hands in his. "She loves you both and, Lord knows, your mother has enough passion in her, so when she loves, she really loves. I hate men who try to discredit their wives when they split up. Your mother is an amazing woman; look at all she's done, look at what she does for you."

Charlie had thought of her friend Suzy, whose mum would sit on her bed at night and ask about her day, then tell Suzy how much she loved her and how proud she was of her. Charlie would have liked that, but it wasn't the sort of thing Mum did. Plus, Mum despised Suzy's mother.

"The woman's a nightmare!" Kitty had exclaimed. "I don't know why you have to pal around with Suzy. She's such a milk-and-water child. Oh, I give in. Go to her house, if you must—but when I come to pick you up, be waiting at the gate for me. I refuse to be subjected to her drivel about how fabulous Suzy is and how they're all going camping or something ghastly for their holidays. Who the hell goes camping? Well, we girls camped that time in Paris—but that was different. We were part of the Women and Power demo, and we were broke." There had followed a litany of fun had at the time, including a night in Montmartre with a man who chain-smoked Gauloises and said he was going to sculpt her.

And, oh, there was a fabulous dress shop in a backstreet in the Marais where Kitty had bought a secondhand Schiaparelli dress that everyone just adored. Men dropped like flies when they saw it. Simply *dropped*.

"Your mother sacrificed a lot for you girls," Dad continued. "Don't forget that. She'd be devastated if she didn't have you. I wouldn't dream of doing that to her."

He had seemed lost in thought for a moment, and Charlie could tell he was thinking how ungrateful she was. He was right— her mother must be wonderful, really. Children didn't leave their mothers. That was a sin. Being a mother was hard, and if a mother screamed sometimes, it was because she had kids who drove her to it. So Charlie was a bad person for even *thinking* of leaving her mother.

She looked at her father and saw that his eyes were wet. Just then, she felt a bit of her curl up and die. She'd revealed something bad to her darling dad and he was upset with her. She felt so ashamed.

"I love you, Charlotte," he said as he left.

Charlie had nodded and said nothing. She daren't, in case she started to cry. Telling the truth couldn't be good when what you felt inside was so bad.

When she was twenty-four, she'd met Brendan, and he'd changed everything. He'd made her feel treasured and special. From their first meeting, she'd known he was the love of her life. Accustomed to her mercurial home where tension ratcheted up and down at speed, Charlie realized upon spending time with Brendan that people could be calm and kind to one another. Nobody in Brendan's home screamed at anyone else because they were randomly in a bad mood.

Six months after meeting, they moved in together. A year later, they were married.

"You're throwing yourself away," her mother had said furiously. "He's only a bank clerk. He'll never amount to anything."

But it's not his job to amount to something on my behalf, Charlie had thought but never said. Surely that was the very tenet of her mother's much-vaunted campaigning: there was no use pretending to be Cinderella and waiting for the prince to arrive. You had to be your own prince.

She had a good job with the phone company. Together, she and Brendan had enough money to put a deposit on a house. Together they could do it. Now her mother was saying that together wasn't the key: Brendan had to be able to support the pair of them all on his own for it to count.

She'd given up work when Mikey was born, another bombshell.

"You can't give up work now! What's wrong with using daycare?" demanded Kitty.

"It's expensive. I'd be going to work purely to pay for the daycare, and paying for daycare so I could work. It's a vicious circle. We've decided that I'll stay at home until Mikey goes to school, that's all."

"Your career will be ruined! Have I taught you nothing?"

As it turned out, Charlie's career hadn't been ruined, though when Mikey had started going to school, she'd looked for work with more than a little trepidation. After all, who would want to employ her? When the phone company told her it had no vacancies, it seemed her mother had been right. But Organic Belle, a fledgling company, and Kenny's were willing to take her on. It transpired that Charlie had a gift when it came to selling cosmetics. She had done so well that a year ago she'd been appointed supervisor for the Organic Belle line, which meant more money and more responsibility. Charlie loved her new role.

Brendan too had moved up the promotion ladder, but the bank had yet to make him a manager, which was about the only job his mother-in-law would have respected.

Mikey was the center of their lives. As he grew, Charlie grew too, realizing that while she wasn't precisely the high-performing career woman her mother desperately wanted her to be, she was the most special person in the world for one little boy and for his father, and actually, that was all that mattered.

Motherhood had taught her to trust her instincts. And it taught her another lesson she'd quite like not to have learned: that there

were many ways to be a mother, and that letting children think
their mother had sacrificed her fabulous life for them was probably not top of the list. That thought simmered away in the re-
cesses of her brain. A person could be wonderful at one thing, say
campaigning for women's rights, and yet be hopeless at another,
like being a kind and caring mother.

There was no law saying a person had to be both. One was
enough. But understanding one's own abilities in these areas was
a vital part of life. Charlie had been raised with the independent-
woman ideal, but had found that parenting was the career that
fulfilled her most. What hurt was having her mother treat this
important part of Charlie's life with such disdain.

During a lull in business, Charlie took a moment to ask Karen,
the woman she was training, how she was getting on. Charlie
enjoyed working with trainees: there was a buzz from being
with someone learning about Organic Belle, particularly when
they were doing as she'd done and rejoining the workforce after
having children.

Karen was forty and still very anxious about her new job, even
though she'd worked as a personal assistant to a high-powered
businessman before leaving to have children.

"That was then, this is now," she said to Charlie. "Ten years is
a long time to be out of the workforce. I feel like I'm masquerad-
ing as a person with a job. I half-expect customers to tell me to get
out from behind the counter and fetch a real salesperson to help
them."

"You're great at this," Charlie said. "You're good with people,
too. I felt the same when I started; I was just as nervous."

"That's very kind of you, Charlie, but you're only saying that,"
said Karen, still anxious. "There's no way you were nervous. Look
at you—you're so calm and professional about this. I'll never be
like you."

"Trust me," Charlie said, "I was incredibly nervous. If you
don't believe in yourself, Karen, believe me, and I'm telling you
that you're well able to do this."

Karen went to serve a customer, and Charlie reflected how strange it was that her coworkers thought she was calm and professional, while her mother thought she was dithery and unambitious. It was the family-box syndrome: your family put you in a certain compartment when you were small and, once you were in it, you weren't supposed to leave—not in their minds, anyhow.

Charlie had been stuck in the *quiet, will never make anything of herself* box, and that's where she was supposed to stay.

Well, now she'd decided she wasn't staying in any box, for anyone.

Today was her late shift at work, which meant Brendan would pick Mikey up from his friend's house at six and together they'd make dinner. Brendan was teaching Mikey to cook, and they were slowly working their way through a Jamie Oliver book. In fact, Mikey showed great flair for cooking and was improving at such speed, that he'd soon be better than his dad.

"Dad, like this," Mikey had said the night before, taking one of the sharp knives and cutting a zucchini slowly but expertly. "You do them all sideways. They're supposed to be straight, all the same." Mikey was dark like his father, with big hazel eyes and spiky hair that fell over his forehead as he worked. His tongue stuck out a little as he concentrated on slicing the zucchini, and that, combined with the intensity on his young freckled face, made Charlie's heart contract. He was growing up so fast.

"When you get your restaurant, we'll go there every night," Brendan said proudly.

"If you do," replied Mikey, still busy chopping, "you'll have to pay like everyone else. I have to make money!"

"Right, then, we'll join the huge queues waiting to get in," Charlie suggested.

Mikey considered this. "No, it's all right, you can skip the queue."

"Why?" demanded Charlie, ruffling his hair. "Because we'll be too old and wrinkly and will ruin the look of the place?"

Mikey giggled, a big smile creasing his face and making his eyes dance. "No. Okay, you can eat for free."

"Same deal as here, then," his mother said with a laugh. "Everyone eats for free."

They were making a beef stew tonight and Charlie was looking forward to it. To add to the whole thing, she'd bought some apple strudel in the food hall and there was cream in the fridge. No matter how enormous the main course, Brendan and Mikey were always like wolves for dessert. Mikey had shot up in the past year, was nearly as tall as his father, and could eat to Olympic standard and still remain lanky.

It was after seven when she reached her car, a battered Citroën she was passionately attached to despite its decrepitude. Throwing her bag in, she switched on the heater to take the February chill from the air, then phoned home.

"Hi, love," she said as Brendan answered. "How was your day?"

"Hello, Charlie. Oh, you know, the usual. It's over, that's the thing. How was yours?"

Charlie thought of the news Shotsy had imparted. She usually told Brendan everything—well, almost everything. She lied by omission sometimes when it came to her mother because Brendan wouldn't stand for some of the things Kitty said. But tonight, she didn't want to ruin their evening telling him about DeVere's. She'd tell him tomorrow or at the weekend, perhaps. "Fine," she replied. "Has the chef started?"

"Braising beef as we speak."

"He's amazing," she said in wonder. She knew so many people with teenage sons who talked about them as if they were juvenile-delinquents-in-waiting, and here she and Brendan had this wonderful son who cooked them dinner once a week. Sure, he grumbled sometimes, and left smelly socks and cycling gear all over his room, and was totally deaf when he was at his PlayStation, but he never shouted that nobody understood him or told his parents he hated them, which was apparently the norm. Charlie felt so lucky when she thought about her beloved Mikey.

"I didn't know how to braise beef when I was thirteen," Brendan said.

"Nor I," Charlie agreed. Hardly a surprise, she thought, given that cooking wasn't a premium in the Nelson household. "And I may never have to do it again, now that Mikey's taken over."

"He's better at cooking than either of us," Brendan added ruefully. "Did you get anything for dessert?"

"You only love me because I work beside Kenny's food hall," Charlie teased.

"Is that a yes?"

"Yes, greedy guts. I love you."

"Love you too. You're on your way?"

"Yes, just leaving."

"Drive carefully."

Charlie hung up, then deleted the missed-call symbol on her phone. Her mother had phoned twice, once at five minutes to three and again half an hour later. Staff on the floor at Kenny's weren't supposed to have their mobile phones on their person during working hours unless there was a specific reason for it. So Charlie, along with most people, left hers in her locker with her bag. Brendan, Mikey, and Mikey's school all had the number for the direct line into the Organic Belle department, and could reach her in any emergency. The only person, therefore, who left urgent messages on her mobile was her mother.

"I'm at the doctor's in the waiting room. I felt faint and I got a taxi to take me. There's a long queue, mind you. But I'm sure Dr. Flannery will see me quickly. He knows my heart's not good, and that's more serious than what's wrong with most of the people here. Call me when you have time. I may need a lift home."

Charlie felt the familiar tightening around her temples that foretold a massive tension headache and wondered if she had any ibuprofen in her handbag. Only her mother could leave such a message, dismissing everyone else's ailments as nothing compared to hers, with the entire waiting room listening.

The second message was more succinct:

"Dr. Flannery wants to do cholesterol tests on me. He's worried. So am I. I knew this morning that something wasn't right. I'll be at home, if you can spare the time to phone."

Charlie clicked off, then switched the phone off totally. Was that what Shotsy meant when she said "detach with love"? Charlie wasn't sure. Between the news about DeVere's and her mother's double volley at either end of the day, Charlie felt wrung out. She wanted to go home, eat dinner with her darling family, and not talk to anyone else. What she didn't want was to be at her mother's beck and call. Was that too much to ask?

Four

When you're annoyed, don't speak from that place inside yourself that nurtures all past hurts. That will just make it all worse.

Friday was Valentine's Day. Passing a man carrying a big bouquet of red roses on her way to work, Ingrid thought of her daughter getting ready to go to Lizzie's wedding. At the television studio in Dublin, the security guard at reception was hauling a big bag of fan mail with red envelopes spilling out of the top through the inner security doors to the offices.

"Valentines for Ken Devlin?" she asked.

"Don't know what they see in him," muttered the guard, panting. "He's got a face like a robber's dog. And he's a midget, you know. Five foot two is all. A midget. Looks taller on television, of course."

Ingrid nodded noncommittally, thinking of Marcella. One person's midget might be another person's love god.

It seemed there was no escaping St. Valentine, even in the office. The *Politics Tonight* team was divided into two camps: those who thought Valentine's Day was a ruthless marketing ploy by flower shops and card-makers, and those who saw the public declaration of love with the gift of flowers or chocolates as an expression of pure romance.

Ingrid found that where people stood on the matter largely depended on their current experience with the opposite sex. Martin, one of the producers, was in the throes of a vicious divorce and was muttering grimly about having been nearly knocked off his racing bike on his way to work by a fleet of flower delivery vans.

"Waste of time and money," he was heard to snap. "It's not as if it even makes any difference. Buy her flowers, cut your wrists, whatever! Like the bitches actually care."

Ingrid had enormous sympathy for Martin; reliable rumor had it that his wife had hired one of the country's top divorce lawyers, a woman whose motto was "Take him for everything he's got." It wasn't a snappy motto, but it worked. Outraged soon-to-be-ex-wives were queuing up to hire her.

Meanwhile, Jeri, the show's production assistant, was deeply in love with a new man she'd met on a blind date—a teacher who was "kind and funny, has a dog, and does triathlons!" She was walking around in the glorious haze that only came from receiving a public display of affection that showed her colleagues she was Someone's Special Person.

"Twenty-four red roses," whispered Gloria, Ingrid's personal assistant, "and a teddy bear holding a red satin heart that says 'I Heart U.'"

"Gorgeous," said Ingrid with pleasure. She hoped it would last. Jeri was a sweet girl and deserved someone nice.

"Wait till you see your bouquet," Gloria added.

Ingrid was surprised. David didn't normally go in for the whole red-roses shtick.

"Unless it's your secret lover," Gloria went on, seeing the surprise on her boss's face. "I just assumed they were from David—"

Ingrid burst out laughing. "Secret lover, indeed! Where would I find the time, Gloria? And can you imagine the fun the political parties would have if I did have a man hidden away somewhere? They'd never answer a question of mine again—they'd be too busy smirking at me on-air, ready to say, 'Don't ask me anything, Ms. Fitzgerald, until you tell viewers where you were last Saturday. . . .'"

Gloria giggled.

Ingrid's first thought on seeing the arrangement of creamy

Vendela roses was that only a secret lover with exquisite taste and pots of money would send flowers so beautiful. Displayed in a cut-glass vase, with pale pink crepe tissue and a hand-tied satin bow around them, they were lovely.

She surprised herself at how touched she felt as she read the card: *Happy Valentine's Day—Love, David.*

She hadn't got him anything; they rarely exchanged Valentine's Day cards or gifts. David wasn't prone to romantic gestures, and, anyway, romance shouldn't be confined to one day in the calendar, a theme Ingrid had elaborated upon many times. And yet here she was, feeling as moony as a teenager at the sight of her beautiful bouquet.

David was amazing. He could still surprise her after all these years.

She wished she could meet him for lunch to say thank you, but she was seeing her sisters today. They met up every month for lunch and she couldn't let them down.

But she could make a special dinner tonight, perhaps ask Mrs. Hendron, their housekeeper who came twice a week, to buy some fish so that Ingrid could make her special fish pie, which David adored but which she rarely made anymore because it took so long and was so fiddly. She phoned David's direct line at Kenny's, and Stacey, her husband's assistant, answered.

"Hello, Stacey," Ingrid said, surprised. David's personal line was sacrosanct. It was unusual for anyone else to answer.

"Hello, Ingrid," Stacey trilled. "Mr. Kenny's at a meeting. He won't be long now. I'll tell him you rang as soon as he gets back."

"Oh, not to worry," Ingrid replied. "I just wanted to thank him for the flowers."

She felt that shivery thrill again, a lovely feeling. The man in her life had sent her flowers. Was she finally turning into a girlie-girl in middle age?

"Did you like them?" Stacey asked eagerly. "They're part of the new line in the last-minute gift department, came in last week, and I hear they're flying off the shelves today. It was all Claudia's idea.

That girl is a marvel. She's only been with us a few months, and she's smashing, worth her weight in gold. She insisted all the men send the flowers to their wives," Stacey went on guilelessly.

Ingrid recovered in an instant. "Yes, they're lovely," she said automatically. "What a marvelous idea of Claudia's."

"She's so young and so sparky, and she never stops," Stacey continued. "Here till all hours at night, working on new stuff. I don't know what Mr. Kenny would do without her."

"No, me neither," Ingrid replied.

She found it hard to concentrate on work that morning. At the preproduction meeting for the next night's show, a special weekend broadcast because of the by-election, all the talk was about what the wrong result would mean for the government. Old surveys and political swing sheets were reprinted, and comparisons were made with the last time the government had lost a by-election. Ingrid found her mind drifting, running back over David's strange mood and the flowers sent, ostensibly, by Claudia. Something felt not quite right, but she couldn't put her finger on it.

David loved her, she knew that, but he was anxious about something and not sharing it. He wasn't the sort of person to cheat on her with someone else. She'd bet her life on that. But there was something.

It was tied up with the store, and he was keeping it to himself. She knew business had been tough over the past year. She was a director of the company, albeit not an active one, so she'd seen the profit-and-loss statements. But if there had been a serious problem, David would have called a directors' meeting and she'd have been invited, along with Tom, the company's chief financial officer, and Lena, the marketing director. And he hadn't.

"Men!" she muttered.

"Ingrid?"

Everyone around the coffee-ringed meeting table was staring at her.

"Just remembered that the computer repairman is due at my house today," she improvised.

Everyone nodded. Repairmen and their cosmic black-hole schedules: they all understood.

Ed, the director, put in his own story about the dishwasher repairman who needed wooing to get him to come at all.

"That's what you get when you have a fancy dishwasher with two separate compartments," teased Jeri.

Finally, the meeting ended.

Ingrid had plenty of work to do, but she couldn't imagine doing it while her mind was elsewhere.

She dumped her stuff on her desk and picked up her bag. "Gloria, I'm going to lunch early."

"With your sisters?" Gloria had met Flora and Sigrid many times. They were nothing like Ingrid, of course; she was unique. But they were lovely women, with enough of the Fitzgerald eccentricity for Gloria to see where it had come from.

"Yes, I might be late back." Ingrid had a plan: she'd drop by Kenny's after lunch. There was nothing urgent she had to do, nothing that couldn't wait till tomorrow, broadcast day. And this was . . . well, it *felt* like an emergency.

All the way down to Ardagh, Ingrid kept the radio turned up loud to a talk show because she couldn't quite bear to be alone with her thoughts. But they invaded her mind anyway. It was that niggling feeling she'd had for weeks now that something was wrong with David.

Ingrid never acted on impulse: she was thoughtful, careful, considered. But not today.

She knew about Claudia. David never kept anything about Kenny's from her. Claudia was second-in-command to the unflappable Lena, who ran the company development office. Lena's job was to come up with new marketing strategies for the business and to protect its core brand. If anyone had an idea, they went to Lena, and she made sure it passed the Kenny's branding test.

Claudia had been hired to strengthen Lena's team. Ingrid could recall the recruitment process, with David poring over CVs in their living room. Ingrid loved reading curricula vitae; to her, they were glorious pictures of people and their lives.

"I didn't know anyone still listed hang-gliding in their interests section," she'd said, leafing through them, fascinated. There had been a time when everyone professed to like skydiving, deep-sea diving, and reading out-of-print French novels in the hope it would make them sound more interesting. But now the interests tended to be more realistic, and if someone put "traveling round India on a bike," chances were they'd actually done it. Unlike the mythical skydiving.

"Show me." David peered through his glasses at the CV in question. "No," he said, "I didn't like him. Too cocky. Didn't say thanks to Stacey when she brought in the coffee."

Ingrid laughed. If only the guy had been trained by Marcella, he'd have known that how one treated the people who theoretically weren't important was a very useful tool in grading candidates. Being rude to the person serving tea was fatal. She'd never hire someone like that.

"Now, *she* was good," David went on, passing another CV to Ingrid.

Claudia Mills was twenty-eight, with a master's in marketing and another in business development. She'd worked in the States for a year and was keen to move back home.

"Pretty," Ingrid said, admiring a professional color photograph of a dark-eyed girl with a knowing expression, a glossy brown bob, and shiny lips. "Sexy, too."

"You'd have to ask Lena that," David had said without pausing. "She notices if they're cute—I just watch out for who can do the job."

David had never cheated on her in his life. Ingrid had never worried for even a moment on that score. But now the notion that the newest member of the staff had insisted that every man, including the boss, send his wife flowers on Valentine's Day set Ingrid's sensors on full alert. Only someone flirtatious or very sure of her position in the company would do such a thing. What's more, it was a calculated insult to the women involved, like saying, "Your husband wouldn't think of doing it himself, but I asked him to send flowers to you." A very subtle insult, but an insult all the same.

Ingrid's sisters, Sigrid and Flora, were ten and twelve years older respectively. She'd been the baby of the family, an adored "accident" who'd grown up feeling loved and surrounded by kindness.

Flora's passion in life was music. She taught piano and lived in blissful happiness in a cottage in Wexford with Brid, a violin teacher. Flora had been married, had three grown-up children, and had stunned them all when she'd left her bemused husband, Paul, for Brid.

She was fifty-five then; now, on the final approach toward seventy, apart from a dodgy back, she said she'd never been happier. Her children brought the grandchildren to visit, Paul came round every Tuesday for dinner, and Brid and Flora were planning to accompany a group of adult music students to Rome in April.

"We're going to a special Mass in the Vatican, too," she said. "I can't wait." Brid's cousin, who was a priest at the Irish College in Rome, had organized it. Neither Flora nor Brid seemed to find it in any way odd that two women living very much outside the rules of the Church should visit the Holy See, for all its vehement disapproval of lesbian relationships.

But then, Ingrid knew that nobody was likely to throw them out of the Vatican, since they looked for all the world like two genteel music teachers whose idea of a good time was a bit of Mozart followed by a mug of cocoa.

She was careful not to say this in Flora's hearing, for anyone who leapt to such conclusions would be told in no uncertain terms that Flora and Brid enjoyed a perfectly healthy sexual relationship, thank you very much. "Why do young people think that they invented sex?" she once protested over dinner. "It's like playing the piano—you get better with practice, and though you mightn't have as much stretch in your fingers as you get older, you've got the technique to make up for it."

David had choked on his soup. "Do you think they're still at it?" he'd asked Ingrid later.

"Why not?" she replied. "We are, aren't we?"

Sigrid had the family's dodgy back, too, but she ignored Flora's litany of fabulous new osteopaths and kept supple with yoga.

Yogalates was her latest fad, although she had to travel to Dublin once a week for classes and all that driving was playing havoc with her sacroiliac joint.

Sigrid's only complaint was that T.J., her husband, had no interest in keeping supple and was going to fuse to his old armchair one day while sitting there listening to horse racing on the radio.

"If I were to drop dead tomorrow, he'd have to look at the *Racing Post* to see what time he could bury me between races," she said, but it was a joke. Both Flora and Ingrid knew that if anything happened to Sigrid, T.J. would follow her into the grave within the week. They might mutter and moan at each other, but they were practically joined at the hip.

The sisters sat in the Speckled Trout pub at a corner table beside a roaring fire and looked at the menu in between catching up on the gossip of the past month.

"Brid and I named stars after each other for Valentine's Day," Flora said proudly when the waiter had left.

"How gorgeous!" said Sigrid, delighted. "I should get T.J. to name a horse for me! You can do that, you know, name horses—you just have to put up some money for the training. Not that we could, but still—"

"That's lovely, Flora," Ingrid said, conscious of that whiplash of anxiety again.

Her nearly-seventy-year-old sister was getting better Valentine's Day gifts from her lesbian lover than Ingrid was from her husband, and the comparison was making her sad. But why? She had no time for Valentine's Day commercialism. Never had. But thinking she'd been given something wildly romantic had stirred up the desire for such gifts. If David was going to send her flowers, he should have done it off his own bat.

When lunch was over, she drove to Kenny's and parked in the

store's public car park instead of using the staff one. Without quite knowing why, she wanted to see David at work without him knowing she was coming.

She entered the shop through the front entrance and let the whole Kenny's experience flow over her.

"Red is gorgeous on you!" she heard a woman in a flowery shirt say to her friend as they stood in front of one of the cosmetics counters. The friend, wearing a slash of shiny red on her lips, was looking aghast at her face in a small mirror.

"No, it's awful!" She began wiping it off at high speed.

"Bright red is hard to wear," came the gentle voice of the woman behind the counter. "This beigey pink would be nice with your skin tone, and not so dramatic."

Snippets of conversation floated around her.

"Where's the food hall?"

"I'm looking for those suck-it-all-in knickers. What floor are they on?"

The scent of Kenyan coffee mingled with all kinds of perfume, and from every corner of the store Ingrid could hear chatter, laughter, and murmured thank-yous as people were handed back their credit cards and the subtle cream paper bags with the gold font that spelled Kenny's in elegant art deco lettering.

She hadn't been here for ages, she realized. It had become David's work, the same way the television studio was hers—places where they spent huge chunks of their lives separately. She felt guilty at that. No wonder he wasn't talking to her about the store; she'd removed herself from it, and he probably felt he couldn't talk to her about it.

Quietly, she entered the back part of the store and made her way upstairs to David's suite of offices.

The door to Stacey's office was open, as was David's. No sign of illicit meetings there.

"Ingrid," said Stacey delightedly, "how lovely to see you. I was just making coffee for David, would you like some?"

"No, thanks," said Ingrid, smiling and walking into her

husband's office. He was at the big table where he sometimes had meetings, lots of papers spread out on the polished walnut.

"Ingrid," he said, pleased, "what brings you here? Isn't it your day for lunch with Flora and Sigrid?"

He put out his arms to give her a kiss, and Ingrid felt some of her apprehension melt.

"Yes," she said, "I thought I'd drop in on the way back. I haven't been here in ages."

"Stacey's making coffee," he added, going back to his papers.

"I wanted to thank you for the flowers," Ingrid went on. "The roses. I've heard the flowers were Claudia's idea," she said evenly.

"Were they nice?" David asked absently, head still bent over his paperwork.

Ingrid would have growled if she'd been able to, so she said nothing. The silence worked.

David's head shot up and he looked at her inquisitively. "You all right?"

"No," she snapped, keeping her voice low, conscious of the open door. "I am not all right. I am your wife, and today you sent flowers to my office at the behest of your sparky little girl Friday, Claudia. So no, I am not all right. I am very much not all right."

Nobody could ever call David stupid. He got it instantly.

"This is about Claudia?" he asked. "Claudia who works here?"

His look of absolute astonishment was all the evidence Ingrid needed. Nobody could fake astonishment with such utter truth. And Ingrid had seen plenty of people try it in her years as an interviewer. The faintest gleam of bemusement appeared on his face.

"You're worried about Claudia," he said, and she could have sworn he looked relieved, as if there was something else she should be worried about.

The frisson of fear inside her diminished and she felt guilty at having wronged him. "I'm sorry," she said. "I got the wrong end of the stick."

"You did," he agreed, but he didn't laugh with her or even hug her for thinking such a thing. "Claudia and Lena are so thrilled with the whole last-minute gift idea, and yesterday Claudia came up with this plan to share how wonderfully it was going, that's all."

"They were lovely flowers," Ingrid conceded.

Something was still wrong. David hadn't said, "How could you think such a thing?" or hugged her.

"What's wrong? Is it the business? Please tell me, David. Tell me what's wrong."

He shook his head. "Nothing's wrong, Ingrid. Please don't interrogate me, I don't need that."

She never interrogated him. "But you're worried, I can tell. Don't lock me out."

He rubbed his eyes as if getting grit out of them. "Money's always a problem, especially in the credit crunch, but we'll manage, we always do. Now, I need to finish this quickly, love. We can go to the café and have coffee then, if you'd like? I just need another half an hour."

Ingrid shook her head. "I have to go back to work. I was going to make us fish pie this evening."

His face lit up. "Great."

Ingrid wandered round the store for half an hour before she left. She still felt guilty for not having been there lately, and she couldn't help but want to set eyes on Claudia, just to see.

Kenny's was a real jewel, she realized, walking through the homes department with its carefully chosen pieces. The shop couldn't compete with the big department stores in Dublin, so it had specialized in things you simply couldn't get elsewhere. There was unusual china, the gorgeous pottery with indigo glazes, wooden lamps with bases of carved flowers, Tiffany lamps held up by brass fairies, and the Bluestone tapestries that Ingrid adored, even though they were worlds away from the sort of décor she normally liked.

A woman with a baby in a stroller stood in front of the tapestries, fingering a large mermaid one with longing. Ingrid could remember when Molly and Ethan had been babies, and she'd had so little time to meander around shops. She felt a strange yearning to have that time back again, and she'd do it differently. Make more time to meander, like this woman with her baby.

But she'd always been so busy, trying to fit work and house-work into a day that was still only twenty-four hours long.

The woman with the baby turned and caught Ingrid's eye.

"It's lovely, isn't it?" she sighed, meaning the tapestry. "But a bit expensive for me."

"I love them too," Ingrid agreed. "I've actually got one in my hall."

"Lucky you," said the woman.

Yes, thought Ingrid, lucky me.

Five

Life is what happens when you're making other plans.

Lizzie's wedding morning was bitterly cold. Unusually low temperatures for the time of year, the radio weather forecaster said chirpily as Natalie and Molly sat beside the range in Natalie's parents' farmhouse.

Natalie was waiting for her stepmother's porridge, which was slowly cooking on the range and tasted very different from anything she ever heated in a microwave in her flat.

Molly was foolishly having toasted homemade bread—foolishly, because a trio of dogs sat at her feet, making hungry, abandoned expressions and drooling.

"I did tell you," Natalie said. "They think it's their toast, not yours."

"They're sweet," said Molly, who was a sucker for big brown eyes.

The back door opened and both girls could feel icy cold rush into the kitchen. Des, Natalie's dad, came in, and even he was rubbing his hands together.

"This cold would take the balls off a brass monkey. I hope Lizzie's wearing a blanket today," he said, going to the range and holding his hands over it.

"Dad, you know how stubborn Lizzie is," Natalie said. "This is her Valentine's fairy tale, and she's refused all suggestions about wraps and fake-fur throws. She's going to look like a princess, no matter how cold."

"Being covered in goose pimples isn't going to look very nice in the photos," pointed out Molly mildly. She was planning to wear a vintage woolen dress, a coat, and a pashmina to the church, and was already wondering if that was enough.

"You try telling Lizzie that," Natalie said.

"A bit of a mule, is our Lizzie." Des grinned, winking at Molly to show he agreed with her.

Molly loved Natalie's dad, and she loved going to visit Natalie's home.

Part of the charm was that it was so very different from her parents' elegant house with its perfectly designed garden maintained by a gardener who came once a week.

Any grass around Woodenbridge Farm was nibbled low by a pet ram called Sydney, who maintained decent lawn standards and ran to greet visitors when they got out of their cars. Sydney had been hand-reared indoors with milk from a baby's bottle until he got too big. As a result, he thought he was a dog.

The house itself was a small and sturdy stone farmhouse, Natalie's father's family home for generations. It was heated solely by open fires and the giant range in the kitchen, with a few gas heaters here and there for people prone to cold.

Staying overnight in winter had made Molly finally realize why Natalie never turned the gas heating on in their flat. Natalie was used to the cold.

"Here, you put clothes on to go to bed," explained Natalie cheerfully. "When it's really cold, you have to bring two hot-water bottles with you, or else let the dogs lie on the bed. I always feel that people who don't like dogs on the bed have never lived somewhere without central heating."

All the floors were stone or wood, and nobody minded when the three dogs, four cats, and the odd chicken wandered in and out, leaving fur or feathers in their wake. The two old couches and faded threadbare rug in the snug living room were originals and not expensive copies trying to give off a country vibe. This was a working farm, with a small herd of beef cattle grown for the Italian market, and no money for any luxuries. The Flynns ate their own vegetables and the eggs that their hens laid.

The relaxed atmosphere was very beguiling. Bess, Natalie's

stepmum, presided over the house with the easygoing charm of a den mother minding a campful of scouts. She even looked like a den mother: she had a trim figure and always dressed in jeans and long hand-knitted sweaters, her graying hair cut sensibly short as if any messing around with hair dryers or curling tongs was a nuisance she didn't have time for.

There was always homemade soup or some cold pie in the fridge for hungry people. Bess made scones first thing every morning, yet she never pushed her food on anyone. She prepared it, then went off doing things; if people wanted food, they could help themselves. As long as they tidied up afterward, all was well. There was no money for a housekeeper here; Bess did most of the housework and she worked part-time too as a seamstress.

Natalie's brothers, Ted and Joe—a strapping pair of "Irish twins," so called because they were born less than a year apart—clearly thrived in this atmosphere. Unlike most lads of eighteen and nineteen, they could both cook and were good at ironing. Molly knew her mother would approve. Ingrid hated men who looked helplessly at saucepans when they could reach level ten on Temple of Doom.

When the two girls had arrived the night before, the family had shared a lively dinner. This morning, Natalie had to head off to Lizzie's house for bridesmaid's duties. Molly was looking forward to spending the morning going for a long walk around the farm, and perhaps up into the surrounding hills, with some of the Flynn's tribe of dogs. Sparkles, a skinny wire-haired dog with a limp, had taken a shine to Molly and had been following her around the house adoringly. Despite not being the prettiest dog ever, Sparkles had the most beautiful eyes, soft toffee orbs that stared up at Molly beseechingly until she hauled him onto her lap for a cuddle.

They were all due at the church at three, and although Molly wasn't generally a fan of weddings—they seemed to go on *forever*—she didn't mind this one because she was going to be sitting with the rest of Natalie's family.

"Right, I'm off," said Natalie, hugging her father good-bye. "Off to the O'Sheas' to see if they've all killed each other yet."

"Is that one of the rituals of modern weddings?" her father teased.

"It will be in Lizzie's house," Natalie said.

She found a parking space in the cul-de-sac where Lizzie's family lived, and by the time she'd been let into the semidetached house, she knew she'd been on the money about the fight. As predicted, the O'Shea household was in crisis. There were no tea bags or milk, and none of the neighbors squashed into the tiny kitchen for a pre-wedding party seemed inclined to leave the coziness to buy any. The hairdresser had started work an hour ago and was still only putting the finishing touches to Lizzie's mother's hair, which meant she was seriously behind schedule. And the makeup artist hadn't arrived yet.

"Will you phone her?" gasped Lizzie when Natalie came in. Still wearing her fluffy dressing gown, with her hair wet and her face bare, she looked very unlike a fairy-tale bride.

The makeup lady's phone went unanswered, and Natalie left a polite message.

Half an hour late, not good but not fatal yet.

"I'll nip down to the shop to get milk and tea," Natalie said.

"Jesus, no!" shrieked Lizzie. "Get the hairdresser away from my mother. She's hogging her. It's my day, not hers. I need to be done now. They can do without bloody tea. There's a giant bottle of Baileys in the kitchen—they can have that in coffee and feck the milk."

Nearly an hour later, the hairdresser was nailing giant heated rollers into Lizzie's hair to moans of "Ouch, that hurt!"

Anna, who was bridesmaid number two, had turned up, and she and Natalie had been tag-phoning the makeup lady every ten minutes. The woman hadn't replied to either messages or texts.

"She's obviously not coming," Anna said. "We'll never get anyone at such short notice. What'll we do?"

"Don't look at me. You know I'm hopeless with makeup," Natalie said.

"I can do mine, but I've never done anyone else's," said Anna.

"Baileys and coffee, anyone?" roared the mother of the bride from downstairs.

Natalie had a brainstorm. "Charlie from Kenny's—she runs the Organic Belle department—she might be able to lend us someone for an hour. She's lovely, she'd help out, I know."

Charlie recognized an emergency when she heard one.

"It's quiet enough this morning," she said. "I can't lend you anyone, but if I take an early lunch, I'll pop round and do it myself. Will an hour and a half be long enough?"

"You're an angel!" said Natalie gratefully. An hour and a half would get Lizzie and her mother done. Everyone else could fend for themselves.

She went into the bedroom to tell Lizzie the good news and was waylaid by bridesmaid number three, Steve's sister, Shazza, who'd insisted on being a bridesmaid, and having got her wish had been doing her level best to take over. "I think we should all put our hair up," she said.

"What?" Natalie asked, bewildered.

"Up, it's more flattering," said Shazza, holding her own blond hair up to demonstrate.

Shazza had gone against Lizzie's dictate that spray tans would look ridiculous at a February wedding and was the rich brown color of an Italian handbag. Everyone else's skin was pure Irish blue.

One hand holding up her hair, Shazza did a twirl in front of Lizzie. "See? Much nicer with the dresses."

The bridesmaids' dresses were pale baby pink, a color that did precisely nothing for Natalie but suited Shazza perfectly.

"I hate my hair up," Natalie said. "And we agreed that we'd have soft curls—"

"No, you're right, Shaz," said Lizzie traitorously. "Up would be fabulous. Much more fairy-tale. Mum," she called out. "Could I have another Baileys? I'm parched."

"She's only trying to keep the peace," Anna whispered to Natalie, seeing her friend's furious face. "If she doesn't agree, Shaz will rush round to Steve and whine about how his bride-to-be is being mean to her."

"But we're her best friends since we were five," hissed Natalie back.

Anna responded with a shrug and her weddings-are-hell look.

Natalie was shaking with cold and her skull ached from having her hair screwed on to her head with a million hair clips by the time she finally met up with her family and Molly again. The official pictures after the wedding ceremony had taken forever, and most of them had been staged outside in the "spectacular and scenic gardens of the elegant Mount Ardagh Hotel," which actually meant a bit of grass behind the hotel where there was a peeling pergola with flowers twirling round it and a small pond that was no longer viable for actual fish and home to lots of ferny-type things that looked good in photos but were remarkably smelly in real life.

"I promise," whispered Molly, "that if I ever get married, it'll be in the summer and I will let you pick your own dress."

"Never get married," Natalie whispered back, shivering. "Please get me something hot to drink. I am frozen."

Bess handed her a woolen wrap in a dark crimson that immediately lifted Natalie's complexion. "Lizzie should have let you each wear a color that suits you," Bess said, and Natalie felt guilty for silently agreeing with her.

Even her little brother Joe, who didn't notice female attire unless it was on a girl he fancied, nodded in sympathy at Natalie's outfit. "The hair is brutal," he said. "Looks like it hurts."

"It does," Natalie informed him. "But I've got to keep it up for ages."

"Joe only likes long flowing hair," Ted said with a smirk.

Joe thumped him.

"Whose long flowing hair would that be?" asked their father, grinning.

"Nobody." Joe thumped Ted again for luck.

"Joe'll be getting married next," Ted said, getting out of his brother's reach. "You'll have to do bridesmaid again, Nat."

Everyone smiled, and Bess ruffled Joe's gelled hair affectionately.

"Before I buy the mother-of-the-bride outfit, can you tell us who this future member of the family is?" she asked.

Natalie felt a stab of envy. Why? She couldn't understand what would make her feel that way. It was like waking up after a dream and trying to catch the memory of it, feeling it flitting away. Something to do with Joe and Bess and her little brother getting married one day.

"Nobody," said Joe crossly. "Big mouth here ought to watch it, or he'll get another belt."

Sitting at the top table was like being an international peacekeeper, Natalie thought. To cope with the combined masses of the O'Shea and Devine clans, the arrangement had turned into a long table with a big round table stuck on at either end to appease the various great-aunts, grannies, and uncles, who'd have been aggrieved to be seated somewhere less important. Sitting at the cusp of the long table and one of the round ones, Natalie found that she was surrounded by people with a stack of freshly remembered resentments waiting to be aired.

The salmon was not as nice as the salmon at a previous wedding, one great-uncle muttered.

"I wouldn't know, I wasn't asked to *that* wedding," flashed back a gimlet-eyed cousin.

"Who are your people?" demanded Natalie's neighbor, a misleadingly sweet-faced little old lady who'd come all the way from Kinsale for today and had taken against the hotel because there was no kettle or tea-making facilities in her room.

Natalie had heard the whole story twice already.

"They're over there," she said now, looking wistfully at a distant table where her family and Molly appeared to be having fun.

The Kinsale lady peered at them. "Who's that girl wearing the strange outfit with the fandangle on the shoulder?"

Natalie hid a smile. Molly was very proud of her vintage dress, a gray wool 1950s creation with a flared skirt, which she'd accessorized with a patent-leather belt and a large white corsage, à la

Carrie in *Sex and the City,* undoubtedly the fandangle Mrs. Kinsale was referring to.

"One of my best friends," she replied.

"I thought Lizzie was your best friend?"

Natalie's smile was forced this time. "Oh, she's one of them, too."

The introduction of bottles of champagne for the speeches cheered up most of the grumpier people, and Natalie relaxed.

Even the crossness emanating from the tables of relatives hadn't dimmed Steve's love for Lizzie, and Natalie found herself sighing at his speech when he called Lizzie "my best, my always."

"Lovely," said Mrs. Kinsale, taking a good gulp of her champagne before holding her glass up for a refill.

Natalie wasn't listening; she was watching Lizzie and her mother embracing, all the morning's arguments about who got the longer go with the hairdresser forgotten. That was the dream she hadn't been able to touch, Natalie realized. Bess and Joe, mother and son. Lizzie and her mother. The strongest bond in the world.

"Don't worry, pet, it'll be you getting married one day," said Mrs. Kinsale, mistaking the gleam in Natalie's eye for tears over her unmarried state. "But I'd do something different with your hair, pet. That doesn't suit you."

While the hotel staff were rearranging the tables for the dancing that evening, Natalie went to the ladies' to take down her hair. Damn Shazza and her bloody idea. Painstakingly, she took out all the little hair clips until her head was metal-free and she was able to shake her dark hair loose again. She looked better already. With Bess's wrap around her shoulders, she felt like herself and not the horrible fake bridesmaid version.

Despite the cold, she thought she'd venture outside to breathe some fresh air. The smokers had annexed a little outside bar area with heaters and seats, so she went the other direction to stand on the terrace and look out at the coast, where the flicker of the lighthouse lamp broke up the darkness of the sea.

"I was wondering what you'd look like with your hair down," said a man's voice.

"Whatever it looks like, it certainly feels better," said Natalie, turning toward the voice. "I have just taken twenty-seven pins from my head."

"Twenty-seven?"

"I counted every one."

He had a nice grin. Was nice all over, really, with an open, intelligent face and kind eyes. He was probably her own age or a bit older, and even in a very elegant navy suit and gray silk tie looked like he was designed for bashing down doors and had ended up in a tie by mistake.

"I don't do much with my own hair," he added, and unselfconsciously put a hand up to his head, which was shaped like a bullet on top of huge shoulders and totally shaved.

Natalie laughed out loud. "Sorry," she said instantly, afraid she'd offended him.

"It started to fall out," he said, "and I didn't want to be one of those guys who has three long hairs and hair-spray them into place: one to the left, one to the right, and one tossed."

"No, not a good look," she agreed.

"I got rid of the lot."

"It suits you," she said.

"Does it?" he said, sounding as if he'd never really considered such a thing. "It's handy." He shrugged.

Natalie felt a sudden liking for this big, friendly man. "Whose side are you on?" she asked.

"The groom's side. I'm Rory Canavan," he said, and offered her a giant hand to shake.

"I'm Natalie Flynn, bridesmaid number one and school friend of the bride," she said.

"I know," he admitted. "I asked."

"There are men who have to score the bridesmaid at weddings, you know," Natalie said.

"I have heard that," he said. "Not the most noble of aims, is it?"

"No. I wonder, do they have a points system? Three points for the chief bridesmaid, four if she's married and is matron of honor, and ten points and a bonus prize if you score the bride?"

"That is so cynical," he said, but he was laughing.

"You're not trying to score three points?"

He shook his head. "I followed you out here because I saw you earlier and I wanted to meet you, but you seemed very interested in the people at your table."

"If only you knew," Natalie said with feeling. "You could have rescued me earlier."

Rory looked pleased. "Am I rescuing you now?"

"You would be if you sat with me at my table," she said thoughtfully.

Mrs. Kinsale asked all the questions Natalie couldn't.

"What do you do?" she asked, fixing Rory with her most adorable smile and giving him a poke in his substantial chest. The champagne had been round her side of the table many times and she had almost forgotten her grudge against the hotel over the in-room facilities.

"I'm a vet," he replied.

"Ooh, a vet! A professional man," she said, and gave Natalie a delighted poke this time. "Where exactly?"

"About ten miles outside Ardagh," he said, speaking loudly to the old lady. Natalie could have told him that Mrs. Kinsale was so sharp she'd have heard a pin drop on the other side of the room. "It's a big animal practice."

"Big practice or big animals?" asked Natalie, grinning, although she knew very well what he meant.

"Big animals," he said. "Cattle and horses, and some dogs and cats."

"I had a Yorkshire terrier, but she died," said Mrs. Kinsale, getting maudlin. "She was like a child to me, that dog. I loved her like a child."

"Did you get another dog?" asked Rory.

The old lady shook her head. "I wouldn't be up to it, and who'd mind her if I died?"

"You know, if you get her from a good vet, they could promise to do their best to look after your pet if you couldn't take care of her anymore," Rory said kindly. "It's a worry for lots of people, and the veterinary community understands that. And a sprightly thing like yourself will be dancing for many years yet," he added. The band was striking up "When I Fall in Love" "I don't suppose you can waltz? I'm very bad at it."

Mrs. Kinsale beamed at him.

They made an odd couple on the dance floor, the giant of a man supporting the frail lady, and Natalie saw she wasn't the only person looking at them fondly.

Lizzie, who hated slow dancing, wandered over hauling her dress behind her. The skirt was speckled with something dark and reddish. Red wine, Natalie guessed.

"I'm wrecked," Lizzie said, sitting tiredly in Rory's chair. She picked up a full glass of sparkling wine and drained it. "I see you've met Rory."

"He's nice," said Natalie, which was actually an understatement. She'd never gone for those big, Gaelic-football-playing types before, but she could see the charm. You'd feel totally safe with Rory by your side, safe in every sense of the word. There was a decency about him, a sense that he'd protect you from all harm.

"Sure, if you like that type of thing," said Lizzie shortly. Lizzie had always preferred sophisticated men. Steve, with his narrow hips and well-cut hair, could have stepped out of a modeling catalogue. "You can't dress him up, though. He looks ridiculous in a suit."

"Since when do we judge people by dressing them up?" Natalie asked, hurt but hiding it. She hadn't liked a guy for ages, and now she was liking one she'd met at Lizzie's wedding and Lizzie seemed put out by the whole idea.

Besides, Rory looked lovely in his suit. Sexy and rumpled, somehow. She wondered what he'd be like to kiss—

"He's a bit of a caveman," said Lizzie dismissively. "And there isn't an artistic bone in his body. You hate men like that. Remember how much you hated dopey Alan at school?"

"I didn't hate him," Natalie said. "I just didn't fancy him, that's all." Alan was a strapping farmer's son who'd adored Natalie for years, but her constant refusal to go out with him had eventually upset him to the point that he'd called her a "stuck-up cow."

"That was years ago, Lizzie. It's ancient history."

"Just reminding you."

It was as if, Natalie thought, Lizzie wanted their past laminated and untouched so she could visit it from time to time. Lizzie hadn't seen how much everyone else had changed; but then, perhaps she hadn't changed that much herself.

When Rory came back with Mrs. Kinsale, he asked Natalie to dance.

The tempo had changed and the band, which had been warned to mix old and new, was tentatively trying out a version of "Wonderwall."

"I love this song," said Rory as they found a place on the heaving dance floor.

"By Oasis, though?" asked Natalie mischievously.

"This version has its good points," Rory replied, not taking his eyes off her.

"You mean the lead singer's only a teeny bit off-key?"

"No, I mean the company," he said, and Natalie's heart skipped a beat.

He could dance. Not many big men could. Natalie had known many who'd lurched around like fridges on wheels, looking ungainly. But Rory had rhythm. He was fit, too. By the time "Wonderwall" was over and the entire fast Elvis canon had been gone through, Natalie was sweaty and exhausted.

"Let's slow it down," crooned the lead singer, and the drummer went at his drums with brushes as the band launched into a slow set.

Natalie laughed at the corniness of it all and turned to walk back to her seat, but Rory caught her hand and pulled her to him.

"Shall we dance?"

His body was hard and muscular up close, and she felt light as thistledown in his arms, but the effect was ruined by the fact that she was sweating profusely. She'd bet the damn pale pink dress was stained under the armpits and her hair was wet at the roots from dancing. Impossible to feel romantic under the circumstances.

And yet she did feel romantic. Natalie was tall, yet even so, her nose was about level with his chin. There was something beguiling about being with a man who made her feel like a fairy straight out of a children's film.

"I wanted to ask you something, but is it fair to ask without the lady at your table here?" he said. "She's so interested, it doesn't seem right to continue the whole thing without her."

Natalie laughed. "You can ask me anything."

"Can I see you again?"

The pleasurable glow Natalie felt from being pressed close to Rory increased. "I'd like that," she said.

"Great." He stopped dancing long enough to wave over to Mrs. Kinsale. "She said yes," he roared.

Six

It's never too late to stop and change the way you're going. Never.

Marcella Schmidt's mother had always told her she was too picky. If Marcella was given two choices, she wanted a third, just to be absolutely sure. Back then, she'd been Marcella Doyle, a name she couldn't wait to change. Doyle was fine on its own, the same as Marcella was; but together, the two sounded ridiculous. The exotic Marcella teamed with the utterly unexotic Doyle. Her mother, Jane, had defended her choice in children's names.

"Marcella is a name you'd notice," said Mrs. Doyle, who'd hated being plain Jane all her life. There might have been some Janes who lived exciting lives with thrilling things happening to them, but she wasn't one of them. Her children wouldn't be saddled with the same problem. Nobody could forget girls called Marcella, Regina, and Concepta. And if their surname was quite ordinary, it didn't entirely matter. Their given names were the ones people remembered.

Marcella's confirmation outfit had been the source of much drama in the Doyle household. Her mother had wanted Marcella to wear the same cream lace dress her older sisters had worn. Marcella had balked.

Regina, who'd left their small farm in Mayo to work in an office in Dublin, had promised to send a dress from Arnotts' children's department. "A little dress, something in velvet? You'd look very smart."

Marcella didn't see herself looking smart in either cream lace or velvet. She'd spotted a very nice coral pink shift dress and matching jacket, à la Jackie O, in a boutique in Ballina. It wasn't a child's outfit, but she was tall for her twelve years, and it would fit her.

Concepta, who was three years older but shorter, thought it totally unfair that her little sister might look glamorous on her confirmation day, when *she'd* looked like a child in that ridiculous cream dress with babyish white ankle socks and white patent shoes. Marcella was growing up far too fast.

"Regina's going to send you a dress from Dublin," she wailed. "Isn't that enough for you?"

"Regina still thinks I'm a child," Marcella said calmly. "I'm not."

"She has great taste; she'll send you something lovely," Jane Doyle soothed. "And you can't parade down the church in a grown-up's dress, Marcella. You're only twelve. Besides, where are we going to get the money for it?"

"If Regina's going to pay for a dress from Dublin, she can pay for this instead," Marcella said. She'd thought it all out. "I want to look just right, Mum."

"You're too picky, love," her mother had sighed. "It doesn't pay to be picky."

Marcella disagreed. On her confirmation day, everyone had said she looked marvelous in her coral pink. The adult effect of the dress meant the grown-ups didn't talk to her like she was a child, and the older boys she fancied—brothers of the lads in her class in school—clearly fancied her back.

"You always get what you want," said Concepta crossly, as if it was a bad thing.

"What's wrong with that?" Marcella asked, stung. She wanted her sister to approve of her.

"You're a tonic," said their father, smiling at his youngest daughter proudly.

Marcella forget about Concepta's remark and basked in her father's praise. She adored her dad. He didn't think she was picky; he thought she was right.

Thirty-seven years on, Marcella was no longer sure about the benefits of being picky—or discriminating, as she liked to call it now.

It worked in business: Marcella's company was one of the top three in the country in her field and could pick and choose clients. It worked in finance: her portfolio of shares was doing better than most, despite the horrific stock-market downfall. And it worked in clothes: Marcella loved shopping and wore a clever mix of invest-ment clothes alongside generic stuff so that nobody could tell the difference.

But pickiness simply didn't work when it came to men. With men, pickiness meant that you ended up alone.

It wasn't that she'd made a deal with the devil and opted for work success over home and hearth. Marcella had wanted both and would have sacrificed some workplace success if necessary, if she'd met a man who'd wanted less spin doctor and more of a wife. The sisterhood who sang her praises as a feminist might have been shocked to discover this, but it was true. The end justified the means.

But the right man hadn't asked her—either subtly or in an out-right fashion—to compromise her career, and she wondered now if it had been her fault because her criteria for the perfect man were too stringent. Marcella didn't want someone who would "do." She wanted it to be perfect or she didn't want it at all.

So many people seemed to think she had it all, particularly women friends who'd split from their husbands and found them-selves back in the world of dating again. Marcella, they seemed to imply, had everything sussed, knew how the system worked. She went out to dinners and parties, got her picture in the society pages, had a lovely life for herself, and never sat at home mop-ing with a bottle of wine and a DVD. She could guide them, the friends said, happy to have compatriots in their new single life.

Adept at appearing utterly content and in control, Marcella never allowed herself to shriek that of course she didn't have it all sussed; if she had, she'd be sharing a bottle of wine and a DVD with her own man instead of schlepping around town with newly liberated girlfriends.

Ingrid was one of the few people with whom she could be honest. How ironic that her confidante on the subject of loneliness was a woman with the perfect marriage.

"It's not all about a man, Ingrid," she explained. "I have so much and I'm lucky. I have the best job in the world; but at night, the job's not much comfort. I keep thinking that it's a lonely life, that I wanted more all those years ago, that I still want it. Not sex, really, but companionship."

The running joke about telly star Ken Devlin was a part of the game she and Ingrid played to pretend that men were just playthings and a woman like Marcella didn't have time for them. But she did. And when friends like Ingrid spoke about their husbands, idly mentioning that they were going out for a pizza together or taking a spur-of-the-moment weekend away thanks to a cheap flight, Marcella felt horrendously lonely. There was nobody to do those things with her. Nobody to hold her hand during turbulence on a plane, nobody to buy her flu medicine when she wasn't well, nobody to put the dustbins out on rubbish day. It wasn't wild hot sex Marcella craved; it was another body to come home to and somebody to share her life.

"Marcella, I've got Connor on line two. He says it's urgent." Daniel, Marcella's personal assistant, had a mellow voice that was very calming to listen to. He'd been with her for three years, and no matter how frenzied the message he was delivering—and with the nature of their business, he sometimes had to deliver very urgent messages indeed—Daniel made it sound as if they had all the time in the world to sort out the problem.

"Thanks, Daniel," said Marcella, flicking over to line two.

Connor Davitt was her partner in SD International, which stood for Schmidt-Davitt, and occasionally acted as a fire blanket to be thrown over disasters. Today, Connor was out on the road with one of their big corporate clients, which was running a golf fund-raiser and had been blessed with decent weather for it. It was part event management, part smiling and making sure all the right people met all the other right people. Connor could do it in his sleep. Unless someone had hit the nineteenth hole too early in the day and was now running amok with a nine iron and a bottle of scotch, Marcella knew that the problem was likely to be unrelated to today's event.

"Connor, what's up?" she asked.

"It's what's down that's the problem," he said. "Trousers."

"For Chrissakes, not again. Who?"

"Mickey Roche, on a fact-finding jolly in the Bahamas. And the problem, among others, is a woman who says she hadn't been paid and he owes her four hundred dollars."

"Fact-finding jolly in the Bahamas? Why do they persist in sending people like Mickey Roche to the Bahamas?" she asked wearily.

"Fact-finding is less fun in wet cities than it is in tropical paradises," Connor answered.

Marcella hated these fire-blanket jobs. Because people read about them, they assumed it was all a company like SD International did. It wasn't; as Marcella frequently said, their job was making people achieve the best possible version of themselves.

"Has he been arrested?"

"No. They were on the balcony of his hotel room smoking a joint, and he thought it might be fun to sunbathe in the nude, as you do."

"As you do," agreed Marcella, thinking with distaste of Mickey Roche, a councillor who would never be entered in a Mr. Universe contest unless the judging criteria changed to allow swollen beer bellies, forty percent body fat, and lascivious eyes. He was also an idiot. He'd spent a week in an intensive SD International media-training course, and had promptly gone out to do a radio interview in which he'd managed to insult the interviewer by implying that big bosoms had got her the job. Bizarrely, the public liked him. "Mickey tells it like it is," they said proudly.

There was, Marcella thought, no accounting for taste.

Connor continued the story: "He took umbrage when the hotel staff told him to put his clothes on."

"Naturally."

"And then he evicted the lady in question, throwing her clothes off the balcony into the swimming pool area, but neglecting to throw down any of the four hundred dollars he'd promised her. They're sending him home with all the other councillors, who are embarrassed and—"

"—determined to shift any blame from themselves by letting everyone know what Mickey was up to, distancing themselves from the scandal."

"Precisely. Statements are expected by tonight. Only one of them was clued-in enough to phone party headquarters to mention what had happened."

Marcella knew it had been a slow news week. Mickey's fun-packed jaunt had all the makings of a fabulous news story, offering the papers any number of angles, from the waste of taxpayers' money onward. Worst was the fun the tabloids would have with a story that involved public nudity and a man named Mickey.

"Please tell me nobody's got photographs," she said.

"Can't tell you that," Connor replied. "You'll have to make some calls. I'm a bit stuck here."

"No problem," she said. "Talk later."

Marcella swung into action. First, she needed to find out what the fourth estate knew about the problem. She phoned a journalist friend of hers.

"Donald, it's Marcella Schmidt. Can you talk?"

"Private talk?"

"Yes."

"Hold on. I'll take this in the office."

Marcella waited. She'd been in the *Courier Mail* offices often and knew that real privacy was almost impossible in a place where knowing other people's business was the lifeblood of most of the inhabitants. As news editor, Donald had a glass-walled office, but the door was permanently open and, if he shut it, every reporter's eyes would be on it, knowing that something interesting was happening. A few clever souls had learned to lip-read purely for moments such as these.

Donald and Marcella went way back. Many moons ago, they'd

had a fling on a press trip to Brussels, and, for whatever glorious reason, there had never been any awkwardness between them since. They'd both been between relationships at the time, and the following morning they'd lain in Donald's giant bed in the hotel and enjoyed talking to each other just as much as they'd enjoyed making rather tipsy love the night before.

It would never have worked for them to be together properly, Marcella was sure of that. Donald was more married to his job than he could ever be to any woman. Committed journalists were a nightmare—always obsessed with stories, never able to let go of the job. But they'd remained friends, and sometimes they tipped each other off on news the other should know.

"I'm in the dog box," Donald said. "Talk."

"Okay, I hate asking this, but I have a wayward councillor who's in a bit of a bother—"

"Mickey Roche," he said before she'd even finished. "The chief subeditor fancies 'Taking the Mickey.'" The *Courier Mail* was a broadsheet and would never print such a headline, but the office's unofficial bookie, a sportswriter named Chuck, ran a highly profitable book on possible headlines for stories in the tabloids. "My money's on 'Mickey's Mouse.'"

"You've got a picture." Marcella groaned. Only with photographic evidence could such a headline be imaginable. How else would they report that Mickey's mickey was mouse-sized?

Donald laughed. "No," he said, "I don't think there are any pics, but you can't be sure. We haven't got them, anyhow. How are you going to play this?"

"Don't know," Marcella replied. "Not a lot of damage limitation available for a toked-up councillor strutting his naked stuff on a Bahamian hotel balcony."

This time, Donald laughed so much he snorted. "You should be in the office book for headlines," he said. "You have a flair for it. We'll be going soft on Mickey, no pun intended. There's bound to be a reaction from Leinster House, so we'll use that rather than speculate." While Mickey, as a local county councillor, wasn't based at Leinster House, the Irish parliamentary chamber, his party would come in for a few slingshots over its wayward party member. "Are you around this week for a drink?"

Marcella ran through her diary in her head. "Should be," she said. "Friday maybe? I'll phone you tomorrow."

"Great. Now, you've got the inside track with Ingrid Fitzgerald and David Kenny," he went on. "Any truth to the rumor that there are cash-flow problems with Kenny's department store and that DeVere's is going to buy them out in a fire sale?"

For a moment, Marcella's legendary cool deserted her. A fire sale only occurred when financial problems meant everything had to go. "What?" she said.

"I'll take that as a no, then," Donald replied. "Just a very small rumor, Marcella. I heard it last week and there's been nothing else, so I wondered if there was any truth in it. We don't have the staff or the money to run down every tip-off."

"I hadn't heard any such thing," Marcella said firmly, recovering. She cared about Donald, but Ingrid and David were among her closest friends. Her protective instinct went into overdrive. "It's unlikely, very unlikely," she added. "David's a very canny businessman and, from what I hear, things are going brilliantly."

"Right." Donald was thoughtful. "Sour grapes from DeVere's perhaps?"

"Could be. Stranger things have happened," Marcella said lightly. "I'll call you back about Friday. Thanks, Donald."

She got off the phone, the fate of Mickey Roche completely gone from her mind. She needed to talk to David soon.

Seven

*What doesn't destroy you makes you stronger. I just
hope you don't have to go through that process in
the first place. But if you do, it's true. Trust me.*

Two days later, David walked through the front entrance of
Kenny's department store. He often went to the office that
way, pushing open the big brown-and-gold swinging doors the
way the customers did, instead of slipping in through the back
entrance that led to the offices. It was a way of connecting with
the store, reminding him of what he did.

Even early on a Wednesday morning, the store was buzzing.
Scent wafted through the cosmetics hall accompanied by the
hum of people chatting. The music in the store was always discreetly low, Vivaldi today. David hated piped pop and insisted on
proper classical music. Occasionally even opera came from the
speakers. He walked through cosmetics and into jewelry, which
was quiet. The jewelry hall was elegant, with exquisite costume
jewelry displayed alongside a limited amount of the real stuff.
He had recently taken the work of a new designer, a talented
young man from Poland. David looked into one of the cabinets
at Pavel Zaborsky's work, noting with approval how well it
looked. Modern, rounded pieces, cuff links and rings set with
round cabochon semiprecious jewels. It wasn't expensive, but it
looked incredibly expensive—that was the trick. David had been
hooked immediately. It wasn't the sort of thing that Ingrid liked.
She was the epitome of the modern woman, yet her taste in jewelry ran to art deco pieces, marcasite brooches and delicate little
earrings and watches that looked like they might fall off the hand

of some etiolated Viennese countess from the twenties. No, Ingrid wouldn't like Pavel's jewelry, but there were plenty who did.

Molly had told him that her flatmate, Natalie, had nearly finished her first collection. He liked Natalie, admired her fierce dedication to her work and how she was prepared to work hard in the store's café, never expecting anything from being best friends with the owner's daughter. But then, David thought with pride, Molly wouldn't actually be friends with anyone who thought like that. Even at school, she'd hated the clique of what she called "the children of," teenagers with famous, wealthy parents who believed that because Mummy or Daddy worked in big business or appeared on the telly it made them special by association. As Molly used to say: "Not!"

Ethan had been different. David sighed. Ethan was showing no glimmer of interest in either the family business or getting a job. Ingrid pandered to him and had worried incessantly about him flying off to Thailand. When David had been his son's age, he'd been working in the store morning till night, doing all the horrible jobs so he wouldn't get too big for his boots, as his father used to say.

"Good morning, Mr. Kenny," said the assistant behind the jewelry counter.

"Good morning, Laura," he said instantly. "Peaceful in here so far?"

"Yes, it is," she said, "but you know early mornings aren't good jewelry times. It'll pick up a bit later."

"I know, of course," he said with a smile, and Laura's faintly anxious expression relaxed.

David never ruled by fear, a lesson he'd learned from his father. "Kenny's is a family business, and family businesses do better when the sense of family values stretches to the management as well," Andrew Kenny had said.

That notion had been vital in the old days when he'd started the business. In 1924, nobody would have thought that a department store would work outside a big city, and now look at it.

David walked out of jewelry, thinking again about Natalie.

"She's got a lovely collection, Dad," Molly had said. "I can't describe it, but it's all brave and strong."

"Get her to show it to me," he'd said.

"Well . . ." Molly paused. "It's tricky."

"Why?"

"Natalie's very independent. She's got a thing about doing this the right way, going through Paul." Paul ran jewelry. "She doesn't want to use you or the fact that she knows me to get her foot in the door."

David considered this. "That's either very commendable or very stupid. I don't know which."

"Natalie's anything but stupid," Molly pointed out. "If so many jewelers hadn't gone out of business over the past year, she'd have got a job with one of them and a platform for her stuff. She's done brilliantly setting herself up, and she wants to do it all properly. She's like me, she hates all that 'It's not what you know, it's who you know' cronyism," Molly almost spat.

"I just said she could show it to me," David pointed out mildly. "I didn't say I'd buy it from her just because she's your friend. Business is business. Another old cliché." He grinned.

Directly in front of him, the vast wooden staircase stretched upward, gleaming goddesses in the Old Celtic style poised before each banister like the figureheads of ships.

One was Morrigan, the warrior goddess, carved from oak with a jutting chin, trailing hair, and a sword held firmly in one strong hand. Her other hand held a shield decorated with her symbol, a crow. The second goddess was Brighid, healer and keeper of the druidic fire. Her gown was carved with flames, and in her calmly crossed hands she carried one of the woven crosses that bore her name.

In David's father's time, the goddesses had been Egyptian, painted gold, black, and azure. A trip down the Nile in the 1930s had entranced Andrew Kenny, and he'd spent a lifetime reading about Egypt and taking holidays there, staying in the Old Cataract Hotel and photographing the temples.

But when his father's beloved Egyptian women had begun to chip and fall apart, David decided to commission these ancient Irish goddesses, in memory of a time when he'd loved a woman who knew all about the old Celtic religion.

Ingrid, who had no interest in magical imagery, had never even noticed the symbolism of these statues. He'd never told her about Star, either. Women found it hard to reconcile themselves to other great loves in a man's life—something else his father had told him.

David ignored the stairs in favor of the escalator, but as he rose above the floors, the usual glow of pride wasn't there. It was just as well his father couldn't see what was happening, David thought, no longer seduced by the beauty of the department store he'd worked for all his life. If his father hadn't been dead already, it would have killed him.

Just after half twelve, in her small office on the fifth floor of Kenny's, Stacey O'Shaughnessy felt a cool breeze coming from somewhere. Instinctively, she turned to see if David had opened the window in her office while she'd been down on the second floor getting coffee, but it was shut. More drafts, then. Despite all the money that had been pumped into Kenny's, it was still a very old building, full of architectural oddities and quirks that modern, well-insulated places didn't have.

She set David's caffe latte on the tray, added the half a spoon of sugar that he liked, and opened the cellophane on his sandwich. Ham and salad on rye bread. Not that David would notice what he was eating, to be frank. Not these days. Stacey had worked for David Kenny for fifteen years, and previously he'd always loved his food. When she used to bake for her children, she'd sometimes take muffins or homemade scones into the office for elevenses, and he loved them. Of course, Stacey's children were grown now and she didn't bake that often, just cakes for birthdays and such. Except she doubted whether David would want any, even if she'd arrived with some of his favorite soda-bread scones and gooseberry jam. He'd changed; eating his lunchtime sandwich without appearing to taste anything.

She took a sip of her own cappuccino before carrying the tray over to his door and knocking.

"David," she said in her clear voice. "Lunch."

There was no answer. He wasn't there, must have slipped out when she was in the café.

Balancing the tray on one hand, Stacey opened the door.

David Kenny was there, sitting in his chair and facing the open window. That's the source of the breeze, Stacey thought briefly, before realizing that her boss wasn't looking, as he sometimes did, across the town spires to the curve of the coastline and the white-capped waves of the Irish Sea. His head hung down on his chest.

"David!" Stacey dropped the tray and rushed forward. But even before she touched him, she could tell it was too late. There was a gray tinge to his normally tanned face, a whitening around the lips, a slackness to his jaw. David Kenny was dead.

On the second floor of the TV studio, Ingrid was doing one of the things she loved most: research. Every few weeks, she conducted an in-depth interview with a public figure where she got to break the mold. Instead of a straight Q&A where the subjects spouted their views on specific headline-making topics such as crime or unemployment, Ingrid talked to them for hours about what had driven them into politics in the first place or what still motivated them.

"You're a failed psychologist," the producer commented from the doorway, looking in at Ingrid with her dark-rimmed reading glasses on and a cup of cooling tea at her elbow, unconsciously smiling to herself as she made notes.

Ingrid peered at Carlos over the top of her glasses. "You mean because of this lot?" She gestured to the pages spread over the desk: newspaper and magazine clippings, articles printed off the Internet. "Probably," she agreed. "Does that make me a total nerd?"

He laughed. "If being one of the highest-paid broadcasters in the country means you're a nerd, then yes, you're a nerd."

"You ought to print new T-shirts for the show: *Nerd Tonight*," she said, smiling. "What can I do you for?"

"Nothing," he said, but came in and sat down in the chair opposite her desk.

Producing could burn people out easily, and Ingrid liked working with young producers because they brought an energy to the job. She herself was probably the oldest person working on the show, which was marvelous and scary in equal measure.

"Is everything all right?" she asked Carlos.

"No, it's all brilliant. You're brilliant," Carlos added fervently. "Just came in to chat." He picked up a newspaper from her desk and sat scanning it.

Ingrid smiled. Carlos was brilliant too, but quite mad with his wandering around at high speed.

It was flattering that he admired her professionally. She'd never felt that she was an impostor, that one day she'd be recognized as such and fired. Lots of women did, she knew, millions of them, unsure of their own abilities and convinced that they were in high-paying jobs by mistake and would one day be discovered.

Finding out what made people tick was like a drug. Some people got a buzz from sex or drugs; Ingrid got it from finally putting a piece of a mental jigsaw in place, like Archimedes shouting "Eureka!" Earlier she'd been in one of the endless program meetings discussing the rest of the week's output and looking at footage for that night's show. But this, researching a real person, was what she loved best.

Her mobile phone rang. She picked it up and saw that it was David's office number.

"Hello, love," she said cheerfully, expecting to hear that he wouldn't be home for dinner. She'd asked Mrs. Hendron to defrost a free-range chicken and put it in the oven with the timer set to start cooking at six.

"Ingrid—" Not David but Stacey, his right-hand woman.

"Sorry, Stacey, I thought it was the man himself," Ingrid said easily. "How are things? Did he forget to tell me he's due in Ulan Bator tonight and won't be home?"

Stacey didn't pick up on the joke. There was only silence. With an instinct Ingrid hadn't known she possessed, she understood then that something was very wrong. She stood up, clutching the phone in a froze grip.

"What is it, Stacey? What's wrong?"

"Oh, Ingrid, I don't know how to tell you this, but I came in and he was at the window and . . ."

"And?" Ingrid urged in panic.

"He's dead, Ingrid. I've called the ambulance. Dolores is here, our first-aid specialist in the store, but she says there's nothing anyone can do. David's dead."

Ingrid dropped the phone and it banged loudly onto the desk.

"What is it?" Carlos reached over the desk and grabbed her because it looked as if she might faint.

"David," she said blankly. "Stacey says he's dead."

"Fuck."

Carlos helped her into her chair, ran into the corridor and called for help, then returned and picked up the phone she'd dropped.

"This is Carlos Monroe," he said, "a colleague of Ingrid's. To whom am I speaking?"

Ingrid was vaguely aware of Carlos talking, of someone else coming in and hugging her, then leaving to get a cup of very strong, sweet tea.

"Brandy would be better," said a voice.

"Brandy gives you heart attacks," said someone else. "Tea's the best thing, with sugar."

"Whiskey, maybe?"

"Now's not the time to be dispensing drinks. Her husband's just died." The voice sounded exasperated. "We should get a doctor, she's in shock."

"Should we drive her to Kenny's?"

"No, I don't think so. She doesn't need to see his body, not yet."
His body.

"Why the hell did you phone her? Why not phone one of us so we could break it to her gently?" Carlos was demanding on the phone.

Ingrid was conscious of all this conversation, yet she couldn't have joined in any more than she could lift the cup of tea beside her. She felt otherworldly, like she was floating on the ceiling looking down. There but not there. Everything was so unreal. David couldn't be dead, not her David. She must be having one of those fearful waking dreams; perhaps if she was very quiet, she'd slip back into proper sleep again and then wake up to a new day, a day in which David was lying beside her in the bed.

He couldn't be taken away from her. He was so much of her life, the man she loved. She couldn't go on without him. Didn't they know that?

"Ingrid, look at me, please."

She managed to focus enough to see her assistant kneeling in front of her. Gloria was so efficient, she'd sort all this out. David wasn't dead. That was a crazy idea. Nobody who was as full of life as David could possibly be dead.

"You'll phone him, won't you?" she asked Gloria. "Deal with this mess? I don't know what's wrong with Stacey, you see."

Gloria was not one of life's touchy-feely people. She didn't hug people hello or kiss their cheeks twice or three times. But now she took Ingrid's hands in hers and held on tightly, comfortingly. "Ingrid, there's no mess, no mistake. We've spoken to Stacey. The ambulance men are there now and there's nothing they can do. They don't know what happened, probably a heart attack."

Gloria's words made it past the hope that Ingrid had constructed in her mind: *It's going to be fine, David can't be gone. . . .* That hope smashed like a glass dropped on her kitchen floor, shattering and sending shards everywhere.

David was not coming back. She would never see him again.

Ingrid clutched Gloria's hands for comfort, but there was none. She couldn't cry. Instead, she closed her eyes and swayed rhythmically back and forth, keening silently. Nobody in Ingrid's office said a word. There was nothing they could say.

Gloria cleared everyone out, then pushed another cup of tea over to Ingrid. "Please drink some of this one," she said. "You're in shock."

Obediently, Ingrid picked it up and drank. She usually liked sweet tea, but this tasted metallic and strange. She grimaced.

"Keep drinking," Gloria said.

"It's awful."

"Shock," Gloria replied.

"Shock makes tea taste horrible?"

"Shock makes everything horrible. Ingrid, we have a few things to do. What do you want to do first? I mean, we have to tell your children—"

The organizing part of Ingrid's mind flexed into motion like a well-exercised muscle. It was a relief to feel it, a relief to move away from the absolute pain of knowing that David was dead. "The children, I have to tell them. And David's aunt, and my sisters. The children . . . I can reach Molly so easily, but Ethan, it's going to be harder to find him."

It was as if her mind was protecting her by making her think of other people: if she had to focus on her beloved children and what their father's death meant to them, then she didn't need to focus on how awful it was for her.

"I'll phone Molly, then, shall I?" Gloria was ready to do it. "Or do you want to tell one of her friends first, so there's someone with her?"

Ingrid wanted to hold up her hand to halt it all, because if Gloria made that call, then it would be true.

"No, she needs to know now, she'd want that," Ingrid said bleakly. "I should tell her in person."

The idea of telling Molly was shattering. Ingrid buried her face in her hands, trying to calm herself.

"Ingrid, you're not in any state to go to Molly's office. Phone her," said Gloria. "Perhaps there's someone there you can tell first, who can bring her here?"

Ingrid shook her head. "It has to be Natalie—Molly's best friend. She works at Kenny's, in the café."

If Ingrid herself couldn't be with Molly, then Natalie was the next best thing.

"Should I phone her first?"

"No. Molly first."

She let Gloria scroll through her numbers to find Molly's and click the dial button.

She took the phone from Gloria and thought of all the things only a parent was supposed to do. Taking your children to their first day at school, comforting them when they were teased, hugging them when they had their hearts broken. Telling them their father was dead shouldn't be on the list.

"Hi, Mum, how are you?" Molly's voice was happy, and Ingrid winced.

"Molly, love . . ." she began.

"Mum. What's wrong? You sound strange."

"It's your dad," Ingrid said. "We think it was a heart attack."

"What—How is he?"

Ingrid covered her eyes with her hand. "He's dead, my love. I'm so sorry."

Natalie had burned herself on the coffee machine's milk frother again.

"Bloody machine," she said, reaching up into the first-aid cabinet to get the burn spray. She'd done exactly the same thing last week, and steam burns were so painful.

"I think that thing doesn't like you," said Hugh, the café manager, who'd rushed up to see if everything was all right. "I could hit it next time I pass."

Natalie grinned at him. Hugh, according to everyone else in the café, fancied her and was always hovering around her, big hangdog eyes staring with longing. Natalie didn't believe a word of it. Hugh was interested in films and so was she, that was all. And his big love was sci-fi television shows. He'd been to three conventions in the past year and was booked for a whole week for the Science Fest in Killarney in April. He swore he didn't dress up, but Natalie didn't entirely believe him. Hugh reminded her of the kids she used to go to special education with: sweet, vulnerable, and accustomed to being laughed at.

"Shall I spray the sore bit for you?" Hugh asked solicitously.

Natalie's grin faltered. "Er, no, thanks," she said. "It's best to do it yourself, don't you think?"

"Natalie!" roared Siobhain. "Phone call for you in the office."

Natalie sprayed another blast of burn spray on her hand before looking at Hugh to see his expression. He didn't look irritated at this interruption in the working day, the way he might if another staff member had a phone call. In fact, he still looked slightly dopey as he gazed at her. Natalie shoved the first-aid kit away, smiled, and rushed into the office. Everyone was right: Hugh did fancy her. She had a sudden mental vision of Hugh in a *Star Trek* outfit, and shuddered. She needed to mention that she had a date coming up with a gorgeous man named Rory. It was best to let Hugh down gently, because he was sweet.

"Hello?"

"Is that Natalie?"

"Yes, who's this?" Natalie examined the steam burn. She was tired, that was why she'd burned herself. She'd been up late working, and even though Michelle, the chief barista, was of the opinion that any muppet could operate the coffee machines, Natalie knew that staring into space with exhaustion while you made cappuccino was a surefire way to disaster.

". . . Molly's father . . . Ingrid would love you to go to her. Talk to someone in the director's office, they'll organize a cab for you. . . ."

"What?" Natalie hadn't been paying attention.

"Molly's father, David Kenny, is dead, Natalie. I work for her mother, and she wondered if you could go to Molly. She's very upset."

"Oh, my God," said Natalie. "I don't believe it."

"None of us do, but unfortunately, it's true."

Shock made people confused, Ingrid knew this. She'd read about the physical effects on the body and how the stress hormone, cortisol, flooded the nervous system and had an instant impact, raising heart rate and blood pressure. Like so many things she knew, Ingrid had read about it in a dispassionate, removed way, researching a piece on the negative effects of stress on human beings.

She remembered interviewing a politician who'd been widowed a year previously, when his wife died after a long battle with cancer. Ingrid had agonized over her questions, wanting to ask the right ones, wanting to understand his pain without making it worse for the sake of her interview. She thought she'd done it.

"You must miss her a great deal," she'd said, half question, half statement. Enough of a question for a professional politician to answer. That, coupled with Ingrid's empathy and charisma as she leaned toward him, had had the desired effect. No offense had been taken, no frisson that she'd gone too far into a private grief.

"I do," the politician had said quietly. "She was with me all my adult life, and now she's gone. It's fine when I'm out of the house, but when I step back inside my own front door . . ."

Ingrid had let the pause last, waiting him out. In television, the pauses were often what made the best moments.

". . . it's like she's only just gone. I can almost believe she's going to come out of the kitchen to greet me."

The memory of that electric television moment was like a slap in the face as Ingrid stood behind Gloria in the hall and heard the dogs scrabbling around behind the kitchen door, trying to reach her.

Ingrid had thought she'd been as gentle as possible with that man on her show, but now, in her own cold hall with her own husband dead, she felt the politician's naked pain again and wanted to phone him and apologize.

I know now. I understand. I didn't before, but I do now. I'm sorry I asked you all that.

He'd been in absolute agony, and she hadn't understood.

It was as if the world was divided into two camps: those in pain and those not, and the ones in pain could recognize it in each other's hollow-eyed and numb faces. In that camp, you knew the people there understood. But among the untouched, those who hadn't lost everything, you were utterly isolated. If she rang up that politician, he'd understand, and he might tell her what to do next.

"Right," said Gloria, dropping Ingrid's keys onto the hall table.

Once you were widowed, you weren't allowed to open your own door. Gloria had taken her house keys and opened the door for her, as well as turning off the alarm.

"Right," Gloria said again. "Tea—we could make tea. A nice cup would help."

Decision made, she walked toward the kitchen, opened the door, and unleashed two delighted dogs, who at once began leaping up with excitement.

Seeing their eager dogginess made Ingrid want to weep. She'd left them this morning and everything had been fine, normal. She was married to David, she was happy. Now she was a widow. David was gone forever. How had it all happened so quickly?

"Are you all right?" asked Gloria, putting a hand on Ingrid's shoulder, then grimaced. "Sorry. Stupid question. Of course you're not all right, how could you be?"

Ingrid managed to think about the question. All right? She'd never be all right again.

Molly hadn't cried at all when Natalie arrived to pick her up. She was just sitting, frozen, at her desk with an untouched cup of tea in front of her. One colleague sat with her, and Natalie could see the woman's relief when she arrived.

"She's not taking it well, poor love," the woman said. "It's terrible when it's a sudden death. No chance to say good-bye."

Out of the corner of her eye, Natalie could see Molly's face crumple at these words.

"Absolutely," she said, and dragged Molly and her bag out the door and into the waiting taxi. By the time they'd cleared the next set of traffic lights, Molly was crying so hard she was shaking.

"If only I'd known, Natalie," she sobbed, "I'd have phoned him and told him I loved him. But you know what? I can't remember the last time I said it. How bad is that? He's gone, and I can't even remember the last time I said I loved him. What if he was thinking about that? You know he worried about me. And I'd told him I never wanted to work in the store again, Natalie. It upset him,

I know it did. Ethan has no interest and Dad would have loved it if I was interested, but I couldn't fake it, you know. And all the chances are gone now to tell him I'd have done it for him, that I loved him. . . ."

Natalie hugged her and let the words pour out. She could say nothing that would help, but her heart ached for her friend.

And in the midst of the sympathy, there was one glimmer of a thought in her head, a thought so selfish that she felt bad for even thinking it: David was a wonderful father and it was a tragedy she'd lost him, but at least Molly had known her father. Natalie had never known her mother. Was that worse than sudden death, the not-knowing? Or was it easier that way? You couldn't miss what you hadn't known. Could you?

Some staff felt that the store should close for the rest of the day.

"As a tribute."

"David wouldn't want Kenny's shut!" said someone else. "He lived and breathed this place. He'd want the doors open and the customers piling in."

"Poor Ingrid," said another voice.

Everyone nodded. They all liked Ingrid, although some of the younger staff didn't know her that well. She'd been around more when the kids were young, taking them in to see their dad.

"God help Molly and Ethan," sobbed Lena, who was almost inconsolable. "I can't believe he's gone, so what must they be feeling?"

Charlie sat on the roof with Shotsy while Shotsy smoked and cried. She'd known David far longer than Charlie had. He'd hired Shotsy when she was young and, along with Lena, had been a mentor to her.

"It's wrong that someone like David can die, just like that, no warning," Shotsy said, stubbing out one cigarette and reaching for another.

Charlie agreed. There was something strangely shocking about David Kenny dying. As if he was so vital and alive that he couldn't be subject to the same illnesses as ordinary people.

He was a stalwart in life: the boss, the person who calmly ran everything, their father figure. His death opened up a great black hole of doubt: if David could die, then *anybody* could die.

"It makes you think about your own parents," said Shotsy, whose ninety-year-old mother lived alone and was a constant worry to the whole family when she talked blithely about going out to the garden on icy mornings to feed the birds. "Family is so precious. It's only when they're gone that you realize what you had."

"I know," said Charlie automatically.

But David's death hadn't made her think of her mother or father. It made Charlie think of Brendan and Mikey. If anything happened to them, she'd want to die herself. There would be no point to the rest of her life.

If, on the other hand, her mother died . . .

She'd cope. Was it unnatural for a daughter to think that way?

Yes, it was wrong not to feel more. She was wrong, bad. Charlie wished she adored her mother the way Iseult did, but there was a special bond between them, as if they shared some great secret. Charlie felt that if she shared the secret, perhaps she too could share that love.

And then a horrible thought occurred to her—what if that lack of feeling was genetic, what if Mikey came to feel exactly the same about her when she was old?

"Thank you," Ingrid said to Natalie that night. The taxi was waiting outside the house, one from the Kenny's account. It had orders to drop Natalie home. "And feed those damn cats," Ingrid added.

They both smiled, the only levity in the whole day. Molly had stopped crying just long enough to fret about her beloved babies and how they'd be distressed because neither she nor Natalie was home.

"You've been so kind to us both, I don't know what we'd have done without you," Ingrid went on.

Natalie's mind flashed back to the time she'd first met Molly's famous mother and had felt so terribly nervous.

Mrs. Kenny had been so genuinely friendly—"You must call me Ingrid"—and was nothing like the idea Natalie had of a TV celebrity.

"I wish I could do more," Natalie said. Ingrid looked so utterly destroyed that Natalie wanted to hug her. But it felt like too much of an intrusion.

"You were there when it counted," Ingrid said. "That's enough. Thank you."

Natalie walked down the path away from the beautiful house and was glad she was leaving it. The pain and the grief made it too hard to be there.

Gloria was the last to go. Before she left, she handed Ingrid a small plastic pharmacy bag with a tinfoil bubble packet of tablets inside it.

"Xanax," she said. "My emergency stash. I had them when Freddie was having his bypass surgery. I know you're not a tablet person, but they might help you to sleep, and you need to sleep."

Ingrid, who rarely took so much as a headache tablet, reached for the plastic bag. "Thank you," she said quietly.

When Molly's breath was even and slow, Ingrid covered her with the duvet and slid over to her own side of the bed. It was a big bed, big enough for four people almost. David had wanted a big bed because he liked room to sprawl without squashing her.

It was a nightmare getting sheets to fit it. Even Kenny's, which stocked lovely brands of bed linen, had to order in the giant sheets and duvet covers for David and Ingrid's bed. And they always came in subtly luxurious taupes and creams. Ingrid, who loved muted colors for her clothes, adored bright flowery things for her bed. But she couldn't have them. She and David lay on an expanse of mushroom or taupe most of the time.

Would another man's body ever lie beside hers? How odd to think of sex at such a time, yet Ingrid suddenly longed for the feeling of David's naked body on hers and the touch of his hands on her skin. She would never have that again, that love and tenderness. Another loss. Who would hold her in the morning and talk about the day ahead? Who would lean over her shoulder when she was brushing her teeth and kiss her neck softly? Nobody.

The void left by David was so vast she could barely contemplate it.

Gone, he was gone.

The abyss of pain roared before her. Ingrid breathed deeply and willed it away. No, not yet.

The little pharmacy bag lay on her nightstand, beside the book she'd been reading that morning—was it really only that morning? It felt like years ago. Ingrid ripped the bag open, popped a tinfoil bubble, and dry-swallowed a tablet. She lay back against the pillows, refusing to close her eyes. If she closed them, all the agony would emerge. Only by lying open-eyed in the soft light could she hold back the horror of the day and pretend it hadn't happened. She wasn't ready to deal with it, she couldn't. If she let the tears really come, they'd never stop, because she was broken inside and a flood of pain, tears, and hopelessness would come rushing out. Ingrid couldn't bear that. So she held on tight, forcing her breathing to remain calm, pushing back the screams inside, waiting for the tablet to do its work.

Ingrid's first confused thought when she woke the next morning was that this was going to be a busy day. She had a big interview tonight, a tricky one. She stretched and raised herself on an elbow to look at her alarm clock, and then she remembered. She hadn't set the alarm the night before. There was no need, no need for them to wake at seven, rush to have showers, eat breakfast, greet the day.

A sheet of rain slammed against the bedroom windows. Ingrid had loved being inside when it was raining, loved the sense of cozy warmth and security. Outside: rain. Inside: safe.

Except it wasn't true. She'd never be safe again. David was dead. Safety and security were an illusion.

She'd thought that the worst thing she had to fear was something happening to one of the children, and she'd been sure that she'd never be able to deal with that. It was why she'd been so scared of Ethan going abroad.

Ingrid had known loss before. Her parents had died, both after having been ill for many years, her mother with cancer, her father with a lung disease. They'd both known they were going to die, and it had been gentle, expected. They'd been prepared, and death had almost been a release after all the pain and suffering. But this? She wasn't prepared for this.

Beside her, Molly moaned in her sleep and turned over to burrow farther under the duvet. For now, she was safe in the world of sleep. And Ethan, he was safe too, in that he didn't know anything yet. Gloria had called the Department of Foreign Affairs and they were trying to reach him via the consulate in Vietnam, but they hadn't made contact yet.

At this moment, Ingrid was responsible for nobody except herself. There was nobody to stare mutely at her as she let go.

She closed her eyes and let it happen. And then the tears came, flowing at such speed that tissues were soaked in an instant. She abandoned the tissues, just pulled the top sheet up and held it against her swollen face, burying her head between her knees. Rocking herself as she sobbed, keening: *David, oh, David, my love.*

Ingrid felt the flash almost before she saw it. The piercing light fizzed over her retinas, and belatedly she realized what it was: a press photographer taking pictures of her waiting for Ethan at the airport.

Ethan had texted her to say he'd landed and was waiting at the baggage claim, and she knew that it would be only moments until he was with her. She'd longed to hug him for so long, and now that the moment was almost upon her, all she could think of was that she'd do anything to turn back the clock. A few days ago, she'd simply been worrying about him being away; now she was worrying about how devastated he'd be, and about living in hell herself.

And here was a paparazzo, intruding on their private grief. For what? Some picture that nobody needed to see.

Ingrid knew there would be press at David's funeral, partly because he was one of the country's success stories in business, partly because he was married to her. But what paper would have the disregard for other people's pain to want to run this picture of her, puffy-eyed with pain, meeting their son for the first time since his father had died?

This wasn't a human interest story, this was her *life*.

She swiveled and walked toward the photographer, her face set grimly. He gave her a half-smile and began to walk away.

"Please," Ingrid called, "wait."

He stopped reluctantly.

"This is a private moment," she said, using her voice the way she did when she had to be particularly authoritative on television. "My son is a private individual and, while I may be fair game in your eyes, he has a lawful right to expect privacy at this time."

The man blinked at her warily, unaccustomed to subjects who had such a grasp of the legalities of invasion of privacy.

"I'd like you to leave us to grieve in peace." She delivered the last sentence in the measured, hard tones that made interviewees twist uncomfortably in their chairs and suddenly feel that their top buttons were choking them. It always worked. It worked here, too.

"Okay," the photographer said, admitting defeat.

She watched him go, her jaw still set with anger. There were no guarantees he wouldn't come back, but Ingrid would sue anyone who printed a photograph of this moment. When had she ceased to be one of them, one of the press, and become one of the hunted?

"Mum?"

Wild animals knew their young by their cries, Ingrid had once read, and as she whirled round to see Ethan coming toward her amid the throng emerging from the security gates, she knew it was true. Even in the noise of the arrivals hall, she'd picked out his voice.

He seemed taller than before, but perhaps that was just the

tan and the leanness; he was verging on thin, his broad shoulders looking bony under the weight of the massive rucksack.

And Ingrid felt the tears coursing down her face.

She hadn't cried since the morning after David had died, hadn't even cried when she'd talked on the phone to Ethan and he'd sobbed his heart out. Tears weren't enough to signify how bereft and empty she felt. There needed to be something else to show devastation, she thought. Like blood coming out of your eyes. She could see how the ancient Indian practice of suttee worked, the widow hurling herself on her husband's funeral pyre to burn with him and accompany him to the next life, leaving behind hennaed fingerprints on the walls lining the route to the funeral. That had struck her as simply a waste of a life before. But now, feeling like half a person, she found it made perfect sense.

"Mum." He was beside her, holding on to her, and they were both sobbing. "I never got to say good-bye, Mum," he was saying.

Ingrid felt the tenor of her tears change. She had to mother her son now, and her own grief must take a backseat. She wanted to tell him that she'd never had a chance to say good-bye either, that David had left that morning and the heavens had given no sign that it would be the last time she'd say good-bye to him.

But now was not the time to dwell on that. Ingrid let her mothering instinct take over.

"Your father adored you, Ethan," she said fiercely. "He died knowing you loved him and he loved you—never ever forget that."

Eight

Sometimes, you can't fix it. You just have to let go.

Three days after David's death, Star sat on her veranda wrapped in the old cream woolen blanket that had comforted the previous two generations of Bluestone women, clutching a tiny china cup of steaming rose-hip tea to her breastbone. She loved the veranda, with its pale blue painted wooden slats, the gently creaking hanging seat she was curled up on, and the trailing honeysuckle and wisteria vines that clung around the wooden pillars like lovers. Two feet away, a curtain of rain lashed the garden, drenching the earth and flattening her herbs.

The night before, there had been a full moon, and for the first time she could remember, Star hadn't felt relief at the sight of the fertile, rounded moon in the sky. All her life, the moon had calmed her. It had such power over the earth, her mother used to say, regulating tides and women's menstrual cycles. Even seedlings planted in the run-up to a full moon thrived in a way those planted at other times of the month didn't.

Inside the cottage, hanging on the wall above Granny Petra's spinning wheel, was a very old pen and watercolor sketch of the twelve astrological signs. A many-pointed sun, like the one made famous by France's Sun King, glowed crocus yellow. But it was the moon that had always been the focal point for Star. It had been painted in some different medium; it seemed to shimmer like a base metal, appearing different from every angle. To Star's eye, it was the most vibrant part of the picture.

"Perhaps I should have named you Moon instead," Eliza

Bluestone would say when she caught her daughter tracing small fingers across the gleaming moon in the picture.

"I like being Star," Star said. "I might marry a man with Moon as his surname; then I could be Star Moon."

Her mother hadn't replied. Until she lost Danny, Star hadn't realized that Bluestone women didn't marry. There was no law to say this, no writing across the doorway to the wooden house on the headland, but it was true all the same. They didn't marry.

They might, though, fall in love forever.

Star sighed and drank her tea. She needed to get ready for the funeral. Since she'd heard about David Kenny, when Lena phoned in tears telling her the news, Star had felt an ache inside the likes of which she'd never known.

Vibrant, poetic David Kenny—dead? How could that be?

Hanging up the phone, she'd gone outside and put her arms around the rowan tree she'd planted when David had left her life.

"Are you happy?" she'd murmured, her face close to the bark, breathing in the scent of the living wood.

She wanted her gifts of understanding to help her find him, wherever he was, to communicate that he was at peace. But she'd felt no peace, just the roughness of bark against her cheek and a whisper of sadness.

Her magic was no help to her now. People had such confused notions of magic, that it was mere trickery that could produce rabbits out of hats or a power that could kill men stone-dead with a single look. Nonsense. The magic Star and her mother before her knew was a harnessing of what was already out there, a tapping into the energy of this glorious planet.

When Star was tiny, her mother had done her best to put it into words: "There's a life force rushing round this world, swirling between every blade of grass and raindrop, and what we do is allow ourselves to close our eyes—"

Star, age five, had closed her eyes obediently.

"—to understand the world."

"Is it just us, Mama?" Star wanted to know.

"No, there used to be many more people who could do it. Not

so many now. If they turned off their radios and TVs and sat listening to the earth around them, then they could. Of course, they'd have to open their minds, too."

Star's eyes shot open. Open mind and close eyes at the same time? Confusing.

"Some people call it the sixth sense," her mother went on. "There's no word for that in the old Irish language, but my mother used to call it *féth*, the magic lore. It's about getting in touch with what all people once had. That sixth sense—we're born able to do it."

There was huge joy and comfort in being a true part of the earth, in sensing that a terrible storm was going to lash the coast before it came, or waking up into a golden September morning with a feeling that it was going to be a glorious Indian summer day when nothing would go wrong. But it could be horrible, too. Star remembered the times women would creep to their door, pleading for help, and just by taking someone's hand to lead her to her mother, Star would instantly know there was a good-for-nothing wife-beater at home. Eliza Bluestone would do what she could, going to Sergeant Maguire or Father Hely and telling him something needed to be done soon, before the husband ended up killing the woman. Sometimes the wife would come running back down the path a few days later, furious that the police had hauled her beloved away when really all he needed was someone to understand him.

When the visitor had gone, Eliza would sit on the veranda murmuring about responsibilities coming with gifts, and how it was easier to be good at sewing or cooking—anything rather than this. But she'd apologize afterward, sorry lest her words had upset Star.

"It's a great gift," she'd say, "a great gift. We're blessed to have it."

Their abilities in the realm of magic were different—Star's was a pure gift of touch; when she took somebody's hand, knowledge came to her in a rush. Sometimes she saw high-speed footage of the person's life, crammed into a few seconds; other times, it was just one thing, one bright, shining pinpoint: the birth of a child, or touching the cheek of a loved one. And then there were moments when she touched a hand and sensed darkness, as if somebody had pulled the shutters down, plunging her into gloom. Those feelings were the worst. She could see the hurt of the other person and, as it passed through her, she felt it, too—her whole body aching as the pain bounced out of the other person's soul into hers.

Eliza's gift had been less immediate; she could read the lines of someone's hand the way other people read a map, seeing lessons learned and lessons to be learned in every tiny crevice. She could read tea leaves too, although she only did that for fun, with friends who she knew could take it.

According to Eliza, Star's gift of seeing by touch was the most intense any Bluestone woman had had in the three hundred years they had lived on this bit of coast. Passing on tales of these gifts was part of the legacy, each woman revealing to her daughters and granddaughters the special abilities of all the Bluestone ancestors. Bluestone Cottage was a part of it, too, a creaking, living wooden receptacle of all the knowledge and wisdom of those who'd lived and loved there over the years.

Unfortunately, their magic could be somewhat blurry around the edges when it came to their own lives. Or else Star would never have fallen in love with Danny or even with David, and she'd have been spared a broken heart.

"Your heart has to break before it can open up properly," her mother had told her.

It sounded so wise in speech, but it hurt so much in reality.

Now, thirty-five years after David had gone from her life, Star wanted to feel something of him, to touch his spirit wherever he was, and she couldn't.

His death had left its mark on her.

The day after she heard the news, she'd looked in the bathroom mirror and discovered that her blond hair had turned entirely white. Without any lightening golden threads, the effect was stark. Her face looked very pale, too, as if the frost of old age had crept up on her in the night.

For years she'd lived without David Kenny, at peace knowing

that he was happy, and content with her own life. People might think she was eccentric, yes, but her life suited her: the almost monastic seclusion of her home, the solitude of her work, the silence that came from living alone. She'd loved it.

And now, she didn't. She felt uneasy, unsettled. And she didn't know why.

Charlie woke at dawn on the morning of David Kenny's funeral, jolted awake by a hideous dream in which Brendan and Mikey were being swept away from her in a raging river. She was in a tiny boat, screaming their names, reaching for them, but the torrents were carrying them farther away every second, she was losing them—

She sat bolt upright in the bed, heart pounding, covered in a film of cold sweat.

The room was still murky in the morning dark and Brendan was a duvet-covered lump beside her. With relief, she reached out and touched him, barely resting her hand on his body lest she wake him up. It had been a nightmare, that was all. But it had felt so *real*.

Knowing it was crazy but needing to do it anyway, she slipped out of bed and tiptoed into Mikey's room. The normal musky, old-sock smell of a teenage boy was like perfume to her, and she felt the ripple of relief again as she saw her son sprawled in his bed, his marine camouflage duvet barely covering him. Gently, she fixed it, making sure he was warm, for it was a cold morning and the heat hadn't come on yet.

Asleep, he looked even more like Brendan, the same mildness in his face, the same freckles, the same dark hair that stuck up at all angles no matter how it was brushed.

She wondered what he looked like to other people, because to her he was so infinitely precious that she could see only beauty. Everything about him was right, perfect. He was so kind. Even the teachers said so.

That appalling nightmare she'd just had . . . Charlie shivered, as much from the cold on her damp skin as from her dream.

It must have been brought on by the thought of today, David's funeral.

Charlie, along with everyone else at Kenny's, had talked of nothing else since his death a few days before.

How devastated Ingrid must be. At least she still had her children, but still . . .

With the empathy that Brendan loved in her, Charlie tried to imagine the pain Ingrid was feeling, not in a voyeuristic way, but as if by doing so she could somehow send love and light Ingrid's way.

Kitty Nelson had laughed like a drain when, as a teenager, Charlie had tried to explain her theory about empathy and human beings.

"Empathy," Charlie had said, "is like coils of smoke reaching blue tendrils into the air. If they're let go, they can fly wherever they want, reach people, touch them and help. It's a type of global love, the great unconscious doing good."

Kitty had arched an eyebrow, shaded to perfection with her Dior pencil—*only Dior, darling, nothing else will do.* "Global love?" she'd enunciated, as though Charlie had been talking about cockroach love. "What a load of utter twaddle. The only global love I've heard of involved lots of drink, drugs, and very loud Jimi Hendrix music. Where do you get your ideas from, Charlotte? That is the most awful nonsense I've ever heard."

Charlie had been careful to keep her notions about love and earthly frequencies to herself after that. She would have gone on to explain that being kind had a ripple effect, with one act of kindness creating another, and another, until there were waves and waves of them. But she said nothing.

Another unbearable thing about David's funeral was that Kitty was determined to come. She'd known David, she said, from years back.

Charlie had been hearing this since she'd started working at Kenny's, and had lived in fear that her mother might march into work one day and demand to see her old friend David. It was just the sort of thing she would do, but luckily it had never happened.

Today, though, Kitty was convinced that the world should see she'd been a friend of David's, even though she hadn't seen him for years.

"I knew his old girlfriend, too—Star. Very full of herself," Kitty had sniffed.

Charlie had taken this to mean that the unknown Star hadn't been a fan of Kitty's, and made no comment.

Purple would work, one of those full-length shearling coats that screamed the owner was filthy rich and oblivious to funeral etiquette.

Or pink, Schiaparelli pink, making her look wildly glamorous amid the dowdy hens in their black.

Once, Kitty Nelson would have painted her lips pink to match, but those days were gone. It wasn't so much that her lips had shrunk—although, to be honest, they had. It was the furrows around her mouth that made vibrant-pink-wearing a no-no.

Cigarette lines or life?

Kitty had met David in the early seventies, when he was still going out with that Bluestone girl. They'd moved in different social circles: David and Star had hung around with artists and poets, while Kitty was pals with the feminists of the day. But sometimes the two circles overlapped. David had been considered a catch then, heir to Kenny's, though he seemed to be turning his back on the family firm to be with Star.

Kitty had never taken to Star; she looked *through* you, Kitty felt. As if she could see exactly what you were thinking, particularly when it wasn't a nice thought. Star had given Kitty one of those serene, knowing looks when Kitty had been flirting with David. Not that he'd responded, the idiot.

Few men resisted her in those days. But David had taken Kitty's purred "You could buy me a drink someday, *on our own*," and gently batted it back to her:

"That's kind of you, Kitty, but no thanks."

Kitty had been furious, but she'd got over it. Men were strange, there was no doubt about it.

She reached for her cigarettes, extracted one from the pack, and lit it in a single fluid movement. Sitting at her dressing table, ignoring the film of dust illuminated by the February sun, she admired the way she looked in the mirror as she smoked. Who cared what all the bloody doctors said? Smoking was sexy. What could be more erotic than a mouth circling a smooth column, inhaling, and then blowing out a wisp of smoky promise at a man? What man could resist that?

Few of them, that's who. Except for David, and only because he'd been in thrall to Star at the time. Oh, and Anthony. Bloody Anthony. Always her mind ran back to her ex-husband.

Kitty stopped admiring herself in her triple mirror and took a long pull on her Dunhill, wanting her beloved nicotine to wipe him out of her mind.

Yes, if it had been his damn funeral, she'd be wearing pink or purple, or even pillar-box red with a fur collar for sheer extravagance. Anything to show the world that she was still there even if he wasn't.

I'm still here.

She could picture how shocked Charlie would be if she knew what her mother was thinking. "Mum!" she'd say, dragging one syllable into three.

Charlie was so naïve, really.

Iseult, her older daughter, would say nothing. Very little got Iseult going. She was well-suited for the world and its pain. Like herself.

Poor Charlie, alas, wasn't. Hadn't a clue, Charlie. Not a clue. No idea whatsoever how it had been for Kitty. Didn't understand, never would.

Had it been Anthony's funeral instead of David Kenny's, Kitty would be throwing a massive party afterward with unending booze, jazz musicians, and food available only at breakfast for the hardy souls who'd lasted the course.

The house would have been perfect for a wake. *Her* house, that is. The house that went in the divorce settlement and left her living in this box. Though it hadn't been a particularly big house, it was detached, with a conservatory. Perfect for parties.

A hint of heat in her hand made her realize her cigarette had burned right down.

"Shit!" She let the tendril of ash fall into the crystal ashtray and automatically reached for a fresh cigarette.

The momentary sexiness she'd felt admiring herself had gone. That brunette bombshell who made a moue with her full lips had been gone some twenty years. Low-angled sunshine lit up the room and cast a harsh light on her face. Kitty knew that with the right lighting—candles, preferably—and when she'd had her skin freshly lasered and had her fillers in, she could pass for late fifties. Today, in the dark burgundy suit she'd dragged from her closet for the funeral, with her hair still dark against the paleness of her skull, she looked every day of her sixty-nine years.

Suitably deathly for a funeral, she thought, grinning at herself. At least she still had her sense of humor. If you could laugh at life, you had one weapon left. This morning was going to be short on laughs, so Kitty wanted to get them when she could.

Charlie would be weeping beside her, and Kitty hated crying. She'd tried hard to teach her daughters that crying got you no-where. Anger, determination, and feral hunger for survival—now, *those* worked. Nobody taught you that in college.

"It's going to be such an awful funeral," Charlie had said. "He wasn't even sixty, Mum. Poor Ingrid. And the children are in shock. Okay, they're grown-ups, but still, he's their dad. Everyone says Ingrid is very strong, but I don't know how she's going to cope."

"She'll cope just fine."

Kitty picked up a coral lip pencil and began to draw her mouth on. Men left. Better get it over with now rather than later. Better to have your husband drop dead of a heart attack and be able to mourn him, than to have him run off because he "wasn't happy." *Wasn't happy?* In some ways, Kitty would have preferred it if he'd run off with some little madam twenty years younger. At least she'd have been able to bitch about young trollops out to steal other women's husbands. But for a man to leave without there being someone else, for a man to leave because he simply couldn't live with *you*? The humiliation had been epic. Try mourning *that*.

"You're better off without him, Kitty," all her friends had said at the time.

"At least you have your career."

"You're gorgeous, you'll meet someone else like a shot."

Wrong! Wrong on all counts.

Red, Kitty decided—she'd wear red for Anthony's funeral. Red lips and nails, and she'd get more fillers done around her mouth and nose. Pity she couldn't afford another eye lift. Still, one of her old red suits—the vintage ones from the 1950s, when corsetry could give any woman a siren's figure, regardless of middle-aged spread. All his old girlfriends would be there. Not that he'd had many, and mousy creatures, the lot of them. None like herself. And he'd not married any of them. So she'd be the prominent one at his funeral; the ex-wife commanded respect, no matter what had gone before. She'd be the one to whom people would offer their sympathies. And she'd smile graciously and never let on that she was glad he was dead. Serve him right, the coward!

Kitty layered on the second coat of lipstick. The great thing about funerals, she thought, was that they gave her a chance to show people that she was still here. No matter what had happened in her life, Kitty Nelson was still here and still fighting. That had to count for something, didn't it?

Star sat down in the back of the church and looked around her with interest. She'd been in so few churches in her life and she adored them, the exquisite architecture and the beauty of the images around. There was such a sense of holiness here, and she respected the faith she'd grown up alongside. Her best friends had worshipped in churches like this one, and Star had often been shocked when they spoke disrespectfully about their religion yet remained a part of it all. If you couldn't give yourself totally, you were being a hypocrite, she felt.

Still, it wasn't her place to comment.

Goodness and kindness were paramount in her faith; being good to humankind and being grateful for what you had were the main tenets. Not much different from what was preached here.

Only the words and the rules were different, she decided. Religions run by men were always very keen on lots of rules. Rules about behavior in church, behavior out of church, rules about sex—what was it about sex that fascinated them so? Surely the main thrust of any religion should be about kindness and spirituality, not about what people did in the privacy of their own beds?

She watched the mourners file into the church, some somber in black and others clearly making a statement about celebrating David's life by wearing bright colors. Star approved of that. She herself had worn white, the only splash of color a red silk corsage pinned to her breast. It was a subtle tribute to her long-lost love.

A tall woman with glossy dark hair and a dramatic black coat swept into the church on the arm of an older man who seemed to be holding on to her in a bid to calm her down. The woman's eyes were red and her face was drawn. Obviously somebody close to David. A friend of Ingrid's, too, Star decided. Good, Ingrid would need friends now. Star closed her eyes and sent healing and light toward the tall woman.

As she stalked up the aisle with Harry by her side, Marcella ran an expert eye over the funeral guests. Under normal circumstances, she'd have been able to gauge what they were like by their demeanor and their dress. Today, she felt too shocked by the fact that it was dear David's funeral to be professionally distant about it all. He was her friend; he was darling Ingrid's husband. Today, it was personal, and she glared at anyone who didn't look suitably devastated.

Her usual rule of thumb was that people in perfect makeup, exquisite tailoring, and shades were either members of the family determined to put the best side forward despite their pain, or media-savvy types who liked the sight of themselves in the inevitable newspaper photographs of the funeral.

There were some of that latter tribe present, sunglasses on and not a hint of a tear ruining their faces, chattering happily as if they were at a cocktail party where most of the people just happened to be clad in black. Marcella scowled at them.

"Settle," murmured Harry, who knew without being told what was upsetting her.

"That bitch has never had a good word to say about Ingrid or David," hissed Marcella, gesturing to a woman in a leather ensemble with a hint of an Hermès scarf peeping from her collar and just-blow-dried hair tumbling about her shoulders. "She shouldn't even be here. Why are people so hypocritical that they'll turn up at the funeral of a person they had no time for in life?"

"Look at all the people who are crying," Harry whispered. "David was loved, and Ingrid still is loved. There are plenty here for the right reasons."

Marcella tried to stifle her rage. The church was filling up with people who looked genuinely devastated; many eyes met hers across the pews with sad resignation, and many people hugged her in lieu of hugging Ingrid. They knew that Marcella Schmidt was one of David and Ingrid's closest friends.

"I just can't bear any hypocrisy today," Marcella sobbed, burying her face in her ex-husband's solid shoulder. "Not today, not for David. I want it to be real."

"It's real, all right," Harry said, gazing across at the empty pew at the front of the church where Ingrid, Ethan, and Molly would sit.

Star felt Natalie's presence before she saw her. The tiny hairs on her arms stood on end and the back of her neck prickled, and then a slender girl with a waterfall of dark wavy hair walked past, all bundled up in a gray woolen coat with a striped scarf twined around her neck, half hiding her face. It was like stepping back in time and seeing Dara's profile, the same fine-boned nose and cheeks, the same determined chin, the dark sweep of eyebrows winging back over huge dark eyes. All of Star's composure left her and a lump swelled up in her throat. This was Dara's child, and she'd grown into this beautiful young woman without Star witnessing any of it. She thought of the promise Dara had made them all swear, and she felt again how totally wrong it was. People had a right to know where they came from. The past couldn't be wiped out like chalk on a blackboard. Not knowing who you were could rip a person apart just as surely as remembering a painful past could. Maybe the time would come when Natalie would want to find out for herself. Star really hoped so.

Funeral limousines were like coffins, Ingrid decided—bigger and with windows to the outside world, but still coffinlike. Once you were in one, you were totally isolated. People could see you, but they didn't want to look, as if looking might award them a seat beside you and your pain. The funeral home had sent its most luxurious limousine, and she sat in the back with Molly on one side, Ethan in the seat facing, and David's great-aunt Babe on her other side.

Ingrid could barely cope with looking at her children's faces be-cause of the devastation she saw there. Ethan was pale with grief under his tan, and Molly's eyes were a blur of red from crying. In-grid wasn't sure how she looked—she'd made herself up carefully as a tribute to her beloved David, even though she'd wanted to hurl the cosmetics from the window at the futility of ever trying to look normal again, now that he was gone. She knew her hair was clean because she'd numbly gone through the motions of wash-ing it earlier, and she knew the black Jaeger coat and soft felt hat were suitable; but beyond that, she didn't care how she looked. It shouldn't matter today. It might never matter again.

Her sisters, Flora and Sigrid, were in the limousine behind. "Would you like to come in our car?" Ingrid had asked.

"No," Flora had said, "it should be just you and the children, Ingrid love. You in the first car, us in the second. That's how it's done."

Ingrid didn't want to follow any ludicrous funeral etiquette today. She didn't want it to be just her and the children. It felt so lonely, so isolating, which was why Babe's presence was a bless-ing. Ninety-two and still strong-spirited, Babe was physically frail, with a cloud of white hair and pink glasses with wings not unlike those on the back of a Buick. She missed nothing and could be counted on to speak her most private thoughts out loud.

The family knew that Babe's eccentricity wasn't connected to her age in any way. As David was fond of telling them, she'd always been mad.

"The world has to take Aunt Babe on her own terms," David would say with a laugh, describing how Babe had driven his grandmother crazy when the two of them were young because she was forever misbehaving at the tennis club and had a string of unsuitable suitors and a motorbike by the time she was nineteen.

"She's as sharp as a tack," David would add. "That charmingly mad thing is part of her shtick; don't get taken in by it. She's had some life, I can tell you. If only we could get her to write it down—but she's adamant that a lady never kisses and tells."

Today, Ingrid was simply grateful for Babe's presence, even if she was wearing a floor-length astrakhan coat that smelled as if it hadn't been out of the wardrobe since its heyday in 1938. Because Babe was there, Molly and Ethan were trying hard to take care of her, and she was making them smile with endless stories about their father when he was young.

Babe was well used to funerals and had long since learned that remembering the dead person's happier moments made the day pass more bearably.

"Ingrid, do you remember that time David and his friends pushed a bed all the way from Earlscourt Terrace out to Malahide for a bet?" asked Babe.

Ingrid shook her head. "Before my time, Babe," she said softly.

"Oh, but he must have told you," Babe went on merrily, patting Ingrid's hand. "It was him and his nice friend Jonny—you must remember Jonny, he had a bad leg and practically no hair. Bald as a coot by the time he was twenty. Women loved him, you know. No accounting for taste."

The three mourners grinned.

Babe was the one who should have been on television, not her, Ingrid thought. The old lady was doing a marvelous job of making them remember better times, and all so subtly that neither Ethan nor Molly appeared to realize they were being distracted. Ingrid looked down at Babe's fragile, blue-veined hand clasped in hers and thought that perhaps the old lady had had the right idea after all. If you never tied yourself to one man, you could never feel your heart break when that man died.

But then you wouldn't have had the joy of having children with that same man, and the children were the only thing keeping Ingrid upright. Without them, she wasn't sure she could have done this whole funeral thing. It all seemed so horrendously pointless, so . . . nothing. David was gone. No matter what anyone said to her, Ingrid couldn't escape that.

She felt a frail hand on hers. Babe was looking at her, those shrewd old eyes wet with tears. "Chin up, my love," she said. "Although you'll hear it a million times from people who didn't really know David, I can tell you: it's what he would have wanted."

Kitty Nelson—Well, there was a sight for sore eyes! Star thought with a grin. She hadn't seen Kitty for what felt like a million years, yet she seemed virtually unchanged, still walking with that sexy little sashay, still shoehorned into a figure-hugging outfit more suitable for lying on a piano in Vegas than a funeral in Ardagh. Star watched with fascination as Kitty tip-tapped her way up the center of the church, looking imperiously into pews to determine whether she'd deign to sit there or not. She had a fox fur around her shoulders and one hand was toying with the fox's shrunken head, flicking it this way and that as she progressed. Hurrying along behind her was one of her daughters, Charlie, the one who worked at Kenny's. The older one, Iseult, was a famous writer and the image of her mother, so if she'd been here, there would have been *two* women sashaying up the church in improbably high heels deciding where to sit. Once, after she'd split from David, Star had been out with some friends and seen Kitty with her daughters. Kitty hadn't noticed Star; of course, if David had been with Star, Kitty would have noticed her then.

Charlie had come across as a sweet little girl, gentle and

tentative and absolutely the wrong sort of child for a household like Kitty's. In the battle between the sexes, Kitty had been made in the Valkyrie mode, entirely at home in warrior breastplate with a horned helmet, putting the fear of God into hapless men. A thoughtful, anxious child would have curled up into a ball with such a mother. Star's mother used to say that unborn babies picked their parents for a reason. They chose the families they went to because they had a lesson to learn in life. It would be a tough lesson to learn with Kitty. Perhaps that was why Charlie had those soft, hurt eyes Star had noticed when she'd recognized her in Kenny's cosmetics hall.

She watched now as Charlie spotted some friends of hers in the church and had the temerity to grab her mother and steer her back to a pew Kitty had already rejected. Despite the sadness of the occasion, Star grinned. Good for Charlie.

Charlie was crying; she always cried at funerals, no matter who the deceased was. The combination of the sad music, and the sense of the assembled people wishing they could help yet knowing they couldn't—it all touched her in such a way that she wanted to weep.

Beside her, a jaunty black velvet hat atop her platinum whirl of hair, Shotsy's whole body shook as she sniffled into another tissue.

Shotsy was convinced that stress over having to sell to DeVere's was what had killed David. "Those bastards!" she'd said to Charlie. "Look what they've done to him!"

She felt guilty about having doubted his loyalty to his staff, too. "I was bitching about him and he died, and after all he's done for us."

Charlie reached into her bag and plucked another tissue from the packs she'd brought with her. The plus side of her weepiness was that she always came prepared.

"What's wrong with her?" demanded an irritated voice on Charlie's other side.

Charlie wished her mother hadn't accompanied her, but Kitty wasn't about to be dissuaded.

"Of course I'm coming," Kitty had snapped when Charlie tentatively mentioned that the funeral would be attended by close friends of the family and Kenny's employees, so Kitty didn't need to come. "You can drive me. But not in your old wreck of a car. Borrow Brendan's. Better still, we'll get Iseult's car."

Charlie had driven Brendan's car. Iseult was uncontactable.

"Busy, busy," her mother had muttered approvingly.

Charlie had had to turn to her anti-gratitude diary for consolation.

Iseult is busy when my mother can't reach her — I'm being difficult when I don't return any phone call within twenty minutes. Why?

"What's she so upset about?" Kitty asked loudly, gesturing in Shotsy's direction. She lowered her voice a hint. "Was she *involved* with him?"

Charlie closed her eyes and prayed for a thunderbolt to take her mother. Please let nobody have heard. Her mother had always been a nightmare, but at least she used to be a semidiscreet nightmare. Clearly, that was no longer the case.

"No," she hissed. "David wasn't like that, Mother. He was a good man. Shotsy's upset because she cared about him. We all did."

"I was only asking," Kitty sniffed, unperturbed. She leaned forward for a good look, as if trying to work out whether Shotsy might have what it took to be an important man's bit on the side. "You're probably right, Charlotte," she added thoughtfully. "Too thin."

Luckily, Shotsy only heard the last bit. "Who's too thin?" she asked.

Charlie shook her head to imply that it didn't matter.

She wished she could order her mother to leave the church if she wasn't going to behave in an appropriate manner, but since her mother had never behaved in an appropriate manner in her entire life, it was unlikely she could start now.

* * *

"It seems wrong to talk about it, but what happens to us now?" asked Dolores as they filed slowly out of the church.

"Suppose it's down to Ingrid and the kids," Shotsy said.

The Kenny's staff all approved of Ethan and Molly. Both had done lots of summer work experience in the store, and it was clear that they hadn't been brought up with silver spoons anywhere near their mouths. Molly had worked with Shotsy for two summers running, at the end of which Shotsy had sighed and said there was nothing she could do with the poor girl, for Molly had no interest in shoes, bags, or clothes. "Criminal," Shotsy had sighed. "She could be pretty if she made a bit of an effort, but she doesn't. I think she likes that un-made-up look. And as for second-hand clothes—well, that's fine if it's all you can afford, but I don't think you can ever get the smell of sweat out of them."

"I can't believe he's gone," sobbed Lena beside them. Claudia was holding on to her and trying to comfort her, but it was no use. "He was so kind," Lena went on. "Talked to me like we were friends, real friends."

Everyone looked sadly at her. They knew what she meant. David Kenny had been special, there was no doubt about it.

Natalie could remember hearing a snippet of a radio program about country funerals in the old days. Everyone had gone to "see the corpse," as it was called. Young or old, they all went to offer sympathies and drink tea with the bereaved. The person on the radio had talked about having to lean into the coffin and kiss the forehead of the dead person, at which point Natalie had groaned and switched channels. How horrible!

Molly's father's funeral was her first. Apart from that one snippet of radio, all Natalie knew about the procedure came from the TV or films. Graveyards were the preserve of horror movies in which some gang of stupid kids always ended up in the graveyard five minutes before a curse made lots of desiccated hands claw their way up from the earth beneath.

The church service had been sad but uplifting, with a choir

singing hymns she didn't recognize and some lovely Russian-sounding peasant music that a man beside her had murmured was John Taverner. The event had been so triumphant and moving that everyone was smiling, even the people who were crying as they remembered David Kenny.

Outside in the bitter cold of the mountainside graveyard, it was a different matter. The wind raged around the mourners, whipping up skirts and flattening hair. The ground around the freshly dug grave was laid with sheets of fake grass, and Natalie winced at how stupidly false it looked, as if a few bits of pretend grass could fool everyone into thinking this was a soft green bed rather than a dark hole burrowing into the earth where the coffin would lie before being covered with heavy black soil.

Even the things the priest was saying sounded wrong. He was talking about eternal life and a journey to God's side. Natalie loved the gentleness of Mass and the familiar words she'd heard a hundred times before; but here, in this churchyard with Molly shuddering with tears, clinging to her mother and brother, all of them looking as if their lives had been utterly destroyed, this talk of life felt as wrong as the artificial turf beneath their feet. David was gone. Did it matter that he was somewhere else looking down? Who knew that for sure? They needed him here, now, and he was gone. That was the reality.

As Natalie stood beside the grave, it came to her: a memory from some locked-off part of her mind. She *had* been to a funeral before. And on that occasion, too, the wind had played around the trees in the graveyard and the cold had cloaked her. She'd been in her father's arms, clinging to him and not looking down. She hadn't wanted to stand because she was tired, and she could feel rather than see herself wearing a dark green tweedy coat with a soft collar. Velvet, perhaps? And there was a smell, too, some perfume like musk and amber mixed, warm and comforting. Her mother's perfume. Her mother would kiss Natalie when she was wearing the coat, and her perfume had sunk into it.

Natalie thought again about how not having a real mother

made her feel. It set her apart, even though Bess had been such a rock all her life; steady, kind, loving, and never, ever claiming, "I'm your mother." No, Bess had judged that fine line to perfection, something Natalie was old enough to see now. It must be difficult to parent your husband's previous wife's child and love her like your own.

Because Bess had got it right, there had never been a moment in her teenage years when Natalie had screamed, "You can't tell me what to do, you're not my mother!"

Now, as the wind made the stately poplars in the country graveyard groan and bend, with the smell of actual earth rising up from the ground, a powerful reminder of where the body was ultimately going to lie, Natalie thought of another grave with her real mother inside it.

The woman she'd never really known, the woman whose memory was confined to a few photos in a frame in her childhood bedroom, and whose perfume she could suddenly remember after forgetting it for twenty years: her real mother had lived, breathed, and danced, had given her life, and Natalie knew precisely nothing about her.

A deep shame rose up inside her at the thought. She knew nothing about her mother, had never stood at her grave and cried or prayed. Somewhere her real mother lay unmourned and unloved, while she, the person who should have mourned her and loved her, had gone on with her life.

Natalie had never fainted before, so nobody was more surprised than she when she began to tremble and pitched forward onto the artificial turf.

She was hardly aware of the woman who caught her, a tall slender woman with pure white hair who wore a white coat with a red silk corsage on her breast like a splash of blood.

Despite her age, the woman was surprisingly strong, and she lowered Natalie to the ground gently, all the while saying, "It's all right, Natalie, my dear, you're safe."

Natalie did feel safe, strangely, although she could still smell the powerful scent of the earth, and knew what it was like to be her childlike self and cry at another grave. But from the white-haired woman emanated an aura of calmness so strong that it doused the pain.

As other people rushed to Natalie's side, Star Bluestone drew away, not wanting to call attention to herself. Her red silk flower had come unpinned and fallen onto Natalie's dark coat, but Star didn't want to pick it up. Let Natalie keep it. Star had probably worn it twenty years ago when she'd known Natalie's mother. Natalie looked so like her, the same wild, earthy beauty, the same air of vulnerability about her. On this awful day so redolent with pain and memories of what might have been, Star didn't want to look back any further. If only she hadn't made that vow to Dara, she could have felt some peace. Now Dara's death and David's were tied up together in a strange unsettled way. Star hurried away with an overwhelming feeling of unfinished business about both deaths.

Charlie felt a murmur of shock run through the crowd at the graveside. Someone had fainted. Beside her, reeking of smoke and at least half a bottle of Shalimar, her mother wobbled and had to grab Charlie for support. Charlie looked down at her mother's ridiculously high heels, patent leather with ankle straps and stilettos slender as masonry nails. Stupid footwear for a funeral. No wonder she was wobbling.

The funeral party was so large that people were squashed together in the graveyard, some standing on the low stone surrounds of other graves. Standing on actual graves was considered positively blasphemous, but the little walls were fair game. In order to see everything, Kitty had positioned herself on one such wall and was peering over the sea of heads with interest.

Charlie thought that accidents were supposed to happen in slow motion, but her mother falling over the gravestone happened with such speed that Charlie thought she must have imagined it.

One moment, Kitty was standing beside her, long painted finger-nails playing with the sad, shrunken little head on that awful fox fur she'd worn; the next, she was on the ground.

"Curse of the fox?" suggested Shotsy, before Kitty let out a wail that left nobody in any doubt as to whether she'd been injured. "That sounds serious, actually," Shotsy added.

Charlie nodded and girded her loins for helping her mother up.

But there was no helping Kitty Nelson up.

"I've broken something, you stupid girl!" she shrieked at the top of her voice. "The pain!!! Get an ambulance."

The doctor in the ER was pale with tiredness. Under normal circumstances, Charlie knew, her mother would be recommending Yves Saint Laurent Touche Éclat for the bluey-purple shadows under the woman's eyes. Kitty was good on makeup hints, wanted or not. But it wasn't a makeup hint day.

"It's my bloody hip, you moron," she roared, making the poor doctor go even paler.

Charlie knew they were probably used to abusive drunks in casualty, but not necessarily perfectly lipsticked older women with genuine fox-fur collars swearing like navvies.

"Is your mother on any medication?" the doctor asked.

"I'm not an idiot!" shrieked Kitty, getting crosser by the minute. "You can talk to me, you know!"

Charlie could see exhaustion and anger flit across the doctor's face, and anger won.

"We won't treat you if you're abusive," she said firmly, standing up straight. Behind her waited two nurses who had already been on the receiving end of some of Kitty's treatment. None of them looked as if they recognized the stalwart of the feminist movement, a woman who'd often grumbled that she'd be Dame Kitty if she lived in a country where honors were given for services to the state.

"I'm in pain," Kitty whimpered. "It's so bad. . . ." She began to cry.

The nurses relented. "Pain makes us all angry," one of them said gently.

Kitty nodded and grabbed Charlie's hand, an act so rare that Charlie nearly jerked her hand away in shock. "Stay with me," she moaned, "please."

"I'm not going anywhere," Charlie said.

She thought of Shotsy's fear of losing her mother. Charlie hadn't felt like that, and now she was being punished for it. Not loving her mother was an unnatural crime. Being there for Kitty was her penance.

Nine

Be kind to yourself. Love yourself. Nobody else is going to be able to if you don't first. It's a hard lesson, that one.

Six weeks later

The scent of disinfectant was making her eyes water, and Natalie was glad she hadn't bothered putting on mascara or more than a smudge of eye shadow. The operating room was clean, though, and she was proud she'd finished the job so quickly.

"Is this your idea of a romantic date, Rory?" she demanded, putting down the scrubbing brush and wiping the sweat off her forehead with her arm.

"No," said Rory, faking shock, "this is more of a preamble. On the real date, we're going to look at a few horse X-rays and"—he lowered his tone to a gravelly whisper—"I'll show you the thing we use for removing cows' teeth. Romantic, huh?"

Natalie grimaced. "No, don't. Please," she begged. "Let's clean the place again first—anything but cow dentistry!"

"Thanks for helping," he added.

"You're not bad with a bucket and scrubbing brush," Natalie said, "but you still don't have the female ability to clean at speed and talk at the same time. I don't mean that women are better at cleaning, by the way, just that—"

"—you can multitask. I know," Rory said good-humoredly. "It's not an ideal date, but it's the best I can do." They'd been on several dates already, and tonight they had planned to go to a movie and then on for dinner. Then Rory's partner had been delayed on an emergency call to a valuable mare that was having trouble foaling and, at the last minute, Rory had had to cancel their date to fill in for him on some routine operations.

"Unless you'd like to come and wait for me at the practice," he'd said.

"I'd love it," Natalie had said truthfully. "Can I come earlier and watch?"

As a farmer's daughter, she had seen many vets at work but had never watched one operate.

It was simple, Rory said: three sterilization operations, including one on a Jack Russell terrier who sat nervously in her cage, her little pointed face peering up at Natalie. Natalie reached in through the bars and stroked the dog's velvety ears.

It was fascinating to be inside the operating theater, watching Rory expertly inject sedative.

"Anybody can operate on humans," he explained as he waited for the anesthetic to take effect, "but only a vet is legally allowed to operate on animals in Ireland. Did you know that?"

Natalie watched as he carefully swabbed down the little dog's pink belly with disinfectant before slicing through the layer of skin and fat. She marveled that his big hands could be so gentle and nimble. Kind hands.

The operation was quick, as Rory swiftly found the dog's uterus, a pearlescent pink organ like a marble hidden in silky folds, then clamped it off at both ends.

"I'd have loved to have been a vet," she said wistfully.

"What stopped you?" he asked.

"I wasn't good enough at school. I'm dyslexic."

"There's a genetic link with that," Rory remarked, expertly sewing up the dog's belly. "Do your parents have it, or your brothers?"

"My dad doesn't, and Bess isn't my real mother," she said. "I mean, she's like my mum, but she's not, not biologically. . . ."

Rory took his eyes off his furry patient for the first time. "What happened to your real mother?"

"She died when I was little."

"That must have been hard."

Natalie nodded. She hadn't told him how she'd fainted at Molly's father's funeral, and then came to sitting in Lena's car, with a nurse who'd been at the funeral checking her pulse and recommending that she go to her GP to get a full checkup.

She'd ignored the advice. It had been a disturbing day, that was all. Everyone was upset. She hadn't told anyone about the thoughts she'd had just before she'd fainted.

It all sounded so mad—they'd have locked her up. No, there was no point worrying people.

She reached out and stroked the anesthetized dog's ears. The terrier's pink tongue lolled out the side of her mouth. Rory had explained that tongue color was a good sign of the patient's stability. If a pink canine tongue went gray, you were in trouble.

"Was your mother dyslexic?"

"I don't know," said Natalie, and felt the shame again, the shame she'd felt at the funeral when she realized she knew nothing about her birth mother. She could almost smell the earthy smell of the grave.

"You could ask someone if she was dyslexic—or would that not be a good idea?" Rory said.

Natalie met his gaze. Rory had instinctively grasped that there was more to this story.

"My dad has never told me about her," she admitted, still holding the dog's silky ear as if clutching a talisman. "I didn't really ask, either. I knew somehow it was a taboo subject."

There, it was out in the open.

"And you don't know your mother's parents or any other relatives you could ask?"

"My mother's parents are dead, and her only brother lives in Australia. I've never met him, don't even know if I have cousins on that side," Natalie said. "Dad's got brothers and so does Bess—we've lots of family, and that always seemed enough. . . . I'm ashamed to say I didn't really ask about my mum's side. Not that I didn't think about her, my real mother; but you know, when you're a kid, you think people tell you what you need to know. Nobody talked about her. . . ."

It *was* strange. Saying it out loud made it obvious. But Dad and Bess had been such wonderful parents. Bess could have won a Stepmum of the Year award. Natalie always hated watching Disney stories about wicked stepmothers because it was such a cliché. Hers was wonderful. Bess adored Natalie, Joe, and Ted equally. She'd treated all three of them exactly the same, as if Natalie were as much her own as the two boys. She wasn't the sort of woman to want her husband's first wife consigned to the ether because she couldn't cope with the competition. And Dad—he was one of the best men in the world. He wouldn't have let Natalie's real mum disappear without reason, would he?

"What was her name?" asked Rory.

"Dara," said Natalie, smiling. She loved the name. "I have a couple of old pictures of her. She looked a lot like me."

"So you do know something about your mum," Rory said.

After he'd operated on the other two dogs, he began to clean up and Natalie offered to help.

"No," he said, "really, you sit there and I'll do it."

"Get me a mop," Natalie commanded. "If I want to have the whole vet experience, I must do it properly."

When they'd cleaned up both the theater and themselves, Natalie felt pleasantly tired and happy. Content, that was the word. That was what she felt when she was with Rory.

"Should we give the cinema a miss and just have dinner?" she said.

"I could cook at my place," Rory offered.

Natalie smiled. "I'd love that."

The following evening being Friday, she had arranged to meet up with Lizzie and the gang at a pub in Dublin. Rory was on late call, which meant he couldn't come, and Natalie was almost pleased. Not because she didn't want to see him; strangely, she wanted to see him all the time, which had never really happened to her before. No, she was pleased he wouldn't be there because Lizzie behaved so oddly around him. It wasn't that she didn't like him—nobody could not like Rory, Natalie thought proudly. But Lizzie seemed to have a notion in her head that Natalie could do better. And that made it uncomfortable on the occasions when Rory joined them.

When Steve and Lizzie got married, Anna had predicted that would put an end to them hanging out as a group.

"Married couples do different stuff," she'd said with a certain longing, which implied that when and if she and Gavin got married, they wouldn't be sharing pepperonis with old friends; they'd be doing married-coupley things like looking at houses or poring over the IKEA catalogue or sitting at home watching DVDs so they could save up for a deposit on a house.

But despite the wedding, Steve and Lizzie were not holed up in their flat discussing the merits of one type of mortgage over another. They were gung-ho for nights out with their friends, even though they seemed to be permanently broke.

Anna and Gavin weren't out with the gang because they were both broke—not something that appeared to faze Lizzie.

"I've got thirty-five yoyos to last me until payday," said Lizzie, lifting her head from a detailed analysis of the contents of her wallet.

"When's payday?" asked Mark, one of Steve's friends.

"An entire week away," Natalie replied.

Mark grimaced.

"It's fine," Lizzie said happily, "my husband can lend me some cash. What's mine is his and vice versa. Isn't that right, husband?"

Steve liked the "husband" stuff and smiled affectionately at her. "That's right, wife," he said. "I've got a hundred quid."

"Yahoo. Where are we going?" Lizzie said enthusiastically.

"We're broke," Natalie pointed out.

"Spoilsport," said Lizzie. "You'll be as bad as Molly soon."

After Molly's father died, she'd stayed with her mother. Both Natalie and the cats had missed her. The flat was hardly enormous: two bedrooms, one bathroom with a decent shower, and a living-room-cum-kitchen that had a claim to the word *cozy*. But without anyone to share it with, the place felt cavernous and lonely. The cats mewed piteously all the time and had gone off their food, refusing to use their clever timed-feeding dish. They wanted a real live person at their beck and call, opening packets of the most expensive cat food and personally spooning it into their bowls. A few days ago, Molly had finally moved back, but she didn't want to go out at all. Natalie had invited her to join them tonight for a drink, but she didn't think there was much hope of her showing up.

"The pair of you are turning into bloody nuns," Lizzie went on.

Natalie clenched her jaw. "That's offending three groups of people, Lizzie," she said. "Me, Molly, and nuns."

"What do you care about nuns?" Lizzie was mutinous.

"I was taught by some very nice nuns, now that you come to mention it, and so were you. And there's nothing wrong with wanting to stay home on a Friday night, either. And don't forget, Molly's father just died."

"Take it easy, will you—I didn't mean it like that," said Lizzie. "It's just, you know, you're no fun anymore."

"You're the expert on fun, now, is that it?" Natalie's eyes glittered dangerously. "As it happens, I was out last night, with Rory."

She didn't talk on the phone to Lizzie as much as she used to, so Lizzie didn't know how often she'd been seeing Rory.

"Where did you go?" asked Lizzie suspiciously, as if wanting to confirm that the date had been suitable.

"His place, for dinner," said Natalie, feeling herself get angry. "I stayed the night."

Lizzie's mouth was a perfect oval. It was the first time Natalie had ever stayed with a man and not shared it instantly the next day with Lizzie.

"Hello."

They looked up. It was Molly.

"You came, wonderful!" said Natalie.

"Hi," said Lizzie brusquely. "I'm going to the bar," she added, getting up.

Molly sat down beside Natalie, who squeezed her arm in support. "I can't believe you came!"

It was the first time Molly had been out since her dad had died. Natalie knew that six weeks of not going anywhere had to be bad.

"I'm only coming out for a little while," Molly said. "I don't like leaving the cats, they're not used to it. They were so traumatized when I was away living with Mum. Sorry, I didn't mean that you haven't been looking after them."

"No," said Natalie, "that's okay, I understand—they're your babies."

She noticed that Molly's fingernails were bitten down and the brown print dress that she wore now looked too big for her.

"We're thinking of having something to eat," Natalie said. "Chicken and chips? Sausages in a basket? Maybe we should go the whole cordon-bleu hog and have burgers . . ." She was trying to joke Molly into enjoying herself.

"Yeah, that'd be okay," Molly said. "It's noisy in here tonight."

It was. The music had reached migraine-inducing levels and there was a drinks promotion on in the pub. Stunning-looking girls wearing lots of makeup, short skirts, and Mexican hats were rambling around trying to get people to try the booze.

"Do you want some?" Natalie asked.

"No," said Molly, predictably. "Not in the mood really."

Mark, who was one of Steve's best friends, began talking to Molly and Natalie, discussing a movie they all wanted to see. Finally Natalie was able to sit back and relax, leaving Mark to talk to her friend. It was like minding a child, she thought, trying to take care of her until she was happy enough to let go of your hand. Poor Molly, there was no getting over her dad's death. It was the suddenness that hurt.

Natalie's stepmother had said that dying quickly was a blessing for the person who died, but horrible for everyone left behind. "Nobody gets to say good-bye," Bess said.

That's not the only way nobody gets to say good-bye, Natalie thought. Watching Molly grieving for her father kept making Natalie think about the mother she'd never known. She tried to forget the incident in the graveyard. It had been so embarrassing, falling over like that at a funeral as if she were trying to draw attention to herself, when that was the last thing she'd wanted. She didn't even know why she'd found the funeral so upsetting. It wasn't as if she'd been bereaved recently.

She tried not to think about it, except it came into her head at night, particularly the nights when Molly went to bed early; even though she closed the door of her room, Natalie could hear her sobbing.

At the same time that she worried about her friend, Natalie's mind kept going back to her own grief. She'd never cried for her mother, had she?

Natalie had tried knocking on Molly's door and offering, "If you want to talk, I'm here."

"No," said Molly. "I'm okay, really, thanks."

Did talking work? Natalie didn't think so. It was like having cups of tea when you were in shock, or a lie-down—all rubbish. None of it helped. Talking wasn't going to bring Molly's father back. But Natalie wondered—might talking bring her mother to life a little?

Molly and Mark seemed to be getting on well. For the first time in ages, Molly was actually smiling, and when a waitress cruised by and handed out menus, she took one. Brilliant, thought Natalie, she might stay for food and then she'll have had a night out, a night where she didn't sit at home with the cats and stare blankly at the television, not seeing anything. Natalie felt the weight of guilt lift from her shoulders. These days, she felt guilty whenever she went out with Rory or her friends because she hated to think of Molly alone in the flat with only the cats to talk to.

"Oh, my God, that new drink is amazing!" Lizzie threw herself down on two barstools opposite Mark, Molly, and Natalie. Her eyes were glittering and she was positively fizzing with enjoyment and drunkenness. "It goes straight to your head—fabulous!" She giggled and put her feet up on a third barstool. "This is so comfortable, I could stay here all night. No!" she roared as someone else tried to take one of her stools. "You cannot sit down here, I need the three of them."

Natalie could see Mark and Molly looking at Lizzie with

distaste. It was something she hadn't noticed until the hen night, when she'd tried to haul Lizzie out of the club and had seen people move out of the way, looking disgusted at the sight of this young woman absolutely out of her mind on booze. It was horrible seeing that expression, on Mark's face in particular. There was something not nice about having your husband's best friend look at you that way, Natalie thought. Not that Lizzie was noticing.

As for the way Molly was regarding Lizzie with pity . . . well, Molly and Lizzie had never entirely seen eye to eye.

"Move out of the way there," said Steve, shoving Lizzie's legs aside. He sat down on the last stool in the triumvirate and she promptly put her legs across his lap. "Cheap night out," he added, referring to the drinks promotion.

"Yeah," said Mark uncertainly.

Steve didn't look drunk, Natalie noticed. He leaned down and put a hand on his wife's forehead, as if taking her temperature. "How are you doing down there, madwoman?" he said.

"Fine," she roared. "Absolutely fine. Get me a couple more of those drinks, husband, I'm not done yet."

"I think you're well done," Steve said, laughing.

"No, I'm not," said Lizzie. "I want another one—no, make that two more. Get her quick before she goes! Don't forget we're saving—it's much better to get free drinks."

Steve dutifully got up to go in search of one of the Mexican-hatted women for more booze.

"You've had enough, you know," Molly said coolly.

Lizzie propped herself up on her elbow and said, "Don't be daft! Besides"—her face grew grimmer—"it's none of your business, is it?"

Natalie cringed inwardly; Molly had been doing so well, and now bloody Lizzie had upset her. But then Molly surprised her, sitting up a little straighter and speaking in a voice that reminded Natalie, strangely, of Molly's mother.

"Actually, it is my business because you're in my company, and I don't really want to be out for the night with someone whose main aim is to open her mouth and have alcohol poured into it.

Why don't you just stay home with a bottle of vodka and an IV?"

"Fuck off!" snarled Lizzie, and Natalie winced. "I'll do what I want."

She began to get up and her face looked angry and aggressive. Oh no, thought Natalie, she's going to try to start a fight. But suddenly, Lizzie's balance went and she fell off her low barstools onto the ground with a clatter. Mark got up to help her, and Molly turned to Natalie. "You know," she said, "it's quite nice to be out, but I just don't want to be out with her. Do you think we can go somewhere else?"

Natalie looked down at where Lizzie was sprawled on the floor, cursing and refusing to let kind old Mark help her up.

"Go 'way, I'll do it myself. Stupid cow, none of her business, I can drink what I want."

Her diatribe was aimed at everybody and nobody. She didn't know what she was saying; she wasn't the person Natalie knew and loved, she was somebody else.

Natalie grabbed her coat and her bag. "You're right, Molly," she said. "Let's go somewhere else."

"Don't walk away from me!" shrieked Lizzie as they left.

"Hey, what's happening?" said Steve, on his way back from the promotion girls with a tray of booze.

"Lizzie's not much fun tonight," Natalie told him. "We're going somewhere else. Sorry, Steve." She gave him a hug and they left. Let Steve deal with it. Natalie wasn't taking responsibility for her friend anymore.

Lizzie phoned the next day, full of hangover and remorse. "I'm really sorry, Natalie," she said. "Steve said I was an absolute cow, to you and to Molly. I'm so sorry, I don't know what got into me."

"Well, that's funny," said Natalie, "because I know what got into you—half a bucket of cheap drink, that's what."

"Oh, for God's sake," Lizzie said, remorse vanishing at high speed. "I've already had Steve going on at me all morning. What's wrong with everyone? I was just having some fun."

"Well, what's fun for you isn't fun for everyone else," said

Natalie coldly. "And I don't see why your brand of fun has to always mean booze. There is no other fun with you these days. You go out and get absolutely plastered. Show me the fun in that for the rest of us. Clearly it's lots of fun for you, but not for your friends."

"It's harmless," said Lizzie, sounding taken aback at the harshness in Natalie's tone.

"It's not harmless. There's nothing harmless about it. You behaved like a total bitch to Molly. That was her first night out since her father died. We had to go off on our own because we couldn't hang around with your lot. We might as well have stayed at home."

"Oh, yes, staying at home," sneered Lizzie. "You're just like a couple of crazy old lesbians in that flat with your cats."

For a moment, Natalie thought of telling Lizzie that in fact Molly's aunt was a lesbian and lived with her lesbian partner, without the cats though. Then she realized it wasn't safe to tell Lizzie things like that. Molly had to be very careful whom she spoke to about her family because of who her mother was. The old Lizzie might have kept the information secret. The new Lizzie, the one who wanted to get drunk every night and couldn't remember who she was talking to, wouldn't.

"Call me back when you're in a better mood or when you really want to apologize," Natalie said shortly, and slammed the phone down.

Actually, she reflected, it wasn't as if there was a new Lizzie all of a sudden. This Lizzie had been taking over her friend for a long time, creeping in, bit by bit. This Lizzie was the one who had been drunk at their debs ball, the big party when they'd left school. This Lizzie was the one who had sneaked into Freshers' Week at the college with Anna and Natalie and got completely trolleyed on cheap wine made by the microbiology department. This wasn't a new Lizzie; this was the old Lizzie sliding slowly down.

Molly was in a good mood when she woke up. "Last night did me good," she said. "Sort of nice to get out, not sit at home with the box."

"Lizzie phoned and sort of apologized," Natalie said.

Molly shrugged as she put the kettle on to boil. "It's not her fault," she said. "She's an alcoholic."

"What?" Natalie nearly dropped the bowl of cereal she was holding. "She's not!"

"I'm sorry," said Molly. "I thought you knew."

"No, she's my friend, she's just my age." Natalie didn't know what to say. Alcoholics were supposed to be old men in grubby raincoats who hung around outside early-opening pubs, looking all grizzled and wrecked, dying for a drink in case they started to see pink elephants marching down the street. Not her beautiful friend.

"You can't work in the poverty sector and not see a lot of that," Molly said matter-of-factly. "Has anyone tried to get her help?"

Natalie's mind was reeling. "Get her help?"

"You know, get her into rehab or anything like that?"

"I don't know," Natalie said. "I never have."

"Google alcoholism," Molly said. "See what you think then. But just as a stranger's viewpoint, and remembering the state of her when she woke up after her hen night, I'd say it's a pretty good bet."

Charlie had found that routine helped. Intense routines that kept her from making fists with her hands and wanting to punch all the cushions in the house. The morning routine involved getting up earlier than usual and having a cup of coffee on her own in the kitchen as she wrote a bit in her gratitude diary. It was the only time in the day when she was totally alone, and she was doing her best to relish it.

"Me" time was very important, so everybody told her. Apparently, the key to me time was to be able to do your own thing and have nobody making demands on you. Since this was impossible on the average day, Charlie found that six in the morning would have to be her me time. Where there's a will there's a way.

She tuned to some music on the radio—on low since, if it was noisy, it woke her mother—sipped her coffee, and wrote:

Iseult is driving me mad, even madder than my mother. Yes, shock, horror—I know, I never say a bad word about her, but I swear, I will kill her if she doesn't stop being such a cow and help me.

I mean, how DARE she talk to me like that? "I haven't got time for this, Charlie, I'm busy. This is make-or-break time for me. I know you don't understand, but you'll just have to manage on your own."

How dare she? In six weeks, I have done absolutely everything for Mother and Iseult has done precisely nothing, except come into the hospital and make a big fuss—as if Mother wasn't making a big enough fuss already—and annoy the hell out of the staff, so that everyone glared at ME for the whole time Mother was in there. Fine, the hospital wasn't the Ritz-Carlton, but what hospital is? And the nurses were brilliant. Okay, the hip man talked to us like we were a bunch of three-year-olds, but still, they were doing their best. All Iseult's talk of helicoptering her to somewhere else and about how she had a friend in the private hospital up the road and how fabulous that was did nothing but get people's backs up. And it was all rubbish anyway—if Iseult was going to helicopter her somewhere else, why the hell didn't she? Because it was just talk, that's why. That's all Iseult does, talk about stuff. There's no follow-through.

And now Mother is much better, but she's still using the crutch and there's no plan for her to go home yet because she's so weak. So we're stuck with her, and I may kill her.

Hip breaks, the consultant had explained when it was established exactly what had happened, were more likely when the patient got older and had less bone density. Smoking was a prime factor. He'd looked sternly at Kitty as he said this, but Kitty had looked back at him with an insouciance Charlie knew too well.

The doctor was short, balding, and ordinary-looking. Had he been a Dr. Kildare look-alike, Kitty would have been batting her eyelashes and murmuring, "Yes, Doctor," in breathy tones and implying that she only smoked occasionally.

"After sex," she might have added meaningfully.

Charlie was grateful that they'd at least been spared that particular scene.

There had been nobody to flirt with in the hospital, which meant her mother was even more irritable than usual. Flirting suspended normal behavior, and if the flirtee reciprocated, Kitty would remain in a post-flirtal happy mood for quite a while.

But flirty men were thin on the ground. There was the Polish cleaner who spoke little English and looked alarmed when the woman painting her lips red began to make eyes at him and murmur about getting her pillows plumped up. There were male patients in the next ward, but they all looked as if they were on their last legs, and Kitty stared at them with disgust when they shuffled past her ward, slippers flopping on the lino.

There was one male nurse; but according to Kitty, there was something emasculating about a man being a nurse. "Men are doctors," she said, "not nurses."

"That's sexist," Charlie pointed out. "You fought against sexism and the glass ceiling."

"That was for *women*," her mother retorted crossly.

"*That's* even more sexist," dared Charlie, and it was a measure of how tired her mother was that she didn't instantly contradict her.

There were herds of young male doctors roaming around, but they were all too exhausted and busy to notice freshly applied red lipstick or batting eyelashes, and when they stood at the end of Kitty's bed and discussed her case, they focused on medicine instead of the person.

The only other man on the premises was the priest, a spindly man named Father Farrar, who was thinness personified and wore a saintly expression. Priests were among the small minority of men for whom Kitty had no time. They weren't supposed to flirt, so what was the point of them?

The third time Father Farrar attempted to give Kitty Holy Communion, she threw her magazine at him.

"I'm not interested in being converted to your man-god," she screeched. "Come back to me when he lets women into the club!"

Charlie paled. Father Farrar took a few steps backward, and a nurse came in and hauled the curtains around Kitty's cubicle closed at high speed.

"Now, Mrs. Nelson, we've talked about this," the nurse said. "It's not fair to Father Farrar or to the other patients. If you don't want him near you, that's fine. But no shouting."

"I did tell him not to come near me again," Kitty said, shrugging. "He's the one you should be telling off, not me."

Visitors made her worse, bringing out the more flamboyant side of Kitty's personality.

Hospitals in the old days let patients have fun, Kitty muttered, with little parties and a blind eye turned to bottles of scotch being smuggled in with the grapes.

Gwen, an old campaigning friend who arrived with another, quieter woman called Fiona, had a cache of stories from the past. She turned up at the hospital bearing library books, a trailing ivy with dusty leaves, and a bottle of something the color of pee that was clearly homemade, alcoholic, and probably dangerous.

"Gwen!" shrieked Kitty with a delight she'd never shown when Charlie arrived with grapes, chocolate biscuits, and a new audio book for her mother's CD player.

"Kitty, my love!" Gwen threw herself and her belongings onto the narrow hospital bed, and had it not been for Charlie making a grab for the bottle, it would have smashed into pieces on the floor. "Look at you! What have they done with you?"

Gwen had been on the 1970s contraception marches and at a few French riots, and had even lived in a commune in West Cork for a few years until someone nearly died of listeriosis from homemade cheese and an absence of refrigeration, and social services had become involved. Gwen was fond of crumpled linen clothes, henna in her hair, and perfume that managed to combine the scents of a Moroccan souk with full-strength Dior Poison.

"I hope they're giving you decent drugs." Gwen poked around on the small side table looking for bottles with skulls and crossbones on them.

"Nothing decent at all," said Kitty. "Painkillers that wouldn't knock out a mouse. Now, come and sit on the bed, Fiona," she said to the quieter lady. "Charlotte will get us coffee or tea."

Not *"Please could you get us coffee or tea."*

"Of course," Charlie said automatically. She felt a brief stab of pain at being pushed to the sidelines again. If Iseult were here, her mother would have embarked on the litany of Iseult's latest triumphs. Charlie was ordered about like a waitress.

She spent ages getting drinks, and when she came back, her mother was telling Gwen and Fiona a dirty joke.

"And then he said, 'Madam, that's not where I was going to put the thermometer!'"

The three women cackled. Together, they were like the witches in *Macbeth*, only scarier.

When Kitty came home to Charlie's, things had got worse. At least when she was in the hospital, Charlie had been able to leave the premises. Not so anymore. She was a prisoner with a very bad-tempered jailer. As there was no need for Kitty to put on makeup in the morning and nobody to be bright and chatty with, she lapsed into irritation 24-7. Charlie, who'd taken leave from work to look after her, bore the brunt of it.

Without her makeup, Kitty looked her age and then some. The fall hadn't shocked her, but being confined to bed and being unable to get around had. Charlie realized how accustomed she was to seeing her mother in full war paint.

Six weeks on, Kitty was supposed to be much more mobile, but she wasn't improving as quickly as she should be—partly because she hated physiotherapy and often refused to go.

"Charlotte," she roared now, breaking into Charlie's precious early-morning me time.

Charlie sighed and got to her feet. Hello, day.

"I want my tablets," Kitty said when Charlie entered her bedroom. "Then I need my hair washed. It's dreadful. In fact, I need it set. That place on Shop Street *might* be capable of doing it."

Kitty hated Ardagh. She said it was a provincial town with pretensions just because it had a department store like Kenny's. The city, now that's where it was at. People could be themselves in a city, could live wild, vibrant lives and not be shackled by other people's perceptions.

"Since when were you shackled by other people's perceptions?"

Charlie would have liked to ask, but didn't. She couldn't face the inevitable fallout.

"Chloë's, that's the hair place on Shop Street," Charlie said. She loved Chloë's. It wasn't as elegant as the tiny salon on the third floor of Kenny's, but it was great fun. The owner was a fabulous man named Gordon, whom people thought was gay because he wore a brooch and made campy hand gestures. Gordon had told Charlie he was heterosexual but that women preferred gay hairdressers, so he played the part. "The business took off when I changed the name and put the picture of the kitten with eyelashes and a feather boa on the sign," he said. "Camp is comforting, and that's what beauty's all about, isn't it? Comfort."

Charlie wasn't entirely convinced. Gordon was so *good* at being campy. There was no sense he was putting it on, just a feeling that he was totally at home wearing vintage brooches in the shape of salamanders, with a red spotted scarf sticking out from under the collar of his shirt.

"Chloë's—yes, that's it. Stupid name for a hairdresser's. I suppose I don't need an appointment?" Kitty assumed that any establishment catering to the yokels of Ardagh would hardly require advance booking.

Charlie had half a mind to let her mother trail in only to be sent packing, but that would only mean Charlie would have to trek downtown again when they'd made an actual appointment. "You have to book," she said evenly. "I'll phone later."

"Phone now," demanded her mother.

Charlie counted to ten. "It's half six, Mother," she said. "I'll phone at nine."

Chloë's had an opening at ten that morning, and at twenty to, Charlie duly drove her mother to the door.

She would have liked to sit at a mirror and have Gordon fuss over her, clucking at the state of her hair, ordering a treatment on the house, conjuring up a latte with caramel syrup spirited over from Kool Koffee next door.

But having her mother beside her would take the gloss off the experience. It was bad enough to have Kitty in Chloë's in the first place, annoying people with her negative energy, peering down her nose at the place like a cardinal who'd been teleported into a whorehouse.

"Mum's a bit . . . miserable," she said tactfully to Gordon. "She broke her hip and, even though she's mobile now, she's in a lot of pain. Don't mind her if she's grumpy."

"Fine, love, no problem. We'll look after her," Gordon said. He was wearing a spider brooch today, modeled on one the Duke of Windsor had purchased for the Duchess from Cartier. His fine-knit sweater was lemon yellow and his shoes looked suspiciously like ballet pumps, half-implying that he might pirouette across the salon at any moment. "Sure you don't want to wait, have something done?"

Charlie smiled and shook her head. "I don't have a moment to myself, Gordon," she said. "This is the only chance I'll get to run some errands."

She did the grocery shopping, dropped off some dry cleaning, took one of her mother's handbags to the repair shop, and paid a few bills at the post office before racing back to Chloë's with a fine sheen of sweat on her skin.

She was expecting her mother to be in the inevitable mood, but when she walked in, a newly happy Kitty beamed back at her.

"Isn't Gordon a marvel!" she trilled, twisting her head to admire the Medusa curls that clustered delicately around her face, framing it. Gordon had applied color, too, a softening chestnut with paler hints in it to flatter Kitty's skin.

"Lighter strands around your hairline, that's the answer," Gordon was saying, tweaking a curl here and there.

Charlie was shocked at how angry she felt. How dare her mother come in and annex Gordon! She had no right—he was Charlie's friend.

At home, Kitty went off to her room to admire herself, and Charlie phoned work to see what was happening.

Since she'd had to take so much time off, Charlie felt she was missing out on the events at Kenny's. In the first weeks after David's death, everything had continued as normal, apart from the absence of David himself. Everyone said that the systems he'd put in place operated seamlessly and the store ran itself. Tom, the store manager, had stepped into David's shoes, with Lena as his second-in-command.

"It can't last," Shotsy explained on the phone. "Sales are definitely down, like pretty much everywhere else in the luxury market. They're going to have to sell, but Ingrid hasn't been in to talk to anyone yet."

Both women were silent at the thought. Ingrid had phoned Tom and Stacey, but she'd been too grief-stricken to actually venture in.

"Tom's going to see her, though, to talk."

"How horrible." Charlie shuddered. "Coping with your husband's death and his business being in trouble at the same time . . ."

"I hope we still have jobs at the end of it all," Shotsy added.

"I know, but it seems awful to be thinking that way," Charlie said. "We can find other jobs, but Ingrid can't find another David, can she?"

At lunchtime, Iseult arrived, and Kitty's mood improved even more.

"Hello, girls," Iseult said, dumping a bag from the delicatessen onto the table, along with an orchid in a china pot and a stack of magazines. Nobody could ever call Iseult anything but generous.

She hugged Charlie warmly before picking up the orchid and giving it to Kitty. "Flowers for a flower," she said, and Kitty smiled a smile that made her look lit up from the inside.

Charlie stared at her mother, wondering how on earth Iseult did that. Was it the things she said, or the way she said them? Or was it simply that Iseult had a better relationship with their mother than Charlie could ever achieve?

"Your hair is fabulous, Mother," Iseult went on.

"I know, it's lovely," Kitty said, preening. "Had it done in a little place here. I can't believe what a good job they did. From the outside, it looks like a bit of a dump, but they can do hair."

Charlie stifled anger on behalf of both Chloë's and Gordon.

"You look marvelous, too, love," Kitty said to her elder daughter. Iseult was tall and leggy and had long hair bleached to

Scandinavian goddess standard. Tumbling blond curls were her trademark, involving much time with heated rollers. She was also, like their mother under normal circumstances, heavily into grooming, and never appeared in public without nail polish, mascara, and shaped eyebrows tamed with a hint of wax.

"Thanks, sweetie. I'm parched," Iseult said, opening the fridge and looking inside. "I could kill for a cup of tea. Or even a drink. Have you any wine open?"

"In *this* house?" Kitty was scathing. "Divil a bit. There's a decent red in that cupboard by the back door."

Which Brendan bought ages ago and which we were saving, Charlie thought with annoyance, but said nothing.

The wine was opened, tea was made, and a packet of handmade delicatessen cheese biscuits was unwrapped, along with lots of delicious antipasti. And all the while, Iseult entertained them with stories about her new play.

The backers weren't theater people at all, but what were known as theater angels—rich do-gooders, brought in to keep a production going. They hadn't a clue what it was all about. They thought being involved in the theater meant wall-to-wall fun and late nights at the Trocadero trading stories about great plays. In reality, it meant mixing with anxious, jumpy actors who worried over their lines, their roles, and their direction and needed lavish amounts of ego-boosting.

There was *some* fun, Iseult added, explaining how Edwin, the director, had a passion for the female lead's understudy, which was making the lead very cross. And then some screwup with wardrobe had resulted in five corseted gowns needing to be remade from scratch.

"They're raw silk, they cost a fortune, and they're all tiny," Iseult said. "None of them would fit a child, even with the laces fully extended. Jennifer, that's the leading lady, tried hers on just to see, and of course her tits burst out over the top. Then Iarlath, who plays her son in the play and who is a *nightmare* when it comes to women, says he's going to rouge her nipples. He grabs a stick of greasepaint and goes for it. We all laughed like drains, but the costume woman's new and she was white as a sheet watching Iarlath drooling as he tried to rub the greasepaint on, and all the stagehands crowded round like a shot, and someone had a camera phone, so Jennifer's screeching that she turned down photo shoots in the lads' magazines and she's not going into them with red tits in some dodgy camera-phone picture. Leo, who's playing her husband and who can't stand Jennifer, says the magazines would need to be paid to feature Jennifer's tits, and then Edwin has to take her off to the pub to console her and tell her she's fabulous, wonderful, etcetera, etcetera. And it all delayed rehearsals by another two hours."

"I wish I'd acted," sighed Kitty dreamily.

"You'd have been great, Mother," Iseult said obligingly.

"I'd have loved the costumes."

"And the red nipples," said Iseult, laughing.

"God, yes!" roared Kitty, and the pair of them were off, giggling with delight.

When lunch was over, Charlie tidied up around them and felt a certain relief when her mother went outside with her wineglass and an ashtray for a postprandial cigarette.

Iseult patted the chair beside her and motioned for Charlie to sit down. "Are you doing okay?" she asked gently.

"Yes," Charlie fibbed. Then added, "No, not well at all, actually. Mother is not going to win any patient of the year awards, and she's—"

"Yes, but she's still in pain, Charlie," Iseult interrupted. She did it all the time, too eager to say her piece to let others finish theirs. "Think how hard it must be for her to have her routine broken. This is a vision of mortality, too, don't forget that. Imagine falling and having bones break; the vision of the future it presents is simply terrifying." She drew breath, but before Charlie could intervene, she was off again. "It's fascinating, don't you think? It's a story that has to be told, of old age and all it represents. I'm working on a screenplay on that precise subject. Well, it's very rough right now, but the germ of the idea is there. Crash! Your life changes, you start to recognize the prospect of aging, the familiar routines of your life are ripped asunder. . . ." Iseult was no longer seeing her sister. Her eyes were shining, focused on a distant point in her imagination.

"Iseult," interrupted Charlie, "I know all that. I *am* being totally understanding, but my routines are being ripped asunder, too. It's hard for us all. It would be great if Mother could stay with you for a while. I can't take any more time off work."

"Well, I certainly can't. It's out of the question. I'm so manically busy," said Iseult.

Suddenly, for Charlie, it was like being a child again. Three years wasn't a big difference when you were a grown-up, but to a child, it was forever. Iseult had given up playing with baby dolls and dolly nappies and pretend feeding bottles by the time Charlie got into them.

"That's for kids," Iseult would sniff, wrapping a bit of a skirt around a svelte Sindy doll with long legs, a wasp waist, and plastic breasts molded like smooth mountain peaks.

When Charlie eventually inherited Sindy, Barbie, and their by-now tattered wardrobes, Iseult was only interested in her own wardrobe and what to wear to impress the boys in her class.

Whatever Iseult was doing took precedence over everything else. Iseult's first state exams plunged the Nelson household into a quiver of anxiety. When Charlie was doing the same exams, her mother told her, "Exams aren't everything, for heaven's sake. You're only fifteen, Charlotte. It hardly matters at this stage."

Now they were adults, and nothing had changed.

Iseult could be very entertaining, and she was at least interested in Charlie, Brendan, and Mikey in a way that their mother never could be. Yet there was always a slight undercurrent that *her* life and *her* exploits were far more important. Charlie always felt that Iseult's interest was a benign fascination with those less blessed than herself in both the brains and the success department.

There was no way Iseult could take their mother in; Charlie must do it—that was her role.

It was hard to hold in the anger and the hurt, but Charlie managed bravely. What was the point in fighting with either Iseult or her mother? They didn't count her or her life as important. It would take an earthquake in their lives to change that.

Late that night, when everyone was asleep, Charlie sat up in bed and wrote some more in her gratitude diary.

I want it to matter to my mother and my sister that I have a husband I adore who adores me, and a son who lights up my world. That's something precious and I need them to understand.

Charlie stopped writing. This stupid journal suddenly seemed so hopeless, because nothing had changed since she'd started it.

Perhaps her mother and Iseult would never understand. Never, ever. It wasn't as though Charlie could beat it into their heads. It was impossible to change what other people thought. The only thing she could alter was herself and how she dealt with them.

My mother is right: I am stupid. I've spent years thinking I could change her, and I can't. How dumb is that? I'm going to stop now. Stop writing and stop hoping. She is who she is. If she doesn't like me — even writing it felt strange, prickly — then she doesn't like me. I can't do anything about that. There's no law that says your mother has to love or even like you, is there?

Iseult's the same. To her, the only important life is hers. That's always been the way it is. How do I change forty-something years of conditioning? The answer is: I can't.

There was something very freeing about writing this, as if giving up trying to fix the problem was the only answer. Let it go, as Shotsy might have said. Charlie decided to give it a try.

Ten

Live for now. Not for tomorrow or yesterday. Now. You don't know what will happen tomorrow, and yesterday is gone, so all you have is this moment. Enjoy it.

Marcella hated Mondays: waking up early after luxuriating in bed at the weekend, having to rush through all the little pleasures like having her morning tea staring out at the sea from her apartment with its vast picture windows. The traffic on the way to work was always hell, full of men in slower cars who felt their masculinity threatened by a woman in a sleek gray-metallic BMW. They cut her off at lights and glared at her with irritation. Today a motorbike courier gave her a two-fingered salute when she got stuck in an intersection and he had to maneuver illegally to get past her.

"Right back at you, asshole," Marcella growled.

There was so much negative energy about Mondays. She was willing to bet that none of the world's greatest minds had ever done anything brilliant on a Monday. Nobody ever mentioned when Einstein had put the finishing touches to his theory of relativity, or when Marie Curie discovered radium. But it definitely wasn't on the first day of the week.

The mood didn't improve in the offices of SD International. When she opened the door into the normally immaculate foyer of the Georgian building, she saw a disaster zone. The soft blue rug—a murderously expensive handmade thing with the company logo of a maple leaf—was crumpled up by the wall, dripping wet, and the wooden floor itself was a shallow pond with soggy newspapers floating like lilypads. Marcella absently hoped they weren't today's papers; then reality asserted itself.

Julie, the usually beautifully-turned-out receptionist, was on her Wolford-clad knees with a towel, fruitlessly trying to stem the deluge. The water was at least three inches deep. Julie's stockings and the bottom half of her skirt were sopping wet.

"What happened?" asked Marcella, standing just outside the threshold to avoid the water.

"Something burst—a pipe, I don't know," wailed Julie, stopping her mopping. "I came in at eight as usual to find this. I don't know where it's coming from."

"Did you phone the maintenance company?"

"Yes, they say they can't be here until after eleven."

More negative energy zoomed around the room. Marcella growled for the second time that day, rolled up her charcoal-gray trousers to midcalf, removed her spindly heeled boots and her socks, and walked into the wet. It was like stepping into a freezing ankle-deep puddle.

Reaching the reception desk, she checked to see if the water had got as high as the electrical outlets. It hadn't. That was one blessing.

She found the directory, flicked through it to find the maintenance company's number, and got through in an instant.

The man at the other end of the phone didn't sound too worried about it all.

"Ah sure, we'll be there at eleven and we'll have it sorted out. It's the age of the building, you see. Old pipes and whatnot. You'd have had to rip it all out and start from scratch to make sure this type of thing didn't happen."

Marcella had a vision of him sitting back in a chair, scratching his belly, enjoying giving the usual lecture on old buildings and plumbing that he reserved for female callers. She wouldn't have been surprised if part of it included the phrase: "Don't worry your pretty little head about that, love."

"We did rip it out and start from scratch," said Marcella in an icy voice. "Three years ago. I know, because I wrote the check.

I write the checks for your company, too, the retainer that says you get someone here immediately in an emergency situation. The water will reach the electrical outlets soon, and when somebody is electrocuted, I'll be the one suing your company for failing to respond as per your contract. What do you think the insurance company will pay out for a dead person?"

"Er . . . well . . ."

"It's eight-thirty. I expect someone here within the hour," Marcella finished, and hung up.

"You'll have to teach me how to do that," Julie said from the floor.

"That wasn't a very good demonstration." Marcella sighed. "I slightly lost my temper, and you forfeit any moral high ground if you do that."

"But still," said Julie. "I'm sending my boyfriend over to you later so you can tell him those survey results about how working women still do all the housework."

"Can't use the vacuum cleaner?" Marcella said, making her way to the stairs.

"I'm not sure he knows we have one."

"Two options, Julie." Marcella sat on the third step and began putting back on her boots. "You can tell him to pack his bags, but it's better to work with him on the issue of cleaning the house and sharing the chores a bit more. Explain that it's important to you and reach some sort of compromise."

"You mean I shouldn't sit him down and give him the ultimatum?" Julie looked surprised. Her favorite magazines were very keen on dumping the wrong guy instead of wasting time on him. Dump Mr. Wrong and find Mr. Right.

"Ultimatums never work. Compromise does." Marcella zipped up her second boot. "If you love him and he loves you, you'll work it out. But you may have to live with it. I don't know if you can really change anybody. You have to decide whether it's worth it to stay with him and his faults, or to be without him.'

As she made it to the sanctity of her office, she wished that someone had said that to her when she was Julie's age.

Compromise was a dirty word back then. Arguments were all about standing up for your rights and reading the riot act to any man who dared to disagree. Poor Harry, her ex-husband, had felt the blast of her Alexis Colby impersonation many times. Her life might have been different if a wise older woman had explained the facts of life to her years ago. It was too late for her now.

She sat down at her desk and made her daily phone call to Ingrid. "Hello, what are you up to?" she said cheerily, much as she did every day.

She'd learned early on that the clichéd "How are you feeling?" was a disaster; after all, how could Ingrid be feeling?

"I feel terrible!" Ingrid had shrieked at her one day, and Marcella didn't know what was more shocking: to hear her friend cry out in such obvious pain, or the fact that Ingrid hadn't managed the bereaved person's careful lie: "Yes, I'm fine." She wanted Ingrid to be honest with her, yet it was hard to hear such honesty.

"What am I up to? Not much," said Ingrid dully.

Nobody hearing her on the phone would recognize her as the country's bright, intelligent top broadcaster anymore.

"Tom, David's second-in-command, is coming over," she added. "I can't bear to have to deal with it, but I've got to."

"Okay," said Marcella, stuck for words, an almost unheard-of occurrence, as Harry would say. "Would you like me to come by later?"

"No." Ingrid's tones were still lifeless. "I'm fine. Better off on my own. Besides, if I'm up to it, I'm going in to the store in the afternoon, and then Flora and Sigrid insist on taking myself and the kids out tonight before Ethan goes away, which I'm not really in the mood for, so I'd be no company, to be frank."

Marcella hung up, feeling a powerful relief that she'd never loved anybody the way Ingrid had loved David. To witness such naked grief was like standing beside someone with their skin blistering and burning, while you felt no pain apart from mild heat at being close by. If that was love, then it was better that she was on her own. Better that it was too late for her to fall in love.

* * *

On Sky News that morning, there had been footage of a storm in the Pacific. Shots of exotic trees bent double by the wind, and houses tumbled into debris. "Those poor people," Ingrid had said out loud, then realized she'd said it automatically. She didn't *feel* it. She didn't really feel sorry for them because she was too numb from her own sorrow.

Life was going on for other people. They got up every morning, laughed as they listened to the radio, kissed their loved ones good-bye, bought chocolate at lunch and said to hell with the diet, went out with friends, talked loudly, drank red wine, curled up safely in their beds. While Ingrid's life had stopped with a crash as if she'd hit a brick wall.

Just as the human mind struggled to assimilate the notion of infinity, Ingrid couldn't cope with the idea of a world without David. His absence was too huge.

What would she do for the rest of her life without him?

It would have been different if the children were still small; then she'd have had a reason to get up every day. Mothering, being the lioness guarding her cubs, she could have done that.

Being the mother of adult children was different. Her children were able to get on with their lives and come to terms with their grief on their own.

Ethan was dealing with it the way he'd dealt with all emotional crises since he was a child—he rushed into the rest of his life to fill up the space where his father used to be. He went to parties and gigs, out to clubs with friends. He spent hours on the computer in his room or playing with his Wii, the rumble of music from his bedroom the only sign that he was there.

For a while Molly had moved back into her old room at home, leaving Natalie minding the cats. She'd kept order in the house because Ingrid was no longer able to.

When Ingrid couldn't sleep at night, a common occurrence, she sat up and watched Sky News and CNN, searching for worse and worse stories, because only then could she rationalize her own suffering. Other people lost loved ones, in bombings or storms or famines. They had to cope, so she must too. Only when dawn crept into the sky was Ingrid finally able to sleep, which meant she often didn't come downstairs till noon, bleary-eyed and exhausted.

Molly had taken compassionate leave, and when that was over, she used some of her holidays so she wasn't at work all the time.

"I'm going in for half a day," she'd said one day at noon, when Ingrid was standing in the kitchen in her dressing gown, stuck halfway between the coffeemaker and the fridge, wondering what she needed to do next. Even making coffee presented too much choice.

"Is Ethan about?" Ingrid asked. She'd heard the deep rumble of his voice in the kitchen just before she came downstairs. But now there was no sign of him.

"He's gone out," Molly said quickly.

Ethan was avoiding her, Ingrid realized.

"He's keeping out of my way," she'd said tearfully on the phone to her sister Flora. "It's as if he thinks it's my fault somehow, that I should have looked after David better, or realized he was ill. . . ."

"Ethan loves you, Ingrid," said Flora gently. "He doesn't blame you in the slightest, I know that. *You* know that, really. I think the problem is that he can only cope with his pain and not yours too."

Ingrid had been stunned. It was true, she realized. Her grief was so overwhelming, people backed off from it. Only the staunchest friends were able to go the distance, and Ethan simply wasn't experienced enough to handle it.

That was when she realized why Molly had moved home: not for comfort from her mother, but so she could give comfort to her mother.

The ultimate role reversal.

Despite being grateful for dear Molly's love, Ingrid felt another weight settle painfully on her shoulders. She wasn't the feisty mother lioness anymore; she'd become a burden to her cubs, needing their protection.

She told Ethan and Molly she wanted to talk to them over

dinner one night, and roused herself enough to cook properly instead of heating yet another microwave dinner and leaving it half-eaten. She made roast chicken, stuffing, and roast potatoes, and when she cried as she was making it, she turned the news on loudly to dose herself with more there-are-other-people-worse-off therapy.

She opened a bottle of wine, put out her favorite red napkins, and rearranged the position of the table in the kitchen, pushing one end against the wall so that the empty space where David used to sit was not so obvious. "This is our new family unit," she was trying to say without using words. She didn't accept it herself, but it was time to do a little mothering and help her children believe it.

"You need to go back to your apartment," she told her daughter firmly. "We have to move on, Molly."

Ingrid hated it when people said that to her—move on. As if David's dying were a little blip in her life instead of the biggest agony she'd ever lived through. Move on from the man she'd loved for more than half her life? What an insult.

But those words could be useful.

"I'm fine, Molly—well, as fine as I can be," Ingrid amended.

"I like being here, Mum," Molly protested.

"I like having you here, my love, but you've put your life on hold, and you know Dad—he'd have hated that. He was so proud of you in every way, and he'd want you to go on living, not staying here trying to keep me on the straight and narrow."

Molly half-laughed, half-cried. She nodded.

"And Ethan, I think you should go back to your traveling. The rest of the gang are in Australia now, right? If you leave soon, you'll still have at least three months with them."

Ethan fiddled with his fork. "I'd love to, but it seems wrong. . . ."

"It's not wrong," said his mother briskly. "You can't give up your dreams for me. Dad would have been so upset. You know how he used to tease me for worrying about you, wishing you'd e-mail more often."

They all smiled fondly, and Ingrid felt her heart ache. What she wouldn't give to return to that time when they were still a family, when worrying about what *might* happen to Ethan was her main anxiety. She hadn't appreciated that properly. Why was happiness only obvious when it was gone?

"You'll have to e-mail more, that's my only stipulation," Ingrid went on, wondering where she was getting the strength to play this tough-but-happy-mother person.

"I promise," said Ethan eagerly.

Ingrid made herself look at the storm on Sky News for a little longer, then switched it off. When Molly phoned, she was looking into the wardrobe and thinking about getting dressed.

"I can cancel going to the launch, Mum," Molly said. "If you're going in to the store for the first time today, you need someone with you. There's no problem with me canceling, they'll understand—"

"No, don't cancel anything," Ingrid replied. She'd picked today precisely because it was a hectic and unmissable day in Molly's office involving the delivery of an important report to the media. She wanted Molly to slip back into her own life and not feel that she had to be Ingrid's shadow. "I'll be fine, honestly. Besides, Tom is coming round early and we might go together."

She didn't say that it was unlikely she'd travel to the store with Tom. David's former second-in-command was a sweet man, but without a shred of charisma. Tom had wanted to visit for ages now, but she'd kept putting him off.

He'd said he understood if she preferred not to meet at Kenny's—"too many reminders," as he'd put it.

But he was coming here today, and there were far more reminders in the house she'd shared with David. Every little thing told her he was gone.

She'd cried the first night she'd remembered to put out the rubbish bins. That had been David's job. There was nobody to read a bit out of the paper to, nobody to drink the second cup of coffee in the percolator. The unconscious things were almost worse. She felt helpless at night when she didn't know when to go to bed, when to switch off the TV and end the day. They'd done that to-gether. Now it was her choice and hers alone.

She had just dressed when the doorbell rang at half past nine. Sighing because Tom was early, she opened the door and found Carlos, her producer from work, on the step.

"You're not returning my calls, so I thought I'd surprise you," he said, giving her a hug.

"Coffee?" she asked, flustered at this intrusion into her den.

"Yeah," he said, putting a patisserie bag holding some cakes on the table.

As usual, Carlos got straight to the point. "Do you think you'd like to come back soon?"

He walked around the kitchen as he talked, the same way he did in the office. Perpetual motion, that was Carlos. He'd wander around picking up pictures, looking at them, putting them down, sweeping a bit of dust off a shelf, craning his head to look at the spines of books he'd looked at just the other day. Some people found it disconcerting, but Ingrid understood that high-energy thing. Today, however, his energy was jarring. It reminded her of the life she used to have—a reminder she wanted to avoid. The comparison was too painful.

"I don't know," she said. "I don't know if I'm able to come back yet." It was, Ingrid knew, the wrong answer. The right an-swer was, *Yes, I'm desperate to leap back into the saddle again and be the current-affairs queen of a flagship TV show,* but her heart wasn't in it. She'd read the books on grief—well, she'd flicked through them and thrown them down onto the big pile of reading matter by her bed. But the bits she'd read said that getting back into the real world was an important part of recovering your life. Your beloved might have died but you're still alive, was the general theme, and Ingrid understood it perfectly—in theory. In reality, it was different. She simply didn't care.

Unbelievably, she didn't watch the show she'd once lived and breathed for. She scanned the newspapers because they were still delivered to the house, but she looked at the headlines with little

interest. Political scheming, by-elections disastrously lost, earth-
quakes, coups—she didn't care. She didn't even get the papers on
Sunday, the one day they weren't delivered. It had been part of the
routine, to go to the shop and get them, then pick up croissants
for breakfast. Why bother? Ingrid had decided that, quite frankly,
the world could carry on without her.

"I just wanted you to know that they're grooming Joan to take
over," Carlos went on.

"Oh," said Ingrid. "Joan. . . . She probably won't be bad at it.
She needs to work on her *s*'s though; too much sibilance when she
talks."

"God, I know," he said. "Nobody's that keen on Joan, and you
know she'll want a wardrobe allowance."

Ingrid laughed, the sort of laugh she did now, a hollow one.
She could count on one hand the number of times she had really
laughed since David had died. "Wardrobe allowance? She should
be so lucky."

Ingrid had had a tiny wardrobe allowance. Even someone who
had to appear on-screen twice a week and look grave and intelligent while delivering major news stories had to pay for pretty
much all her own clothes.

"She's thirty-seven," Carlos added.

Once, that would have been the clincher for Ingrid. Not anymore.

"Pretty, too," Ingrid commented. She wasn't that keen on Joan
herself. Not a team player; she appeared to have no understanding
that the show came out twice a week because of the hard work of
a lot of other people. Ingrid had always been aware that, while she
was the public face of the show, there was a whole team behind it.

"I thought you'd be more upset," Carlos said, studying her now
with an expression of appalled concern.

"So did I," she said. "I'm sorry, Carlos."

"They're going to make a decision by the end of next week.
So if you still want the job, you need to come back. You need to
phone in, talk to someone, talk to the director-general," Carlos
said. "I hate seeing you like this, Ingrid."

"Yeah, me too," she said bitterly. "Thanks, you're a good friend. Shut the door on your way out, will you?"

The bell rang again about half an hour after Carlos had left. On her way to open the door, Ingrid caught sight of herself in the hall mirror. Not a good look, she thought, realizing, although not caring, why Carlos had seemed so shocked at her appearance.

Her hair was sort of brushed, but she hadn't been to the hairdresser since before David died and her roots were that streaky silvery-brown that suited nobody, certainly not herself. She wore no makeup and her face gleamed with the excess moisturizer she'd slathered on to make her skin feel less taut. Ingrid couldn't be bothered with dressing well either. Today, she wore black tracksuit bottoms and a comfortable sweatshirt of the sort of pale pink Marcella called "nursing-home chic."

"Throw it out," Marcella had advised, seeing Ingrid wearing it once. "It makes you look like you're on your way to get a blood transfusion."

Perversely, Ingrid had kept it, and today it seemed like the right thing to wear. She might not need a blood transfusion, but if they could give her a life transfusion, a David transfusion, then maybe she'd be okay.

Tom, at the door, clearly had absolutely no idea what to say to her. "Ingrid, my dear." He tried a brief hug, which felt extremely strange because Tom wasn't a hugger.

He refused tea or coffee and sat at the dining-room table opposite her, all business. Ingrid steeled herself to cope with it. All mention of the business reminded her too much of David; she'd had to force herself to visit the solicitor's office to talk about David's will, and only went through with it because she was the executor.

The company auditors were desperately keen to talk to her, but she couldn't face them yet. Perhaps when probate was sorted out, she thought miserably. Then she could look at the company and consider how she was to run it, given that David's will had given her the controlling interest.

Tom started off with pages of figures from the quarterly report about where the company stood, and Ingrid, who had always had a good head for numbers, found that she couldn't concentrate on any of it. The numbers looked bad, though. Surely that couldn't be right. Kenny's was doing well; that's what David had told her. Was that why the auditors had been phoning so often, to give her this appalling news? She didn't want Tom beside her telling her bad news; she wanted David saying it was all going to be fine.

Finally, she'd had enough. "I can't concentrate today, Tom," she said. "What's the bottom line?"

"Well," he said cautiously. Then he appeared to make up his mind, and it was like watching someone leap over a cliff. "I'm so sorry to have to tell you, Ingrid, but the company is in financial trouble. It's nothing that David was doing wrong. It's just that Kenny's is a luxury department store, after all, and people have less money at the moment. We're all being squeezed. No matter how many brilliant ideas we come up with to market luxury goods to people, ultimately they have to have the money to buy them in the first place."

Ingrid managed not to gasp. Kenny's in trouble. And David hadn't breathed a word to her.

"Right," she said, as if she'd known all along. "What was David's plan? You know, the finer details of what he thought would work?"

She would not admit that she knew nothing about any of this.

"I don't know," Tom said. "To be frank, I didn't know things were this bad, or how hard the banks were squeezing us, until David told me that he'd had lunch with Stanley DeVere. I knew that meant something."

"Right," said Ingrid again, trying not to betray her shock. David had disliked Stanley DeVere and the whole DeVere ethos. In fact, *dislike* was too mild a word.

"And did he tell you how that went?" she asked. "From a business perspective."

"No," Tom said, "it was more of a 'feeling their way' meeting. You know how David was: he liked to keep his cards close to his chest."

Ingrid bit back the word *evidently*.

"Yes," she said. "I know." She hadn't known, but she was learning fast. "I'm sorry I haven't been up to coming in, Tom, and that I'm not up to speed on what's happening, but what would you do in my shoes?" she asked, letting her defenses down for a moment.

"Sell," he said bluntly. "Let's face it, running Kenny's is a massive full-time job. It was getting too much even for David."

"But it was his baby," Ingrid said wistfully. "He loved the store. It was in his blood. He was like his father—for him there was a story attached to every part of it, every door, every window, every floor. . . ."

"But that's being sentimental, Ingrid," Tom said, "and in the current economic climate, we can't afford to be sentimental. This is a very valuable business, if you sell it now. If you put your heart and soul into it over the next couple of years and still run it into the ground, it won't be so viable. I'm sorry," he went on, seeing her stunned expression, "I know that's probably the wrong thing to say to you, given the way you must be feeling, but I would be doing David a disservice if I told you anything else. He was a brilliant salesman, a brilliant ideas man, and it was hard even for him. Ingrid, this isn't your forte, and I don't think the children want to run the store either."

"True," she said.

Once he'd broached the tough news, Tom was all set to chat, but Ingrid gently got him to leave. Two visitors with bad news was more than she could cope with in one day. Besides, she needed to be alone to think. If David had been contemplating selling his beloved department store and hadn't told her, what did that say about them, their relationship? That he was trying to protect her, or that he couldn't share things with her? She didn't know.

She let the dogs out for a final pee, pulled a coat on over her blood-transfusion sweatshirt, and left to drive to Ardagh. She didn't want to face Kenny's without David, but it had to be done.

"Can I get you anything?" Stacey hovered behind Ingrid. She'd been hovering ever since Ingrid arrived at Kenny's. Ingrid felt sorry for her in a dispassionate sort of way. There was no etiquette for dealing with the first occasion your dead boss's wife came to the office after his death.

"No, I'm fine, thank you," said Ingrid, then thought she was anything but fine. But somehow, despite all the parts of her that had been destroyed by David's death, there was still some compulsion saying, *You must be nice to other people, not let them see your pain.* They couldn't see it anyway, even if you laid it out in front of them.

She remembered the neighbors who'd dropped into the house to give her Mass cards, funeral flowers, and lasagnas, all saying sorry and that David was wonderful and wasn't it tragic and awful and could they do anything? If she tried to talk to them about him, they backed off or changed the subject. They simply couldn't cope with it. The rituals of death were a glorious part of tradition, but God forbid that anybody should have to engage with the actuality of death once the person was buried.

No, best to move on, find a new life and some peace; that was the trick they expected of the bereaved. Ingrid didn't know how to make a new life for herself. She'd been happy with the life she had.

"I could get a cappuccino from the café, or tea, or maybe water," Stacey went on.

"Thank you, Stacey," said Ingrid, "I'm fine, really. Just give me a few minutes here."

"Of course," said Stacey quickly, and scurried back to her desk.

Ingrid stood in the doorway of David's office and looked around. How odd to be here without him; she felt she was an interloper in his private space. It was all so unchanged. Exactly the same as he'd left it. How? How could it remain the same when the person who created it all was dead and buried? There should be a scientific disintegration of someone's things when he was dead, a physical manifestation that mirrored the loss of the person. His papers should crumble at the edges, his special cup develop deep cracks. It was wrong that physical things remained intact when those who loved the dead person were falling apart inside.

The desk still shone and a faint scent of polish was in the air. The old-fashioned blotter David liked still sat perfectly square on the desk, his mouse mat to its left, the computer, sleekly white beside it.

There was nothing for it. Ingrid walked into David's office and shut the door behind her. This was his space, where he'd spent so much of his time when he wasn't at home with her. There were pictures of her, Molly, and Ethan in beautiful wooden frames, paintings, a couple of old framed maps. He'd loved those old maps from when the boundaries of countries had been so different, the sorts of maps great explorers had used to trek to the poles. David had always fancied taking part in an expedition with sleds and huskies and clothes that could withstand polar temperatures. "I'm too old now," he'd said the last time he talked about it. "No you're not," said Ingrid. "You're never too old; age is in people's heads." She smiled now at the thought of it. Then the smile disappeared. Age might be in people's heads, but bodies gave in when they aged. Your mind might be twenty, but your heart—now, that could be old.

Most of the filing cabinets were in Stacey's office, but David had kept some beautiful walnut cabinets in his. They'd been locked, Stacey said, but she had the keys to most of them, and today she'd left them open. Ingrid pulled out the drawers one by one, thinking of the last person who had opened them. David. She slammed them shut and went to sit in the chair, where he'd died. She wouldn't cry; this wasn't what his life was about, this chair. He wouldn't have had time to realize, his doctor had said. With such a massive heart attack, it would have been very quick. No sitting in the chair thinking of everything he was going to lose, thinking in pain of her and the children.

She sat back and closed her eyes, wishing to be close to him; but there was nothing. It hurt, feeling the emptiness where he used to be. The priest had talked about another world and God and love; yet she sat here in this room where David had spent so much time, where he'd died, and there was nothing. She would never see him again; he was gone from her forever.

Her sister Flora had such great faith and had come many times over the past weeks, sitting quietly with Ingrid, listening to her talk, hugging her while she cried, and telling her it would get better. She often held Ingrid's hand, occasionally patting it gently. Ingrid wanted to feel comforted, but she couldn't. Nothing comforted her now.

"You have to have faith," Flora would say. "We don't know God's will or what he wants from us. This is a way of testing your faith, Ingrid—"

Ingrid couldn't listen to her any more. She removed her hand.

"I know you're trying to help, Flora," she'd said, "but it's *not* helping. How am I supposed to have faith now? I'm not like you; I wish I were. If something happened to Brid, you'd be able to cope with it and make sense of it all. You'd see her in heaven—what did they say at the funeral about God's house having many rooms? Well, that'd work for you, but it doesn't for me. I don't have your belief. Having faith in God when your husband has been snatched away doesn't make sense to me."

In her grief, Ingrid thought about God and his plans all the time. The priest at David's funeral had talked about how believing in God would take her through this, and how David was with God.

But David wouldn't want to be with God—he'd want to be with them.

After the funeral, when the mourning party had retired to a hotel in Ardagh for coffee and sandwiches, the priest came round again and sat beside her on a stool, almost like a schoolboy ready for a grilling from a teacher, Ingrid thought.

He was young, perhaps thirty, and at any other time, Ingrid would have liked him. Flora had whispered that he'd worked in South America for three years, and before coming to their parish he'd been employed in a maximum-security prison.

"Do you know for sure that David's happy?" she said. "I can't feel it. I can only feel that he's gone from me, and that absence is huge, huge and total. He's not coming back. I am never going to see him again." She put her hands over her face and took a deep breath. "You say I will, but how do you know?"

"We don't know. That's what faith is: trust in the Almighty."

"How can I trust the person who took my husband from me?" Ingrid demanded.

The priest, clearly used to this type of discussion postfuneral, took it in his stride. He talked of love, belief, and the Holy Spirit guiding the bereaved.

He had no answers, either, Ingrid decided.

Now she pulled at the drawers on David's desk, looking for something, something she could touch that would bring him back to her. The first two drawers contained stationery, but the third drawer was locked. Presumably Stacey hadn't found the key. She dragged at it, but it wouldn't open. This was too much, too painful; she shouldn't have come in today. She got up and left the office, shutting the door quietly behind her. She wasn't going to cry, not in front of anyone.

"Stacey, I feel a little weary. I think I'll go home now," she said.

She slipped out one of the side entrances. She didn't want to walk through the administrative offices and talk to everyone, have them hold her hand a touch longer than normal, have them look at her with sad eyes, thinking, Poor Ingrid, how is she coping? That made it worse. Not the kindness—that was wonderful, and people were so terribly kind. But the pity, people looking at her and seeing her empty life ahead of her; that hurt. She knew, because she'd done it herself to men and women who'd had loved ones ripped away from them before their time; she'd looked at them with the same eyes, thinking, *Poor you, I'm glad it's not me.* Ingrid wasn't ready for that today.

On the main street of Ardagh, she breathed in the cool, fresh air. It was a beautiful day, still cold, but the sun was shining. She walked down the street, past a glitzy hair salon called Chloë's where the nylon scent of hair spray filled the air, and into a small florist's, where she bought a large bunch of freesias.

"Are they a present?" asked the girl in the shop as she expertly wrapped them in cellophane.

"Yes," Ingrid said. They were a present—they were for David.

On the headland where the church and its graveyard were

situated, it was still a beautiful day, but windy. She could hear the sea crashing against the dangerous rocky crags below known as the Twelve Apostles, deadly to swimmers and boats alike. The church was called the Black Abbey by the local people because it was built of dark stones and looked as if it had been cut right out of the earth; the color of wet slate, its thin, pointed spires reached up to the sky.

Discussing where they wanted to be buried hadn't been high on Ingrid's list of topics for enjoyable evening conversation, but they had talked about it once and David had said that this was the place for him. It wasn't the church so much, he'd explained; it was the graveyard. It was beautiful, Ingrid had to admit, if any graveyard could be called beautiful. It clung to the side of the hill as if the church were the centerpiece and the graveyard a cloak spread beneath it. It contained many beautiful Victorian memorials, stone angels with lichen clinging to their soaring wings, and giant tombs that hadn't been opened in a hundred years, all gothic and beautiful and wild. Ingrid could see why David would want to be buried here—and she would be buried here too, she thought with a shock. She'd bought a plot for two. One day, she'd lie here with him; and that was frightening because, even though she wanted to be with him again, she didn't want to lie in this cold ground.

She pulled her camel-hair coat tighter around her and walked down to the grave. It still had the signs of new grief about it. Amid the remains of the funeral flowers and the big bunch of daffodils she'd brought the week before, there was a tiny arrangement of red roses, placed as if they were lying on David's heart. Ingrid stared at them. There was no card, nothing to say whom these flowers had come from. She looked at them for a long time. Who had left red roses for David?

She closed her eyes to pray, but couldn't concentrate. Abruptly, she picked up the red roses and hurled them far off over the cemetery wall where they could bounce down into the sea. *She* was the person who got to leave red roses for David—nobody else.

* * *

That evening at dinner in a small restaurant on the far side of Ardagh, Flora was talking about a program she'd heard on the radio about bats. "Absolutely fascinating," she said. "It turns out they aren't as blind as scientists originally thought."

"Really, Flora," said Sigrid, "we're eating our dinner. I don't want to think about bats."

"Well, I'm interested," said Flora.

Ingrid could almost hear David's voice saying, "She is a bit bats; perhaps that's why she likes them so much," and she had to try not to laugh.

"I love this place," Molly said, looking around her. She gave her aunt a hug, defusing the bat row. "Thanks, Aunt Flora."

"I decided we shouldn't avoid places where we went with David," Flora said firmly. "We're not going to do the 'avoiding' thing, we're going to do the 'celebrating the life' thing."

"Fine," said Ingrid. It was better not to argue with Flora when she was in that sort of mood.

"I think Aunt Flora's right, Mum," said Molly. "We should be celebrating Dad's life in every way."

"Yes." Ingrid thought of her meeting with Tom and the discussion about selling Kenny's. Her husband had had a meeting with the head of DeVere's, and he'd never told her. "Yes," she agreed, "we should celebrate his life."

She tried to smile at her family, patting Ethan's hand where he sat beside her, smiling across the candles at Molly. They were all so good, but she felt too empty to enjoy it.

Ingrid couldn't taste the food. It looked beautiful, even smelled nice. They were having Wicklow lamb with an herb crust and fresh vegetables, and it all tasted like cardboard animal feed marinated in brackish water. She went through the motions of eating and trying to smile because she didn't want to be the specter at the feast. Everyone was trying so hard for her.

Ethan's eyes had been suspiciously red when Flora had handed him the wine list and said, "You choose, darling. Your dad taught you all about wine—go on, you pick."

David hadn't really taught him all about wine, Ingrid knew.

They weren't big wine drinkers, definitely not wine snobs, and Ethan's knowledge was about on a par with her own: pick something midrange from the list and you couldn't go too far wrong. She'd seen, though, how he was grateful to Flora for saying that, making him feel in some way his father's successor.

At the beginning of the meal, Molly had been doing what she used to do as a small child when she was nervous, twirling her hair endlessly with her right hand, twirl, twirl, but as the evening wore on she stopped doing it. Everyone was able to relax except for Ingrid. What would they feel if she just got up to go and said, "I'm really sorry, this is kind of you, but I can't do this. I'm not ready yet."

There were flowers on the table, carnations. She hated carnations and their peppery scent. On the next table was a yellow orchid, much nicer, and farther along at a big table for ten there were red roses. Something sparked in her mind. Red roses . . . She remembered the roses on David's grave. Nobody would leave red roses except somebody's wife, somebody's lover; yet there they were, a little bouquet, beautifully tied.

"I went to David's grave today," she said, and they all looked up, sad at the image she conjured up. The widow with no life beyond her husband's grave. "There were lovely red flowers there, but the card had blown away. Were they from you, Sigrid?"

"No, sorry," Sigrid said. "I've some plants I thought we could put at the head of the grave, but I haven't brought them yet."

"Not me," said Molly.

"Sorry," said Ethan guiltily. "I meant to buy something today. Can we go to the grave before I fly off?"

Nobody here, none of the people closest to him, had left roses for David.

He'd had secrets from her; she'd found that out this morning from Tom. And there was a locked drawer in his office desk for which Stacey didn't have the key. Something was being hidden from her.

Ingrid thought she might be sick. She shoved her chair back

from the table. "I'm sorry," she said, and stood up, napkin spilling on the floor, everyone looking at her. "Headache."

"I'll come with you, Mum," said Molly, leaping to her feet.

Ingrid controlled herself long enough to say, "No, love, you stay here. Please."

Somehow she managed to get out of the restaurant and into her car. It would take five minutes to drive to the store, that was all.

The Kenny's security man, Abel, clearly thought she was under the influence of something. "There is nobody in, Mrs. Kenny," he kept saying gently, as though he were speaking to a small child.

"I know," Ingrid hissed, doing her best to maintain her calm public persona. "There's something I need to check."

"They'll all be here in the morning—"

"Now—I want to check it now," Ingrid snapped.

"Of course, madam." Abel's professional mask went up. He was polite, a tall, immaculately turned out man from Sierra Leone. David used to say he had the intelligence and gravitas of a judge. What might he have done with his life if circumstances hadn't brought him and his large family to Ardagh, where he had to work the shifts that nobody else wanted? She wondered whether David had come here late at night. Had Abel been accustomed to letting him in with someone else clinging to his coat, laughing at their daring—No, she wasn't going to think that way. Not until she was sure.

Her mobile phone rang as she was inserting the key into the door of David's suite of offices. Probably Flora, checking she'd got home all right. Flora was unlikely to be comforted by a message that read: *Not home yet, decided to go to dead husband's office to see if my instinct that he was hiding something from me is correct.*

It would probably be padded-cell-and-soft-focus-drug time if Flora got *that* message.

She checked her phone. The text was from Molly, seeing if she was all right. Whatever was going on, Ingrid didn't want Molly involved.

Nearly home, sorry for rushing, headache bad, talk in morning. Love Mum. She sent the text.

Lying was actually an okay thing to do when your husband had just died. If you told people the truth about how you felt, they'd have you locked up.

Ingrid flicked on all the lights, swept through Stacey's office, then found the correct key for David's. The Lucite lamp on his desk lit up jewel-green when she pressed the switches on the wall. Clever. Like everything David did, it was all perfectly organized— no fiddling around with desk-lamp buttons; just flick two switches and everything worked. Attention to detail was David's trademark.

Which was why the red roses on his grave and the locked drawer sounded a discordant note in Ingrid's mind.

The drawer was still locked. Ingrid pulled it again to make doubly sure. No, still firm. She looked around the office for something with which to pry it open, but there was nothing obvious lying around.

She wrenched open the drawers on the other side of his desk. They contained paper, files, pencils, even, ominously enough, one of those big suction corkscrews, but nothing useful. Next, she tried Stacey's desk and hit pay dirt: a lethal-looking letter opener.

"Perfect," Ingrid said grimly.

It took about ten minutes, much longer than it took thieves in action movies. But then, they always had delicate picklocks and she was hammering away at the keyhole with the tip of a letter opener. Finally, the lock broke. She threw the blunted letter opener down. Stacey would wonder what had happened to it. Not Ingrid's problem.

For a couple of seconds, the opened drawer looked like any other drawer in David's desk: an innocent space with neat piles of stationery. She'd been picturing something awful. Grief did terrible things to people. Made them imagine all sorts of wrongs.

She poked through the paper with a forensic eye.

And there it was: a neat pile of handwritten letters. She lifted them out.

The goddess of clichés was kind today. The letters weren't tied up in ribbon or—she sniffed them—scented with perfume. But they were love letters just the same, written on decent-quality writing paper in a looping, feminine hand:

Darling, I dreamed about you last night. I woke up and thought you were here with me. I hate it when that happens. America seems such a long way away, and I want you beside me, making love to me. Love and kisses, Me.

David's wastepaper bin was made of metal, which was just as well because Ingrid had to throw up into something and she didn't want to ruin the carpet. This thoughtfulness seemed odd under the circumstances. Her heart was destroyed, why not the carpet?

Once she'd got rid of the beautiful dinner that had tasted like sawdust, she sat back against the wall, weakly holding the bin, her legs spread out in front of her, eyes closed. She didn't want to move because, if she moved, she might feel sick again. She had so many feelings inside her, all jostling for recognition, that she couldn't cope with any more.

After a while, she felt strong enough to put the bin down. She wiped her mouth on the sleeve of her gray cashmere cardigan, and thought how incongruous the scene would have appeared to an onlooker: Ingrid Fitzgerald sprawled on the ground, a wastepaper bin of vomit beside her, a smear of sick on her cardigan. She hauled herself onto the desk chair.

She laid the pile of letters to one side. David had kept them together with big paper clips. No red ribbons. He'd never been a romantic, had he? There was a modicum of pleasure in the fact that his lack of romance stretched to both of his women. She'd look at them later, when she felt able.

There was something else in the drawer—credit-card receipts that told the story of the affair. Lunches at beautiful restaurants on the outskirts of Dublin, nights at exquisite hotels where nobody ever went for business meetings, a three-day stay at the George V in Paris. That stung, despite the barrier Ingrid had created around herself. Paris, their city, where they'd gone when the children were small, and again for their first adult-only holiday after Ethan and Molly left home.

They'd had coffee in the George V but never slept there. Instead, they'd stayed in the Crillon, where they'd lain in an antique French bed made up with endless pillows and snowy sheets, enjoying room-service champagne and the hotel's famous breakfasts.

They'd visited Paris many times since. Ingrid's favorite shop was the beautiful Anne Fontaine shirt shop where elegant salesladies had sat David in an armchair, plied him with coffee and *Le Monde,* and patted him in an understanding Gallic way, so he was happy while she tried on exquisite blouses that fitted as though made for her.

"If we go bankrupt because you like that shop so much, we'll be able to say: 'We'll always have Paris,'" David said once, and laughed heartily at his own joke.

"We won't go bankrupt with you working such long hours," she'd joked back.

Not so funny now.

Ingrid stared at all the receipts, some with faded printing, through the small reading glasses she never wore on-air because she felt they made her look old. If she tried hard enough to distance herself, maybe it would be like reading the research compiled on a cheating politician.

She would be at her desk with Gloria bringing in the details, and everyone in the office would wonder about the ethics of using such evidence. Was the moral life of a politician open for public consumption?

But this evidence wasn't about a politician for whom she felt nothing. It wasn't about a poor politician's wife, waiting patiently at home while even the dogs in the street knew her husband spent more time than was necessary with a colleague. Ingrid had always felt so sorry for the women who kept the home fires burning, hauled children to and from school, and answered phone calls from irritated constituents while the man himself was wined and dined in Dublin and Brussels, making it all look so easy. It was easy because of his wife, and he was cheating on her.

Now Ingrid was in exactly the same position. It hurt so much.

What really surprised her was the anger, pure and sharp, that roared through her. How could David have done this to her? She had never nagged him the moment he got home, irritated by his life, bored by her own. She was a career woman, damn it. She dealt with big issues every day, wasn't afraid of responsibility.

If he wasn't happy, he could have left; but *this*—having someone else who wrote him adoring letters and missed him so much in a needy way—this was sheer betrayal.

Ingrid would have fallen to pieces privately if he'd asked her for a divorce; but if David had said "I'm in love with another woman," she'd have given him his divorce. Only a fool or a masochist would try to repair the cracks in a marriage after that.

Except he'd never said it. He'd gone on playing happy family. He'd died letting her believe he was true. She'd stood at his grave and sobbed her heart out for a man who loved someone else.

If David hadn't been dead, Ingrid could have killed him with her bare hands.

She bent and threw up again, bile this time. There was nothing else left in her stomach. She closed her eyes until the nausea passed, then got up and went to the small fridge in Stacey's office. It held cans of fizzy lemonade, and she drank one.

Slowly, Ingrid felt her energy return, along with a little bit of herself.

Stacey would wonder what had happened if she saw the bin, the ruined paper opener, the drawer. There was no hiding her presence in the store—Abel, the security man, would have to report anyone who'd come into the building. Ingrid knew she had to handle this carefully. She emptied out David's drawer and closed it neatly, then took the bin to the bathroom and washed it. When the place looked more or less as she'd found it, she wrote a note for Stacey:

Stacey, David had some letters of mine and I knew they were in his desk. I came to get them last night. They were so personal, I just wanted to have them. Ingrid.

Not a bad excuse, she thought grimly. Men may come and go, but the ability to lie lasts forever.

She roamed the fifth floor until she found an empty cardboard box. As she piled in the evidence of David's betrayal, she had a sudden thought. The only drawers she'd tried were in his desk. What if there was more for someone else to find? She opened the elegant wooden cupboards that hid filing cabinets where he kept his personal records and tested the drawers. Among all the innocently open ones, there was one that was locked.

"More shit," she muttered as she wielded the letter opener again. This lock broke easily. There were more credit-card statements going back further. Ingrid scanned the first sheet, then scooped the whole lot out and into her box. She closed the drawer and pulled the cabinet door across. She hoped the note would satisfy Stacey's curiosity. But then, perhaps she'd been in on it with David.

"Tell my wife I'm in a meeting—I've got another secret date with my girlfriend," David might say, and Stacey would wink at him in time-honored personal assistant style, knowing it was her job to keep everything a secret.

Or perhaps the other woman *was* Stacey. "Let's lock the door; nobody will know. . . ."

Damn David! She had to know who it was or she'd go mad, suspecting every woman in his life. But she had to be subtle about it. The media would love to hear that a television star like Ingrid had been betrayed by her supposedly loving husband. It would destroy the children if they were to learn of the affair. Ingrid would do everything she could to hide this other woman's existence from Ethan and Molly. But first, she needed to find out who she was.

There was only one person she would trust with this pain: Marcella. Among her many talents, Marcella knew how to lock a secret into her mental strongbox and keep it there forever.

Marcella sat curled up on her couch picking hard skin off her feet and watching an episode of *Sex and the City*. She'd seen this particular episode many times before and owned the box set, but deciding to watch a show from your own DVD collection was somehow never as enjoyable as finding it randomly on television. During the ad break, she ran out to the kitchen and made herself another cup of decaf tea. She'd drunk pints of tea every waking hour of the day until her acupuncturist told her that caffeine late at night was fatal for sleep and, as someone with sleep issues, she needed all the help she could get.

The doorbell buzzed loudly.

Instinctively, Marcella looked at her watch: quarter past eleven. Nobody called without warning at that hour. Either it was some emergency—surely whoever it was would phone instead?—or it was a crazy person selling religion or junkies armed with syringes wanting to break into her house. They'd picked the wrong woman. She grabbed her alarm remote and her mobile phone, dialing in 999 just to be ready. Then she peered out the window beside the door and saw, to her utter astonishment, Ingrid standing there.

"Ingrid!" Marcella wrenched open the door and stared at her friend in alarm. Carrying a large cardboard box, her face a strange gray color, Ingrid looked as if she hadn't slept in a hundred years. "Come in. What's wrong?"

Ingrid didn't speak as she carried the box indoors and set it on the giant glass coffee table. Marcella noticed that all the scaly bits of dry skin she'd picked off her feet were on the table beside the box, waiting to be binned. Normally, that would have horrified someone as house-proud as she, but she simply swept it all onto the floor. From the look on Ingrid's face, it was clear that bits of skin were hardly important in the grand scheme of things.

"What's wrong?" she repeated.

"This," said Ingrid in a monotone, gesturing to the box. "There were red roses on David's grave earlier today, and a locked drawer in his desk. I knew something was wrong."

Marcella sank bonelessly onto one of her armchairs. "Roses?"

"Red roses—not from me, and without any card saying who'd sent them," Ingrid said, opening the flaps of the box with great calmness. She began taking out sheaves of paper and placing them in neat piles on the table. "I was out at dinner tonight with my sisters and the kids, and the memory of those red roses kept coming into my head. That and the locked drawer I discovered when I went to David's office today."

Marcella reached forward to put a comforting hand on her friend's arm, knowing how hard it must have been, and how Ingrid had been putting off the visit to Kenny's.

Ingrid flicked her a brief, wry smile. "I thought I was being brave, too," she said. "I went in today because I knew Molly couldn't come and I didn't want her to be with me when I went through his things. I didn't want to make her into a handmaiden of death, having to be with me all the time, worrying about *me*. Her father died—that's enough to deal with. She shouldn't have to deal with my feelings, too. Do you understand?"

Marcella nodded, although she didn't understand. She had imagined that the children would help Ingrid get over David's death, because there would always be three of them who'd lost him. But she still couldn't quite touch what that would feel like, being a mother. She stuffed that ache away in her mind.

"I'm glad Molly wasn't with me," Ingrid went on, and resumed emptying the box. "*She'd* have noticed a locked drawer."

"Where was the key?"

"I didn't have the key," Ingrid replied. "Stacey hadn't found it. The whole thing kept nagging at me through dinner. I decided I had to know for sure. I drove to Kenny's and broke open the damn drawer with a letter opener. Every office should have one," she added with fake brightness. "This is what I found—"

"In one drawer?" Marcella looked at her coffee table, which was now obscured by papers.

"There was a locked drawer in a filing cabinet, too. I haven't gone through the stuff I found in there." For the first time, Ingrid's brittleness appeared to crack. "I read one letter from his desk drawer. He was away in America and she missed him. There's a date on it, last June."

"They might be someone else's letters," said Marcella, clutching at straws. She looked through the piles for the handwritten stuff.

"David was in the U.S. last June," Ingrid said flatly. "And why would he hide someone else's letters? No, they're his."

"I can't believe it," Marcella said, searching. She found the letters and held them carefully in her lap: Exhibit A, Your Honor.

The flowers you gave me are nearly dead. I'm not going to throw them out until the very end. It was such a lovely weekend, wasn't it? When I'm with you, I feel safe and protected.

When I was little, I used to press flowers, and I'm going to press the roses. . . .

"What's this rubbish?" Marcella said, furious. "All this little-girl stuff: 'I used to press flowers.' I used to have a bloody Barbie, but I don't go on about it now."

"I told you, I only read a bit of one of them," Ingrid said. "I brought them here so you could do it for me."

Marcella took a deep breath. "Red wine?"

"If I drink anything at all, I'll cry, and I don't want to cry, not yet."

"Good point."

Marcella went to the kitchen and returned five minutes later with a pot of coffee and biscuits. "We're going to be up all night anyway, so we may as well imbibe."

She put on some music—Tina Turner, because no woman could fall to pieces with Tina singing "What's Love Got to Do with It" in the background—and began looking through the letters. It was a mammoth task: the unraveling of the myth of David and Ingrid. Like a fairy story in reverse. Like *Sleeping Beauty*. Except in this case, the prince hadn't woken Ingrid from a hundred-year sleep—he'd made her age one hundred years in a moment.

* * *

Ingrid poured herself a coffee, sank back on the couch, and stared at the television. She liked this show; it was fun and thoughtful. Samantha, Charlotte, Carrie, and Miranda were having brunch in their Sunday-morning restaurant. Whatever panic they were going through, it was over. It had been made up. Ingrid felt a bit made-up herself. Her life hadn't been real at all. What she'd thought was real wasn't.

She thought back to all the times she'd smiled indulgently at David at parties when women flirted with him. They might have thought they were being discreet—smiling, twirling their hair, touching him when they spoke—but she saw it all. And smiled at it. She trusted him. Believed he'd never betray her, that it was their private joke: all the women in the world could throw themselves at him and he'd do nothing, because he loved Ingrid, and true love beat all corners.

And all the time, *this*.

She felt bleak; there was no other word for it. As if all the light had been leached out of her life, out of her. All the time she'd thought it would be her career that would fall out of love with her when she got old. Not her husband.

Ingrid's exhausted mind drifted back to an episode from a year ago, the first time a woman she knew had been subtly shunted aside on a television show. Ingrid had been shocked, even though she'd seen it coming.

Grace Reynolds was a fortysomething former model who'd moved into television and charmed people with her sense of fun and intelligence. She'd cohosted the breakfast program for five years, patting the hands of reality TV victims who'd come on to present their sides of the stories, smiling comfortingly at people raising funds to fight diseases that had killed their loved ones. She'd mothered people, and viewers had loved it. Except that the show's producer felt the need for younger blood, a child-bride co-presenter for the male host—the craggy Jeff—who was at least fifteen years older than Grace.

The new presenter he found was twenty-three and fresh out

of college, with the looks of a Victoria's Secret model, all honey-blond skin and honey-blond hair with a flawless complexion and glossed bee-stung lips that some at the TV station uncharitably suggested had already been clamped around certain parts of the producer's anatomy. She started immediately, and Grace, displaying the characteristics of her name, bowed out, obediently following the script: she was tired of the early mornings and wanted to spend more time with her children and her husband.

That had infuriated Ingrid more than anything else: like making a hit-and-run victim admit that it was all her own fault, that she'd wanted to be smashed by a car, honestly.

"You should leave," David had said furiously when he'd heard. "They'll do the same to you, Ingrid, and you can't give them the satisfaction."

She'd felt a rush of love for him, her man, who didn't want her hurt. It was true that she feared the axe falling and the shame of being shunted into the background for a crime that was pinned only on the female of the species, but she didn't want David to know her fear. He'd worry more, and he had enough to worry about as it was, running the store.

"Darling, I'm a lot stronger than Grace—it wouldn't be so easy to get rid of me," she said. "Besides, I've made my peace with it all. I don't want to go on working forever. I've got all those book ideas to work on, like the one about the cult of feminism in pre-Christian Ireland. I can't do it now, not with the show; but when the time comes and they decide they don't need me and are ready to pay me a stinking great disappearance fee, well, I'll be gone in a flash. No point hanging around telling the world I didn't like working nights anymore. I refuse to get pushed out of the way like poor darling Grace."

"You sure?" He'd still looked worried, and Ingrid burned with anger at the idea of anybody in TVland having the power to make her family sad or worried. They would *not* fire her the way they'd fired Grace, by the stealthy guerrilla attack. That only worked on employees compliant enough to smile bravely and go quietly.

Ingrid wouldn't go quietly, and the powers in the organization damn well knew it.

"Course I'm sure. TV's a young person's game. If I retired, we could travel more. Perhaps do that tour of Australia we've always talked about."

It worked; David relaxed.

"You're some woman," he'd said, shaking his head. "I thought you'd be angry over it all."

"I'm furious—for Grace. But not worried, love. It won't be like that for me, promise."

"But what if it *is* like that for me?" she had asked Marcella on the phone later. "What if they force me out and bring in some kid to do my job?"

"They won't do that to you," Marcella counseled. "Grace is a sweetheart, far too nice for television, to be honest. She should have come to me, and I'd have shown her how to handle it."

Ingrid laughed. "Does that mean I'm not nice?"

"You're a total bitch—didn't you read the editorial the *Irish Times* ran on the subject?"

They both laughed this time.

"No, you're a professional, that's all. Grace isn't. She's a lovely, gifted amateur, and you cannot get on in this job and be an amateur. You need the armadillo plating of a professional."

"She wasn't fired for being an amateur," Ingrid reminded her friend. "She was fired for committing the cardinal sin of getting older. And she didn't even age like a normal person. She's aged like a model. You could grate cheese on her beautiful high cheekbones, and her skin is fabulous."

"How Grace looks was at least fifty percent of why she was hired," Marcella pointed out. "For all that you're on the 'Fabulously Hot at Fifty' list in *Woman's Way* magazine, you weren't hired for your looks."

"True. So why could I be fired for those same looks getting older?"

"Beats me, Aged Wise One," Marcella had replied.

* * *

Marcella read on. If Ingrid hadn't been there, albeit in a strangely calm state staring into space, Marcella would have allowed herself to curse as she made her way through the pile of handwritten love letters.

Of course they could have been sent by a crazy stalker lady who had yet to move on to boiling rabbits and kidnapping Molly and Ethan, but Marcella didn't think so. She might not have the corresponding letters from David to this mystery woman, but from every detail, it was obvious that she was David's lover.

It hurt her to think of David doing this. What must it be like for Ingrid?

None of the letters was signed by name, and she wasn't sure if that was because the writer specifically wanted to maintain anonymity or was merely part of some game.

Darling David, thank you for the most wonderful evening ever. I wish it wasn't over. I wish you hadn't had to go back to her. . . .

Marcella couldn't bear to think of Ingrid reading this one.

. . . I know it's complicated, I know it can't be sorted out in a minute, but I wish things were different. My darling, why does she get to have you and I don't? It just seems unfair—she has everything. I'm sorry, David, I didn't mean to write that. It's just I'm upset. Perhaps I should blame all that champagne. But I feel so lonely, sitting here on my own, wearing the gorgeous negligee you bought me, wishing you were here to see it. . . .

Marcella scanned it quickly. She'd been wrong; *this* would kill Ingrid if she had to read it. Negligees, and talk of "she," clearly

---

meaning Ingrid. Appalling stuff. There were dozens of letters. They said thank you for meals, nights out, lovemaking—together they represented everything David had stolen from Ingrid.

"Well?" asked Ingrid, after what seemed to Marcella like forever but was actually only an hour.

"Well, we should go to bed," Marcella said. "This will all be here in the morning, but we'll look like two mad old hags if we don't get some sleep." As soon as the words were out of her mouth, she regretted them.

The woman who'd written the love letters had never given away her age, but Marcella would bet a year's salary that she was much younger than Ingrid.

Ingrid, however, merely smiled at her friend and said, "More of this coffee in the morning will soon sort us out."

"I'm your woman for that," said Marcella, smiling back.

At a few minutes after seven, Ingrid woke up and felt instantly alert. And rested. She'd only had five hours' sleep, yet she'd slept more deeply than on any night since David's death. Strange. Death and betrayal after death scored differently on the interrupted-sleep scale. She must tell David that—

It happened a lot, thinking of how she'd like to tell him something and then remembering he wasn't there to be told. Most of the time, bleakness washed over her and she wondered if this pain of loss would ever go.

But today, the realization was different. Today, there was tremendous anger in the mix. Being angry with David was so much easier than mourning him.

In the bedroom's en-suite bathroom, she washed the sleep from her face. She hadn't taken off her makeup the night before, despite Marcella's offer of toiletries. She'd scrupulously washed makeup from her face all her life, and she'd had enough of it. It was all camouflage, a cover to deflect attention from aging and betrayal. All the unguents and creams in the world couldn't change this.

She found an elastic hair-band in the cupboard under the sink, scraped her hair back with her fingers, and tied it up. It didn't suit her—she looked like a medieval dowager, banished to a convent.

But today, this suited her mood. She had been playing the wrong role for too long. She'd believed she was a vibrant woman with the best years ahead of her; she'd actually looked forward to a time when she could go on long holidays with her still-adoring husband. It was clear now that she should have been playing the crone all along.

One desire consumed her: to find the identity of David's lover. But unless Marcella struck gold in the reams of papers, she didn't know where to start. She felt lost. Lost and alone.

Eleven

Fight for who you are. It takes a long time to find who you are, but when you do, take care of that person. She's one of the most precious friends you'll ever have.

People who came to Star's front door were always surprised to see the two red Chinese Fu dogs guarding her door. The house, with its pale clapboard façade and wisteria-covered veranda, seemed an odd setting for the exotic lion-dog faces that stared out at the pathway. Once visitors entered the house, they understood a little better. It was a cornucopia of wonderful and unusual things from all over the globe.

Star's house was anything but ordinary. Walking in, the first thing a guest noticed was the scent: a combination of cinnamon, ambergris, and frankincense cut through with the sharp, tangy aroma of lemongrass. Then the person would walk across the beautiful Persian rug that was older than Star could ever tell anyone, and hear the whitewashed floorboards creak underfoot. The third and seventh floorboards in the hall were the creaky ones, which Star would say was lucky. Then a guest would admire all the treasures the Bluestone women had collected over the years.

On the hall console table was an old sextant from a seventeenth-century Dutch sailing ship alongside a wooden model of a boat that had sailed from Plymouth Rock. On the walls were Star's tapestries, their vibrant colors contrasting perfectly with sepia photographs of other Bluestone women with strong faces and long blond hair, taken in Morocco, Scandinavia and Alaska.

Shelves in an alcove held an exquisite Tiffany lamp and a wooden bowl, carved hundreds of years before by French monks.

In the long sitting room that stretched along the entire back of the house, there were even more treasures: massive couches, tightly packed bookshelves, watercolors of rare flowers, and a collection of unusual teacups in translucent bone china with rich, gilded colors. Pride of place went to Star's great-grandmother's wooden rocking chair, still with its original lace cushions, and the 1940s gramophone that played Count John McCormack records beautifully but refused to play anything else.

Lena had been to Star's house many times before to discuss the tapestries and Kenny's plans for the line, and she loved everything about the place: the flower beds in bloom beneath the windows, the beautiful orchids in the tiny conservatory with its cast-iron chairs from another era and the floral cushions a person could sink into. She loved the rag rugs and the old chintz armchairs, the copper pots that hung over the huge stove in the kitchen. Today, she was showing this gorgeous home to her colleague Claudia.

"If I lived here, I'd never want to leave," Lena said to Claudia as Star showed them into the hall and they were immediately enveloped in the golden sense of comfort that was Bluestone Cottage.

"It's so beautiful," said Claudia, looking around in wonder. "And the smell is . . ."

"Oh, just some things I've been making," Star said. "Special coffee and cinnamon muffins—does that sound good?"

"Lovely," said her guests.

"This is Claudia," said Lena suddenly. "Sorry, didn't introduce you properly."

Claudia blushed. "Sorry," she said too, and held out her hand.

Sometimes people thought that Star was standoffish. When she met people on the street, she didn't rush to hug them or kiss their cheeks or take their hands. She stood back a little, a trait that many over the years had assumed to be a sign of reserve. That wasn't the case. Touch was so important to Star. Touching a person could help you see into his or her soul, or so she had found,

ever since she was a tiny child. Now she carefully took Claudia's
proffered hand and held it in both of hers.

"Lovely to meet you, Claudia," she said, and drew a deep
breath.

The feelings she experienced were subtle at first. From Claudia,
young, pretty, and smiling, there came just a soft warmth, happiness, contentment. Suddenly, Star could picture a young man who
loved Claudia and had asked to marry her, had given her a ring, a
tiny square-cut something—not a diamond, but some special older
jewel.

She sensed all this, but "Lovely to meet you Claudia," was all
she said.

She wouldn't say anything about what she'd seen. Claudia
probably wanted it kept a secret. Star had learned at an early age
that not everybody appreciated the Bluestone women's gifts.

Granny Star, for whom Star was named, had been able to sense
the light in what she called found objects, things that were special.
If someone handed her a watch or an item of clothing belonging
to a loved one, she could feel the person's energy, know where
they were, what was wrong with them. It was a powerful gift,
especially at a time when the magic most rural people looked for
was the cure for various ailments.

When a traveling woman named Madeline had come to Ardagh
selling pots and pans, people had flocked to her as word spread
that she could cure bad backs. Nobody quite knew how she did
it, but once they had been to see her, whatever back problems
they had were gone. It was a simple, crude magic, but it worked.
Granny Star told her little granddaughter how she and Madeline,
recognizing the sixth sense in one another, had talked about the
way their powers set them apart.

"People fear what they don't understand," Madeline had said.
"They want it, and yet they fear it."

"Is it easier when you're moving from place to place all the
time?" Granny Star wondered.

"It is and it isn't," Madeline said. "Traveling is all I know. People welcome you when they need you, but when they are better, they want you gone. When that happens, it's horrible to feel they don't like having you around."

"I understand," Granny Star had said. Her gift had been brought into the open many years before, when she'd used it to find a missing woman. Since then, many people had come to her; but afterward they would hurry away, eyes shifty, afraid someone might see them. They needed her help, but they didn't want anyone to know they'd turned to a Bluestone woman rather than falling to their knees in church.

Star's own experience had taught her that this was as true today as it was then, so she was careful about letting people know what was revealed to her when she touched them.

Holding lovely Claudia's hand, Star stiffened suddenly. Something came to her like a pulse of electrical current, something to do with a woman and David—her David. She tried to work it out, but it was hazy, the way things were blurred when the person didn't know what was going on. Whatever it was involved David and a woman close to Claudia, but Claudia was innocent of it all. Suddenly Claudia took her hand away.

"It's a beautiful house," she was saying. "I love those old maps, and those teapots are just adorable." Everyone admired Star's teapots. She'd been collecting them since she was a small child and there were scores of them: blue-and-white willow-patterned ones, a colorful hand-painted one from Greece, a couple decorated with delicate chinoiserie that she'd acquired on her travels. Most precious of all to her was a tiny handcrafted pottery one with a slightly uneven spout and a willow handle. It was very old and had been her great-great-grandmother's. Tea drunk from that pot could give the drinker a vision of her destiny. Star had only used it a few times in her life. It should not be abused, her mother had said.

"Star has an amazing collection," Lena agreed. "Is this a new one?" she asked, running a finger over a fat rose-colored teapot with a chipped handle.

"I bought it in an antiques shop," Star said blankly. Her mind wasn't on teapots; it was on Claudia's hands and what she'd seen, a flicker of another woman who was close to David. The woman hadn't been Lena or someone who worked closely with David; it was a different kind of closeness, something to do with love— but that didn't make sense, because the woman was linked to Claudia, and how could David be in love with a woman linked to Claudia?

She felt the urge to touch Claudia's hand again, but it mightn't work a second time. Her magic was strange like that: it delivered its gifts when it felt like it, not on request, and especially not when her need to know was so strong.

Star felt shaken and clumsy, which was unlike her. She spilled the tea leaves when she was making the tea, then knocked the jug over so that milk flooded the wooden kitchen table, almost reaching one of the tapestries she'd laid out for the visitors to see.

"Sorry, sorry," she said, quickly grabbing a tea towel to mop it up.

When they were all seated, enjoying tea and some of Star's muffins—though Star, in her troubled mood, barely noticed their taste—they talked briefly about David.

"It's such a cliché, but I can't believe he's gone, I just can't," said Lena mournfully. "It was so sudden. One minute he was here, and the next he was gone."

"I know." Claudia put down her muffin as if her appetite had vanished.

Star watched her. There was something strange going on, she could sense it. No, not strange so much as sad. Sad and full of pain. For someone.

In the cool of the shed-cum-studio beside the farmhouse, Natalie hammered away at copper coils, bending them into shape with the tiny jewelry hammer. It was satisfying work normally, pounding away with purpose. Today, it was painful. Her hands hurt, from the tendons in her wrists down to every flexor in her fingers. The dull ache seemed to come from the inside and was like nothing she'd ever felt before.

It had been the same all week: she'd feel normal in the morning; then at intervals during the day as she worked at Kenny's café, the pain would return, throbbing, pulsing into every sinew. Nighttime was the worst. No matter how tired she was, she'd wake at least once every night from the awful ache, and it would be worse than it ever was during the day.

Kneading her hands, stretching them, doing odd bending exercises—nothing helped. She wondered whether this was what it felt like to go slowly mad: feeling something strange that you couldn't explain to anyone else, but that constantly haunted you.

"How's it going?"

Her father stood in the doorway, clad in his usual work uniform of worn corduroys, Wellington boots, an ancient sweater, and a rain jacket. He brought the smell of the barn with him, a mixture of the scent of animals and silage. Natalie loved the smell. It was the smell of her childhood and somehow infinitely more precious than any other aroma, although, if pushed, she'd say that Bess's apple-and-blackberry crumble came a close second.

"Not too bad." She laid down her hammer.

"Bess said you were in bad form," Des said.

Natalie allowed herself a small smile. Her father never beat around the bush. "I am a bit, I suppose."

"Why? Is it Rory?"

Bess and her father had met Rory and pronounced him very agreeable. Even better, the family dogs—wise barometers of human beings—had adored him at first sight, and the ram had gone berserk outside the kitchen door wanting to join in the fun.

"Dr. Dolittle," her father had said cheerfully. Coming from him, it had been a compliment. From Lizzie's mouth—"You're not seeing Dr. Dolittle again, are you?"—it had been a slur.

"No, it's not Rory, he's great."

He was great, too. Kind, sexy, funny, generous: he ticked all the boxes. But despite that, Natalie hadn't allowed herself to fall totally in love with him.

It was, she thought wryly, the perfect example of "It's not you, it's me." It *was* her. He was lovely. She was the one who wasn't sure, although she had no idea why. She simply didn't feel like herself these days.

What with not sleeping well, she felt jumpy and achingly sad. She couldn't bear to hear the news on the car radio on the way to or from work, and she hadn't been able to look at the latest batch of leaflets for Molly's antipoverty organization either. The main picture was a black-and-white shot of a small child curled up in one corner of a bare room, looking lonely and scared. Natalie had felt tears well up in her eyes the first time she saw it.

"You're sure it's not Rory?" her father went on. "We all think he's a great fellow, but if he's misbehaving, I can rush round to the clinic and pretend to knock all his teeth out. He'd win, you know, but I'd go through the motions for you."

"No, honestly," Natalie said, laughing.

"Right, so," said her father, serious again.

Natalie wished she could summon up the courage to say, "Actually, Dad, could you tell me about my mum, she's been on my mind a bit. . . ."

But she didn't know how to begin. How did you start a conversation you'd been waiting your whole life to have?

"I'm not trying to pry. If you don't want to talk, don't. But I'm here if you need me," he said.

She couldn't do it.

"It's Lizzie," she said. Well, it was partly true; Lizzie's behavior was upsetting. But since Natalie had been keeping out of her way, she hadn't witnessed any other drunken nights. Still, let Lizzie take some blame now to get Dad off the scent.

"What's she done?" he asked.

"It's hard to explain. She's my friend, and I don't want to be disloyal—"

"I promise not a word will go further than this room." Her father sat down on the scarred wooden bench that had sat in the farmhouse's kitchen for many years before being relegated out here. In the olden days, he'd told Natalie, they called it a "firm."

She thought of all the things he'd taught her over the years. He'd been a wonderful dad, but there were things he had kept from her, things she needed to know.

"What's Lizzie done?" her father repeated.

"Molly says she's an alcoholic," Natalie said, and even to her ears, it sounded shocking. "I don't know, Dad, I can't get my head around it. She does drink a lot. But she has a job and everything, and she's not living in a cardboard box. It's not as though she drinks every day. I've seen her keep to soft drinks when she's the designated driver—"

"It's not always easy to see it," her father said, and Natalie had the feeling that she'd said something to upset him. He got to his feet quickly. "You know, I think I left the light on in the garage. I'd best turn it off while I remember." He laid a hand on her arm. "Look, Lizzie's a nice girl, but you don't know what goes on in people's lives. Don't let it mess you up, love." And then he was gone. Natalie was hurt at his abruptness.

No longer in the mood for work, she tidied up, then headed to her bedroom to change. Her precious photos of her mother were in the bedside bureau, and she took them out and looked at them. There were three photos of her mother, two with Natalie when she was only a baby, and another when Natalie was perhaps two and a half. Her mother looked just like her, the same lanky body, the same long dark hair and eyes that looked black in old photos. Her smile burst out of the pictures, though, and she looked as if holding baby Natalie was the greatest joy in the world.

Natalie ran her thumb over her mother's face, as if touching it would somehow impart knowledge of her.

"Mum," she tried. "Mum."

This woman was her mother. And she knew nothing about her.

"Hey, Nat." Joe wandered in. Her youngest brother never waited to be invited in, just sort of threw himself against the door in a half entrance, half knock at the same time. Natalie shoved the pictures under her pillow quickly.

Joe's hair was all gelled up and he was wearing an awful lot of aftershave.

"You going out?" she said.

"Yeah. What do you think of this look?"

He was wearing an old rock-band T-shirt and the hoodie she'd given him for Christmas. It was Diesel, very cool; he loved it.

"Fabulous. You'll knock their socks off. Or her socks off . . . Is it a date?" she asked.

"Yeah," he said, still in full-on cool mode. He admired himself in her dressing-table mirror, posing, putting his hands in his pockets and striking a moody look.

"What's her name?" Natalie asked.

"Sarah," he said. "She's really different, not like Kylie at all."

Kylie, his last girlfriend, had been a major mistake, in Natalie's opinion. A blip on Joe's previous record, Kylie measured worth in terms of Louis Vuitton handbags and was scouting around for somebody to keep her in the style to which she wished to become accustomed. Natalie had disliked her on sight, and the feeling had been mutual.

"What's Sarah like?"

"She's sort of pretty, has long hair and . . . you know. She's into music. She's sound," he added.

Natalie grinned; a man of few words was her brother. She loved him, even if he didn't have that much to say. She'd go out and kill Sarah with her bare hands if she wasn't nice to him. Actually, she owed Kylie a bit of a thumping too, now that she thought about it. Anyone who dared upset her little brothers would have her to contend with.

"You look great," she said, "but I'd wash off a bit of the after-shave, just a small bit, you know."

"Too much?" he said anxiously, a little boy again.

"Sort of."

"Okay, sis—bye."

When he was gone, and his overpowering miasma with him, Natalie looked at her photos again briefly before putting them back in the bureau. There were no more answers there.

But after closing the drawer, she had second thoughts. She opened it again, took out the smallest photo, and put it in her handbag It would be comforting to carry it around with her.

* * *

The next morning, Natalie was on the early shift at Kenny's. Although the store didn't open until nine, the café opened to staff at half past eight for breakfast. The first person in that morning was Charlie.

"How lovely to see you," said Natalie, smiling. She hadn't seen Charlie for an age; someone had said her mother had had an accident and Charlie had taken time off to take care of her. The place wasn't the same without Charlie around. There was something so friendly about her smiling face and shining eyes. And she'd been a lifesaver at Lizzie's wedding when the makeup artist hadn't turned up.

"Hello, Natalie. Can I have a large cappuccino and"—she scanned the pastries on the countertop—"I fancy one of those maple-syrup muffins, even though I shouldn't." Her hand patted her stomach. "But I haven't had one in weeks."

Natalie plated a muffin and began to make the cappuccino. "Your mum was sick?" she said with her back to Charlie.

"Yes, I was taking care of her, and today is my first day back."

"Welcome back. Very worrying, was it?"

"You could say that," Charlie said slowly. "Perhaps I'm not cut out to be a nurse. It's hard taking care of someone, and my mother's not the most patient patient in the world."

"It must have been tough for both of you," said Natalie automatically.

"Yes, it was," Charlie said, following the approved script. She sighed and abandoned the script. "It was a nightmare, actually. I thought I'd never get back to work. My mother and I don't really get on that well. Throw a broken hip into the mix, and it's a recipe for disaster."

They both stopped what they were doing—Charlie fiddling in her purse for coins and Natalie wiping the bottom of the cup with a paper towel—and stared at each other, Charlie's honest words still hanging in the air.

"Sorry," Charlie said suddenly, looking chagrined.

"No," Natalie said, "don't say sorry. If that's the truth, that's the truth."

"I shouldn't have said it," fretted Charlie. "There must be something wrong with me. Other people don't talk about their mothers that way, do they?"

"I don't know—my mother died when I was little," said Natalie.

"God! I've made it worse." Charlie groaned. "I'm really sorry—"

"No, stop." Natalie placed the cup on Charlie's tray. "I'm glad you said it. I've spent my life thinking I was intrinsically different from the rest of the world because I don't have this classic mother person. I mean, I have Bess, my stepmother, and she's wonderful, but I don't call her Mum. Everyone and their granny seem to have marvelous relationships with their mothers, so it's nice to hear someone say she doesn't get on with hers."

"Is it?" said Charlie doubtfully.

"Of course. It makes me feel less out of place. If all you've ever heard about mothers is that they're wonderful, then you feel even more left out. People tell you the good stuff, and that's what you see mostly. And even when they do have their quarrels, everyone says: 'No matter what happens, your mother loves you.'"

They both considered this.

"It's not easy being a mother," said Charlie. "You're afraid of getting it wrong all the time. Whenever I get angry with my mother, I look at my son and wonder if, when he's my age, I'll be driving him nuts and he'll want to murder me. Like it's a cycle and, no matter what you do, your kids'll end up groaning about the mistakes you made. Do you mind me asking, what happened to your mother?"

"She died when I was three. I don't really know the first thing about her," Natalie said.

Charlie recognized that Natalie was about to cry. "Sit down with me," she urged.

"I can't—"

"You can. If anyone else comes in, you can hop up and serve them, but sit now."

Charlie went behind the counter and poured a cup of coffee for

Natalie, then carried the whole lot over to a table. "Go on," she urged, sitting down.

It was strange. Natalie thought of all the people she could have talked to about this, yet Charlie was just the right person. And here in the coziness of the café, where only people from Kenny's would come in, was the right place.

"David's funeral really upset me," she said, "and I began to think about her. I did some research on the Internet about being motherless, and some things began to make sense. Like everything that was hard when I was growing up, stuff I didn't understand at the time. I remember when my friend Lizzie—she's my best friend, sort of—had long talks with her mum about periods, and her mum gave her a book. I borrowed the book and then, when I started my periods six months later, I didn't even ask Bess about it. It was like this was something mums were supposed to do, and it was safer to hold it all inside than ask. Does that make sense?"

Charlie nodded.

"This website talked about the defining moments in your life and how they're hard when you've lost a parent. And in my house, nobody talked about my mother."

"So you feel you can't ask your dad about her?" Charlie prompted.

"Exactly. He's never spoken about her to me. He gave me photographs when I was small, but that's it. I don't want to dredge up painful memories."

"You have to ask him," Charlie said.

"I should," Natalie said unconvincingly.

"Listen, I spent years not getting on with my mother and feeling guilty because of that. I didn't learn to deal with it until I started writing down how I felt in a journal. It really helped. Keeping it in your head makes it worse. I did something, and you need to do something. You have to find out as much as you can about her. She's your mum, you're entitled to know. It's unfinished business otherwise."

"I've got a picture of her with me," Natalie said.

She ran to her locker in the kitchen, found the photo of her mother she'd popped into her bag that morning, and came back.

"She looks so like you," Charlie said, staring at the beautiful woman with the long dark hair and wide smile, holding her precious baby close to her heart. "Maybe your dad doesn't talk because it's too painful, rather than because of anything he wants to hide."

"If you were my stepmum, would you be upset if I wanted to know about my real mum?"

Charlie shook her head. "Of course not. You said Bess is a wonderful person and she loves you. She and your dad have probably been waiting for you to ask. It's like people who adopt children—they know that one day the child will want to know about its birth parents. Just ask them."

Natalie nodded tremulously. "I will," she said. "Soon. What about you and your mum?"

"Don't think there's anything I can do," Charlie said wryly. " 'Detach with love' is what Shotsy says to me."

"Is it that you fight a lot?"

"Not really. More that she disapproves of me. I didn't become what she wanted, although my older sister did."

"What did she want you to be?"

"Somebody important."

"Must be difficult."

Charlie sighed. "Yes, it is. Maybe one day I'll find out what makes my mother tick, and then I'll work it all out. Wouldn't that be good?"

The rest of that day, Natalie thought about how simple Charlie had made it sound: just ask. She would, tonight, she decided.

As it turned out, it was the perfect night to discuss things with her father. When Natalie phoned during the afternoon, Bess said the boys would be out and she had to visit a client for a fitting for a wedding dress.

"I hate missing you," said Bess. "Tell you what, I'll ask if I can see the girl earlier and then—"

"No," said Natalie quickly, hating herself for not being truthful with dear, kind Bess. She felt that her father would find it hard to talk about her mother with Bess present. "I was only dropping in for coffee on my way home from work. Just a five-minute thing. Don't rearrange your fitting."

When she walked into the kitchen, her father looked up from eating shepherd's pie. Natalie thought how brilliant a wife Bess was: even when she was going to be out late, she fixed dinner so her husband could sit down after a hard day's work and eat the sort of food that he liked, with the paper at hand and the dogs clustered around his feet.

Natalie wondered if she'd ever have this sort of relationship with Rory. Would they settle down to the point that she'd cook in advance for him, so that, when she was out, he could eat something she'd prepared? It was strange to think about that. But she found herself imagining living with him, waking up beside him, sitting on the couch with him at night, taking calls for him when he was out with a sick animal. . . .

"Natalie!" said her father, surprised. "I didn't know you were coming. Bess never said anything."

"Just thought I'd drop in," she said. Now that she was here, she didn't know how to start this. Anything she said would sound like a criticism of her father and Bess, which wasn't what she wanted.

"Sit down—have you eaten? This is delicious," he said, waving his fork toward the shepherd's pie. "I'll have to cut back, though," he added. "My cholesterol was up last time I went to the doctor."

"Was it?" Natalie asked, slightly alarmed, thinking of David Kenny.

"Ah no, only a little bit," her father said. "Nothing to worry about, love. Sit down, have some."

"No, I'm not hungry," Natalie said. She busied herself making a cup of tea she didn't really want, then finally sat down opposite him.

"How's Rory?" he asked, then grinned. "Bess reckons it's

serious. Is he it—the One? I have to say, I'm fond of him myself. He's a decent lad."

Natalie smiled, thinking of other conversations about boyfriends over the years. He'd never been the interfering sort of father, the sort who'd stand over visiting lads with a grim face and a threatening look in his eyes. "Rory's great," she said.

"But you're here to talk to me about something?" her father said, still eating. He knew her so well.

"Yes."

"What's wrong, Natalie?" he asked. "There's something wrong, I can tell."

"No, there's nothing wrong," she said quickly. "Not exactly."

"Well, what is it?"

Now that the moment was here, Natalie toyed with the idea of fibbing about being broke (though that was true) or something else; anything to put off the conversation. But no, she'd waited too long.

"It's about my mother," she blurted out. "I just need to know a little about her—" She broke off, seeing how stricken her father looked. It was there in his eyes: an expression that wasn't fear, but something else. Sadness?

"I'm sorry, Dad. I don't mean to hurt you or Bess, but—"

"No," he said. "It's my fault." He put his knife and fork together and pushed the plate away.

"Don't stop eating," Natalie said.

"I've had enough," he murmured. "I'm really sorry, Natalie, I should have spoken to you before, but there was never a right time."

"That's it exactly," Natalie said, grasping the opportunity. "There's never been a right time, Dad. I've wondered so often over the years what she was like. I don't really know anything, and I've so few pictures, and you don't talk about her and . . ."

"And you felt it would be disloyal to Bess and me to ask," he finished for her.

"Exactly, but I need to know. I need to know why we never talk about her. Was it so awful, her dying? Or did you just want to put it all behind you and start again? I need to understand, Dad."

Now that she'd started, she couldn't stop.

"Molly's father dying has made me think about my mother. That day at David's funeral when I fainted, I think—" She broke off; it sounded crazy to say it out loud. "I think I was remembering my mother's funeral." She barely dared look at her father, thinking how painful this must be for him.

"My darling Natalie, I'm so sorry," he said, and reached across the table to take her hands. "It was never meant to be like this."

"But you understand, don't you, Dad? And Bess will understand? It's not that I don't love the two of you, I just need to know about my real mum."

It felt weird to even be saying *mum*.

She'd always thought of her mother as her real mother, but not as *Mum*. That was what you called someone you saw every day, hugged and kissed.

"I knew that Molly's father's death had affected you," her father said quietly. "It's the same graveyard, you see. When you told me you'd fainted, I wondered if you'd remembered something."

"The same graveyard?" Natalie was stunned.

"I can show you. I can take you to see the grave."

Natalie's hand flew to her mouth. She hadn't been going crazy—those had been real memories of her mother's burial. "I was there when she was buried?"

He nodded. "Natalie, it wasn't my idea not to tell you all this."

"Was it Bess?" she asked cautiously. It would be so unlike her stepmother to want to wipe out Natalie's mother from everyone's memory, and yet, it could have been. Maybe Bess had found it too hard to live with the memory of her predecessor.

"No, it wasn't Bess. She thought it was the dumbest idea she'd ever heard. She was against it when she found out. It wasn't right, she said, to keep your mother a mystery to you. No, it wasn't Bess; it was what your mother wanted, Natalie."

"My mother?"

"Your mother," he said. "She was an amazing woman. God,

I loved her. Her dying was just about the worst thing that ever happened to me; but she didn't want you to be . . ." He was clearly trying to find the right words. "Sorry, love—if you knew how often I've had this conversation with you in my mind. I had it word-perfect when you were little, but it's one thing telling a small child this stuff, and entirely another telling a grown-up. Your mother had a hard life, and she worked very hard trying to escape that. She wanted you to escape it too. That was the plan; she didn't want the past to destroy you."

Natalie looked at her father in bewilderment. "She didn't want the past to destroy me?" she repeated. "What past?"

"I'll try to explain, love."

Twelve

The Past

DARA

Dara Murphy loved watching television. Her favorite shows were *The Waltons* and *Little House on the Prairie*— programs about families in which, no matter what disaster occurred, they were there for one another at the end of the day.

Her friend Ruth had read the *Little House* books, and she said they were a lot different from the television series.

"More stuff happens in the books, and they're about setting up home in tough places, sometimes with no school or not a lot of food. There's no Nellie Olesen in the books, well, not that I saw."

Dara didn't read much, had never found reading easy. She occasionally took out books from the library, but books didn't fare well in her house. They went missing or had food spilled on them.

Her father hated books. "Bloody priests," he'd say every time he saw one.

In his mind, the written word was linked with education, which was linked to the Christian Brothers who'd taught him in school. These educationalists were infamous for their love of corporal punishment, and there were many former pupils who had no time for the Christian Brothers and their messianic fondness for the leather. Dara's father, as usual, took this dislike to the nth degree. If they were on the bus and passed by his old school, he'd spit out the window. Greg, Dara's brother, used to laugh. "It's not funny," Dara said.

"You might as well laugh," said Greg.

He was better at laughing than Dara was.

"I'd like to live in a world like *Little House on the Prairie*," Dara said to Ruth. "Imagine a place where everyone cares about everyone else. On the TV show, if somebody's being horrible, everyone in the whole town knows by the end of the episode."

"It's only television," Ruth said. "Real life isn't like that."

"Yeah, I know," said Dara, "I was just saying."

The two friends talked about most things, but there were some topics that were untouchable. Like what happened to make a boy's mickey get inside you if it was all floppy normally, or why Eric, who lived beside Ruth, did drugs when he was so clever and could have gone to college and everything. Dara's dad was another topic in this forbidden area.

Sometimes Dara talked about what would have happened if her mother hadn't been killed in a car crash when Dara was six. This was fantasyland, where Dara, her mum, and Greg lived in a big house with lots of dogs—Dara loved dogs—and had a big telly and heating that worked.

"If you live in the big house, what about us?" Ruth would demand when Dara dreamily went into fantasyland.

"I'm only kidding," Dara would say. "Wouldn't I go mad if I didn't have you!"

Ruth lived across from Dara in a sprawling Dublin estate where the blocks of houses were arranged around small playing greens. The streets had beautiful names, like Snowdrop View and Daffodil Avenue, obviously thought up by someone with a supreme sense either of irony or of optimism. Ruth's and Dara's houses on Snowdrop Park looked exactly the same on the outside: small, two-story redbrick houses with Post-it–sized pieces of garden at the front and yards at the back. Ruth's dad had racing pigeons in his yard, and her mother used to complain about them all the time.

"Those damn birds—the smell and the noise of them," she would mutter.

She didn't mind them really. Complaining about the pigeons was part of the tradition of the whole sport, Ruth's dad liked to say. If women couldn't grumble about their husbands' hobbies, what else would they have to occupy their time? One of the pigeons was called Lulu because Ruth's dad reckoned it sounded the way Lulu did when she screamed the first syllable of the song "Shout."

"I swear he loves those pigeons more than he loves the rest of us," said Ruth's mum.

She was only kidding, though.

Ruth's mum and dad and two older brothers filled the house with good-humored squabbling. Ruth's mum was a terrible cook, but nobody minded. Dara loved eating there because she felt welcome.

Inside, the houses were as different as chalk from cheese.

If houses could be colors, then Ruth's home was a deep rose, full of warmth. Dara's house was gray, a cold gray like endless rain. Her favorite room was the dining room because her father rarely went in there. He preferred the living room with its fire and the big chairs where he and his cronies could sit for hours drinking. Dara always knew when they were there: she'd come home from school and the atmosphere in the house would be so tense and threatening it scared her. On those days, she'd sometimes run over to Ruth's house and stay there for the afternoon. But she didn't like to impose too often. Ruth had her own life. Dara didn't want to rely on her friends too much; it wasn't fair.

Most grown-ups were no use either.

"What happened to your homework?" Miss Daniels would say, examining the empty copybook.

"Dunno, Miss," Dara would say, looking as blank as the pages. She spent a lot of time looking blank. And nobody picked up on it. No teacher came to their house asking why she never did her homework or why she was so tired in class, or even why her lunch consisted of a packet of crisps. Teachers didn't notice much, or if they did notice, Dara decided, they didn't want to get involved.

* * *

Her brother Greg fancied Ruth. Dara wasn't sure how it had happened. They saw each other often, living across the green from each other as they did, and sometimes Greg traveled to school with Dara—something that was almost unheard of in Greg's school, St. Dominic's. Big brothers didn't usually walk with little sisters. But Greg and Dara were different; they were very close— they had to be. They didn't have anyone else, just their dad and no mum. On those walks to school, Ruth and Greg somehow fell for each other. Greg was tall and good-looking, Dara could see that. And Ruth was pretty, even though she didn't have good clothes or much money for makeup. She had a glow and a beauty that came from the inside.

Dara wasn't jealous; she loved them both. But she didn't want Ruth to know everything, especially when it came to what really went on in their house. Dara had never told her. It was too shaming. And now if Greg was going out with Ruth, he'd tell her everything.

"You won't, will you, please?" she asked him.

"Don't be daft, Dara," he said. "What am I going to say?"

"I don't know," she said quietly.

"She is your best friend," Greg went on.

"I just don't want her to know," Dara said, "that's all."

"Don't worry, I won't tell her."

At night, when all the kids in the neighborhood played soccer on the green or sprawled on the grass, Greg and Ruth sat on the low wall near the swings and talked. Sitting on the wall was like taking out an ad in the newspaper: *We're going out*. It was the couples' wall, dotted with people sitting beside each other, not always touching, but close. There was never too much open affection between the couples on the wall. They might be laughed at. The boys playing five-a-side would jeer; rude jokes would be made. They might roar lustily that the girl needed an aspirin for contraception: "Keep it between your knees," they'd shout. "If it falls out, you're fucked!"

Dara went in early the first evening Ruth and Greg sat together on the wall. Not that Dad cared what time she went home. She could come home at three in the morning with the Rolling Stones trailing behind and he wouldn't mind. The more the merrier, especially if they brought booze.

When Dara left school, she went to work at a bank. She both loved and hated the bank. It was her first proper job—working Saturdays in the supermarket near home didn't count. She loved that people weren't allowed to shout at you no matter what happened; but she hated the groaning inevitability of it. The long, slow slog of the week would be followed by a veritable tidbit of a weekend, like a teeny taste of chocolate cake, and you'd barely have enough before the week was back, dull and tiring.

Work itself was a disappointment to Dara. Everyone wanted a job in a bank. Pensionable and safe in a time of uncertainty, it was a dream job—according to everyone else. But they didn't have to put up with being a junior in the Inchicore branch of Harp Bank, and spending their days sorting the reams of post into piles according to the eight-digit account numbers and then matching each item with a piece of microfiche—a four-inch-by-six-inch piece of see-through plastic that could be viewed through a magnifier—onto which eight sheets of paper could be copied. The letters were then taken to the microfiche department for transferring onto the tiny plastic sheets. Once copied, the letters were delivered to their destinations within the bank, and Dara had to file the microfiche in the correct filing cabinets. This process had to happen within one day. It was tortuous work, and searching through boxes of microfiche hurt like hell when the hard plastic scratched her fingers. Worse was trying to decipher people's writing on their letters. Possible account numbers had to be checked against their microfiche matches to determine whether a number was supposed to be a 6 instead of a 0.

"Why can't people write clearly?" complained Dara's friend Elaine. "How hard can it be to write their account numbers legibly? Monkeys would write better than most of these idiots."

"Hey, some of my best friends are monkeys," joked Dara. Then she moved on to their favorite subject: "What are we going to do for lunch?"

Elaine stopped filing and looked thoughtful.

Sometimes the whole staff piled into cars and went up to Kitty O'Shea's, which was always fun. The problem was getting the last customers out of the bank before it closed for lunch at 1:25 p.m.

On Kitty O'Shea's mass exodus days, there was always some mad old bat who came in at precisely 1:24 p.m. with sackloads of ha'pennies to be weighed. The counter staff would then have to stay at their posts, smiling and trying to look as if they didn't mind the stench of dirty coppers when what they really wanted to be smelling was vegetable soup and a ham sandwich.

And the people without cars, like Dara and Elaine, had to hop from foot to foot, waiting for their lifts.

"We're broke," Elaine reminded Dara now. "We brought in sandwiches, remember?"

"Cheese on its own, because I've no butter," said Dara gloomily. "I hate my own sandwiches. They always taste horrible. The same thing in a pub is delicious. Why is that?"

"Because you can't cook?"

"You don't cook sandwiches."

"Okay then, because you can't have a lager with your sandwich if you eat it here," Elaine pointed out.

"Yeah, that's it. Magic ingredient in sandwiches is lager."

The uniform didn't help. Harp Bank's women's uniform was kelly green, with an ill-fitting A-line skirt clearly designed by someone who'd never seen a skirt before, a cream polyester blouse with little green harps scattered over it, and a jaunty little green scarf tied like a bow at the collar. In summer, the polyester made the wearer smell of perspiration; and in winter, it made her shiver with cold. The plus of the uniform was that it transformed the most unbanklike person into a demure office worker because it was simply impossible to look either cool or uninterested when wearing kelly green harps. The color went well with dark hair like

Dara's, and Elaine believed that the bank hired more brunettes than blondes or redheads because of this.

"You'd have been fired long ago if you were a blonde," she said sometimes.

"If I were a blonde, I'd be sitting on the manager's lap all afternoon—and nobody who does that ever gets fired," replied Dara. The bank manager had never so much as flirted with her, for which she was profoundly grateful. She didn't know what she'd do if he did. Her defense was a bold, slightly confrontational stare and a slash of dusty purple shadow blazed above her brown eyes. *Don't mess with me* was the message from both the stare and the cosmetics.

"Where should we start tonight?" Jean asked Dara and Elaine.

It was Friday, the cue for major partying. Dara had been astonished and thrilled to find that people who worked in banks were mental. Once the clock hit the magic number five, the whole place cleared out.

"Dunno," said Dara.

Jean was new and was not entirely allowed into Dara and Elaine's little gang of two, but she was nearly there.

"Captain Americas?" said Jean.

"Ace," said Dara, relenting. "I love that place."

"I'll phone Jason," Elaine said. "It's only a quarter past, he'll still be at his desk." Jason was Elaine's sort-of boyfriend. He worked in a bank in town with lots of people who also loved to party.

When Elaine had mustered up a crowd, they took turns in the small women's bathroom, changing clothes and applying makeup.

Dara owned one fabulous going-out coat: a long velvet frock coat, the sort of thing Siouxsie Sioux might wear. With her crocheted fingerless gloves, plenty of eyeliner, and her fishnets, Dara felt she could do Siouxsie better than Siouxsie herself. Her hair wasn't the right color and her eyes weren't as feline, despite the eyeliner, but still.

Jean, who had forgotten to bring black tights to replace her work tan ones, almost spat with jealousy at the sight of Dara in her finery. "You look cool! I look like a dork."

"You look fine," Dara said. "You could buy black tights when we're out."

Jean grimaced. She was saving up to buy a moped and had her eye on a lilac one. She'd be mobile, no more waiting at bus stops. "It's a waste when I've so many black ones at home."

Dara shrugged. Saving was an alien concept to her. She never had a penny to her name. As soon as she got paid, the money was tied up: on rent, on paying people she owed, on going out.

When she was dressed, she went back to her desk to collect the rest of her stuff.

"Where are you and your peachy little friends going?" asked James. James was three levels above her in the bank hierarchy, and therefore couldn't be cheeked. He perched on the edge of Dara's desk, leaning ominously over her. Dara's radar fizzed when he was near; she couldn't quite get a reading on him. Was he harmless and interesting, or dangerous?

"Out," she said crisply. Less was more with the likes of James.

"Out. Interesting," murmured James, leaning so close that she could smell his breath.

She felt a flash of fear at his closeness, the sense that he was a feral beast and the normal rules of human behavior wouldn't apply to him. But she cast it off. Fear was deadly. If you let them know you were afraid, then they'd won, they'd take what they wanted.

Dara grabbed her stuff. "Yes, out," she said, and gave him the benefit of her Siouxsie glare. *Go away,* it said.

Jason's friend Felippe held her arm as they stood by the side of the road at Stephen's Green, one of the busiest thoroughfares in Dublin, even at half past midnight. Dara tried hard to concentrate, but it was too difficult. Her vision was cloudy, and no matter which eye she closed, she still couldn't see properly.

"Gotta get a taxi," she managed to say. "It's furry late."

"Sure," Felippe said.

Together they weaved their way into the middle of the road and started hailing cars. As if they were stones in a river, cars swerved to avoid them.

"They're not taxis!" shouted someone else from the footpath. "They're ordinary cars."

This was unbearably funny, and Dara collapsed onto the road laughing, trying to haul Felippe down with her. "Not taxis!" she giggled. "Ordinary cars!"

"You're sooo funny," Felippe said. "Oooh, look, I think the Green's open." He unhooked his arm from hers and wobbled over to the other side of the street, where he began to rattle the Stephen's Green park gate in the manner of a person trying to get out of jail.

"Get off the road, Dara," shouted someone. "You're going to be run over."

Offended, Dara got unsteadily to her feet. "No, I'm not. Look. Up. Not run over."

A car came perilously close, skidding in a flash of steel to avoid her. "Oops," she said, and that was very funny too, so she had to sit down again for a minute.

"You'll be killed, you stupid cow."

Somebody sounded angry, and whoever it was had grabbed her and was pulling her back across the road to the safety of the pavement. It was Lawrence, another friend of Jason's, a very boring straight-arrow person who didn't know how to enjoy himself. But cute, Dara thought. Hard to tell because he was so wobbly in front of her, but she thought he might be cute. Nice shirt, striped and with purple in it. She liked purple. He'd got her a cab and was holding the door open and trying to shove her in.

Charming.

". . . please take her, she won't get sick in the car—"

"I won't," Dara said loudly. "I'm not drunk, you know. Not even a little bit. I could drink much more, but I have to get up for work in the morning."

"Tomorrow's Saturday, you moron. Shut up, Dara, will you?"

She was facing Lawrence, and she had a nice idea of how to say good-bye to him, a memento of the evening. Swiftly she pulled up his purple-striped shirt, found his nipple, and bit it. "Good night," she said, and let herself slump into the backseat of the taxi. "Home, driver, and don't spare the horses."

Morning slammed into her consciousness. No gentle opening of the eyes but a rapid sit-up-in-the-bed moment as her pulse thumped drumbeats through her body. Where was she? What time was it? What . . . ?

In her own bed and in her own clothes, which was good. She felt carefully and found she was still totally dressed, everything on. No items of clothing gone—that was always scary. But fully dressed. In her own bed, and she was—she looked around with anxiety—alone. No sign of another person, and since she was still clothed, it was unlikely she'd brought anyone home. People in her home, men, meant she'd have taken some of her clothes off; and even if she couldn't remember anything actually happening, it was always there, the possibility. On those days, she'd shower for ages, scrubbing with the loofah she'd bought in the Body Shop until her flesh was raw. Like monks from the olden days, scrubbing away their sin. Today, though, she was dressed. No man, no body snoring beside her.

Which was one good thing; but instantly she began the roll call of possible bad things, piecing together the night before. Where she'd gone, what she'd done there. Sometimes the receipts in her handbag were the only clues, clues that added up to lots of her salary. Being broke never upset her when she was drinking. Then she was rich as J. R. Ewing, ready to order wine no matter how expensive or how awful it was.

She'd done it again. She'd only meant to have one drink, just the one, and what had happened? Millions of drinks, shots and tequilas and you-name-it pumped into her.

The wave of shame that rose up in her was physical. Shame could be physical. If flirtation made a person blush a rosy hue, then shame was a fire of pain.

* * *

Rhona had been at the bank longer than Dara and had moved on from microfiche filing to answering telephone calls about deposit accounts.

"You don't drink like the rest of us," Rhona said.

Dara felt the hairs on the back of her neck stand up. "Whaddaya mean?" she blurted out. *Stupid*, that sounded wrong, like she was worried about it, which was the wrong impression to give. "I mean, how does everyone else drink?" she added, managing to sound a bit blasé.

Rhona kept her unwavering gaze upon Dara. She wasn't one of Dana's favorite people: she was too sharp, too ready to say what she thought—a very annoying habit.

"Like you're going to drink the bar dry."

"I don't do that," Dara said, and laughed. Convincing, no?

"If you say so." Rhona shrugged.

When she was gone, Dara thought about the stupidity of the whole conversation. Wasn't that the point of drinking, to drink the whole bar dry? Dara scanned her mind for that moment in the pub when the alcohol was sinking into her and she was sinking into it, when she'd stare at the jewel-colored bottles racked up behind the bar and want to finish every single one of them. Surely everyone felt the same, didn't they?

Dara lived in a bedsit near the bank. It was small but reasonably clean, and it was her own. That was the best thing about it.

Des Flynn lived near her. Dara liked Des—not that he was her type. He was always in the company of a gang of other lads, equally strapping, all muscled sporty types with big bags that held soccer jerseys and sneakers, and probably damp towels that housed billions of bacteria and hadn't been washed for years. Friendly blokes who drank a couple of pints of beer on a night out and danced badly to Dexy's Midnight Runners. Not the type who knew how to roll a joint or where you could get a bottle of absinthe, therefore not her type.

She'd watched him sometimes as he went out with his pals.

Sitting with the window all the way open and her legs hung out in the sun, with a glass of wine beside her and her skin tanning, she could see all the way down the street. She could see the little old man who came slowly out of his house every afternoon, shuffling in the direction of the bookies and perhaps for a pint in Horgan's once midday Holy Hour, when all the pubs closed, was over. She could watch the young mother with two small kids come shouting and panting out of her front door, one child holding on to her reluctantly, the other crammed into a stroller, face screwed up and crying. The park, Dara decided, they were going to the park, and the mother would stop screaming and they'd all sit on the grass by the swings and the children would smile at the dogs rushing around, sniffing everything, in the sun. She didn't know if all this really happened, but she liked imagining people's lives.

And the boys, she watched Des and his mates.

"How's it going?" Des called up to her.

"Fine," Dara said. She wanted to say something else but couldn't think what to add, so she gave him a little wave. That looked stupid, she decided.

They were in the pub again after work. It was a Thursday, so nobody wanted to be out late. Well, not that late.

"Tequila slammer," she said.

"Way-hay!" yelled Stanno. "Atta girl, Dara. Let's all do tequila."

"You're so boring when you don't drink," agreed Mark, who worked at the counter and charmed all the good-looking mummy types who came in to pay off their husbands' credit cards.

"I hate boring people," sighed Michaela. "The salon was full of them today."

Everyone smiled indulgently. Michaela owned a nearby hairdresser's and was often to be found in the pub because she hated the smell of perming lotion and needed little drinkies to cope with having ten staff and annoying clients.

She was older than the rest of them, midforties at least, and had curly hair the color of blackberries. There were three shot glasses lined up in front of her. Peach schnapps. It was her latest favorite, discovered when she drank a Vestal Virgin, of which schnapps was the major ingredient. Nobody was too sure what the others were, but it was mind-blowing.

The tequila arrived, dumped on the table by a waitress who was too busy for niceties.

"Just one lemonade," said Dara quickly. No point paying for lots of mixers when they only wanted to spend cash on booze.

The waitress silently took the extra lemonades away and collected an assortment of coins from them.

Dara grabbed the lemonade first, splashed a bit into her tequila, held her hand over the glass to shake it, then slammed the glass onto the table. The drink obediently fizzed up, and she knocked it back in one.

The bite of the tequila rasped her taste buds. It was hideous stuff, but oh, the effect. Her eyes closed, she waited. The warmth spread from the depths of her belly into her limbs and, most important, into her head, lapping at the anxiety and fear like a soft lake gently drowning her. She opened her eyes and smiled at her friends with relief. She felt safe and loved.

"Haven't you guys started yet? I'm ready for another."

James and a few other older guys from the bank had been sitting on their own having grown-uppy conversations, but as the evening wore on and the fair-weather drinkers left, they joined Dara, Elaine, and the young gang.

James made a beeline for Dara as usual, and for once, she didn't mind. He was harmless enough, she decided from the delicious safety of several tequila slammers.

"Having fun?" said James, sliding onto a barstool beside her and waving a hand at the barman at the same time.

"Yes," said Dara happily.

"And on a school night, too," James added. "You are a wild child."

Dara grinned. Wild child: she liked that. She liked to think of herself as untameable. Nobody tried to capture or hurt wild things. He obviously understood that much about her.

"Another drink?"

Dara considered having another slammer. They hurt her stomach after a while. She'd had a couple of chips when one of the lads got sausages and chips in a basket, but she never ate much when she was drinking. Food soaking up the booze was such a waste of good alcohol.

"Have something else," urged James, seeing indecision in her eyes. "I'm having brandy."

That was the smell around him, she realized. A rich, fiery smell. She liked it.

"Okay," she said. "I'll try one."

Slammers made her feel high, but brandy made her buzz. Her pulse raced and she felt full of energy, wanting to dance when someone put Salt-n-Pepa on the jukebox; but they weren't allowed to dance in here and she had to content herself with standing at the bar, moving her hips in time to the music.

Dara focused on her reflection in the mirror behind the bar. She loved how she looked when she was drunk; it was the only time she did. Otherwise, she felt ugly and, no matter how often people like Elaine or Ruth told her otherwise, fat.

"You're skinny," Elaine would shriek. "If you're fat, what does that make me, you idiot?"

"But you're taller than me," Dara would reply. Elaine was gorgeous; there was no comparison. She could be three hundred pounds and she'd still be gorgeous. It wasn't about weight, not for other people. Only her. She was wrong no matter what.

Ruth and Elaine never gave up, though. "You have to say, 'I'm a beautiful woman and I have a secret,'" said Ruth, who was much taken with a new fad about how to walk into a room and look in control and mysteriously gorgeous at the same time.

Dara had pretended to do it, but she didn't believe it for a moment. They were just words. She wasn't beautiful, although she had plenty of secrets.

Right now, she was feeling a little bit not-so-ugly, which was not even in the same time zone as being beautiful. The lighting was dim, and in the mirror Dara saw a small face with big dark eyes and lashes so long they looked false. Her skin was a warm tone, and she had a dusting of freckles across the bridge of her nose and her cheeks. Any lipstick had long been smeared off, so she rubbed Body Shop strawberry lip balm on her lips. Sexy, that's what she looked, with her large dark pupils and the trails of long, thick espresso-colored hair curling around her shoulders.

James met her in the hallway as she emerged from the ladies'. "I just had a thought," he said. "This place is boring. Let's go somewhere else. Closer to town, more fun."

Dara wavered. She wanted to stay with Elaine, not go off with James. She didn't really like him, despite the brandy.

"I've got your stuff," he said, holding up her handbag and coat. "Come on."

He gripped her hand and led her outside, whereupon he began to run, pulling her along behind. His car was a red MG. Dara had never been in such a car.

James fired it up, did a U-turn in the middle of the street, and began to drive in the opposite direction from the city.

"This isn't the right way," Dara said.

"We're going the back route. Don't want to get caught by the cops."

Briefly, Dara wondered if it was a good idea to drive after so many drinks. How many could you have and still drive? She didn't know; she didn't have a car, and there was no limit on drinking and taking the bus home.

James put in a cassette and turned the music up to full blast. "Pink Floyd," he said.

After a few minutes, they pulled into a small, heavily graffitied car park with lots of cans and broken bottles scattered around and got out. The pub was a solid redbrick square with blocked-up windows that had bars on them.

"This is a great joint," he said.

It didn't look it, but Dara followed him in. The pub was busy. Every other customer was male. They stared at Dara with her velvet coat and heavily kohled eyes. She shuddered. This was the sort of place where her father would be right at home, bursting with men full of bitterness and whiskey, angry with life and everyone who looked crossways at them.

James seemed to know the barman, and he sat comfortably at the bar and ordered double brandies. "Get that down you," he said when the drinks arrived. There were no rounded brandy balloons here, just plain glasses that looked dirty. Dara drank, but the brandy didn't make the fear go away.

"I don't like this place," she whispered to James.

"Don't you, honey?" he asked, putting a proprietorial hand on her leg.

She shifted uncomfortably, but James moved his hand higher.

"Drink up, then, chickie, and we'll go."

"I'd like to go home," Dara said when they were in the car.

"Sure," he said vaguely. "I'll go the back way again."

"No," she said, panic coming from somewhere, "drop me at a taxi stand. I'll get a taxi."

"No, no way," he said. "You wouldn't be safe."

The brandy and Pink Floyd were giving her a headache; it was like being on a magical mystery ride in the middle of nowhere. James drove down strange streets along the docks, past big empty buildings and boarded-up blocks. Then he wheeled the car rapidly into a small cul-de-sac in a warren of dockland buildings. James stopped the car and grabbed her, shoving his face into hers.

"James, no!" she yelled, pushing furiously.

"Yes," he murmured, forcing his tongue into her mouth at the same time that his hands were wrenching her coat away and pawing over her blouse. "God, you're something else," he said, ignoring her struggles.

"No," she shrieked, pushing at him as hard as she could.

He was on top of her now, having somehow pushed her seat down and moved himself over the gearshift to pin her down.

"You want this," he said hoarsely, "you know you do."

"Not like this," she said desperately, hoping to stop him with subterfuge. Maybe she could get him to come to her flat, and then she'd scream, then people would hear her.

But it wasn't working; James was at her breasts now, his breath hot on her bared flesh.

"I'm the wild child, you can't do this," she begged, trying to shock him out of his frenzy.

"Wild child, yes," he groaned, and then he was holding her down even more forcefully. Dara hadn't known he was so strong, or that she was so much weaker than she thought. Her strength was nothing compared to his; he could break her with one hand.

"Of course you want this," he panted. "Why else did you stand beside me dancing to that music, waggling your ass in my face, asking for it?"

"No!" she roared, but he put a hand over her mouth, pushing so hard she felt she might black out.

"You want this."

The weight of his body on top of hers, the force and the fear, brought her back to the bedroom on Snowdrop Park when she was small. Another man, another heavy body on her little one. "No," she breathed inside her head.

"No!" she tried to scream, but James's hand muffled the noise.

There was only one thing left to do: Dara went inside herself. Lockdown time. It was about more than closing her eyes. She closed her heart and her soul; this was a shell of a thing being raped, not her. And the shell could cope with anything.

"You all right?" asked Mrs. Davis, who lived in the bottom flat. Her front door was in the hall, right beside the phone, and she'd opened her door to take her dog for his morning walk.

Dara had her eiderdown pulled around her and she was as white as snow, except for the raw redness around her eyes from crying all night.

"Fine," muttered Dara, huddling close to the phone. She hadn't the coins to drop in, so she was tapping out the number on the little receiver buttons at the top of the phone. It didn't always work, but sometimes it did and you could make a call without paying.

Mrs. Davis sniffed and went to the front door with her dog.

Dara leaned against the wall, clutching the phone close to her skull.

Elaine answered. "Good morning, Harp Bank, Inchicore branch," she said cheerily.

Dara didn't have to fake a hoarse, sick-sounding voice. She could barely speak, whether it was from the trauma of trying to shout or just plain trauma. "Elaine," she rasped, "it's me, Dara. I'm sick, a bug or something."

"Yeah, right," said Elaine. "Brandy, that's the something. Did you sneak off with James?"

Dara had to hold on to the wall to steady herself. "No, I went home. I felt sick then, just had to go."

"Oh." Elaine sounded a little more convinced.

"Tell them I won't be in," Dara said, and hung up.

There was no hot water for a bath this time, although she'd had a scalding hot one last night when James had dropped her home, smiling as if they'd had the date of the century, seemingly oblivious to Dara sitting mutely beside him, her hands shaking as she held her ripped blouse together. She'd half-fallen out of the car, leaving her shoes in there somewhere, shoved off. She didn't care; she'd stumbled barefoot up the steps of her building, holding her handbag and herself together until she was safe.

She lay in the cool bath, not wanting to look down at the paleness of her skin in the water. Her legs were bruised, and she had a bite mark on one breast. Her neck hurt from the force of being pushed back, and her spine ached where James had shoved her round the car, lying on her, forcing her down onto the gearshift once.

She knew what she had to do next.

The doctor at the women's clinic was a woman, for which Dara was grateful. She couldn't have coped with being alone with a man.

Dara sat looking at her knees as she asked for the morning-after pill. The nurse had all her details and her blood pressure had been taken; now it was down to the doctor.

"You may feel nauseated," the doctor said matter-of-factly

when she'd scanned the blood-pressure results and the alleged reason for needing the pills: getting confused about the safe period. It was the excuse Elaine had used when she'd taken the morning-after pill and it had stuck in Dara's head, to be remembered today when her mind was blank.

Dara nodded. "I know."

"It's not a form of contraception to be used every month," the doctor went on. "It's for emergencies only; you should remember that."

Dara still didn't look up.

The doctor handed over some pink pills and some white ones. "The white ones are for nausea," she added.

"Thank you."

"Is there anything else you want to talk about?" There was a slight softening in the doctor's voice.

Maybe she'd seen the scrapes on her knuckles, Dara thought as she reached the door. No, nobody could help her. Not here.

"No thanks," she said, and left.

The white tablets didn't kill the nausea caused by the pink ones. Dara knelt on the floor of the bathroom and retched dry heaves. When each session was over, she lay with her cheek on the tiles, and she could see all the dust and dirt that had accumulated in the corners. Bits of cotton wool, burnt matches, a glitter of a piece of broken glass from one time she'd been having wine in the bath and dropped the tumbler. When she'd got out of the bath, she'd cut her foot on a silver of glass, and even then she'd laughed. Hopping around the flat, leaving bloody drops everywhere, she'd found it funny because she was drunk. Only the next day, when she was sober, had she realized how sore her foot was.

Drinking had brought her here. Drinking had led her to James, too much brandy and being raped in his car. Drinking meant she was as culpable as he was. Nobody would let her cry rape when she'd had so much alcohol inside her.

"She was pissed, Your Honor," they'd say in court, and everyone would look at her with disgust, the drunken floozy who had danced in the pub with the accused, had drunk brandy with him, had gone off happily in his car. Nobody had forced her; nobody had put her in a headlock and said, "You must go with this man. You must drink this brandy."

"What can this young woman's word be worth, Your Honor? Nothing at all. She cannot be trusted."

Niall, one of the guys in the house, was having a party on Saturday. Mrs. Davis was away, and she was the only one who told the landlord about parties. Everyone else in the house would come and have fun.

"You've got to come down, Dara," he said, leaning in her door and looking curiously at her, still wrapped in her eiderdown. Niall was friendly and he had the maddest hair: bright red, and it stood up like a brush.

She shook her head at him.

"Ah, go on," he said. "You'll be over your bug by tonight, and we need some fun people to liven it up."

By nine that night, Dara had barely eaten anything and the thirst for something alcoholic was vicious. She had not one single thing to drink in the flat. Nothing.

Pulling on jeans and a big woolly jumper despite the warmth of the evening, she went downstairs to the party. She needed a drink, just the one. A single drink couldn't do her any harm, surely? Just enough to damp down the fear, and then she'd be fine.

By midnight, the party had spread into the back garden of the house. Dara was in a happy place now, warmed by vodka punch. She was smoking a cigarette and holding a can of beer as she stood beside the wooden shed in which the house owner kept spare furniture. There was a ladder leaning against the shed. Looking at it made Dara think about flying.

She could fly, she was sure of it. She did it all the time in her dreams: just launched herself and slid her arms and legs out, a bit like swimming.

Sometimes when she woke up, she was so sure she could fly that it was a shock to realize that she couldn't.

Being earthbound was horrible, no freedom to it. But tonight, she could fly for sure. She was invincible. Running her hand along the smooth skin of her arm, she could feel the muscles beneath, sleekly ready to propel her above the ground; and then she'd be able to skim along on hot currents of air like a bird, free. She could launch herself off the shed.

It was a marvelous plan.

She began to climb the ladder.

"Whaddaya doin'?" said someone. Niall. He looked funny, Dara thought. His hair was weirder than usual.

"Hair?" she said. She'd sort of meant to say "Your hair," but the words weren't coming out right. She tried again, but still no joy. Words were bound up in her mouth, clumsy. She hated feeling clumsy and shook her head to clear it, as though shaking might realign everything, but the clumsiness remained.

Niall was holding on to her now.

"Stop," she mumbled.

"Whaddaya doin', Dara?" he said again. "Don't do anything crazy, or we'll all be out on the streets."

At least, she thought that's what he was saying.

"Not crazy," she replied and got him off her by the simple motion of slapping him on top of the head.

"Ouch, that hurt!" he cried.

Dara giggled and kept climbing the ladder. She'd say sorry properly when she was flying.

She felt as if she were dancing now. On top of the shed was a bucket of dirty water. The roof itself was coarse wood. Dara barely noticed. Her skin felt so alive that she didn't care about earthly things like pain; she was above all that.

From below, she could hear shouting. She smiled indulgently; they didn't understand. At the edge of the shed roof, she looked down.

"Dara—Jesus, Dara, what are you doing up there? Get down," roared Niall.

"Ohmigod!"

Dara felt the rasp of the wooden roof as she slid one foot forward. They'd understand when they saw her flying. She leaped, waiting for the whoosh of the currents of air under her body, the glorious lift of becoming airborne.

It never came. There was a sudden screech of fear and a stomach-whooping sensation like being in a roller coaster, and then nothing but darkness.

"It's hard to know what she's taken. . . ."

The words drifted into Dara's consciousness.

"Drinking, all of them. . . ."

"Never seen anything like them. . . . Police are here. No, she did it herself—told them she could fly. I have no idea how nothing's broken. Badly sprained ankle, though. She fell on the bin bags, else she'd be in bits."

The words receded as pain hit Dara like a hail of bullets. Sharp, stinging, aching, unbearable. At least it took her mind away from the other pain, the one in her heart. Physical pain was easier to deal with. You knew where you were with it.

The small front room smelled of wood fires and stale sweat. When Dara had lived on Snowdrop Park, she'd never realized how dirty and drab the house was, with wallpaper that had been the same all her life. The paper in the front room might once have been small blue flowers on a cream background. She pictured her mother choosing it and urging Dad to wallpaper the room. Now it was yellow, the flowers faded into nothingness, more yellow at the top from years of smoke, and with large strips of paper torn off the chimney breast, the result of an argument some night.

"So you're back." Bernard Murphy sat in his old chair beside the fire, his cigarette-making paraphernalia beside him on the stained card table and the ever-present glass in his hand. Clear liquid sat in the glass; therefore Dara knew he'd got poteen from somewhere. The illegal Irish spirit was very strong, beautifully sweet and mellow if made properly. Made incorrectly, it could make a person go blind. But Dad wouldn't care about that. He was with Machiavelli on that one: the end justified the means. Good or bad, if it made you drunk, it worked. All the rest was immaterial.

"I'm back," she echoed, although she didn't want to say anything. It was bad enough to have to move home. She didn't want
to have to talk to her father. She and Greg had discussed it.

"He's not so bad these days," Greg had said. "He doesn't drink
at home so much, goes out a lot. Makes it easier."

"Would make it easier if he'd drop dead," Dara growled at her
brother.

"It would make it easier if you hadn't got thrown out of your
bedsit," Greg said flatly. "You going to tell me about that?"

"No, it was a misunderstanding about rent," she lied. How
could she tell him the landlord had asked her to leave after that
last crazy party? She'd have found another place if only he had
given her the deposit back, but of course he hadn't.

"You crazy or something?" he'd shouted at her, gesticulating
with his hands. "You want your deposit back after all the trouble
you've caused me? I've had the police round, and next it'll be the
tax man. Get out of here and don't come back."

With no money and nowhere else to go—she'd asked some of
the girls if she could bunk with them, but they'd all said no—Dara
was left with no option but to go home to Snowdrop Park.

She'd thought she'd never fit all her possessions back into her
own bedroom, but strangely, she seemed to have less stuff than
she'd thought. She'd unpacked one of the trash bags and had
begun to put things into the dusty wardrobe, but she'd felt too
dispirited to finish it. Instead, she'd left the other bags on the bed
and gone downstairs.

"Want a drink?" Her father pointed to a bottle on the floor.

There were no glasses, only a couple of dirty cups on the man-
telpiece.

"Hospitality the Murphy way," she said cynically.

He gave her the thousand-yard stare she'd grown up with, the
dangerous stare.

At a certain stage of drunkenness, the stare would go from
anger to pure rage in a millisecond, and he'd move across the
room to slam his hand into her face. Incredible how a man so
unfit could move at speed when he really wanted to.

Other times, he'd just glare at her and tell her to fuck off.

Once, Dara had known the precise difference between those two stares. She'd worked it out, as if it were a mathematical formula: $x + y$ = disaster/mild indifference, with a variant of k.

But she couldn't be bothered to analyze his mood today. Let him hit her.

He couldn't touch her on the inside anymore; nobody could. What was another fist in the face from her father? She was used to it. After the first ten years, you became nicely numb. Dara had never hit back before. She didn't know why. Your dad was supposed to protect you—was that it? Was it some race memory of what was expected of a relationship between parent and child that had rendered her too shocked to respond?

Either way, she'd always let him hit her.

But that wouldn't happen anymore. Her old room in the house might be the same, but Dara had changed. She would fight back; and with the animal instinct he'd always had, he knew it.

"Suits me," he said, shrugging. "More for me if you don't drink."

The mention of the word made her thirsty in a flash. Thirsty for the cozy warmth inside her, the warmth that nobody could take away.

"I've changed my mind," she snarled.

She grabbed the bottle from the floor, unscrewed its top, and drank from it. It was good stuff, all right: soft and sweet, like mellow Japanese rice wine, only cold.

"Jesus, I didn't say take it all," he said, watching the bottle upend further.

The poteen hit the spot, many times. Dara was so tired; she sat in the armchair staring blankly at the television as her father watched a soccer match, and thought about summoning the energy to climb the stairs to bed.

"I'll help you," he said abruptly when she got up and swayed on her way to the door.

Somehow they made it up the narrow stairs. In her bedroom,

her father hauled her over to the bed and Dara slumped onto it, toppling black plastic sacks to the floor.

"I'll sort you out," he was murmuring, lifting her feet onto the bed and pulling off her boots. He shoved the covers back and nudged her farther into the single bed, so there was more room. "There's my girl," he said.

Dara's eyes sprang open. With fear came a blast of sobriety. He was drunker than she was, she could tell. He drank so much that it happened faster now, from nought to sixty in a few glasses. That was what forty years of heavy drinking did to you.

"That's my girl."

He had his hand curled around her neck, his fingers sliding down to the curve of her breast in the cheap acrylic polo-neck she wore.

The memories crashed back.

"Get off me!" she roared. "Get off me!"

"Jeez, I was only—"

Dara kicked him as hard as she could, and he fell off the bed. "Out!!!"

He scrambled up off the floor and lurched out the door.

The shaking began, and Dara slid off the bed, searching frantically through her possessions for the bottle of vodka. She could remember it all, and she hated remembering.

"Let's have a bath and get you nice and clean."

"Okay, Daddy."

The bath was too hot for her, but he pulled her in anyway. "You're a great little girl, d'ya know that?"

There were no bubbles, just water, so she could see his spindly legs and the boniness of his body. Only his belly, soft from beer, was fat, a white mass resting on the flaccid penis.

Boys in school made jokes about willies. Padraig, who was nearly ten and therefore older than the rest of them in third class, had drawn one, and the teacher had thrown him out of the class. Dara had said nothing. She could have drawn one too.

"It's dirty, so Daddy can't touch it. Wash it for Daddy, there's a good girl."

She'd done it before. She'd done worse. What happened in her bed when he was really drunk was worse, wasn't it? Although he said it was their special time. Special time hurt Dara. She'd close her eyes for it, go into that place in her head where nobody could reach her. That was a safe place.

Dara found the vodka bottle hiding in her box of albums. She drank half of it, not even feeling it touching her throat as it rushed, fiery, down. It would take awhile to work. It always did now. The instant-hit days were over. It took more and more vodka to send her into the warm, safe place. But she had to get out of here now. She couldn't stay. She stuffed some clothes back into one of the black plastic sacks, got her handbag and rucksack, and stumbled downstairs. The keys to his crappy car were thrown at the bottom of the stairs. She scooped them up. She didn't know where she was going, but she had to get away, out of town.

By the time the city had disappeared, Dara was lost. She found herself on an old road in the middle of nowhere, with a grass bit in the middle of the road and the sea ahead of her. The car was making a strange noise. There was a problem with the clutch, she knew. Piece of crap. Typical of anything her father owned. She swerved, and the car launched itself at the grass-choked ditch, making a jarring crunching noise.

"Fuuuck," she hissed, banging the steering wheel. It took ages to open the door because she couldn't find the lever. When she did, she half-fell onto the roadway. Eventually, she got herself the right way up. Planes had the same problem, didn't they, working out where the horizon was and which way was up. Being a plane hadn't worked for her, though. Oops. No flying for Dara.

She focused, vaguely recognizing her surroundings. She'd almost reached the headland that jutted out over the sea. Another bit of a drive maybe, and she'd be there. The road narrowed to a sliver somewhere ahead and ended abruptly, with a few meters of scrub grass and then nothing but the sea and the rocks below.

There was a wooden fence at the point, she remembered, and if you picked your way carefully past that, you could walk a little farther across the scrubby grass until you came to the absolute edge, where you could stare down at the frothing water and imagine yourself landing there, impaled on the jutting rocks, homes of a million barnacles.

There must be a house nearby, because there was a sign with a postbox that said *Bluestone* in script writing.

Was that a name or a description? Dara wondered, then stumbled and fell against the hedge opposite her car. The hedge was surprisingly soft, with fragrant moss damp from the rain earlier that day. She let herself sink into it. She'd close her eyes and have a little rest.

When she woke, she was stiff and cold. Daylight had leached from the sky and an evening mist was rising from the ground. Dara moved her head and groaned. The buzz had worn off and she was in that place she hated most: where she loathed herself in every way. There was almost no point in moving—why would she move? Where had she to go? Nobody wanted her, and she wanted nobody.

Eventually she had to move because she needed to have a pee; but when she hauled herself to her feet, she could feel that the leg of her jeans was wetter than the rest of her damp clothes. Head thumping, she reached down to check and smell. Urine. She'd peed on herself already. Revulsion swept over her, a headier dose this time.

She crouched beside the car to relieve herself and grimaced as she pulled up her wet jeans. She was disgusting, nobody had to tell her that.

The car disgusted her too. She'd taken *his* car. How could she do that? How could she have moved back in with him after everything?

After what he'd done to her.

And James, she'd never forget what he'd done. Dara had told nobody; after all, who'd believe her? Who would take her side or have sympathy for her? She had none for herself.

She began to cry, a soundless sobbing that hefted great lumps out of her soul. And eventually, she stumbled in the direction of the ditch again and lay there on the moss, lost and alone in her misery.

Oblivious to the footsteps coming along the driveway of the house labeled Bluestone, it was a moment before she became aware that somebody was watching her. It was a woman, tall and slender, with a long woolen cardigan whipping against her in the wind. She had long skeins of silvery blond hair flying about her face, and her expression was strangely concerned. Why was that? Dara wondered. There was only herself around, and who could worry about her, when she'd done it all to herself? There could be no sympathy for someone who'd brought all her misfortune on herself.

"Can I help you," the woman said. Not a question exactly. An offer of help.

Dara shook her head and felt more water fill her eyes.

The woman crouched and edged nearer, the way a person might approach a feral cat injured on the road. "What's wrong?" she asked.

"I want to die," said Dara. And she did. Right now. She might as well be dead; it would be easier, less painful. There was nobody who would really miss her. All right, Greg would, and she loved him so much; but they'd been there for each other as children and he was an adult now, he'd found someone else to love him—Ruth. He'd be safe. He wasn't like her.

"You could get better," the woman said. Again, it was an odd thing to say, Dara realized.

"Could I?" Dara asked, wondering.

The woman tilted her silvery blond head to one side, like a bird, and Dara saw that she had the most unusual eyes: long rather than round, and slanting up at the corners as if her ancestry held a hint of Asia. And they were the most amazing shade of green: not a smudgy color, but the true green of peridots, with a strong dark line around the irises that defined them.

The woman took Dara's hand almost before Dara realized. Two

things happened: the woman closed her eyes and sighed, and Dara felt a surge of heat through her palm as if her hand were lying on a stove. Heat burned through her, up her arm and into—and here, it was getting very strange—her heart. That's what it felt like. Still holding on, she struggled to sit up and touch her chest with her other hand. Yes, there was a feeling of heat where her heart was supposed to be. Normally she felt nothing there, just deadness, or sometimes dull pain. But now there was this warmth and it was lifting her—

"You've been hurt so much, you poor child, but you could get better," the woman said, letting go.

Dara gasped, but the beautiful, comforting heat inside her remained. She stared down at her hand, but it looked the same as ever.

"I'm Star Bluestone," the woman said. "I was making supper. Would you like to come in and have some with me?"

Two years later

Sofie, Lorelei, and Dara left the meeting, calling good-bye to all the smokers who'd lingered to light up.

"We're going to my place for coffee," Lorelei said to the smokers.

"We'll be there in a mo," one of them replied.

The three women walked down the lane away from the community hall and came upon a bunch of young fellas kicking a ball against a wall.

"What's going on in there?" roared one of the lads. "Youse are always there on a Monday night. What's it about?"

Dara eyeballed him. "We're a Christian group," she said, "Ordinary People Against the Devil. Look"—she poked around in her handbag—"I have leaflets. You could have some. You only have to do ninety prayers a night, and promise not to lose your virginity until you're twenty-one; it's really easy."

The young fellas were looking at her with horror.

"But you have to give up smoking, drinking, and girls. Oh"—she gestured to the ball, which had now stopped—"and soccer. Soccer is particularly the work of the devil. I mean, come on—a team called Arsenal? It's obvious."

She produced some papers from her bag—really brochures on aerobics classes from the new gym down the road. "Here are the leaflets. You'd love it."

"Bunch of weirdos," muttered the lads, running off with their ball.

The three women burst into laughter.

"We could show them the work of the devil," Lorelei said, chuckling.

"And then some," sighed Sofie, who was three years sober and still shivered when she thought of what she'd been like. "If only they knew."

Lorelei's home was a five-minute walk away, a two-up, two-down she lived in alone. Dara had spent many evenings there since she started going to the Alcoholics Anonymous meeting in Inchicore.

It was all thanks to Star Bluestone, she knew. If Star hadn't taken her in, comforted her during the hellish withdrawal phase, and driven her to AA meetings, she wouldn't be here at all. Dara could never thank Star enough.

"You did it yourself," Star replied every time Dara said this.

"I couldn't have done it without you," Dara protested. "Without someone to believe in me."

"You want biscuits?" asked Lorelei now as she boiled the kettle.

"No," said Sofie. "I'm trying to diet. I'm on the F-Plan."

"I've given up on dieting," Lorelei said cheerfully. "I take too much sugar in my tea to bother dieting."

Lorelei had stopped drinking twelve years ago. For her AA birthday a month before, she'd thrown a party for the Inchicore group, which was her home group. AA birthdays were precious, more so than belly-button birthdays. When you stopped drinking, Lorelei said, it was like being reborn.

She was the polar opposite of what Dara, years ago, would have considered an alcoholic. For a start, she came from a wealthy, privileged background. Her husband was a well-known surgeon, like her father and brothers, and she'd had a wonderful career in physiotherapy herself until she'd destroyed it with drink.

Nobody looking at the discreetly dressed gray-haired woman now could imagine Lorelei out of her mind on vodka, hammering on her own front door and screaming at her husband to let her into the house because she had to mind the children, a performance that had been reenacted every night for a month after he'd thrown her out. His mother had taken on the care of the children, and Lorelei had been drinking at least a liter of vodka a day to wipe that fact out of her mind. Once it was satisfactorily wiped out, she would go to the house and begin hammering.

"That was me," Lorelei had told Dara when they first met. "I had no home and I was living on the streets. I hit my rock bottom with a good, solid bang."

Looks shouldn't be important, but Dara knew that she judged people by them: That person with the nice car and the gentle manner couldn't possibly have been addicted to heroin. That lady with the manicure and beautifully coiffed hair couldn't once have been the sort of person to piss herself in the middle of the road and roar abuse at passing strangers until she was picked up and taken home by the police. But this was how these people had been. Looks meant nothing. What counted was the inside.

"How are you getting on with Des?"

Dara was caught off guard.

"You're blushing!" said Sofie.

"Stop it!" said Dara, blushing some more.

"It must be love."

"Oh, pee off," Dara replied, but she smiled. "Okay, it's love. Happy now?"

Half an hour of talk later, Dara finished her coffee. "I'm going home," she said, and slipped out of her place at Lorelei's kitchen table. She opened the door to leave, then whispered back at Lorelei and Sofie: "To spend time with my lover!"

"How was your meeting?" asked Des when she got home.

He was cooking. He was a marvelous chef but a terrible clearer-upper. He and Dara had worked out a system whereby he cooked—she had no experience whatsoever, having been raised on a diet of tinned spaghetti, beans and sausages, and white bread—and she cleared up afterward.

"Very good." She put her arms around him from behind and spooned herself into the hardness of his back. "What's that?" She sniffed.

"Cod in a lemon sauce." Des had got his hands on a second-hand copy of one of the Galloping Gourmet's books and was working his way through it.

Dara sniffed again. "You're sure that fish isn't off?"

"Fresh off the boat," Des said indignantly. "I got it in McKee's this morning."

"Sorry, it smells funny."

They both put their heads down to the pan and inhaled deeply.

Dara reeled backward. "Think I'm going to pass out," she muttered, and everything went black.

She was lying down when she came to. "What happened?" She tried to sit up, but her head still felt woolly.

She was in their bed, and Des was sitting beside her, his face a mask of worry.

"You fainted." He was almost accusatory.

"I've never fainted in my life," she snapped back.

"Dara, now's not the time to prove how tough you are!" Des growled. "You fainted, take it from me."

"Why would I faint?"

"I don't know."

They glared at each other.

"Sorry." Des lay down on the bed with her and hugged her so tightly she felt her ribs crunch. "I'm worried about you."

"I'm fine."

"You're not. You're going to the doctor."

Next morning as they sat in the waiting room, Dara worried about paying for the doctor. They were broke; how could they afford this? They were only just managing to live and pay the rent as it was.

"We should just go home, darling," she said. "I feel fine now."

"No," he said firmly. "You're going to see the doctor—you're sick."

In the examination room, Des sat on a chair and looked anxious while the doctor calmly checked Dara's blood pressure, asked her questions, dipped a couple of sticks in her urine sample, and prodded the glands in her neck.

After a while, she held up a skinny white tube.

"It's not a urinary tract infection or a kidney infection, but I think I know what it is."

"What?" Des looked as if he was expecting the worst.

"You're pregnant," the doctor said with a smile.

"Jesus!" said Des.

"Pregnant?" Dara repeated in wonderment, then said it again in her mind: *pregnant? Her?* Then she felt a wonderful joy seeping up from her toes to the top of her head. Pregnant! They were going to have a baby; how absolutely incredible.

Des grabbed her and kissed her fiercely on the lips.

"I'd tell you two to get a room," joked the doctor, "but it's clear you've already gone past that bit."

The day her brother was marrying Ruth, Dara woke to a beautiful April morning. The wedding had been arranged with some haste because Greg had got a contract to move to Sydney with his company, and who knew when he and Ruth would be home again to marry with all their family and friends present?

"Are you ready?" Des called up the stairs to Dara.

They'd found a small house in Ashbourne, and even though it was a long way from Des's work, it had a garden and plenty of other families with young children around. Perfect for when the baby was born.

"Ready as I'll ever be," Dara said. Her hair shone and her cheeks glowed with a rosy quality that was just her, not powder or cream blusher; and even if her voluminous black cotton dress and flat sandals were hardly high fashion, she knew she looked as well as she ever had in her life. Like a goddess, ripe with power and love.

"Because of you," she murmured to the baby inside her belly. "Because of you."

Without her child, she didn't know how she'd be able to cope with this day.

She could smell her father's breath as soon as he opened the back door of Des's car, the sweet, honeyed smell of an early-morning drink mixed with the heady aroma of yesterday's booze soaking out of his pores. Dara said nothing as he got into the backseat, just smiled hello and kept her hands closed over the swell of her belly. There was something diseased about the smell of old alcohol. They told pregnant women not to breathe in other people's smoke. There should be a similar warning about smelling a hard day's drinking on somebody.

"Never thought I'd see this day," her father said happily.

He was always happy when he'd had a few early-morning beers, Dara thought with anger. Happy when there was a party where he could play hail-fellow-well-met to all and be the life and soul. No wonder so few people had ever realized that Bernard Murphy had a serious drinking problem. All they saw was charm personified at parties, followed up by a little slurring of words and a fondness for sitting at the piano and singing Percy French songs. Where was the harm in that?

They didn't see the anger that surfaced when the party was over, or the damage he could do when there was no admiring audience to watch him, just the unwilling audience of two: his son and daughter.

The car jerked to a stop at a red light.

"Sorry," said Des apologetically.

She gave him a small smile. He was as nervous as she was about the day, only because he wanted it to be right for her.

Dara could feel her heart racing with anger. It was bad for the baby. She forced herself to breathe deeply and let the rage evaporate. No, she wouldn't let anything bother her today, she vowed.

Today was Greg's day, and for him and her beloved Ruth, she'd go to the wedding, smile as if they were indeed a normal family where the only son was getting married, and even dance with her father when the time came. She'd do it for Greg and Ruth.

The actual wedding didn't trouble her. It wasn't the church where she and Greg had gone as children—that would have been hard, sitting in a pew looking at the same stations of the cross on the walls and falling back into that dark place of childhood where there was always fear and tension. Thankfully, Greg and Ruth had chosen a church near the hotel where the reception was being held. It was comfortingly unfamiliar, with a choir of schoolgirls who sang at weddings and played the guitar as accompaniment. It held no memories.

The hotel itself was pretty and ivy-covered, managed by a charming couple who must have had a new bridal party every weekend but carried on with delight as if the Murphy/Keogh wedding was the highlight of their hotel's entire calendar.

Nothing was too much trouble. They dragged out an armchair with a footstool and an armload of cushions so Dara could sit in comfort during the sherry reception in the small bar. Most people were standing, so Dara was at a lower level to them all, giving her the opportunity to sit back and watch. She saw her new sister-in-law swirling around the guests in her pretty cream silk gown, the baby roses in her hair drooping prettily in her fair curls. She watched Des talking kindly to Ruth's elderly great-aunt, who'd been anxious about not knowing anybody outside of the wedding party, "and they'll all be too busy to have time for me."

She watched Greg's eyes following Ruth round the room, and saw how he'd held a glass of beer at the start but put it down without drinking more than a sip. And she saw her father talking to Ruth's dad, standing beside the bar with pints in front of them. Bernard had one foot balanced on the footrail, a position he adopted so frequently that Dara wondered whether the muscles in one leg were shorter than the other. One pint became two, followed by whiskey chasers. She couldn't hear from where she was sitting, but she knew the script: "Ah, sure, it'll be a long time till the dinner and the wine. Let's have a couple of short ones to keep us going."

At dinner she and Des drank mushroom soup, ate wild Irish salmon, devoured a beautiful meringue confection topped with raspberries, and occasionally held each other's gaze during the speeches. As father of the groom, Bernard Murphy wasn't due to give one, but that had never stopped him before.

Yet he sat happily beside Ruth's mother, without any visible sign that he'd drunk enough to flatten any normal human being.

"It's been a beautiful day, hasn't it?" Ruth's father said to her as they sat at the side of the room while the tables were reorganized for dancing. "We were lucky with the weather, although I'm sure you would have been happy if it hadn't been so warm."

Dara smiled at him. "We were lucky in every way," she said.

In the end, it was the dancing that got to her. The band played cover music, and the first dance was Ruth's favorite song: Billy Joel's "Just the Way You Are." The singer had a good voice, Dara thought absently as she watched her big brother guide his beautiful bride gently around the dance floor.

Ruth's mother and Dara's father began to shuffle round the floor, and then everybody else was up too, and all the formal bits of the wedding were finally over. The band wove the end of one song into the next, and Louis Armstrong's "What a Wonderful World" began.

"Come on, pet, let's shake a rug."

Dara refocused to see her father standing beside her. "I'm not dancing, Da," she said. "Ruth's dad asked me if I wanted to give the whole family dance a miss, and I said yes. I'm too pregnant."

"Nonsense." He had a firm grip on her arm and pulled her to her feet. Strange how he could look so gentle and yet be so strong. Deceitful. "A little dance will do you good."

He put one arm around her and held her other hand in his, looking down to concentrate on his waltz. He always prided himself on his dancing; he could even do the foxtrot, he said, although Dara had never seen a sober rendition of it.

She set her face and let him manhandle her round the floor. She refused to let him see how it hurt.

"You'll come and see me when the baby's born, won't you, pet?" her father said.

He stumbled a little, but she was holding him, so she kept them both upright. He was still a tall man, although his muscles had run to fat and his belly was as swollen as hers from years of drinking beer after beer. Followed by whiskey chasers, of course.

Dara wanted to say, "Of course, we'll visit you," but she couldn't. She couldn't lie, not now, not with her baby inside listening. There had been enough lies in the Murphy household, and there would be no more.

"It's a great day," he went on, "a great day indeed. Not many a man can see his son and daughter married within a year of each other and think he did it all himself. I wasn't a bad old father, now, was I?"

He was waiting for her to agree. Waiting for her to say, "Yes, Da, you were the best. You never screamed at us till we hid, or threatened us with the strap, or drank your wages till we had no food and had to run to Ruth's mother for sugar sandwiches, or—" She stumbled on the "or." It was so big, bigger than ever, now that she was pregnant.

"Wasn't I, Dara?"

Dara could no longer bear it.

She realized she had been waiting for something, some connection that would make the past a safe place again, some moment when her father would transform into the mythical daddy he'd never been. Like a dream that receded when she woke up, she could almost touch the vision of this past. She reached out and it was beyond her grasp.

Nothing could change the past, not her wishing with all her heart, and not this day of happiness when she watched a truly happy family together, seeing them smile at one another and not set their faces into the tight masks of people doing their best not to remember.

Dara was sitting in Star's conservatory watching Star sort out skeins of dyed silk when the contractions started.

"Oh," she said in shock, hands rushing to hold her belly as the pain ripped through her.

"Is it the baby?" asked Star, concerned.

Through the pain, Dara nodded. When it had receded, she leaned back in her chair, gasping. "Ouch!" she said, and laughed with relief. "It must be Braxton Hicks contractions."

She and Des had spent hours poring over their pregnancy guidebook.

Star didn't look convinced. "That's not the feeling I'm getting."

"No, really, your water needs to break first," Dara began, then stopped as a flush of liquid spilled out of her. "Then again . . . Sorry about the floor."

It was Star's turn to laugh. "This floor has seen plenty of water breaking, I can tell you. My mother delivered eight babies in her time."

"And you?"

"None—yet."

Des was at his uncle's farm down the road and came speeding over to Star's house.

"Relax, the contractions are twenty minutes apart," said Dara, who was now lying on a couch in a sea of cushions. "We've ages to go, and remember what they told us in the prenatal classes? If we come in early, we'll just be sent home again. Better to stay here where we're comfortable."

"Okay," Des said dubiously.

An hour later, Dara suddenly howled in absolute pain. "Des, it's more than a contraction, don't know what it is, but help. Help—"

"Let's get her to the hospital, quickly," said Star. "I'll drive."

Dara's labor was long and intense, and the midwife suggested pethidine.

"No," gasped Dara. "No drugs." She squeezed Des's hand even tighter. No drugs, not now.

And then there was Natalie, with her head of silky dark hair and her outraged screaming at having been hauled out into this freezing, very bright world.

" '*Send me back inside!*' she's saying," crooned Des as he held her, screaming, in his arms.

And Dara, worn out yet full up with joy, smiled at them both.

Star cried when she held little Natalie in her arms. Dara didn't think she'd ever seen Star cry before.

"Sorry," wept Star. "It's just that she's so beautiful, so precious."

Bernard came to the hospital the day after Natalie was born. Des had been with her almost all day and now he'd gone; visiting time was nearly over, and along came her father. He was drunk. Dara didn't care. She was happy, insulated in a bubble of happiness. Her father was never aggressive or abusive when there were other people around; and here in the six-bed hospital ward, with Natalie snug in her little crib beside the bed and other mothers on either side and nurses and doctors walking up and down, Dara knew she was perfectly safe from him. Besides, he couldn't touch her in any way, not physically, not psychologically, anymore.

"Look at the baby," he said, clumsily banging into the crib, reaching in as if to pick Natalie up.

"No," said Dara quickly, "you can't—she's asleep."

Miraculously, Natalie stayed asleep despite the ruckus. Perhaps she knew her mother was willing her to keep her eyes closed so that her grandfather would not pick her up and hold her to his drunken face. She slept deeply, those long lashes dark and heavenly on her soft cheeks.

"Ah, she's beautiful," said Bernard. "A beautiful baby. I had a few with the lads, just to wet the baby's head."

"Yeah," Dara said. Any excuse: drinking to wet the baby's head, drinking because somebody had died, drinking because the sun had shone, drinking because the sun hadn't shone. She understood it, all right. Her father hovered at the end of the bed, as if he could sense the armor-plating Dara had put around herself and the baby.

"I meant to bring you flowers or something, but I forgot," he said.

"That's fine," Dara said calmly. She had the gifts she wanted, a

card and roses from Des. She'd told him he shouldn't buy her anything, they needed to keep the money for the mortgage; and then
he'd come in with beautiful white roses, twelve of them, and she'd
loved him for it.

Bernard sat on the end of the bed, and Dara instantly pulled
her feet away. Even though she had stitches and it was uncomfortable, she sat up straight; she wanted to be formal with him,
to move away from him, not lie there and relax. Worse, Natalie
would wake up soon and need to be fed, and there was absolutely
no way Dara was going to breast-feed her baby with her father
watching.

"She's the image of your mother," Bernard went on, peering
mistily at the baby in the little crib. "The image of her. And what
a great head of hair she has. It'll be lovely to have a baby around
the house again."

A wave of absolute revulsion hit her. It would be lovely to have
a baby around the house? A baby who would grow into a child,
a little girl, to be touched and used in the same way she'd been
used? Was he crazy? Did he not remember what he'd done to her?
Had he managed to put it out of his mind so easily, or had alcohol soddened his memory so much that it was as if the abuse had
never happened?

A bell rang, the warning that only fifteen minutes of visiting
time remained.

"That's it, Da," she said. "You'd better head off—they're very
firm here."

He didn't need any more urging. "I said I'd go back to the pub
and meet the lads—they want to buy me a few rounds for the
baby. What are you going to call her, anyway?"

"I haven't decided," Dara said, which was a lie; but giving her
father the baby's name was like giving him a bit of her soul, and
she didn't want to do that, not just yet. He lurched forward for
a kiss, and Dara felt her stomach curdle. She moved her head so
his unshaven cheek cracked against hers. "Bye," she said, and he
staggered off, no doubt happy with himself. Everything was fine in
Bernard's world.

Her grandfather had no sooner gone than Natalie woke up with an adorable mewling noise like a kitten, waking and stretching.

"How are you, my darling?" Dara said, picking her up, wincing only slightly at the pain from her stitches. Natalie's rosebud mouth settled around her mother's nipple and she began to suck. Breast-feeding was incredible, Dara thought; nobody had told her it would be like this. She knew it could be difficult, that some women couldn't manage it and others shuddered at the thought, thinking their boobs would end up around their knees. She'd been lucky: Natalie had latched on instantly, and even though her breasts could be sore and the baby's little gums hurt sometimes as she squirmed around trying to get a good hold, there was something primeval and amazing about it. It was like this was what her body was made for. This sense of an animal minding her young was the most powerful, intense feeling she'd ever had in her whole life. She cradled Natalie's dark head, closed her eyes, and let the sense of rightness ripple through her body. But her father's visit kept rattling back into her brain. He had to come in; he had to come and ruin every feeling of goodness and happiness.

No matter what she did, he'd always be there. She hated him sometimes. Even though she was supposed to let go of the past, not blame anyone, she did blame him. She couldn't put the light of forgiveness around him because what he'd done to her was so appalling. When you had a child, it was your duty to love it and protect it. That was her instinct with her beautiful little Natalie in her arms. Her father had betrayed all that parental love and had done the most unparental thing there was. How could he come in here and talk about how wonderful it was to have a baby around the place again and not remember what he'd done to his own baby when she'd grown into a little girl?

Dara stroked Natalie and vowed that she'd never let that happen to her darling baby. She'd never forgive her father for what he'd done.

Natalie was the most amazing baby in the whole world; Des and Dara told everyone so. She slept through the night at five months and moved on to solid foods with absolutely no problem. Puréed carrots were her favorite, and she squealed with delight when she got the first spoonful of puréed apple.

She was crawling around the room at high speed about a month before the books said she'd be with both her parents hovering protectively, making sure she didn't bang into things or hurt her head on something. The only slow bit of her development was that she loved sleeping in her parents' bed and refused to move into her own cot.

"We should have been tougher when she was tiny," Des said ruefully when yet another attempt to get Natalie to sleep in her cot was met with outraged screams.

"But she's so little," said Dara, who felt almost physically sick when her baby cried. "She'll learn, she will."

"You're making a rod for your own back, letting that child sleep with you," said Mrs. McGuinness, who lived in the flat downstairs and whom they often met in the morning when they went out for a walk. Mrs. McGuinness was an Expert on Everything: the government, taxi drivers, the price of food, those noisy lads who lived next door and had wild parties. . . . Des and Dara had discovered that asking her opinion on anything was a mistake, as she would usually respond with a PhD-length lecture.

"I know," said Dara hastily. "It's just that she's so happy when she's in with us and she goes back to sleep, and at least *we* get to sleep. If we put her back in the cot, she screams for ages. Just like her dad, I say." Dara smiled down at her adorable daughter and tickled her under the chin. "When she decides she wants to do something, that's it."

Mrs. McGuinness looked sagely at Dara. "I'd say she takes after her mother as well. Something tells me that when you make up your mind, Dara, you don't like to change it."

"I used to be like that," Dara said softly. "But not anymore."

Saturday mornings were the best, when Des didn't have to get up early for work and the two of them could lie snug in the double bed with Natalie between them, squirming and wriggling, happy being adored by her parents.

When Natalie was seven months old, Dara's breast milk dried up, and she decided to get a tattoo. When she checked with the GP to make sure it would be safe, the GP said, amused: "What are you getting? A butterfly?"

"Something like that," Dara agreed.

It was a tiny tattoo on the inside of her wrist, and was actually made up of three dates written in a spiral. They were three of the most important dates in Dara's life: the day she'd stopped drinking, the day she'd met Des properly, and the day Natalie had been born. Natalie was fascinated by the tattoo and rolled her fingers around the delicate tracery of the writing on her mother's narrow wrist.

"Where would I be without you, darling?" Dara murmured to her daughter, stroking Natalie's soft cheeks, holding her fat little hands, watching the light in her beautiful eyes. "You're everything to me, my love, you and your dad."

They were so happy, the three of them; it was a golden time. Dara had never known so much happiness.

Des hated working in the furniture shop. Dara knew he'd like nothing more than a bit of land somewhere, for he was never happier than when he was mucking around in the fields at Pinewood, the farm his uncle owned in Wicklow.

Whenever he visited Uncle Phillip, Dara brought Natalie to visit Star.

Natalie loved crawling around on the floor, reaching up to grab all the fascinating objects in Star's house. Dara followed her anxiously, worried things would break.

"Stop worrying," Star would say. "It's all replaceable."

Dara laughed. "Nothing in this house is replaceable; it's all so special or old or priceless."

They sat on the veranda, letting Natalie sit on the grass and wriggle her bare feet, and talked.

Dara wanted Star's opinion on how to convince Des to move to Wicklow.

"He loves it here, but he says he knows I'm a city girl. I don't care where I live, Star," she added. "As long as I'm with Des and Natalie, I could happily live in a box on the motorway." She rushed over to pick a fat, juicy worm from Natalie's grasp. Natalie, who'd been considering eating the worm, squealed with temper.

Star laughed. "Tell him that," she said.

Two short years later, Star knew there was somebody in the house before she unlocked the door. Everything looked the same, but she just knew.

She walked quietly into the kitchen and out onto the veranda before she found her visitor. Dara was sitting on the swing seat, wrapped in the old cream woolen blanket, holding a cup of tea loosely in one hand. A small teapot rested on the table beside her.

In one glance, Star knew everything was very, very wrong.

She sat down on the other side of the seat and looked into Dara's face. She was deathly pale, her lips bloodless. "What's wrong?"

Dara shook her head. "Can't talk," she whispered. "Can't."

"Tell me."

Dara's eyes flickered to the teapot. It was the oldest teapot in the house, one that had been passed down from Bluestone woman to Bluestone woman for more than three hundred years. Dara knew what it was, for Star had told her. Tea drunk from it could tell you your future, if you knew how to ask it correctly.

"Why did you use it?" asked Star.

"The mark on my arm, the funny black spot," Dara said. "Remember it? The tattoo guy said I should get it looked at, but I didn't get round to it until I was in with Natalie for that little cough she had and the GP said he'd best remove it. He did, and he phoned me, said it's skin cancer, a malignant melanoma. It's been there for so long. . . . I didn't know, Star. I didn't know it could be dangerous—"

"How dangerous?"

Star daren't touch her yet in case something terrible sprang from Dara's soul into Star's mind, something that meant bad news.

"I went to the hospital for a scan. It's everywhere. I have spots on my liver. Des doesn't know yet; I couldn't tell him. The doctors want me to come back with him so they can talk to us. . . ." Dara bent her head. "I kept thinking it was something to do with my drinking, and I couldn't tell him. Like I'd done it to myself, like it was my fault. I thought if I came out here, you'd be able to tell me it was going to be all right. *Then* I could tell him, because I knew the ending."

Star knew what she'd say next.

"You weren't here and I was desperate to know—"

"You used the teapot."

"I used it. I don't have six months, Star. They said I might, but I don't, not even that. It's cold at the funeral, you see. I saw it, and everyone's in winter coats." She paused. "I can't leave Natalie. I love her so much. I've a pain in my heart now," Dara said quietly. "It's like an ache, a dull, huge ache that spreads from my throat down."

"There must be treatment," Star said, but even as she said it, she knew it wasn't true. The magic of the Bluestone teapot didn't lie. What Dara had seen was the truth.

Dara shook her head. "It's not cancer pain," she said. "My heart is broken. That's what the pain is. Natalie will grow up and I'll never know her. All I can think is that I'm damaged, dangerous. All I bring to people is pain—pain to poor Des, and now pain to Natalie. Perhaps if I'm gone, the pain will be gone from my family—it will all be wiped out, and Des and Natalie can start again."

"How can they start again without you?"

"They can move on, forget me, find a new life," said Dara fiercely.

Star took her hands then, and she could see that Dara meant it.

"I want her to be happy, and my history never made anyone happy. She deserves a fresh start, with good parents. With Des and somebody else. Not me with my darkness. What sort of a dead mother would I be? A crazy one that no child would want to be like. 'Who was your mother, Natalie? Oh, an alcoholic, the daughter of an alcoholic, who was abused and raped and tried to self-destruct.' That's no role model for a person. No, better she has a fresh life without me."

"But you got better."

"I tried," Dara said quietly. "I did my best, but it's still in me, the darkness—why else would this happen to me? I love them both so much; my love will always be there for her, whether she knows about it or not. I'll be with them in spirit somehow." She half-laughed. "You'll feel me, Star, although nobody else will."

"Natalie has a right to know about her past."

Dara shook her head. "Some pasts are best left buried."

Thirteen

Only one person can change your life, and that's you. Don't wait for anyone else to do it, Prince Charming or otherwise. Be your own prince.

*M*orning rain had lashed Ardagh with floods of water, but now, as evening light turned the sky opalescent pink, it was mercifully dry. The rosy rays of the dying sun looked for all the world like a medieval painting, and Natalie reflected that all the scene needed was the figure of an angel hovering over the coast for the look to be complete.

She was silent as her father drove his old pickup truck out past Ardagh on the road to the Black Abbey. He might have thought she was locked in darkness and confusion, yet it was merely that she felt unnerved and otherworldly. After all this time, she knew something about her beloved mother, Dara. What a story it had been, even if that was just a short version of it.

"Star will tell you more," Dad said.

He'd told her how much he loved her mother, how devastated they'd both been when they found out she was going to die. But there was a lot of darkness in her mother's life, things, he said, that even he didn't know.

"Dara went through a lot of awful stuff when she was a child, and she didn't want me to know everything," he'd said. "Kind of like how she felt it would be better if you didn't know about her, because she said being the daughter of a dead alcoholic from a dysfunctional family wasn't any legacy to talk about."

Natalie had just nodded; she felt too emotional to speak. This woman from the photograph had become a flesh-and-blood person to her, a person who'd traveled a hard path.

And now she was going to see her grave.

The car rounded a bend and the dark shape of the church and its surrounding graveyard were visible in the distance, under a threatening dark blue cloud bearing rain. To the right was a narrow road that led farther down the headland. As teenagers, Natalie, Lizzie, and Anna had sometimes gone there with boys, scrambling down the stony outcropping to reach the rocks below, where they'd sit, dangle their feet in the water, and flirt. It was very beautiful and wild, and there was a thrilling, dangerous feeling that if you weren't careful, you could slip into the frothing waves and never be seen again.

Her mother had spent a lot of time with Star; had she wandered around these rocks too?

As the Black Abbey got nearer, Natalie could barely see it because her eyes were blurred with tears.

"She didn't want me to know about her pain . . . because she loved me?" she asked, when they'd parked and he'd switched off the engine.

"She adored you, Natalie," he said, his voice cracking. "I could talk forever and I'd never be able to get across how much she loved you. That's the only reason she didn't want you to know about the past—because it might hurt you, and she wanted to protect you from all that."

Natalie's father held her hand as they made their way across the grass and gravel of the graveyard, out past the carefully tended newer graves—one of them David's—to the wilder part at the back. Here, they were closer to the sea and the ground was strewn with rocks, as if the sea were slowly claiming it back.

Natalie's eyes darted to and fro; she wanted the satisfaction of identifying the right grave before her father told her.

"It's this one," he said, stopping beside a small mound with a plinth and a white marble angel. The angel's beautiful carved head was bowed in prayer, and the white eyelids were closed. Her hair was a plait tied around her head, and everywhere she was slender, from the nape of her neck to her folded hands.

There were pretty plants in containers sitting neatly under the angel, and Natalie wished she'd brought something to lay at the grave. It must be Star who kept it tended.

Above the flowers, on the plinth, was the inscription:

DARA FLYNN, DIED AGED 28. DEEPLY BELOVED WIFE OF
DESMOND AND ADORING MOTHER OF NATALIE. MOURNED
BY FAMILY AND A LARGE COMMUNITY OF FRIENDS.

Natalie's hands flew to her mouth. It was written here, everything she'd ever wanted to know or feel.

"She only wanted a simple headstone," Des said hoarsely. "Nothing fancy. But I saw the angel in the stonemason's, and I knew it was right for her grave. She was an angel, you see. My angel."

Natalie knelt down at the base of the grave and began to pray. She wasn't a frequent Mass-goer, but right now she felt the holiness of the church and the graveyard flowing through her.

For the first time in her life, she allowed herself to talk to her mother.

Mum, I'm so sorry this is my first time here. I should have asked sooner. I thought it was easier to say nothing, let life go on; but now I know differently. I want to know you.

There was no sign that anyone was listening. The wind made the vast trees in the graveyard shudder, and large drops of rain began to fall.

"Come on, we'll be wet through," said Des, hauling her to her feet.

They made it back to the pickup just before the rain came down properly, huge raindrops bouncing against the roof and windows.

"Let's go see Star," he said.

* * *

Star's house smelled deliciously of seafood chowder. She'd woken that morning with an intense longing for the dish and had gone to the quays in Ardagh to see what the fishermen had brought in.

"I haven't seen you down here for a while," said old Liam as he worked on the wet quay beside his boat, the *Lady Anne*, named after his wife.

Anne and Star had gone to school together and enjoyed a comfortable friendship. Years before, when the *Lady Anne* had gone missing one evening after a storm, it was to Star that Anne had run, needing to know that Liam and his crew were safe.

"I woke up with the notion of fish soup in my head," Star told Liam now.

"I wake up like that every day," said Liam. "What would you like?"

Star went home with some mackerel, pollock, and a small sack of mussels. She spent an enjoyable half an hour scrubbing the mussels, then cooked her mother's special seafood chowder. She never knew why she got random urges to do things like this, but when they came, she acted upon them. There was a reason for everything.

She was reheating the chowder on the stove now, and had turned on the table lamps and lit the fire in the living room, enveloping the room in a golden light. It was a nice contrast to the thundery rain lashing down outside. Star liked rain sometimes, but tonight it seemed intrusive.

Instead, she felt in the mood for music. She flicked a switch on the CD player and let the pure, clear music of Delibes fill the room.

Lena from Kenny's had been surprised to see Star's high-tech CD player.

"We used to have a windup gramophone," Star had teased her, "but I got tired of winding it."

"No, it's just that everything here is green, organic, and—"

"—and very old. Myself included." Star laughed. "I love old things, but not exclusively. When a modern piece of equipment makes sense, I'm first in the queue."

She'd applied that principle to the conservatory where she worked. It had been a very old structure, made of metal coated with chipped green paint, and when the wind blew, the panes of glass rattled. With the money she'd made in her first three years with Kenny's, Star had finally been able to renovate the conservatory with modern materials so that she didn't have to wear layers of clothes. Now Delibes followed her from room to room, melting into the very beams of the house.

It was a strange evening, rain pelting down outside and dark purple clouds rising ominously in the background, while over to the right the sun shone through the clouds into the conservatory, bathing Star's precious orchids in light. She loved orchids. Lady's slippers were her favorites, so delicate with their silken membranes and subtle colors. As the chowder heated, she wandered around the conservatory, checking the soil for dryness, watering here, spritzing mist there. Her beautiful Victorian terrarium sat in state in one corner with another orchid inside. Star gave it a little pat as she walked by. The chowder must be nearly ready; she could smell it. Then she heard the crunch of a car's tires on the drive—that was the great thing about the pebbled drive, you could hear anybody coming a mile away.

She peered out the kitchen window and saw a man get out of a pickup, a tall, lanky man, and then a young woman.

"Dara!" Star collapsed against the window. She had to grip the sill so she wouldn't sink to the ground. No, it wasn't Dara—it was Natalie, darling Natalie, and Des.

Des looked so much older—didn't they all? Star thought wryly. She hadn't seen him in more than twenty years. Her heart swelled at the thought that Natalie was finally here. Star had never tried to look into the future; but somewhere deep inside, in the most magic part of her, she had known that Natalie would come here one day.

No matter that Dara had tried to wipe the effects of her painful past from Natalie's life—the truth would make its way out, like the tendril of a plant through dark soil. People deserved to know their histories; that was what made them what they were.

* * *

"I'm a bit anxious, Dad," said Natalie, grabbing her father's hand as they walked to the front door.

"Don't be, love," he said calmly. "You're going to love Star, she's wonderful. She always was wonderful. I'm sorry I haven't seen her for so long."

The door flew open and Star stood there, smiling at them, her arms held out wide.

"It's you—you helped me at Mr. Kenny's funeral," said Natalie, startled, recognizing the woman with the long, bright hair who'd held her when she'd fainted that day. "And you knew my name then, you called me Natalie."

"I nearly called you Dara," admitted Star. "You look so like your mother."

"Do I?"

"Oh, you're the image of her, it's almost scary." Star reached forward and put her arms around Natalie. "This was sort of your mother's other home, so welcome home, Natalie." She included Des in the hug.

Natalie closed her eyes and let herself cry. Why did this feel so good when she'd just experienced something so utterly sad, her mother's grave? She remembered the little plants that grew there, and how she had known instinctively that Star had left them. It was wonderful to think that Star had tended the grave.

"She's never been forgotten or unloved," Star said.

Natalie jerked away, shocked. "You knew what I was thinking. How?"

"I don't really. I was touching you, and I can see things that way," Star said. "It's my gift, my magic."

"Magic?" Natalie stood with her arms wrapped around herself, watching Star warily. "If you have this magic, why didn't you come to me all the times when I wanted to know about my mother, when I cried myself to sleep—where was the magic then?"

She didn't see her father hang his head, looking heartbroken.

Star put a hand out to pat his shoulder. "It's not that sort of magic, Natalie," she said.

She reached out with her other hand to Natalie. "Please come inside."

At Star's touch, Natalie felt the energy run from her body to Star's; it wasn't frightening, just a pleasant ripple that seemed to come from deep within her, calming her. "What are you doing?" she asked.

"Very few people have any idea I'm doing it," Star commented. "Your mother did too. Knew instantly, that first night I met her crying out here on the road."

"She was on the road crying?" Natalie echoed. Her father hadn't told her that. He'd said Dara had lived with Star in those early days when she'd given up drinking. And it hurt in an almost physical way to think of her mother's suffering. How could she have gone through so much and Natalie not know any of it?

"You can't tell a life story in an hour," Natalie's father pointed out.

"I know. It's simply that I feel . . . cheated," Natalie said. "Angry almost, that you all knew and I didn't."

"It's complicated," said Star. "Let's go slowly, and I'll tell you what an amazing woman she was and how much she loved you. There was a lot of pain in your mother's life, Natalie, but you can hear that after I tell you how she turned it around, changed it utterly, and how she adored you and your dad. That's what you need to learn first about her. The other stuff, the childhood stuff, the things she wanted wiped out—you can hear about them when you've found what sort of person she really was."

"Was her childhood really awful, then?"

"The worst," Star said calmly, leading Natalie into the kitchen. "Unloved and betrayed. What happens when you're a child shapes you as an adult, and if you're scarred as a child, you carry those scars always. Dara overcame her childhood experiences, but when she found out she was dying, she was afraid that all you'd know of her was the bad parts of her past."

Star and Des exchanged a look.

"Perhaps she was right. A small child can't understand a grown-up's pain and shouldn't have to. She wanted the best for you, a happy family, no shadowy past, nothing but normality. But I knew you'd come one day." It was Star's turn to feel her eyes brim with tears.

The chowder on the stove began to bubble ferociously, and Star was glad of the chance to turn away and see to it.

"I don't suppose you like seafood chowder, Natalie?" she added. "I had a sudden impulse to make it this morning; it was your mother's favorite."

"That's uncanny," said Natalie. "I love seafood chowder—it's one of my favorites, too. How did you know?"

"I didn't." Star took three earthenware bowls from the cupboard. "My magic is a law unto itself. I woke up with a longing for seafood chowder, so a deep part of me knew you'd be coming tonight. There are times when I'm just the conduit."

As they drank their soup and dipped buttered bread into the steaming bowls, Star and Des talked about Dara.

Natalie listened, wide-eyed, as she heard about Dara's pleasure in motherhood, how she'd adored Natalie and Des and wanted to do everything for them. She heard too about her mother's upbringing in the sprawling council estate with her brother, Greg, and their alcoholic father. Star skimmed over the years when alcohol possessed Dara, but Natalie could read between the lines to the misery therein.

"Dad, that's why you were upset when I told you about Lizzie," she burst out. "Lizzie's my friend, used to be my best friend," she explained to Star. "But she's drinking too much and I can't cope with it. It's so upsetting."

"You were so angry with Lizzie," said Des, "and all I could think of was your mother when I first knew her and fancied her, but she was locked in that prison too. Just like Lizzie, maybe worse. I thought of how disgusted you were about Lizzie, and wondered how the hell you knew to loathe the idea of alcoholism. Race memory?"

"Or some older and wiser instinct?" suggested Star. "Your mother and I talked about alcoholism being in the blood, but she could never allow herself that, felt it was a cop-out. She said if anyone should not want to drink, it should have been her."

"But there's a genetic link, for sure," Natalie said. "My flat-mate, Molly, told me to go online to investigate what I should do or say to Lizzie, and it's a genetic disease. Everyone in Lizzie's family drinks like a fish."

"I hope it's passed you by," Des said gravely. "You've no idea how closely Bess and I watched you when you were a teenager, Natalie, in case you went out with your pals and got terribly drunk. It's a dreadful legacy. That was partly what your mother wanted to protect you from."

"But what about my granddad and my uncle?"

Again, Des and Star caught each other's eyes.

"Your uncle lives in Australia. Greg is a lovely man. Leaving Ireland was a bit of an escape for him," Des said. "I'm sure he'd love to meet you one day and introduce you to your cousins. Your granddad is dead, I think."

"You know, Natalie, Dara grew up without a mother, and that was a tremendous loss in her life," said Star. "She wanted more for you, and she thought that Des would marry again, make a new life, and you'd have a mother."

"I love Bess, but she isn't my real mother. I always knew that," Natalie said, grabbing her father's hand and squeezing it to show she meant no offense to Bess.

"You were nearly five when Bess came along," Des said. "You knew she wasn't your real mother."

"I have a lot of Dara's things in the attic," Star said, "all wait-ing for you."

"Mum's things," breathed Natalie.

"There's a lot of stuff up there, Natalie," Star warned. "Lots of people have given me secrets to keep. It will take me time to find your mum's—I can't do it tonight."

"Okay," said Natalie, downcast. Now that she was here, she wanted to know it all right away.

"Let's sit and talk about Dara," Star suggested. There was

another reason she was in no rush to show Natalie all the things Dara had given her: Natalie needed time for the information to sink in. Better to learn it all gently and slowly.

"I love your house," Natalie said, looking around. "It's so beautiful. I feel at home here."

"You were nearly born on this floor," Des said, smiling.

"Let me tell you all about that," Star said, and she began to recount the story.

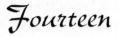

Fourteen

Trust your instincts. I didn't trust any part of me, so I discounted my instincts too. But when I thought about it, nine times out of ten my original instinct had been right. I just hadn't paid attention to it.

Grief took many paths. Ingrid had flicked through a book that described the Kübler-Ross method of defining loss. This tracked various stages of suffering, including anger and ending up, it was hoped, with acceptance.

Abra, the kind psychologist Ingrid had been seeing, explained that there was no set time frame for this.

"Grief is a journey through a changing landscape, and it takes everybody a different amount of time to travel it," Abra explained. She was older than Ingrid, the perfect Woody Allen–film version of a shrink, with serious glasses, a wise face with shrewd dark eyes, and a wardrobe of simple but unremarkable clothes that said she was at home with her internal vision of herself and didn't need the fashion industry to define who she was.

They'd started out with Ingrid sitting in a chair opposite her; then, one day, Abra had suggested that Ingrid might like to try lying on the couch with Abra seated behind her.

And Ingrid, who'd been used to people looking at her all her professional life, found it very freeing to lie and stare out the window and talk, knowing she was being heard but not having to make eye contact.

It was a relief not to have to look at Abra the day she told her about David's infidelity. She trusted Abra and her wisdom, but it was almost more than she could bear to have another person hear this awful story. Marcella was different, almost like a sister. She took Ingrid's battles as her own. In fact, Ingrid hadn't even told her own sisters. She wasn't sure why. Perhaps she couldn't face the pity, or perhaps she couldn't face them hating David.

She wanted to understand how she felt about him before she told anyone else. _If_ she told anyone else.

"I can't mourn him properly because I'm so angry," she explained to Abra. "He lied to me about everything, because to live another life like that, you have to lie about everything. Every thought, every feeling. Every time we made love, it was a lie."

The idea of David making love to her and to another woman didn't hurt as much as it had that first night. It wasn't the thought of sexual cheating that pained her—it was all the other sorts of cheating. The subtle lies about where he was and how he felt, the lies that fueled their day-to-day lives: _that_ was pure agony.

Why hadn't he just told her about the other woman? Why keep on living with her, yet deny her a chance to face this threat to their marriage? Was he in love with her or with the other woman? Was indecision the reason he'd never made a clean breast of it?

Now she would never know.

"I might write a book to follow the Kübler-Ross ones," Ingrid told Abra. "_When Grief Isn't Enough—When Only Screaming Will Do_. It could be a unique reference book, when someone doesn't fit the standard grief model."

Abra didn't smile much. But she was smiling now, Ingrid could tell from her voice: "Yes, that sounds like a good idea. You're certainly doing the master's course in it."

Ingrid felt a sense of pleasure at making a joke. Was she getting better? She hoped so.

She'd made progress in other areas of her life, too. She'd met the auditors to talk about the store and had been to a board meeting where she and the two other directors discussed interim plans for running Kenny's until probate had been resolved—at which point Ingrid, Molly, and Ethan, who'd also inherited shares, would be able to plan what to do in the future.

It was a bleak future, from the store's point of view. Kenny's was just about profitable.

"If it goes on like this, we won't be trading next year," Tom said gloomily.

Ingrid had felt a little of the old fire in her belly. "Kenny's isn't finished yet," she said.

Ingrid and the two dogs waited for a break in the traffic. It was the last leg of their four-mile walk, and they were all tired. It was also the part of the walk that she liked the least, because they had to cross a couple of busy roads and she preferred walking along nice quiet suburban streets.

Today, she was too tired to hurry across the road.

A girl with long legs, a miniskirt worn over black tights, and a cute black knitted hat perched jauntily on top of her blond hair stood a few yards away, also waiting to cross. Despite the cool of the morning, she wasn't wearing a coat. She was maybe Molly's age, an age, Ingrid thought, when girls were impervious to cold and went out at night to parties wearing teeny little dresses and no jackets. This girl looked so happy, so young and fresh, her skin glistening in the morning sunshine, and Ingrid noticed that the drivers slowed a minuscule amount to look at her until, finally, a lorry flashed its lights, urging the girl to go. She gave a grateful wave and skipped across, leaving Ingrid and the dogs standing there watching her.

Invisible, Ingrid decided: that was what she had become. She had some hope when her hair was fluffed up and her makeup was done and she was wearing her good work clothes; but now, her face gray and bare of makeup and her hair a tousled mess, she almost didn't exist. To the lorry drivers and other motorists, she was just some crazy old lady walking her dogs, possibly going home to sit in front of a fire and grumble bitterly about the world in general and young people in particular. That's what people thought of her now. She'd crossed a line that made her invisible.

When she got home, she slammed the front door behind her, and the dogs jumped with shock.

"Sorry, doggies," she said. "Didn't mean to frighten you, but I've got to do something."

She phoned Marcella.

"I want to go back to work," she said as soon as Marcella answered.

"Hallelujah. When?"

"Tomorrow?"

There was a pause. "You'll need your hair done. Beg your hairdresser to fit you in today. And I'll get a makeup artist to the house in the morning. You need to look amazing."

"Does she do surgery too?" quipped Ingrid.

"Good point," Marcella said. "How are the lines? Do you need Botox?"

Ingrid could quite happily have lived the rest of her life without ever getting another injection in her forehead, but she understood where Marcella was coming from.

"I'm still fine," she said. "My forehead's smooth—it's the rest of me that looks crap."

"See you at nine," Marcella said. "Ingrid—I am so pleased you're doing this."

"I know," murmured Ingrid.

By ten the next morning, she looked a lot more like her old self. First, the blond was back in her hair, newly streaked and blown out with a ton of volumizer on it. She decided she looked like an American television anchor.

Marcella had convinced her to wear her charcoal Armani skirt suit. It was now too big for her because she'd lost weight, but Armani cleverly hid this.

The makeup artist Marcella had sent to the house had managed the impossible. Ingrid's face looked dewy, shiny, and alert, as if she'd had some magic potion to drink.

"God, you're brilliant," Ingrid told the young woman when she'd seen herself in the mirror. "You're a miracle worker."

"I can be when I have a lovely canvas to work on," the woman said.

Ingrid had been about to make a joke about the wrinkles in

the canvas, but decided against it. There was self-deprecating, and then there was self-destructive.

Driving through the gates of the television studio, Ingrid felt anxious and shaky, that same jittery feeling she'd had returning to work after the children were born. It was the same, she supposed: death, birth, they were all linked. Great events that rocked your world and left it changed utterly. She wasn't sure if she had the mental strength to go in and say hello to everyone cheerily, as if she'd just been away on a two-week holiday instead of for three awful months. Yet it was important that she do just that. If Ingrid was going to come back, everyone needed to know. As Marcella had told her—although Ingrid knew it damn well herself—perception was everything in their business.

Three months off with Joan filling in for her, strictly on a temporary basis, was just about reasonable. Any longer, and it might be considered career suicide.

The office even smelled the same, she realized, as she quietly walked in. It smelled of coffee, croissants, a myriad of perfumes, and that elusive but unmistakable scent of people rushing around. Not sweat, but energy. She'd missed it.

"Oh my God, Ingrid!"

There were screams of delight, and then people's voices dropped a little, as if they were remembering why she hadn't been there.

"Oh, Ingrid," people said sadly.

"We missed you," said Jeri, the production assistant, and hugged her.

Ingrid thought of Jeri receiving all those red roses on Valentine's Day, almost the last day of Ingrid's old life. She hoped the romance was still working, for Jeri's sake.

"Great to see you back," said Martin.

She wondered how his difficult divorce was going. "You too, Martin."

She went from desk to desk, talking, smiling, and not lying when people said, "How are you doing?"

There was no point beaming and saying, "Oh, wonderful,"

which was what some people seemed to expect after three
months' grieving.

Instead, she said, "I'm doing okay," and all the while she
thought, If only they knew. . . .

And then standing in front of her was Gloria, who was in on
her plan.

"Ingrid, wonderful to have you back at last. We missed you,"
said Gloria, and everyone nodded in agreement.

"It's wonderful to be back," Ingrid said, and walked into her
office as if she had never been away.

"I mean it, it really is terrific to have you back," Gloria said
when the door was shut. "The place was half-dead without you."

Ingrid's office looked different. It had been painted, and the
desk had been shifted to face in a different direction.

"I hope you don't mind, but I thought it would be difficult
to come back and see everything exactly as you'd left it," Gloria
began. "It would be like it had been before. . . ."

It looked almost like a different office. A new place for a fresh
start. Ingrid loved it.

"Thank you." She grabbed Gloria's hand. "It's wonderful."

"Phew, I wasn't sure," Gloria said. "We could put it all back the
way it was before, it would only take an hour—"

"I don't want it the way it was before," Ingrid said quickly.
Nothing would ever be the same.

"Ingrid, how wonderful to see you!"

Jack, the head of current affairs, got to his feet and came
around from behind his desk to shake her hand gravely. Ingrid
turned her star quality on full blast and gave him her most glittering professional smile. "It's lovely to see you, Jack."

"You look fabulous," he said.

Ingrid was aware that the look she presented was more artifice
than anything else, but she was happy with that. She wanted a little piece of her life back, just a sliver. Most of it was gone—it had
died with David and his locked drawers—but there was still one
part that she could access and pretend that nothing had happened,

in a way she couldn't with Ethan and Molly. Here in the television studio, she could pretend it was all the same; and for now, that would have to be enough.

"Thank you, Jack." Ingrid kept smiling. She'd never liked Jack and she was entirely sure that he returned the favor, but they had worked together quite well. Joan, who was ready to hop into her shoes, would be much more his type of news presenter: young, malleable, and willing to go along to his parties like a pet, tamed and ready to be on show. Ingrid had never been that person. She wasn't going to be now, either, but she was prepared to give a little to get what she wanted.

"You look good too, Jack," she said. "How's the handicap, still in single figures?"

This approach always worked; Jack was a golf fanatic and he liked talking about his game.

"Oh, you know, I don't get much chance to play these days," he said.

Liar, thought Ingrid, who knew damn well, via Gloria, that Jack played three times a week—the working week, that is. One rule for the boys and one rule for the girls. She wondered how many female executives got to skip work three times a week.

"You've been so kind with compassionate leave," she added. "It was wonderful, I really needed it. But I'm ready now." Another lie.

"You're sure you want to come back?" said Jack.

Ingrid gave him the megawatt smile she saved for television and said, "Of course, Jack, that's what I'm here to talk about."

"How was it?" asked Gloria when Ingrid had made it safely back to her own office and shut the door.

"Okay," said Ingrid tightly.

"Just okay?"

"I hope I haven't left it too late."

"Don't be silly," said Gloria. "Of course you haven't, Ingrid. You *are* the show. Every week we're getting hundreds of e-mails and letters wondering when you're coming back. I've not been able to deal with them all."

"The people who write the e-mails don't run current affairs," Ingrid said. "That's what this is about. It's also about the fact that Joan has an agent, an agent who's very friendly with Jack."

Ingrid had never had an agent, mainly because when she'd started on her television career the talent didn't have agents; but now everybody did. She had stuck to managing her own career, with a little help from David when it came to the numbers. He was always able to draw up fantastic proposals for salaries. But just what had he been thinking when he was drawing up those proposals? she wondered bleakly. His betrayal still hurt so much. Most of the time she tried not to let the pain in, tried just to think that David was gone and that she had to cope without him. But sometimes it got past her, the absolute torment of knowing that not only was he gone but he'd betrayed her too, and she would never be able to find out why.

"What's the plan now?" Gloria asked.

"Well, I'm going to ease myself in gently," Ingrid told her assistant. "That's the way I put it to Jack. I didn't want to make it sound like I was taking over the planet, so I said I'd come in, see how everything is, and start working properly next week."

"Carlos wants you to come along to today's editorial meeting," Gloria said.

Ingrid nodded. In for a penny . . .

It was like she'd never been away, except for the presence of Joan, who was more groomed than Ingrid remembered. Her hair was blonder, sleeker, and her clothes were sharper. She sat at the exact other end of the boardroom table and watched Ingrid the way Wile E. Coyote watched Road Runner.

When did I become the enemy? Ingrid stored it up to discuss with Marcella later. She could remember mentoring Joan a few years ago, when Joan came into the show after being at the coalface as the station's court reporter. Joan had been eager then, fond of wearing anoraks to fend off the cold of live outside broadcasts, and admiring of Ingrid. Not anymore. She wanted Ingrid's job.

The queen is dead, long live the queen, Ingrid thought. Well, this queen was very much alive. And would kick if necessary.

The first story was about the energy crisis, although Martin, who'd clearly had a going-over from his wife's divorce lawyer, had a solution to the problem: "The venomous soon-to-be-ex-wife power supply," he said balefully. "Who needs nuclear energy when you have first wives going nuclear all on their own? It's an endless supply of rage. Could power a whole country."

"Martin, enough," groaned Jeri.

"You wait," he snapped, "until Mr. Perfect Triathlon says he made a mistake, that you probably shouldn't have ever got together, but at least you've never had kids and could you possibly be civilized about the breakup. . . . Then you'll lose it."

"Martin!" Carlos rarely raised his voice, but when he did, people listened.

"Sorry." Martin got up and left the room.

Ingrid stared at his departing back. Did all spurned wives turn into nuclear power stations of fury? Would she have done the same if David had given her the option and left instead of dying?

She'd have hated to become that kind of person.

The meeting ended with a discussion about a forthcoming interview with the Minister for Finance. Without a word being said, everyone turned to Ingrid as they spoke about this. She knew it was because she had the most experience interviewing him; she'd done it many times. She could see Joan's face, cold with anger. Ingrid was back and had slipped effortlessly into her old role without anybody saying "But what about Joan?"

Once, Ingrid might have gone to Joan afterward to discuss this, but she had no energy left in her for such things. If Joan stuck around long enough, she would have the job one day. Ingrid herself knew she didn't have forever. But right now, she needed it more than Joan did.

"It's yourself!" the mailroom man exclaimed, catching sight of her as she crossed reception on her way out. "We've got a pile of post for you in the mailroom. Bags of it." He suddenly appeared to remember what the post was likely to say. "I'm sorry for your loss, Ingrid," he added. "You've been missed around here."

"Thank you," she said, and she meant it.

Today, she was able to be grateful for even the small things. She'd come back to work, she had a big interview to do next week, and people had missed her. It wasn't everything she wanted, but it was enough for today.

Fifteen

Life seems so long when you're in the middle of it, but when you know it's going to end soon, you realize how little time we have on earth. Don't waste it.

Kitty, *Brendan, and* Charlie sat in a box in the theater, waiting for the curtain to come up. It was the first night of Iseult's new play, *Dancing with Their Lives*; the theater was groaning at the seams, and Iseult had arranged for an enormous bottle of champagne in an ice bucket to be delivered to the box, a bottle that Kitty had made Brendan open as soon as they'd arrived.

However, Iseult, the guest of honor, wasn't with them. She was backstage talking to the cast and the director. Kitty was quite cross that she'd only been allowed backstage for five minutes before being gently, but nonetheless firmly, ushered out by Iseult. Charlie had been surprised to see her mother return so quickly.

"You weren't long," she said, taking in her mother's flushed cheeks, which matched the burgundy raw-silk dress she was wearing.

Her mother looked great, she had to hand it to her. Nobody would have guessed that a few weeks ago, Kitty had been hobbling around after breaking her hip, devoid of makeup and despondent.

Tonight, her hair was a triumph of the hairdresser's art, with lots of little Medusa curls clustered around her face. Her makeup looked amazing, and Charlie figured her mother had definitely had some cosmetic work done, although she would undoubtedly deny it if asked.

"Good genes, taking care of myself," she liked to say if anyone asked.

Whatever, the effect of Botox or fillers was now slightly ruined by the irritated look on her mother's face.

"There's some sort of palaver going on backstage," Kitty said crossly, settling herself in the box like the Queen Mother at a command performance. "They don't want outsiders there. As if I'm an outsider!"

Behind her, Charlie and Brendan exchanged a grin. Charlie reached out and took his hand. It was lovely being here with Brendan. He calmed her so much. She had been dreading tonight. Not that she wasn't looking forward to seeing the play itself—Iseult was so talented, and the play was bound to be fascinating. No, it was more that she knew her mother would be in I'm-the-playwright's-mother mode, with attendant airs, graces, and tantrums.

Kitty had been delirious with joy earlier in the week when a profile of Iseult was printed in the *Irish Times*. In it, Iseult was quoted uttering the immortal words: "My mother has been such an inspiration."

When Charlie and Brendan picked Kitty up from her house to take her to the theater, the cutting had been taped to the fridge. She'd probably frame it, Charlie thought crossly, and then was angry with herself for sounding bitter and resentful.

Detach with love. She had to let go. Her mother's relationship with Iseult was their business, and if it was strong, lucky for them. Neither of them had what she had, which was a wonderful marriage and a wonderful son.

Her new mantra was that you couldn't change how people carried on or thought, you could only change how you reacted to them.

Well, that was the theory. No matter how often she told herself these things, in reality it was different.

"Relax," Brendan mouthed to her across the box.

She stuck her tongue out at him good-humoredly, and he did the same back. What was it about being in Kitty's presence that made them feel so juvenile? Charlie could think of no other circumstance where she'd dream of sticking her tongue out.

It was the Kitty effect, for sure. Brendan was amazing. He tolerated her so well, given that he had nothing in his past to help him understand someone like that. His family was totally normal.

At the weekend, they'd been at his parents' house for Sunday lunch, and it had been so relaxing. Jenny and Stephen Fallon were retired schoolteachers. Stephen was a quiet man who said little and smiled often, like Brendan himself. Jenny was a lovely, strong woman who'd reared six children and gone out to work, which hadn't been easy. She was a stalwart of the local church, a fabulous cook, and very involved in her children's and grandchildren's lives, but never in an overbearing way.

Needless to say, Kitty hated her.

"She's very pious, isn't she?" Kitty would say. "And the hair. You'd think she could do something with her hair!"

Jenny's hair was short and wispy and never saw the inside of a hairdresser's salon.

Kitty's dislike of Jenny had upset Charlie for years, but not anymore. The gratitude journal must be working, Charlie decided. Reading back over things she'd written helped her understand them. She now understood, for example, that her mother's dislike of Jenny was more to do with jealousy than anything else. Kitty was always going on about women's rights and the importance of work, yet she hadn't worked outside the home after getting married.

Jenny had raised her family while succeeding at a full-time career that saw her ultimately become vice principal of a national school. It wasn't superiority that made Kitty dislike her, Charlie thought; it was a sense of inferiority.

"Is this damned play ever going to start!" snapped Kitty now.

Yes, Charlie decided, her mother was merely upset at having been sent away from the backstage excitement. She was like a child denied fun. Understanding did help.

By the end of Act Two, Charlie had forgotten her mother's temper and was riveted to the stage. The central character of the play was a dying woman who was looking back over a life that took in one world war and many deaths, marriages, and love affairs through a series of flashbacks. Her family was at her bedside, and through each person's eyes, Iseult's play examined their relationship with their mother. The play had such depth and the actors were so marvelous that Charlie found it hard to remember the funny stories about rehearsals that Iseult had told them. All those things were forgotten as she stared at the stage and watched this amazing story unfold in front of her.

One strand of the play that absolutely fascinated her was the story of the youngest daughter, the person who sobbed most at her dying mother's bedside. Slowly it became clear that she didn't share the same father as the other children.

Her father was the mother's true love—a man she had to love in secret but adored more than anyone else. That, Iseult seemed to be saying, was why there was this special bond between mother and child.

"Oh, I see," breathed Charlie out loud, although nobody heard her because everyone was watching the stage.

The theater seemed to recede, and she thought suddenly of the first time she'd had an ultrasound when she'd been pregnant with Mikey.

Brendan had been beside her, holding her hand, the two of them watching the screen as the sonographer traced the shape of the baby inside Charlie's womb. On the screen, the picture looked like lots of random speckled dots; and Charlie, desperate to see what her baby looked like, couldn't work it out.

"Now, there, that's the head. See?" said the sonographer, reaching out and touching the screen.

Instantly, it had all made sense. Charlie could see her baby's fragile face, then one little hand stretched out with tiny stubby fingers, and the legs, all curled up.

Charlie had got the picture. Like now. Iseult might claim, as she had in the *Irish Times* interview, that she was writing about a fictional family, but there was something at the core of this play that was very dear to her. She might convince everyone else that it was fiction. In fact, she might believe that herself. But even though no other character and no other scenario in the play bore any resemblance to Iseult's life, Charlie was quite sure that her sister's heroine was really Iseult herself. Which meant that she and Charlie weren't both Anthony Nelson's children.

The producers had taken a suite in the Merrion Hotel for the after-show party, but before the cast, director, and playwright even got there, drink was flowing in the stars' dressing rooms.

Charlie hadn't wanted to go to the dressing rooms; she was still reeling from what she'd seen onstage. Was that what Iseult and her mother had been hiding from her all these years? Was that the simple, crude answer to why she had no loving relationship with her mother? Had Iseult's father meant more to Kitty than Charlie's had? When had Iseult found out, and why hadn't she shared the knowledge with Charlie? Charlie burned with anger and impotent fury. To think of all the years she'd spent worrying about pleasing her mother, trying to be the perfect daughter, and it had all been in vain. There was nothing she could have done to be Kitty's favorite: that role had been assigned by the simple, unchangeable circumstances of their births.

"I don't feel well, I've got a headache. I'm going home," she told her mother as they left their box. She couldn't face looking at Kitty for the rest of the night.

"Nonsense!" said Kitty, refusing to brook any opposition. "I've got some painkillers in my bag, you'll be fine—come on." And she dragged Charlie along behind her, with Brendan following.

Charlie looked back at Brendan helplessly.

"Are you all right?" he said, looking worried.

"No," Charlie mouthed at him. "I'm not."

She wanted to sit down and cry in the middle of the theater, but there was no hope of that because Kitty had her in her grasp, a surprisingly strong grasp for somebody who not that long ago had been very frail. Kitty blazed a path backstage, where the triumphant sound of champagne corks popping mingled with shrieks of excited relief after a successful first night.

"They loved it, loved it!" roared somebody.

"They loved *us*!" echoed somebody else.

"You were fabulous!"

"No, *you* were fabulous!"

"Was I really, darling?"

Charlie had never resented Iseult's success for a moment. Still didn't. But tonight, she didn't have the heart to cheer this particular play, still in shock at having an important secret about her life revealed to her in front of hundreds of other people. If only Iseult had told her about it beforehand; if only Kitty had.

As soon as Kitty spotted Iseult's tall figure, her blond Valkyrie head visible above so many other people's, she ran over to her, shrieking, "Darling, it was breathtaking."

And Charlie watched them embrace, feeling angry and excluded.

"Mrs. Nelson, you must be so proud," said a woman with a notebook in her hand and a photographer beside her. The notebook was pressed close to Kitty's face, as if it were a microphone.

"Yes, I am," Kitty began. "It's nights like this that you remember the hardship of bringing up a child alone."

Even Iseult looked a bit stunned at this. Their mother had hardly reared them alone. Iseult had been eighteen when Anthony moved out. And why "child" and not "children"? It was as though Charlie didn't exist. She felt angry tears prickle.

"I am so very, very proud of my daughter," Kitty went on, flicking back a bit of hair so she could elongate her neck for the photographer. It was too easy to look pudgy in a close-up.

"Proud of both your daughters, obviously," said the reporter smoothly, catching sight of Charlie.

Kitty blinked as the flash went off. "Well, yes, of course, both," she said, entirely wrong-footed. She flicked a mascara-lidded gaze over at Charlie, who turned and stalked off.

"Mother!" hissed Iseult.

Kitty kept a smile glued on her face. "Yes, darling?"

Teeth only slightly gritted with the long practice of many years talking to journalists, Iseult managed to steer her mother out from under the newspaperwoman's nose.

"Excuse us," Kitty said, still smiling her glued-on smile.

"Mother!" Iseult said when they'd reached a nook where nobody could hear them. "What did you say that for? Look at poor Charlie; you know it must be hard for her when everyone is congratulating me. You can't say that you're proud of me and talk as though you only have one daughter with her standing beside you!"

"Don't be ridiculous," Kitty said. "She didn't mind." But she wasn't so sure. Charlie had looked very upset.

Iseult saw someone she needed to talk to and moved off, leaving Kitty feeling something quite alien to her: guilt.

She didn't do guilt. It was a complete waste of time. She and Mairead used to talk about it all the time, usually over Kitty's favorite vodka martinis.

"Why do guilt?" Mairead would say, waggling her glass for a refill. "Only women are supposed to feel guilt."

The reason they could talk about guilt so successfully was that they both rarely felt it.

But now Kitty did. Charlie had looked stricken. Kitty hadn't meant that she was only proud of Iseult; of course she was proud of both of her daughters. But Iseult's success was so much more obvious—people could see it. That did make it extra special, slightly more wonderful. Besides, Charlie was probably just going to get headache tablets and she'd be back in a moment to drive Kitty to the party. It would all be fine, Kitty knew it.

Charlie didn't come back. Kitty had to hitch a ride with Iseult, who hadn't brought her own car and was being ferried around with the producers in a big black limousine, which surprisingly barely had room for Kitty to squash in. She felt quite affronted, particularly when, just before they got into the car, the journalist she'd been talking to earlier tried to corner her to talk about her feminist days, and Iseult shuffled her along murmuring, "Not now, Mother, you've done enough damage!"

"What do you mean, 'damage'?" Kitty demanded, when they were packed side by side in the limo.

"That woman writes a gossip column, and anything you say will be twisted," Iseult snapped. "This evening is supposed to be about the play, not real-life warring families. It's been bad enough, you implying that you're only proud of one daughter."

"Why didn't you warn me about her?" said Kitty crossly. "It's not as if I haven't talked to the press before. I know what to say."

"Oh, Mother," sighed Iseult. "The only time you talked to the press was when you were a cog in the feminist wheel. You were hardly the president. That was then, this is now!"

At the party, Kitty felt adrift. It would have been nicer to be there with Charlie. Brendan and Charlie wouldn't have known anyone either; they were hardly fashionable people. But Kitty could have hung about with them and started conversations with people who caught her eye. It was always easier to join conversations when you were already with people; it looked lonely and sad if you arrived on your own.

In addition, she was disappointed because people didn't seem to recognize her. They should know her—her face had been quite famous in the seventies. True, she hadn't been one of the leaders of the feminist movement, but she'd been so glamorous and the papers had always liked to take her picture when they'd been doing features on women's liberation. "You make a change from all the ugly auld women's libbers who want to burn their bras," one photographer had said winningly. She had been important; she was somebody. But no one here seemed to know it.

She looked around the party in disgust. Who did she know, apart from Iseult—who had long since gone off chatting, smiling, flirting, doing all the things Kitty herself would have done in the same position. For the first time in a long while, Kitty felt her age. No, she felt more than her age. She felt decrepit and unloved.

She made it over to the bar, where one of the cast members was camping it up happily, doling out drinks and banter.

"Vodka martini," snarled Kitty, leaning on the bar.

"You'll have to give me a kiss first," he growled.

Kitty glared at him. "Consider yourself kissed," she said. "No, change that. Consider yourself fucked. Now, give me a bloody martini!"

He gulped. "Coming right up."

Kitty stood at the bar and drank her martini. She wanted a cigarette, but smoking indoors was now forbidden by the health and safety fascists, and she felt too tired to go out onto the terrace. Why did she feel so tired all the time? It wasn't fair. In her mind, she was still eighteen and raring to go, adept at throwing come-hither glances at any man who passed her way.

If someone had asked the eighteen-year-old Kitty what she'd be doing when she was in her sixties, she'd probably have shrieked with horror. She'd be dead by then, she'd have said breezily. Forty was ancient; sixty-plus was a hideous thought. Sixty was ancient Aunt Tilda with her mothy old mink, the hint of thermal underwear visible beneath her blouses, and a reddened complexion from being outdoors in all weathers deadheading flowers and separating the irises.

Tilda was mouthy, bossy, and to be avoided at all times. The second martini—super-strength, because the idiot at the bar had finally copped on—made it all clearer to Kitty. Normally vodka didn't make her maudlin, but tonight it did. Kitty wondered if *she* had turned into Tilda. She wasn't the sexy dame of her youth: she was the irritable woman who'd managed to upset both her daughters. Well, one far more than the other.

Bloody guilt. It wouldn't go away. Kitty found her cigarettes and lit up. Let someone try throwing her out for smoking in the hotel. Anyone foolish enough to try clearly didn't know Kitty Nelson very well.

Sixteen

The Past

KITTY

*W*hen *Kitty was* young, men were said to be after only one thing. If you gave it to them, you were entirely ruined, and only foolish women did so. Even in the slightly rarefied and unconventional atmosphere of Cardinal Martinez House, the boarding school that Kitty attended, everyone believed this to be the case. Go the whole way with a man at your peril.

Kitty was reasonably aware of how animals procreated. After all, someone who came from a farm and had older brothers could hardly be ignorant of that. So she knew what this was all about. But what she couldn't understand was the power the sexual act appeared to give men. They were in charge of it all, not women.

"Why is it that men are always supposed to be looking for sex?" she said to her friend Dervla. "It's like we're cattle, stupid things who don't know how to say no. Or"—she paused, because this was a very shocking idea to even consider—"is it all a ploy to stop women considering that we might enjoy it ourselves?"

Dervla and Kitty were friends partly because they were on the same wavelength, but also because they were considered by the school staff to be the biggest troublemakers in their class and therefore spent a lot of time together, sitting outside classroom doors, having broken some rule or another.

"You never hear anything about anyone enjoying it," Dervla said thoughtfully.

"That's part of the conspiracy," Kitty said with spirit. Dervla was on her side. "They tell us it's supposed to be no fun at all, like they say about having a drink or a cigarette. No fun at all. But what if it's great fun?"

Kitty knew of a girl from home who'd gone the whole way and actually had a baby. She'd never met the girl, because Kitty was the daughter of a wealthy farmer and the girl was from the cottages down by the railway where, Kitty's mother remarked with disdain, "they breed like rabbits." There didn't seem to be much sign of anyone enjoying sex there, despite the obvious evidence of it going on. When Kitty went past the cottages, there was an air of squalor and poverty about many of them. They were not like most of the rest of the town, where people took pride in their homes and gardens.

Once Kitty saw the girl with her baby and, for one moment, thought of going up to her and saying "Hello" or "well done." Kitty couldn't imagine the hell at home if she became pregnant.

But the girl looked bone-tired, with untidy fair hair and shabby clothes, and the baby was crying loudly, a noise that gave Kitty a headache. She gave a half-smile and walked away. There was no sign from the girl that an important step for women had been made either in having sex or in having a baby outside the marriage department. Kitty overheard a friend of her mother's saying that the parish priest had been down at the girl's door, hammering on it and demanding that her parents cast her out or else they'd be in on the sin. Incredibly, they'd refused. Kitty knew without a shadow of a doubt that if the priest had hammered on her parents' door, they'd have shoved her and her pregnant belly out the door like a shot.

When Kitty was nineteen, she got a job in the office typing pool with her father's accountant in Dublin. There had been war when she said she wanted to leave home, particularly after the trouble she'd got into in France the year before. She'd visited Bordeaux on an exchange program and had begun a lifelong love affair with all things French. A few girls from school had gone too, but it didn't seem as if they had any fun at all; too prim and proper, they'd been. All of them determined to be indoors whenever Madame said they had to be. Blind obedience to rules held no interest for Kitty. Rules were made to be broken.

Madame had thrown her out when she discovered that Kitty had seduced her "sweet and innocent" seventeen-year-old son, Charles. Charles wasn't the slightest bit sweet or innocent, but his mother thought he was, and that was what counted.

"Out!" she shrieked, shoving Kitty and all her belongings out the door. "You 'ave to leave. We never vant to see you again."

Charles, the coward, had looked miserably out an upstairs window as Kitty trailed down the drive, carrying her suitcase. His papa was peering out another window, looking equally miserable.

Kitty had had high hopes for Papa, too. She fancied the idea of an older man; but it was not to be.

It was then that Kitty went to Paris for the first time. Paris in 1959 was where it was at. There was no provincial carrying on like at home in Ireland, where people you barely knew would comment on your behavior in the street because they were "older and better," and hence perfectly entitled to tell you off for smoking or wearing red lipstick. In Paris, you could smoke, wear red lipstick, and kiss whomever you wanted wherever you wanted, and nobody took the slightest bit of notice. Kitty fell instantly in love with the city. She was also broke and, after two weeks, ended up at home with her wings clipped.

"You're a little tramp!" her mother had hissed. Mother had received a letter from Madame about Kitty, leaving her in no doubt as to what had gone on. "Did you have relations with that boy?"

Kitty considered lying, but decided against it. Truth was important. "So what if I did?" she said. "We were careful."

Charles had been more than careful; he'd been wonderful. Kitty wrote Dervla a letter telling her what they'd suspected all those years ago: "Sex is fantastic!!!"

When Kitty made it plain that she was going to Dublin to work with or without her parents' help, they relented, and her father found her both a job and a room in a house where other nicely behaved young girls lived with a widowed ex-teacher who had strict rules and permitted no carrying on. Nora Slattery foresaw trouble with Kitty, but it was hard to pin anything on her. Kitty always appeared to be home at curfew, and she was always off to work on time in the mornings, hair perfect and wearing a nice, if a little too tight, twinset.

But there was *something* there, Nora knew.

At work, Kitty engaged in mild, girlish flirtation with the senior partner, but she reserved her serious seduction skills for the junior partner, the very handsome and very married Mr. Lynch. With Mr. Lynch's admiring eyes upon her, Kitty's skirts got shorter, her sweaters got tighter, and her lipstick got redder. She didn't bother too much with the work itself, much to the chagrin of the dignified spinster who ran the typing pool. Miss Roche never lost her temper when Kitty arrived late back from lunch. Miss Roche had seen it all. Young girls came and they went. Once they got married, they left for good.

"It's not fair that we have to stop working just because we get married," Kitty pointed out. "Most of the men in the office are married, and they keep working."

"Married women have to look after their husbands," said Miss Roche, who'd never had the chance to marry and therefore enjoyed the one area of 1960s society where not being married was a positive.

"Why can't men look after themselves?" said Kitty crossly.

"That's women's work," Miss Roche said.

"Rubbish," snorted Kitty. "As if a man can't cook if he puts his mind to it."

Kitty's favorite reading at the time was a battered copy of *Married Love*, which explained the mysteries of the female menstrual cycle and when it was safe to make love without getting pregnant. Unfortunately, Mr. Lynch's favorite reading was *Fanny Hill*, the eighteenth-century erotic masterpiece, which meant they failed to pay proper attention to the advice Kitty was getting in *Married Love*.

With Mr. Lynch's car parked down by the beach and the dome light on, they sipped whiskey from the bottle and read passages of *Fanny Hill* to each other. Kitty felt that she was finally reaching the glory of her time in Paris again. This was what life should be about: being wild and free, avant-garde, enjoying fabulous lovemaking with a fabulous man. Who cared if he was married? Such strictures were for the old guard, and Kitty was one of the new, modern people.

"I'll pull out in time," gasped Mr. Lynch. Kitty didn't care what he did, as long as that glorious rippling feeling continued arching through her.

When her period failed to come and her breasts swelled up painfully, Kitty cursed *Fanny Hill*, the beach, and *Married Love*'s so called "safe period."

"Are you insane? I'm not having a baby with you," hissed Mr. Lynch, looking less like an Adonis and more like a man on the verge of apoplexy. "Get yourself sorted out. London's the place. You can get it"—he paused and gave her the gimlet stare she'd only ever seen him give a very rude client—"*fixed* over there."

"*Fixed?*" Kitty demanded. "That's your baby you're talking about."

"How do I know who else you were sleeping with?"

Kitty stared him down. "Nobody, you bastard," she hissed.

"You're the one with the bastard, not me," he snapped. "What about that green young college bloke you go out with? It could be his."

She'd told him that she'd never slept with Anthony Nelson. Anthony had been raised to respect women; he treated his elder sister like a lady. He would have passed out with shock if Kitty had laid a hand on his knee, never mind any higher.

"You talk about this, and I'll tell everyone you're a little tart and you've been after me for months. Who do you think they'll believe?" he taunted her.

Kitty didn't see the point in answering. It seemed he wasn't a modern person after all. Kitty thought of her parents and the shame they'd feel if she arrived home pregnant.

It was time to phone Anthony. They might go on a date, a long one that ended up on the beach.

Kitty's little girl, Iseult, and Lisette's little girl, Saffron, went to the same nursery school, and Kitty, Lisette, and some of the other mothers had got into the habit of having coffee together in the mornings after they dropped off the kids.

It was Kitty's turn to play hostess, and she'd left Betty Friedan's *The Feminine Mystique* open on the coffee table so that perhaps they could all talk about the ideas in it. Betty was right—women weren't the only ones who could iron and cook. Women had so much power in them, but the patriarchal society had kept them in chains. It wasn't fair. Women like Kitty had so much promise; yet here she was, stuck at home with nothing to do but buy luncheon meat for Anthony's sandwiches and keep the house clean. She adored Iseult, who was funny, clever, and the image of Kitty herself, but there had to be more to life, hadn't there?

Lisette didn't want to talk about books, but had no problem talking about patriarchy.

She had three children and a husband who felt he deserved a medal if he occasionally made a pot of tea. " 'There you go,' he says whenever he does anything, *anything*. And if he puts a cup away or sets his plate on the drainer, he expects me to thank him."

"You think that's bad?" snarled Phyllis, a onetime teacher who'd had to resign because of the state decree that female civil servants had to give up their jobs when they married: the so-called marriage bar—"yeah, called that because it drives you to the bar for a drink," she used to say. "Seamus told me that if I budgeted the housekeeping money better, I'd be able to buy myself a few fripperies. All because I said I was fed up with having nothing nice to wear, ever, and that I'd be the only one at the office party in the same dress for the fourth year in a row."

Kitty was conscious that Anthony wasn't in this band of smug husbands who thought their contribution to married life stopped at earning money. He often cooked, saying it relaxed him, and he was good about tidying up afterward, because he knew he used four times more saucepans than she would. Kitty wasn't a fan of cooking, and she was fond of the dinner-in-a-pot where you threw a bit of cheap meat, vegetables, and stock in together and cooked it slowly. The *Thrifty Housewife* book said it should turn out tender and delicious. Kitty found that cheap meat still tasted like leather no matter what she did with it, but the recipe only used one pot and that was the whole point.

Still, Anthony was a man, responsible for slowing down her progress in the world. Without him, she'd have achieved something big, like Simone de Beauvoir or another woman of note.

The women talked about another mother who was pregnant with her fifth child.

"Poor cow," said Phyllis. Phyllis had two kids and felt that was enough, but neither the Church nor Seamus agreed with her.

Seamus came from a long line of devout Catholics and thought interfering with fertility was like dancing with the devil. Phyllis had tried to get the contraceptive pill from her doctor on the grounds of regulating her cycle, but he too had turned out to be of the doctrinaire variety.

"Mrs. Maguire, children are God's gifts to us. It is against God's law to tamper with procreation. I'm surprised at you. . . ."

Phyllis had retreated before he got going properly.

"We should get it abroad. London, that's the place for it," said Kitty. She was scared at the thought of getting pregnant for the second time. She hadn't messed up on the safe period again, but it was tricky.

"Isn't the Pill bad for you?" wondered a new woman in the group.

The others glared at her.

"What's bad for you is dropping a baby every year," snapped Kitty. "One's enough for me, thank you very much."

* * *

Kitty called the conservatory her space. It wasn't much of a conservatory, more of a lean-to with pretensions, but it had a glass
roof and plants, and it was where she kept her books—*The Female Eunuch* and some of her Virago Modern Classics. She'd read
them all but hadn't found anything new she wanted for ages. One
of the mothers had made the fatal mistake of giving her a bodice-
ripping historical romance to read, and Kitty had been spitting at
the next coffee morning.

"It's a fairy story, for God's sake," she'd shrieked. "That's
what's wrong with women today; we were all raised on fairy tales,
and most of those are totally misogynistic. The men are always in
charge of things in these books. Ludicrous, that's what it is!"

Things had never been quite the same at the regular coffee
mornings since the great orgasm talk, when the speaker that Lisette and Kitty organized, a woman named Pandora, concluded
her presentation by passing around small mirrors and inviting
people to find a quiet corner or, if they were totally comfortable
with their femininity, "just do it in the middle of the room," and
examine their female beauty.

"You mean, look up my you-know-what with a mirror?"
squawked a girl called Rita.

"Naming your body correctly gives it dignity," intoned Pandora, clearly used to such interruptions. "Embrace your woman-
hood; admire your labia, your vulva, and your vagina."

"Thought a vulva was a car," sniggered someone else, who'd
drunk too much and kept dropping the little mirror on the floor.

Even Kitty, four martinis and a cigar along—mere coffee wasn't
enough for this morning—wasn't entirely sure about the self-
examination bit. It wasn't that she hadn't seen herself; she had.
During one of her early love affairs, she had studied herself using
a cheval mirror, considering what she saw with the thought of the
man in question looking at it later. But that was different, in the
heat of lust. She was no prude—she'd had lovers, and she knew
it was all in working order in that department—but she felt that

Georgia O'Keeffe's painted flower versions of female sex organs were prettier than the real thing. Men's bodies—now, they were beautiful.

Kitty was bored, she realized. Bored with her life and bored with not having a job. But, as her friend Mairead bluntly pointed out to her one day, she wasn't really qualified to do anything.

Only Mairead could get away with saying such a thing, Kitty reflected.

Mairead was not the sort of woman to attend a ladies' coffee morning. She worked in an architect's office, kept all the architects doing what they were supposed to be doing, and knew she was generally considered a bit of a bitch.

"Women are called bitches if they're strong and powerful," she remarked. "Men are just ambitious. Talk about double standards!"

The conversation about Kitty's boredom and lack of practical work skills was now over. Anyway, Kitty consoled herself, Anthony earned enough that she didn't have to work. As per her feminist beliefs, they had a joint bank account, and there was never any talk of Anthony "giving" her money for the housekeeping.

Kitty had once tallied up how much a housekeeper/laundress would cost to keep their house running and shocked Anthony with the amount.

"That's what I should be paid," she'd said proudly.

Anthony hadn't argued at all.

"Unlike most men, he clearly recognizes your worth," said Mairead.

But Kitty wasn't so sure. Still, the Nelson family had enough money to get by, and now that the children were older, she might go to college as a mature student and get herself a degree. That would be exciting.

She was better off without him.

She'd find somebody much better.

The words echoed in Kitty's ears as she sat alone and miserable in her kitchen. They were what her friends had said when Anthony packed his bags and left.

"A woman needs a man like a fish needs a bicycle!" That was from Gwen, who loved slogans and was going through a phase of displaying words on her T-shirts that most people were shocked to read, never mind say out loud.

"Kitty, you're fabulous; you were tied to him for far too long." That was from Mairead, who thought that marriage was a form of legal slavery and couldn't understand why women put themselves through it in the first place.

Kitty blocked out the fact that, mere months before, Mairead had been delighted with Anthony for not behaving like the average chauvinist pig and for appreciating Kitty's worth.

What was wrong with living in sin? demanded Mairead. Sin was entirely fabulous—at least, it was fabulous the way Mairead explained it. Kitty always felt it was a little disloyal to think it, but Mairead and her boyfriend, Timmy, didn't *look* like wild, free souls who were at it like knives every night, dancing around their semidetached house in the nude, having rampant sex so loud that the neighbors called the police in alarm.

Still, if Mairead reckoned that living in sin was where it was at, maybe she was right. Maybe Kitty had made a huge error in marrying Anthony all those years ago when she'd been pregnant with Iseult. But Anthony had had a good job; he'd offered a solution. Kitty had always been pragmatic.

"Find yourself a decent man who understands who you are and doesn't want to live his life within the confines of a patriarchal society," Mairead counseled. "He'll need to be the sort of fella who'll take on the kids as well."

This, Mairead added, could be the big stumbling block.

Mairead wasn't that keen on children herself. She never went on with any of that "Timmy and I weren't blessed with children" malarkey. She saw it as more of a benefit to be without them. You couldn't parcel up a small baby and take it along to a rock festival, could you? Precisely.

Because of that, she didn't quite understand what Kitty was

going through. Mairead might proclaim that Kitty should get herself another man now that Anthony had upped and left her, but who was going to take on a woman with two children? Nobody, that's who.

Iseult was eighteen and Charlotte was fifteen, nearly a grownup, but they still carried on like children. Kitty thought back mistily to when she was eighteen. God, the things she'd done! Her mother hadn't had a clue.

"Mum," a timid voice broke into her reverie. It was Charlotte. If there was one thing Kitty hated above all others, it was timidity, and Charlotte was very timid. Kitty was always trying to knock it out of her. Charlotte took after her father. Not that he'd been timid when it was time to leave, stupid bastard.

"Don't squeak, Charlotte!" she roared. "You're not a mouse."

"I'm sorry, Mum," said Charlotte, sounding even more terrified. "I just wondered about dinner, and I have to get you to sign my homework notebook."

"Sign your homework notebook? What have you done?" demanded Kitty. This was a turnup for the books. Charlotte never normally put a foot out of place, and the signing of homework notebooks was usually a device to alert the parents to some misdemeanor.

"Oh, it's just to say that you got the letters about the Inter Cert mock exam," Charlotte said.

I should have known, thought Kitty. Now, Iseult—there was a girl who was always putting a foot wrong, bless her. She'd been suspended in her final year for giving cheek in English class. Well, she'd been perfectly right to do so, in Kitty's opinion. That mad old bat who taught the class hadn't a clue. It was important that Iseult could express her point of view about what they were studying, and an honest argument, well, that was hardly rude, was it? But the school had been very upset, and so, typically, had Anthony.

"She's got a bit of fire in her belly, that's all. Takes after me. What's wrong with that?" Kitty had demanded.

"Nothing," Anthony had said dully.

She should have known then that he was going to leave her,

should have seen the signs. God knows why the coward didn't do it earlier.

The day he left, she'd been on the verge of telling Anthony that Iseult wasn't his child after all. God, she'd have loved to do it, but a moment of sanity prevailed. All right, Anthony was an old fuddy-duddy, and as he'd believed Iseult was his daughter all these years, he'd undoubtedly stand by her. Probably stoically say fatherhood was about more than biology. But it would be messy if she told him, messy and involving questions about why she'd married him in the first place. And it might affect his willingness to put his hand in his pocket and maintain them all.

"You won't suffer financially," he'd said as he left.

Damn right she wouldn't.

Well, she'd show him, she'd get another man. Mairead was right, that's what she needed—another man and a bit of wild sex. That would show bloody dried-up old Anthony that he should never have left her.

Rex was perfect. Sexy and a bit wild, despite the suit and old school tie. He was also a wonderful lover. They would meet when Rex could escape from the office at lunchtime while Charlie was at school. Kitty had briefly wondered if the neighbors thought it was odd that the handsome man dropped into her house so often in the afternoons, staying for an hour or so, but then she stopped wondering. Let other people with their dull lives think what they liked.

It went wrong, though. One day, they lay in the bed where Anthony used to lie—Kitty liked that; it made her feel better. The sex had been fantastic. She liked this bit too, this lying nude and talking.

Kitty lifted one leg high like a ballerina testing her extension and admired it. Rex admired it too.

"I love your body," he murmured, and ran a hand down her bare leg till he reached the apex of her thighs, where she was still damp for sex. "You're always ready for it, aren't you?"

Kitty's leg lowered a little.

"I hate those women who don't like sex—stupid cows. You're a real woman."

Kitty stretched her calf again, luxuriating in his praise. Rex was the most amazing lover, and praise from him was praise indeed.

"You're almost like a man, do you know that? I think that's what makes you special."

The ballerina leg dropped. "What do you mean?" she demanded.

"You're tough, you're like me—that's a compliment," Rex said. "You're not one of those women who whine that they want to be loved or taken care of—do they have any idea how off-putting that is, that neediness?" He was warming to his theme, and he sat up and reached for his cigarettes. "Want one?"

Kitty sat up too, pulled the sheet over her bare breasts, and took a cigarette. She felt she needed one. The nicotine hit the spot.

"What do they mean, anyway, that 'I need to know what you think' rubbish?" he went on.

Kitty seldom felt out of her depth either talking with men or in bed with them, but she was beginning to feel this scene was leaving her grasp.

"What does *who* mean when they say that?" she asked.

"Oh, this other woman I'm seeing. Well, a girl," he said.

Kitty made a mouselike squeak and pulled the sheet closer. "Girl?" she muttered.

"Don't worry, lover, she's not like you, nothing to you," he added, patting her fondly. "Just a little romance I have going—a man has to settle down sometime. But she's not in your league, Kitty, my love. Doesn't do sex," he said, and smiled wolfishly. "Her mother would kill her, and she'd never be able to go to Holy Communion again. For the love of God, what's her mother got to do with it? Or the Church. It's not like I asked her to screw me on the back pew!"

He seemed to find this hysterically funny. Normally, Kitty liked hearing him laugh. He was a great big bear of a man and his laughter was like a bass drumroll; but now Kitty felt bleakness wash over her. She was his bed person, someone he had sex with, she saw this only too clearly. Because she didn't ask any of the usual female questions, in his eyes she wasn't so much a woman as an honorary man.

Her enjoying sex on the same level as a man meant he didn't need to treat her with any emotional kindness. Enjoying unencumbered sex, which she thought of as striking a blow for her own feminism, made Rex think she wasn't interested in love. She was fine for sex but nothing more.

It was a horrifying thought. Where was the equality legislation now?

Seventeen

Get down on your knees every day and say thank you. Even if you don't feel grateful all the time, practice it, and one day you will appreciate all the good things. And that's one of the greatest gifts of all.

The morning following Iseult's triumphant first night, Charlie used her skill in the makeup department to hide her exhausted face and red-rimmed eyes.

When they'd got home the previous night, she'd sobbed her heart out to Brendan and told him about the implications of the play.

He'd held her tight while she cried. "Your mother really is the limit. She's a crazy woman sometimes," he said, which was shocking, coming from Brendan.

"You've never said anything like that before," Charlie sniffled.

"It's tricky with families," Brendan murmured, kissing the top of her head. "If I moaned about your mother, I'd never be able to take it back. It would always be there. So I don't. But she is a bitch sometimes. I know you want her to be proud of you, Charlie, but you don't need it. You're a much better mother than she's ever been, for a start."

"Am I?"

He held her at arm's length, astonished. "Of course. You're a brilliant mother. You know the way she has a thing about my mother, because she worked and reared all of us at the same time?"

"Yes," said Charlie slowly. They'd never actually talked about this, and she'd nurtured a vain hope that Brendan had never over-heard Kitty's rude mutterings about Jenny.

"I reckon it's the same with you. You show her up because you're such a good mother and she wasn't, despite all her talk of how she gave you and Iseult the chance to be who you wanted to be. That's all crap. She wasn't cut out to have kids; she's far too selfish. But you are, and it kills her to have anyone do anything better than she did."

"Is that what you think?"

Brendan nodded. "Mikey adores you. So do I. I know that might not be enough—"

She stopped him by putting her finger up to his mouth. "It is enough," she said. "Absolutely enough for me."

"And the only way you're going to know the truth behind Iseult's play is to ask one of them."

Charlie would have to pluck up the courage.

She'd barely slept at all, lying in the dark in a burning rage as she thought of all the things she wanted to say to her mother and Iseult, and never had.

She'd drifted off to sleep at half five. Brendan woke her at seven with a cup of tea and toast and marmalade.

"I love you," he said, sitting on the bed as she blearily stared at the tray and tried to focus properly.

"I know, love, thank you." She gave him a grateful smile. What was wrong with her? She had a wonderful husband and a wonderful son. It was about time she stopped hoping for approval from her mother and sister. They were locked in their own little world of two. Let them stay there.

The atmosphere in Kenny's that day was gloomy. Nobody knew anything for sure, but there was a sense, a frisson, that all wasn't well. People from the fifth floor had been heard murmuring the DeVere name. Longtime Kenny's staff shuddered at the notion of their beloved department store becoming a part of the DeVere empire.

Everyone had a story about something they'd heard from someone on the fifth floor—don't tell anyone else, but the auditor's report was bleak. Kenny's was in serious trouble.

"Selling to DeVere's is probably the only way we can survive," Shotsy said to Charlie as they shared an early-morning coffee in the Hatbox Café.

"Perhaps a total change is the answer," said Charlie blithely. "Sell it all, and start again."

Shotsy blinked. "What's got into you?"

Charlie was cutting her muffin for something to do. She wasn't even hungry, didn't know why she'd ordered a muffin.

"No, let me guess," Shotsy went on. "It's your bloody mother again, isn't it? What's she done now?"

Everybody, it seemed, had seen that morning's gossip column where Iseult and her mother were shown looking at each other adoringly. The columnist hadn't actually reported Kitty's proclaiming how proud she was of one daughter, while the other daughter stood beside her looking aghast. At least she only hinted at a family row, didn't say it outright:

_The Nelson family turned out in force for Thursday's first
night: Iseult, her mother, the redoubtable Kitty, and her
sister, Charlie. One does wonder where the talented Iseult
Nelson gets her ideas for family squabbles._

"Probably thought you'd sue," Shotsy said, when Charlie filled her in on what might have been written. "Pity you don't sue your mother, old bag."

Charlie giggled. It felt good to laugh.

"What was the after-show party like, anyway?" Shotsy asked.

"I was so angry with her, I didn't go. Said I had a headache and went home."

"Well done, you!" said Shotsy approvingly. "A bit more of that is what your mother needs. Proud of one of her daughters, indeed."

"It was horrendous, I felt about two inches tall," Charlie admitted.

"Iseult should have said something," Shotsy went on crossly. "She's almost worse, Charlie. Your mother's always been mad as a bicycle, but you'd think Iseult would stand up for you now and then."

"It's not really Iseult's fault—"

"Has she been on the phone this morning, asking if you're all right, then?"

"No."

Iseult hadn't bothered to phone and find out how her sister was feeling, seeing as she'd missed the after-show party. According to the papers, the success of the play had directors queuing up to work with her, and she was in talks about a new play at London's Donmar Warehouse theater. Too busy to phone her sister and answer the questions Charlie dearly wanted to ask: "Is it true that you're not Dad's daughter? And if so, when did you find out and why didn't you tell me? Don't I deserve to know?"

"There's a pair of them in it," Shotsy said. "Kitty and Iseult."

And you don't know the half of it, Charlie thought.

"Hiya, Shotsy and Charlie."

Dolores put a tray down beside them, two chocolate brioche buns on her tray. "Might as well make use of the staff discount while the store's still open," she said.

"Don't be defeatist," said Shotsy, shuddering at the sight of the buns. She was having a triple espresso, as usual.

"It's not defeatist," Dolores said. "I overheard Lena speaking to Tom about a meeting with the auditors, and she said something about Ingrid having to make a decision soon. See? They're not talking about whether to repaint the façade. They're talking about selling—they have to be. It's been like a ghost town since David died. If they close the place down to revamp, we could all be out of a job."

Charlie thought about this and found that, strangely, she didn't care all that much. She loved Kenny's, loved the family atmosphere; but since sitting through Iseult's play and feeling her life shift on its axis, she realized that you could survive change. Nothing stayed the same, after all. What was important was how you managed the change. That, and having the people you loved around you, was what mattered.

Charlie was due to work on Saturday, but woke up feeling ill.

She lay listlessly in bed, unable even to sip the tea Brendan took up to her.

"I'll phone and tell them you're sick," he said decisively.

"No, I'll be better—"

"No," he said. "You need to stay at home in bed. It's all your bloody mother's fault," he added.

Privately, Charlie agreed with him.

Mikey had soccer that morning, and once the pair of them had gone off, Charlie lay there with the remote control in her hand and flicked through the channels. She was deep in *Oprah* when the phone rang.

"Hello, Charlotte," said her mother. "I've been phoning your mobile, but it's off. I thought you worked on Saturdays. Are you sick?"

"You missed your calling as a private investigator," snapped Charlie, and they were both a little surprised. Charlie never spoke like that to Kitty.

"I need to talk to you."

"Well, I don't need to talk to you," Charlie said.

"I'm coming over," Kitty went on.

God, she was a one-woman army, Charlie thought. She decided to hang up, but it was too late: her mother had already done so.

Charlie had, on occasion, put on makeup before her mother arrived because she didn't like the inevitable "You look shattered!" expostulations when she didn't.

Today she stayed in bed, wrapped in her dressing gown, a bulky cream terry-cloth creation that was very cozy but did nothing for her face or figure.

When her mother's furious doorbell ringing started, she went downstairs, opened the door, and marched back up to bed.

"You're not well," said Kitty in surprise as she followed Charlie up.

"What are you here for, Mother?"

Again, Charlie surprised herself. Where had this tough-cookie character been hiding all her life? Perhaps she'd always been there but obscured, because Charlie had thought that being a chameleon was the way into her mother's heart. She'd tried so hard to make her mother love her, trying to be everything her mother wanted, blending to fit in with every backdrop, and she'd always failed. Now that she knew it was pure DNA that had altered the picture, the please-everyone chameleon was gone.

"I thought you were upset the other night," Kitty said lamely, and sat on the bed.

"I was upset for two reasons," Charlie snapped. "Can you guess what they were?"

"I didn't mean to say it like it sounded to that reporter," Kitty began. "Of course I'm proud of you—"

"*Of course!*" roared Charlie, and suddenly she didn't feel ill anymore; she felt invigorated. "What do you mean, 'of course'? You've never told me you felt proud of me, never. It was always Iseult—and I love her, don't get me wrong, but it's hard to always come second-best. And now I know why."

Under her usual layer of makeup, Kitty blanched.

"My father isn't Iseult's father, is he?"

It was like watching the energy go out of a prizefighter. "I don't know why she put it in the play," Kitty said.

"I doubt if she knew she had," Charlie said. "But it was what made you love her more, wasn't it? Whoever he was, you loved him more than my father, and you love her more than you love me."

"No I don't!" roared Kitty. "I love you too."

"You don't!"

"Yes I do!"

They glared at each other furiously.

"All right, I screwed up!" Kitty shouted. "I was never Mrs. Perfect Bloody Mother. Iseult was easier because she was more like me. Tougher. You were so gentle; I could see you watching me with those big sad eyes when I did it wrong. Nobody else needed to point out my failings in the mothering department—just one look at your little face was enough. Motherhood is supposed to be instinct; we're all supposed to be able to do it. Bloody monkeys do it—why couldn't I?"

"Is that it?"

"That's enough!" Kitty said. "You're not considered a woman if you're a useless mother, never forget that. Well, you're good at it. Mikey worships the ground you walk on."

It wasn't a false compliment. Kitty meant it, Charlie realized.

"He does, doesn't he?"

"I never had that, not with either of you."

"What about Iseult's father?"

"I was pregnant when I married your father. He doesn't know, never will." She didn't plead. Kitty held her head high. "I love you, Charlie, and I'm sorry about the other night."

"How did Iseult find out?"

"I told her once when I was drunk, told her not to tell you."

At least that solved the mystery of why Iseult hadn't shared that information with her sister.

"Stupid mare for putting it in a play," Kitty went on. "Iseult has no sense when it comes to some things. You'd never have done that. You can keep a secret, at least."

Charlie couldn't help herself: she burst out laughing. It was as close to a rapprochement as anyone would get with her mother.

Kitty laughed too, then took advantage of the change in mood. "Would you get rid of that hideous dressing gown, Charlie? I know Brendan's not the type to stray, but merciful hour, no man would stay with a woman who wears that to bed."

Charlie looked down at the dressing gown. Brendan had given it to her a few years ago for Christmas. She loved it.

"No, Mother," she said cheerfully, "it's like the rest of me: take it or leave it."

When her mother was gone, Charlie felt unaccountably better. Lighter, almost. She showered, dressed, and, on impulse, picked up her anti-gratitude diary and read it from the beginning. It was strange to read her own words, yet time lent a dispassion to her reading. From this distance, she could see glimpses of the child who'd always wanted to please her mother and had grown up not appreciating the value of pleasing herself.

Both her mother and Iseult said what they thought and did what they wanted to, irrespective of whom it hurt or affected. Charlie ran every sentence and every action through her mental filter first to see if it might hurt anyone else.

But since she'd been writing this diary, she'd seen the patterns in her behavior and learned, slowly, that she really couldn't please all the people all the time.

She needed to start pleasing herself first.

The phone rang, and she answered it automatically.

"Charlie?"

It was Iseult, and she didn't sound like her usual wildly confident self.

"Hello," Charlie said coolly. She might be feeling better about the whole thing, but she wasn't letting Iseult get off scot-free.

"Mother just phoned me. Oh, Charlie, I never meant you to find out this way. I didn't think anyone would realize . . . well, I almost didn't realize it myself. I wasn't writing about us, but—"

"Iseult," interrupted Charlie, "I'd rather not talk about this over the phone. Can you come round?"

"Well, I'm busy, and I have a stack of meetings this morning because everyone's so excited about the play . . ."

There was the pause where Charlie knew she was supposed to say that *of course* Iseult was too busy, Charlie must have been mad even to ask; after all, Iseult could see Charlie anytime. But Charlie said none of these things. She merely said, "Oh," and waited calmly.

Iseult, used to picking up inflections in people's voices, grasped the extent of that "oh." "I'll be round in half an hour, is that okay?" she said.

"I'll brew coffee," Charlie said, smiling into the phone.

Marcella was feeling miserable and unsettled. Her entire view of life had taken a battering. Up to now, the planet could self-combust with bitterness every day over the price of oil and budget cuts, and she could handle it; but there needed to be a few constants in her life. Ingrid and David had been that. Their existence proved that true love could exist—that there were nice, decent people out there, and good things came to those who waited.

All entirely false, as it turned out.

Ingrid's life had been based on a lie, and David, dear David, whom Marcella had simply *adored*, had been seeing someone else.

Even worse, there was nobody she could discuss this with, because Marcella simply had nobody else in her life to trust with such sensitive information. If she'd had a partner or a husband, she could have talked to him about it.

Poor Ingrid—thank God we have each other. She imagined lying with her beloved in bed holding hands, simply being glad that they were together and weren't ripped apart by infidelity.

But she didn't have that. No man to hold in bed and talk with quietly about how horrible it was for dear Ingrid.

No prospect of a man in her life, either. It wasn't that she needed romance or rampant sex—companionship was all she craved. David's very existence had made her think there were decent men out there and that perhaps one day she might find one. Well, she'd found Harry; but she and Harry were too different, and that had never really worked. But *another* decent man. There was little hope of that now.

The plumbing system in the office had broken down completely, despite the speedy fix-up job when the reception area had been flooded.

"The whole thing?" said Marcella when her business partner gave her the bad news.

"Heating, sanitation—the works. It'll cost thousands," Connor said grimly.

"We spent thousands getting it installed in the first place," Marcella said.

"We can sue," said Paul, Connor's assistant, who was new and hadn't yet been jaded by life.

Connor and Marcella exchanged a will-you-tell-him-or-will-I glance. Marcella got the honor.

"We probably will sue," she said, "but suing is a little like Dr. Johnson's description of marriage—a triumph of hope over experience. And we still have to sort out the problem now."

"In other words, we need a good plumber," said Connor in a voice that implied Dr. Johnson's remarks might have been on the money when it came to plumbers, too.

This, Paul could do. "My cousin's a plumber. It's his own company; he set it up and he's doing very well. No discounts for cash or any dodgy business. He's your man. He's very ambitious— wants to start his own empire, we all say."

"Get the emperor to come in and give us a quote," Marcella said. "I have to go out for a meeting. I'll be a couple of hours."

Her meeting had gone on for ages, and Marcella stormed up the stairs of SD International, coat flying, thinking about the cost of fixing the office plumbing. The expense would be stratospheric. She'd kill those other incompetent muppets if she got her hands on them.

With a wrench of the door onto the second floor, Marcella walked headlong into Connor, Paul, and another man deep in conversation. Her handbag hit the floor as she cannoned off Connor and stepped clumsily back into the third man, who grabbed her arms to steady her.

She shot away from him as if she'd been scalded. She was not in the mood to be grabbed by anyone.

"This is my cousin, Lorcan McNamara," said Paul in a squeaky, surprised voice.

"Oh." Marcella whirled round to glare at him. If he so much as *looked* at her with an expression that said she didn't understand plumbing, so help her God, she'd—

Her brain gave a little cavewoman throb of lust.

"Hello," she said. *This* was Paul's cousin?

It had been a long time since Marcella was jolted by a man. Longer than she could remember. But *this* man, he was something else. It wasn't entirely his looks—although Marcella could imagine Julie from reception muttering that she wouldn't kick him out of bed for eating crisps, which was high praise indeed and few men earned it. He was dark-haired, the type of darkness that brought heavy eyebrows that could beetle in a moment and stubble that needed two shaves a day to control it. His eyes were blue, glinting a smile at her, and he was at least ten years younger than she, far too young to be giving her such a knowing smile.

No, it wasn't any of that, not even the lean perfection of him, narrow hips encased in old denims, broad shoulders in a plaid shirt. It was the air of absolute confidence and control, the sense that he did things his way and if anybody didn't like it, that was fine; unless he was in charge, in which case it wasn't fine, and the entire place would march to the beat of his drum no matter what, and he'd make it happen by sheer force of will.

The bit of her brain still operating gave her cerebral cortex a good shake.

"Pleased to meet you," she said, with a stab at a normal voice. "So you're taking on the mammoth task. What's the verdict?"

"It's an interesting job," he said, eyes assessing her. Even his voice was sexy. "I'm beginning to think it may take longer than I initially thought," he added.

Marcella realized he was flirting with her, in such a subtle way that nobody else noticed. She felt a rush of total lust that made her whole body burn. Suddenly she was far too hot and her skin was misted in sweat, and she felt sure everyone could see it. But the training kicked in. Her own training.

People aren't looking at you all the time watching for imperfections. You'd be surprised what they don't notice. If you hiccup, sneeze, or flush beet red, they often don't notice; and if you carry on as if you haven't noticed, then they will carry on, too. . . .

Her own words mocked her as the heat increased. Satellites in space could probably detect it.

"I'll leave you boys to it," she said, and backed off into her own office. *Leave you boys to it?* What did that sound like? Not the independent career woman, that was for sure.

She picked up her desk calendar and fanned herself with it. Had that really happened? Had she just felt herself fall head over heels in sheer lust with Paul's plumber cousin? She was really losing it now. It was time to give up work, move to a remote island, let her hair grow long, and pin it up in a bun with knitting needles.

She kept the door shut all morning and only ventured out at lunchtime when there was no noise in the rest of the office. She didn't know if Lorcan was starting work that day, but the less she saw of him, the better. She'd die of embarrassment if she reacted like that again. Imagine if Connor had noticed. Paul wouldn't— Paul was clueless—but no matter how clever she was at hiding it, Connor would eventually cop on.

With luck, it would be a quick job and Lorcan would have his team of people doing it, rather than him hanging around the office looking broodingly handsome and flirty.

She made herself coffee, took a banana from the kitchen fruit bowl, and was on her way back to her office when Lorcan appeared.

"I was looking for you," he said.

"Oh?" Hanging on to her banana for dear life, Marcella kept walking until she reached the safety of her office. He followed her.

"Can I help you?" she asked. She was hot again. She couldn't fan herself; it would look like she was having a hot flash, which was the kiss of death to a woman in her forties. "Connor seems to be out, but if you want to wait until he's back—"

"I don't want to see Connor. I came up to ask you out," he said, staring at her with ferocious calm.

"To ask me—"

"—out, yes," he said. "You're unattached. I asked. I'm unattached and I find you incredibly gorgeous, so I'm asking you out. Is there a problem with that?" He put his lovely dark head to one side, and Marcella had a vision of that head nuzzling her throat with her hands grasping his skull, his mouth moving down farther to suck her nipples.

The heat soaked through her sleeveless white top this time, and she hoped it wasn't making the fabric cling to her, because this bra

was so see-through, entirely the sort of thing a woman might wear
to bed with the intention of having a man rip it off her later, with
his teeth perhaps. . . .

"What is it with you?" she demanded. "You, you—"

One of his eyebrows arched.

"Out where?" she asked abruptly.

"Dinner."

"When?"

"Tonight?"

"I'm busy," she snapped.

"Tomorrow night?"

"Fine. Where?"

"I'll pick you up," he said.

Marcella shook her head. "No, I'll meet you there."

"I'll pick you up," he said again. "When I take you to dinner, I
take you. Eight o'clock? You tell me where."

"Are you always this pushy?" she asked as she wrote her ad-
dress on a piece of paper.

"Only when I really want something," he murmured.

When he left, Marcella went to the window and wrenched it
open, standing with the breeze flowing over her skin until she
cooled down. She would get him out of her system. He was probably as thick as four short planks. Nothing turned her off a man
like stupidity.

He wasn't thick. Quite the contrary. They ate at a small Italian
restaurant in the city, and Marcella found that she could listen to
him talking all night. Not that he did talk all night: he let her talk,
and he listened. But when he did talk, it was clear that a serious
brain was behind those sexy blue eyes.

He'd completed a degree in finance before turning to plumbing
when the investment bank he'd worked for went through a rocky
patch in the late nineties.

"But why plumbing?" Marcella asked.

"Why not plumbing?"

"With your education, you could do anything."

"Do you think that what I did in college means I should want something better than to be a plumber?" Lorcan said, smearing brie on a cracker for her.

Marcella, realizing that he was going to feed it to her and shocked that she liked the idea, blushed.

"If you don't hold it against me that I'm a plumber, I won't hold it against you that you work in PR," he said.

"I love my job," Marcella said.

"I love mine and I'm proud of it." He held the cracker delicately to her lips, teasing her with it, allowing her little bites. "I have a growing company with forty employees, and I won't tell you my turnover because I don't know you well enough yet, but I'm earning more money than I earned in finance. You're not an intellectual snob, are you?"

Marcella blushed again.

"Intellectual snobbery is a real nineties thing," he said. "I'm more of a twenty-first-century guy, and I don't look down on anyone because of their education or what they choose to do with it. Ambition and success have nothing to do with that. Some of the most successful entrepreneurs of the nineties didn't go to college at all."

"Don't rub it in that I went to college a million years before you did. I'm old enough to be your mother," she said anxiously, taking a sip of wine.

"That's not possible, not unless my mother had me when she was eleven," he replied. They'd already had a conversation about age, in which Marcella had told Lorcan the truth, half-expecting him to run away at the news that she was forty-nine to his thirty-eight. He'd said it didn't matter in the slightest.

"And I don't go out on romantic dates with my mother," he said now. "Except when we're planning to appear on *Jerry Springer*."

Marcella laughed loudly, spraying wine everywhere.

"Sorry," she said, reaching over with her napkin. She dabbed his face and then his throat, and it felt as if they had both stopped breathing.

"If you go any farther down with the napkin, we'll never be able to come to this restaurant again," he murmured.

"I've had enough cheese," she said.

"Me too."

They both made gestures to the waiter to bring the bill, but he won the battle to pay.

He drove slowly, not speaking, and Marcella felt the tingle of anticipation grow inside her. At her apartment, he parked the car and they sat in silence for a moment.

"Do you want to come in for coffee?" she asked.

"Do you want me to come in?" The blue eyes bored into hers. "If I come in, I don't know if I'll be able to leave."

Marcella wondered if she was stone mad, but she reached up and touched his cheek where the five-o'clock shadow was breaking through. Like a cat, he moved his face so that the line of his jaw was cupped in her hand.

"You don't have to leave," she said.

Marcella had never kept a secret from Ingrid in all the years they had been friends. No matter what happened, they talked about it. But Marcella couldn't tell Ingrid about this; this was like breaking all the commandants of being a good friend, enjoying yourself when your friend was devastated and betrayed.

Enjoying yourself with a younger man made it worse.

When she thought about the age gap, she felt like Hugh Heffner with one of the Playboy girls. She thought of how she and Ingrid had spoken of such men, the sort who grew older and older, got covered in liver spots, had frail bodies and wrinkly skin—and eyes that still gleamed when they saw nubile flesh.

"They're disgusting," Marcella used to say. "Why don't they date women their own age or thereabouts? Why twenty-year-olds?"

"It's about power," Ingrid would say sagely. "Having a young girlfriend signals to the world that the man has the money and the power to attract such a woman. If he didn't have that, he would just be an ordinary, much older guy."

So doing it in reverse, dating a younger man, made Marcella feel hypocritical and secretive.

But, oh, he was wonderful.

Lorcan. Marcella rolled his name around in her mouth.

Her younger lover. In the media world she belonged to, that made her a cougar—a woman in her prime with a younger lover.

When she was with Lorcan, laughing with him, making love with him, they were just people.

Thinking of herself as a cougar changed that; it smacked of desperation, for all that articles in magazines always made being a cougar sound fabulous: have a younger man as your lover, let him appreciate your inner beauty as well as your experience.

But in reality, it felt different. Like a secret she needed to keep. Nobody could know, not anyone at work, not even Ingrid.

If Lorcan had been less good-looking or even worked in a different field, it would have been different. But there was a *Lady Chatterley's Lover* quality to falling for the plumber. She couldn't tell anyone that, truly, he was one of the smartest men she'd ever met. Well-read, funny, clever. In the world of the media—a world where, ironically, people tended to have a very blinkered view of reading and pored over little else but media pages in the papers and articles written by people they knew—a professional woman dating a plumber was a little like a successful man dating a beauty queen.

Trading down.

None of them would believe that Marcella was with him for his mind. They'd disregard the brain cells and look at the sculpted body, the handsome face, and the powerful charisma that emanated from him, and they'd think: Bingo!! Yeah, you're with him for his mind, Marcella. Sure.

On the third date, he'd taken her home to meet his mother and brothers.

That's what you did with someone you were serious about, Lorcan said, and Marcella, who hadn't been taken home to meet the mother of one of her boyfriends for at least twenty years, had thought it was very sweet—until she got there.

Lorcan's family home was a sprawling semidetached house in

a Dublin suburb where his mother, Antoinette, had raised her six sons alone after her husband died. Immaculately presented but comfortable, the house spoke of a warm family life. When they arrived for dinner, three of Lorcan's brothers were there, all nearly as gorgeous and charming as he, making Marcella think they could fill half a calendar of hunks.

Then she'd met Antoinette, who'd come out of the kitchen in an apron, drying her hands on a tea towel.

"Hello, Marcella," Antoinette had said, and Marcella had felt her gut clench.

This was no little old lady with fluffy white hair. Lorcan's mother didn't seem that much older than Marcella was, although miles apart in all obvious ways. Antoinette made Marcella think of what she'd have become if she'd stayed in her hometown and married one of the boys who'd been after her all those years ago.

Antoinette had short hair—Marcella remembered how her own mother had cut hers as soon as she'd hit forty, saying that long hair was for younger women. She wore a cream blouse tucked into a sensible plaid skirt and shoes that were undoubtedly comfortable but positively antifashion.

Marcella had gone for her version of casual, which meant a Ralph Lauren sweater with a white shirt underneath and denims that looked ordinary but were actually expensive ones cut by a former jeans model who understood the female body. Her hair hung around her shoulders in glossy, dark waves.

What was worse, was that one of Lorcan's brothers, Tony, had brought his wife, Sarah, and their eighteen-month-old baby, an apple-cheeked little girl named Lulu. Antoinette was polite to all, but Marcella felt a frost every time Lorcan's mother looked in her direction. Tony, Sarah, and Lulu were a proper family unit, was the silent message. You, older woman taking my boy, are not.

Everyone wanted a go at Lulu, and when she landed on Marcella's lap, Marcella felt the frisson of loss she always felt when she held a small child. No matter that she'd done her grieving for that; it still hurt to have a perfect little creature staring up at her with pale blue eyes and an inquiring face. She would never have this now.

Marcella was good with children. She'd spent a lot of time with her nieces and nephews and was adept at amusing them. It took two minutes of smiling, talking, and tickling Lulu's chubby little hand in "Round and round the garden," before Lulu was hooked.

"Aren't you beautiful?" Marcella crooned as a delighted Lulu examined Marcella's necklace and gave a few exploratory tugs on one of her earrings.

Lulu refused to be passed along and clung to Marcella.

"She likes you," said Sarah happily, and began to relax enough to eat her dinner.

In other circumstances, Marcella would have liked Antoinette; but when Marcella was helping tidy up, Antoinette spoke to her alone and destroyed any chance of happy families.

"I can't say I'm delighted you're going out with Lorcan," Antoinette said, "but he's a man and he knows his own mind. I don't tell him who to see. That said, I'd prefer if he were with a woman his own age, to be frank. You're not going to give him children, are you, no matter how good you look. You're too old for that."

Marcella, who'd faced down fleets of fierce alpha males in the boardroom and chewed up bitchy female types for breakfast, felt close to tears. "No," she managed to say.

She wouldn't say she didn't think she was able to have them now even if she wanted to, no matter how clever Italian fertility doctors were with women well beyond childbearing years. Her grief over not having had babies was her own business, no one else's, not even Lorcan's mother's.

"You're quiet," remarked Lorcan as they drove off.

Quiet? If only he knew how hard she'd fought not to run out of the house and hail a taxi to take her away. "I'm fine," she said tightly, then regretted it. "I'm fine" was classic female hedgehog prickle-speak, meaning *I am anything but fine and you better find out why that is, you moron.*

"My mother likes you," he added.

"She's very nice," Marcella said. What was wrong with her? *Nice* and *fine* were nonwords, used to pad out a conversation that was going nowhere.

"Actually, I don't think she liked me at all," Marcella said, unable to hold it in.

"Trust me, she did. You'd know it if she didn't like you. She made one girlfriend cry." He was smiling ruefully at the memory.

Marcella had to control the urge to beat him around the head with her mobile phone. Typical bloody man: they were all martyrs to their mothers, thinking they could do no wrong. God knew what Antoinette had done to make one poor woman cry. And Marcella was suddenly jealous of this old flame. Was she younger than Marcella? Or the same age, another cougar in a lineup that made Lorcan's family shrug helplessly and wait for the moment he came to his senses and dated women who could give him children?

"I don't like feeling disapproved of," Marcella blurted out. Blast him, he had a strange effect on her, making her say what she felt. No man had ever done that before, not even Harry.

"It's not a good feeling," he agreed. "Sort of what you're afraid of happening to me with your friends, right?"

Marcella gasped. Another thing about Lorcan: he made her totally forget all her neat tricks about presentation. She reacted with him, couldn't hold anything in. "I am not afraid of my friends disapproving of you," she lied.

"Yes you are," said Lorcan. "I'm not, by the way. I'd like to meet them because they're important to you, but I'm not afraid of what they think. That's up to them, and we're up to us. You can't live your life worrying about what other people think."

And with that, he was back concentrating on the road; the conversation was over.

He was such a *man*.

Eighteen

Speak out of love and a desire to make things better.

*I*ngrid had never done nights out with the girls. She hadn't avoided them on purpose; it was simply an aspect of popular culture that had passed her by.

"It's because of who you are, I daresay," Marcella said. "You're too famous for normal people, and if you went out with a group of famous women, there would inevitably be someone with an iceberg-sized ego who would want the conversation to be about her, her show, her publicist, her fans."

Ingrid found herself grinning. Marcella was right. She hated to think of her fame as making her different, but it did. There were people who didn't care how often your face was on television and treated you normally, but there were twice as many who did the opposite, asking personal or rude questions on the grounds that famous people had no right to privacy.

Tonight, Marcella had organized an evening with Ingrid and two other friends, Carla and Nikki, women they both knew and loved.

It wasn't exactly a wild night out with the girls, but Marcella said that Ingrid needed to get out and do things that weren't entirely work-related. Although work was going well and she had slipped back into the driver's seat much more easily than she had expected, Ingrid had been avoiding all social events.

"Your hand will get welded to the TV zapper if you spend any more time at home in the evenings," Marcella had scolded. "Let me organize something nice and quiet."

Carla was a high court judge, married with three adult

---

children. Nikki was single and a successful clothes designer who'd launched an international handbag line to great success. They were lovely women and good friends; but as she and Marcella sat waiting in the restaurant, sipping Kir Royales, Ingrid felt deeply uncomfortable. It was her first evening out, her first nonfamily, nonwork evening since David had died.

There was something scary about it. The safety blanket that had been her marriage was gone. No, she corrected herself mentally, the safety blanket that she'd *thought* was her marriage was gone.

Marcella's BlackBerry beeped with the arrival of a message. "Sorry," she muttered, "must reply to this."

Marcella was distracted, Ingrid thought idly. It must be work. She sipped her drink and looked around the room.

An elegant older woman arrived, flicking an arrogant gaze over Ingrid and Marcella as if to say a party of women was beneath contempt.

Ingrid watched the woman with interest as she joined a wealthy-looking elderly man at a nearby table. She was thin, far too thin really—the thinness of savage self-control at every meal for the past twenty years. Ingrid would have been fascinated to see *her* bone-marrow-density scans. The woman was clad in a subtle shift dress with lots of detailing around the arms to distract from the creping of her skin. She had to be more than sixty, yet her hair was a girlish blond bouffant, combed and fluffed high at the front over a surgically smooth high forehead, with a rounded flipped-out curl all around.

The contrast between the Barbie hair and the rest of her made Ingrid shiver. Was this what getting older was all about? Fighting age with the weapons of girlhood?

Ingrid's hand went automatically to her own hair, and she had a sudden overwhelming desire to have it all cut off. Short, sharp, and sleek, à la Judi Dench. That would be different. Nobody could accuse her of trying to look younger than she was then. Was that where she'd gone wrong in her marriage? Had she assumed she and David would be together forever when, in reality, she should have faced the fact that nothing lasted forever? Had his mystery lover been younger? Of course. Ingrid knew she must be—

"Hello, sorry we're late. Traffic was mental."

Carla and Nikki arrived with a tall, gray-haired man beside them.

"This is Eric Johannsen," said Nikki. "We ran into him in the lobby."

Marcella and Ingrid smiled hellos and shook hands with Eric, whom Ingrid tried hard to place. She'd definitely seen him before. On the business pages, perhaps, or a picture in the *Financial Times*.

He had the keen eyes of a successful businessman, for sure: coolly assessing, analyzing, working out where the next billion was coming from.

"Good evening, pleased to meet you," he said.

His accent was neutral with the perfect enunciation of the multilinguist. Ingrid was always fascinated by men like him, ones who ran empires and could speak Japanese, Chinese, and Russian and had secretaries in every major city, taking speedy dictation.

He lingered only a minute before heading off to his own table, where the inevitable group of men in suits awaited him with bulbous burgundy glasses in front of them.

"If I weren't married . . ." murmured Carla, sitting down.

"Hands off," said Nikki. "Let us free agents have a chance." Nikki had dated a property billionaire from Seattle for a few years, but he'd left her for his masseuse. Since then, she'd sworn off men. "Isn't he a dish?" she asked Marcella.

"Well, er . . . yes," said Marcella.

Nikki whooped. "Marcella Schmidt—you're seeing someone! Tell all."

"I am not," protested Marcella.

Ingrid could see that Carla and Nikki believed her. Marcella was, after all, marvelous at fibbing. But Ingrid had seen her blush slightly and knew better. Marcella must have a new man in her life, and she hadn't said anything. Ingrid felt a pang of guilt. Dear Marcella felt she had to pussyfoot around her, as if any good news would devastate Ingrid. That wasn't true. Just because Ingrid's life had been shattered didn't mean everyone else had to suffer too.

"Where do I know that man from?" Ingrid asked, to take the heat off Marcella.

"Another billionaire property/business/delete-where-applicable magnate," Carla said. "I don't know where Nikki finds them. Is there a dating club for lonely billionaires, Nikki?"

"I wish." Nikki sighed. "Money's not everything, anyway, is it?"

The other three laughed.

"I'm never interested in men because they have money," Nikki claimed. And then she grinned, a wicked little grin. "But they're nicer when they do."

"Maybe not nicer, but the push-off-I'm-over-you gifts are better when they're rich," Marcella joked.

Nikki jangled her bracelet, a platinum and diamond confection that Mr. Seattle had bought her. "Doesn't keep you warm at night."

"Eric might keep you warm at night," suggested Carla. "Where did you meet him?"

"Last year at a skiing party in Courchevel."

"What is he in? Property, the space program, buying other nations?"

More laughs.

"Just your general megarich bloke," Nikki said. "Very nice, actually. Swedish; still has his company's main base in Stockholm. Houses all over the place—you know the drill. I didn't ask what he's in Dublin for. You know these guys, they hop all around the world in private jets doing deals."

The waiter appeared with menus.

"Food, I'm starving!" said Marcella. She was permanently ravenous these days, something to do with being unable to eat when she was with Lorcan. When she was away from him, she ate like a horse.

The evening was very enjoyable despite Ingrid's initial anxieties, and as they left the restaurant, the four of them promised to meet up again next month.

"Are you okay?" Marcella asked her quietly when the other pair had gone off in taxis.

"I'm fine," Ingrid said. "Tonight was fun, like practicing being normal and happy. If I practice long enough, I might remember how to do it."

"You don't have to pretend to be normal and happy," Marcella said. "It's all right to be sad."

"Not every hour of every day," Ingrid said. "It's not good for the soul. But tonight was fun, so thank you."

Ingrid was about to ask Marcella about her new man, but thought better of it. Marcella would tell when she was ready.

The dream woke Ingrid again that night. She was in the front pew of the church, waiting for Molly to walk up the aisle, and she looked across at the groom, seeing him properly for the first time. He looked so like David: the same shoulders, the same look on his face. The groom's mother, a vision in pink who was infinitely younger than Ingrid but still blurry, leaned forward in the pew on the other side and hissed, "Looks familiar?"

Molly was marrying her half brother, Ingrid realized, and she tried to shout it out, to tell her daughter to stop, but the words wouldn't come.

It was at that moment that she always woke up, sweating and distressed.

David couldn't have done that to her, could he? But perhaps he had. Perhaps there was another Kenny child out there somewhere.

Yet if there was, the child's mother would have come forward to claim money from David's estate. Unless David had already set her up with a trust fund or some other type of financial parachute.

It was 2 a.m. Ingrid switched on her BlackBerry and sent a quick e-mail to Marcella:

Need to find out who SHE is. Have to. Priority. I xx

There was no backing out now.

* * *

Marcella didn't mind playing detective on occasion, but this was different. She wanted to make sure that Ingrid knew exactly what she might be letting herself in for.

"If anyone finds out what you're looking for, you're in deep shit, Ingrid," she warned. "Imagine that splashed all over the tabloids."

"I know," said Ingrid. " 'Telly Ingrid's Love Triangle Tragedy.'"

"Not a bad headline," Marcella commented. "Right, leave this with me. I'll have to do some digging myself—this isn't something I'd trust anyone else with. But, Ingrid, are you *sure*? You're focusing entirely on finding out who this woman is. What happens when you know? What are you going to do with this information, assuming I can find out anything?"

"I don't know—look at her and wonder what she has that I didn't have?" Ingrid replied.

"And that will be helpful how, exactly?"

"It will give me closure."

"You've always said you hate all the crap about 'closure,'" Marcella said. "You used to call it mumbo jumbo and complain that the world's full of people seeking closure on everything from a bad day at school when they were four to a row with their kids."

"That was before I understood what it meant," Ingrid snapped. "This woman is holding me back. I'll never stop wondering, Marcella, wondering if every woman in our circle is her, or if he worked with her, or if she's an old flame he went back to. He never told me much about the women before me," she added thoughtfully.

"This is so unhealthy," said Marcella. "I can't believe we're doing this."

"We're doing it," Ingrid said. "I have to know."

Ingrid sleepwalked through her life for the next two weeks. She presented three shows on television and attended her first public function, a lunch for a child-abuse charity at which she was the guest speaker.

"They'll understand if you can't do it," Gloria said.

Ingrid shook her head. "This is different. I said I'd be there, and I will be."

In the mental tally of personal suffering, Ingrid felt that what she was going through was nothing compared to the pain of children who'd been sexually abused. She'd met victims of abuse for a television series and would never forget the sense of pain and betrayal the people lived with, even decades later. Ingrid believed that one day she'd be able to close her eyes and not think of David's death or disloyalty. People who'd been abused as kids could never totally forget.

For the lunch, she wore a black lace shift and posed for photographs with the charity's directors.

"You're so good to be here today," murmured the chairwoman, an elegant brunette clad head to toe in what looked like Lanvin.

"I wouldn't miss it for anything," said Ingrid, and held the woman's hand briefly.

When the chairwoman had had three glasses of champagne and lapsed into the inevitable toying with her lunch, she admitted to Ingrid that this wasn't a pet charity she'd chosen by chance. "Nobody knows why I do it except my husband. He knows I want to help other kids not go through what I did."

Ingrid was shocked. This woman didn't look like someone who'd been abused—but then, who did?

She went home that night and read the book Abra had told her to buy about life and gratitude. It was like homework: read a few pages of the book and explore how she felt. Until now, Ingrid had been going through the motions of reading it. After today, she felt humbled again. Her pain was bad, but there was worse. Much worse.

"Gratitude," the book said, "should be a part of every day of your life."

Ingrid read it again. She closed her eyes and repeated it. Ethan was safe; he'd e-mailed from Australia, where he was hanging out—his words—with his friends in Cairns. Molly had gone on an actual date with a man named Mark, who was a friend of Natalie's friend's husband. Very convoluted. But it had been good.

They'd gone to see a movie at the Irish Film Center and had had dinner afterward. Ingrid couldn't remember the last time Molly had gone on a date, never mind a date she'd enjoyed with a man she wanted to see again.

Ingrid knew she had things to be grateful for. She would say thanks for them. She would try to live her life again instead of hiding in a shell.

After two weeks, Marcella had failed to find out anything about David's mystery woman. Her scheme had been to meet with some of his closest friends on the pretext of discussing how they felt Ingrid was coping and see what information she could ferret out on the liaison.

It wasn't working at all. Marcella was marvelous at getting information from people, but she was convinced, she told Ingrid, that none of them knew anything about David having an affair.

"Obviously, I don't come out and ask 'Did David Kenny confide in you about another woman?'" she said. "But when people discuss how sad it is and how you two loved each other so much, it's easy enough for me to work out if they're lying because they know a different story entirely."

"Thank you," said Ingrid miserably. She knew that Marcella couldn't ask outright, but she was becoming obsessed with knowing more about David's affair. If only she knew *something*, anything, she'd be able to move on.

Part of what made her so good at her job was her interest in what made people tick; yet here she was, knowing almost nothing about a part of her husband's life, and it was driving her crazy. Finally, she had a brainstorm. She'd visit Great-Aunt Babe, David's only surviving relative. David had often visited Babe, and perhaps, with her being so unconventional and not at all judgmental of others, he might have confided in her. It was a long shot, but Ingrid was desperate.

Sheltering Pines was less of a home for the elderly and more of a retirement community for people who wanted to feel safe without having to live cheek-by-jowl with lots of other people. When

Babe had first moved in, around fifteen years ago, she'd occupied a little one-bedroom unit in one of the two-story apartment blocks, with its own balcony and a view of the sea. Now that she'd grown frailer, she'd moved into the big house itself, which was laid out along hotel lines with single- or double-bedroom units, each with a living room and kitchenette. Babe could choose to cook for herself or eat in the dining room with her friends.

She was delighted when Ingrid phoned to ask her out to dinner.

"Marvelous," Babe said. "I'd love that. Everyone will be so jealous."

When Ingrid arrived at Babe's door at seven that evening, Babe was dressed as if for an evening at the opera. She wore a long lilac silk skirt and matching jacket, a white furry collar wrapped around her neck, and a mother-of-pearl brooch on her breast.

"Too much?" said Babe, getting slowly to her feet, which were clad in pink Chinese embroidered slippers.

"Lovely," said Ingrid.

"I hate not getting the wear out of clothes. It's such a waste. I bought this in Madame Nora's in, oh . . ." Babe paused. "I think it was 1973, and it's only been out of the wardrobe a few times since then. Molly can have it when I'm gone; she loves old clothes."

Ingrid winced. "Don't talk like that," she begged.

"We talk like that here all the time," said Babe calmly. "This isn't a health spa, Ingrid. It's where people go when they're too old to live on their own. Next stop: the hereafter. Of course, a lot depends on your vision of the hereafter. Beatrice, who lives next door, has her money on heaven, and she's been to Lourdes twice already this year to be in with a chance. She says I've ruined it for myself because I have a dream-catcher over my bed. Heathen things, apparently!" Babe went on, "I'm toast when it comes to the hereafter."

Despite herself, Ingrid burst out laughing.

"See? I knew I'd cheer you up. Being sad never helped anyone. At least if you try to smile, you're in charge of that one thing."

"How did you get to be so wise?" asked Ingrid, opening the front door of Babe's room and gently helping her into the corridor.

"The benefits of being over ninety," Babe said serenely. "If there are any physical benefits, you're too old to take advantage of them."

"Hey, Babe, I like your friend. She's a hot tamale! Are you going out to meet boys?" whooped one old man as they passed.

Ingrid had never thought she was ageist until that moment, but she was stunned. He had to be a hundred if he was a day. With his frail, hairless skull, he looked as fragile as a museum exhibit, and he was joking about dates?

"Don't talk to my guests like that, Tom, you old rascal," Babe roared back. "I don't date boys, I date men. And if I was going out to meet a man, do you think I'd tell you, with your telegraph mouth?" She whispered to Ingrid, "He's a dirty old man, that one."

"I heard that!" roared Tom.

"Good!" said Babe spiritedly.

Apart from a brief hello from a little old lady shuffling along on a walker, they made it to the lobby unmolested.

"You want to talk about David, don't you?" Babe said. "I can see it in your eyes. I thought people were better at doing that nowadays. When I was younger, you had about six months' grace to talk about them, and then you were supposed to get on with it. Smile, look cheerful, start knitting hats for small babies or volunteering for a charity. The dead were the dead, except in November when it was time for the lists of the dead. Always hated that phrase—it sounds so sad, like there are legions of dead people waiting silently to be put on the list and remembered."

"I think that's the general idea," Ingrid said.

"Sad, so sad. You'll have Masses said for me when I'm gone, won't you?" For the first time, Babe's liveliness deserted her and she looked anxious. Scared, even.

Babe had never been religious. Ingrid could remember sitting beside her at a family wedding and hearing Babe muttering, "As long as this getting married in a church makes them happy. . . . Can't see the need for structured religion myself."

But despite her fighting talk about the hereafter, Babe was frightened.

"Of course I will, Babe," Ingrid said. "Scores of them. I'll get some from those missionary fathers who do whole books of Masses and promise to say them for you for years, okay?"

"Silly of me," Babe said, dabbing at one eye as she got carefully into Ingrid's car. "I'll probably be going down below, anyway. I broke every single one of the rules, and I haven't been to Holy Communion since 1949. It's like being on the Church's Ten Most Wanted List. They haven't got round to excommunicating me, but they have a place for me down there, with fires, pain, and twenty-four-hour sports on the television."

"You don't have to joke," Ingrid said quietly.

"Joking helps. David's dying must have set you thinking about death," said Babe.

Ingrid busied herself fixing Babe's seat belt, then her own; anything to keep from answering. "Yes," she said finally. She was staring straight ahead as she started the car, and she could sense Babe looking at her.

"Because when people you love die, you can't think about anything else, can you?" said Babe, and it seemed to Ingrid that she wasn't talking about David. "I've probably never told you this—well, it's ancient history now, and who wants to hear an old lady talking about past loves? But there was a man I loved, a very long time ago, and when he died I was heartbroken, couldn't see the point of going on. My death, everyone's death was inevitable; it was going to happen, and if I took charge, I could just die myself."

"Babe, you poor pet," said Ingrid.

"That's all I thought about for a very long time afterward. For years, in fact," Babe went on. "When would I do it and how: pills or cutting my wrists in the bath? And finally, I realized one day that I didn't want to die. To be honest, I was terribly afraid that David's death would have the same effect on you. You loved each other so much."

"No, I never felt like that," Ingrid said, and she felt the misery wash over her again. If only she hadn't opened that damned drawer. She wished now she hadn't; she didn't need to know. She could have mourned David properly and not gone through this wondering if everything had been a lie. Babe's lover had died, and she'd been so distraught she'd wanted to join him. All Ingrid could think about was that David was gone and she'd never know why he'd betrayed her and with whom.

She drove out the front gate of Sheltering Pines far too fast and had to brake suddenly as a truck came racing around the corner toward her. "Oh, Jesus, Babe, sorry," she said, her hands flying to her mouth. "I'm so sorry."

"All right," said Babe, "it doesn't worry me."

Ingrid half-laughed, half-shuddered. "If Molly or Ethan had been in the car, they'd be telling me I was turning into a crazy lady and wasn't safe to be out on the road on my own."

"Nonsense," soothed Babe. "They'd never say that—they love you too much. Now, what's really wrong?"

"What do you mean?" said Ingrid.

"Ingrid," said Babe with a shade of sternness in her voice, "I've known you far too long to let you tell me there is nothing wrong. What is it?"

"I can't talk while I'm driving, I'll bang into something."

"Fine," said Babe. "We'll wait till we get there."

True to her word, Babe chatted merrily as they drove, telling Ingrid about the sudoku league at Sheltering Pines and how everyone was becoming wildly obsessive about it. "It's addictive," she said. "Like that crash stuff people take."

"Crack," corrected Ingrid automatically.

"That's it, crack," said Babe.

The old cook had gone, replaced by somebody who shouldn't be let near a kitchen, Babe went on. "Sweet woman, can only do two things with food: boil and boil." Still, Babe didn't mind that much. "I eat so little these days anyway," she said. "As long as I can get my soft mints, I'm fine. There's this sweet young chappie on the second floor who does shop runs for all of us."

Young meant in his seventies, according to Babe.

They settled into the restaurant, a small family-run place where

David used to take Babe and she could get old Irish specialty dishes like coddle and bacon and cabbage.

Babe ordered bacon, while Ingrid, who had little interest in food these days, asked for grilled fish.

"Now." Babe settled herself comfortably in her seat. "Tell me what's bothering you."

Ingrid hesitated, wanting to wait till there was nobody around to hear any of it. But she looked at the clientele and saw that no one was paying her the slightest bit of notice. It was now or never. She took a deep breath and started with the locked drawers and the flowers on the grave.

Babe didn't appear in the slightest bit shocked, merely sad.

"You're sure it wasn't a little fling?" she asked finally. "Sorry— terrible words; an affair is an affair, whatever way you put it."

"It doesn't seem like a little fling," Ingrid said, "not from all the bits of papers and the letters. It looks as if it had been going on for some time, at least a year. I want to know who she is. My friend Marcella has been looking into it."

"No," said Babe fiercely. "No, you mustn't do that."

"What do you mean?"

"This is private," Babe went on. "The more people know, the more chance it has of becoming public knowledge. You don't want that."

"But I need to find out," Ingrid said. "I'm beginning to feel I didn't know David at all, and I can't grieve properly because of this. I don't know who it was, I don't know anything anymore."

"I'm sorry," Babe said. "This must be agony for you, Ingrid, but I don't believe that finding out more about this woman will help you. Humans are complex beings; we can never really know another person, not completely. There must have been parts of you that David didn't understand."

"I suppose," said Ingrid, thinking of when Ethan had first gone away traveling around the world and how David simply hadn't grasped her pain at missing him or her anxiety, worrying about what was happening. She'd hated him for that, thinking that if only he tried a little harder, he could understand. What Babe was saying was that he couldn't, any more than she could understand how he could stay with her and sleep with another woman.

"But the fact he didn't always understand me didn't mean I'd have an affair with someone else," she said.

"He was a man; you're a woman. We're different." Babe shrugged. "For us, love is a huge part of our lives; for them, it's a segment. They have many segments. Think of it this way: was there ever another man in your life who was a better lover than David?" Babe said.

The conversation was moving into wildly shocking waters, Ingrid thought in alarm. "Em, Babe . . ."

"No, bear with me," said Babe. "We've all loved someone and thought perhaps that the previous fellow was a better lover— hopeless in every other respect, maybe a terrible friend, a terrible conversationalist, stupid, but good in bed."

"And . . . ?" said Ingrid.

"And," said Babe, "you sit there and imagine, what if this previous fellow had been like David, except better in bed—" She stopped, seeing Ingrid's horrified face. "I'm not talking about David, but it's an idea I want you to consider. A woman makes do with the package she has. But a man wants that package plus the little bit extra that the previous girl had."

"He wants it all," Ingrid said flatly. "If he can't get it all with you, he gets an extra helping from someone else, and *then* he has the whole package."

"Precisely."

"Do you talk about this sort of thing at Sheltering Pines?" asked Ingrid.

"We talk about everything," said Babe. "Well, some of us do. The rest talk about things like young people running wild and driving too fast, and how grandchildren aren't the way they used to be, and how the money is running out. But some of us do talk about things like this, and the consensus among those still in possession of our marbles is that love is about putting up with the package you've got."

"Right."

The waitress came with the food, and they both stared at it silently.

"So, David wasn't happy with the sex part of our package?" Ingrid said, once the waitress had left.

"I doubt that very much," said Babe. "That was just an example. Perhaps another woman gave him one other thing that you couldn't. But she still wasn't you, and that was why he stayed with you."

"But do you *know* this?" Ingrid asked. "Did he talk to you about it?"

"No, he'd never share anything like that with me," said Babe. "He knew damn well how much I love you. I'd have kicked his backside for him, don't think I wouldn't. Ingrid, love, you'll torment yourself forever if you try to find out why, because you can't find out. He's gone, you can't ask him."

"But if I knew who she was—"

"If you knew who she was, you'd be even more tormented, thinking that she was funnier, younger, better at making muffins. Remember," Babe said, as a thought came to her, "having affairs was in his blood, you know. Blood will out. His father, Andrew, wasn't a faithful man."

"I always thought as much," said Ingrid, "but nobody ever told me for sure."

"Andrew was a decent man, there wasn't a bad bone in his body; but he couldn't keep his hand out of the sweetie jar. He approved of you," Babe said, smiling, and Ingrid could see she'd gone back in time. "He thought you were marvelous. There had been one other woman David was very involved with—wonderful girl, I loved her, but she probably wasn't right for David. He needed someone like you."

"Kathryn, was it?" said Ingrid. She'd heard about Kathryn, a sweet girl David had brought to many dances as a youngster. He'd thought of marrying her, he'd said.

"Lord, no! Not Kathryn, the one after her—Star Bluestone."

"I never heard him mention her," said Ingrid.

"You'd have liked her," Babe went on. "Very wise, even though she was young."

"Do you think it could have been her?" Ingrid said, struck by the thought. "He was having an affair with her?"

"No," said Babe firmly. "But she was an interesting woman. David's mother said she was a white witch, could see into the future and suchlike. David used to get very upset when she said that. We might be a long way from the Salem trials, but the old magic still frightens the bejaysus out of most people."

"Was she a witch?" asked Ingrid, fascinated. She couldn't imagine David being involved with a woman like that. He was straight as an arrow, never so much as read his horoscope, and thought feng shui was rubbish, and she could remember him changing channels when a woman came on the *Late Late Show* and talked about seeing angels.

"No, but she had that long white-blond hair and she was very into herbs and suchlike; that's enough for most people."

"White-blond hair?" repeated Ingrid. "There was a woman like that at his funeral. I saw her: Molly's friend Natalie fainted, and the woman was beside her, all in white—very bizarre for a funeral."

"She did wear a lot of white," Babe mused, then glanced up at Ingrid, who looked bleak.

"I keep finding out more things about David that I never knew," Ingrid said sadly. "What else will I find out?"

Babe shook her head. "You knew the real David," she said briskly. "People have secrets, that's all."

"I don't have secrets," Ingrid countered.

"Course you do! We all do," Babe said. "Just think how boring we'd be if we didn't."

Nineteen

The Past

DAVID

As soon as he heard her name—a name he hadn't heard spoken for many years—the hairs stood up on the back of David Kenny's neck.

"The woman who makes them is called Star Bluestone," said Lena, smoothing a tapestry out on the table in his office. "She's a fascinating person and the tapestries are just beautiful."

Lena was telling him about her newest find, a craftswoman who lived on the outskirts of Ardagh in a windswept cottage on the coast, where she ran a small business producing exquisite tapestries.

"She started off making the dyes herself," Lena explained, detailing the production process as she would for any new line she was trying to sell to David. "Like woad, for example. Did you know it's not some mythical paint people put on their faces in pre-Christian times? It's actually a dye made out of this cabbage-like flower. She grows it in her garden—she showed me. She's so knowledgeable; it's fascinating to hear her talk about it all. As the line expanded, making all the dyes became too difficult and time-consuming, so she buys some from abroad now. But they're still handmade," went on Lena. "There is nothing synthetic in Bluestone tapestries, so that's very good from a 'green' point of view. As you can see, the tapestries themselves are lovely. Sort of mystical, aren't they? She's incredibly creative. What do you think? I've got some more to show you, if you want to see them."

"That would be great," David said, managing not to sound even a little shocked at the mention of Star's name. He didn't want anyone to know about their involvement in the past. "Keep yourself to yourself" was a good motto; not one that his father had taught him, but one that David had learned along the way.

The tapestry Lena had unrolled onto the table was a seascape, a rendition of the Twelve Apostles, the rocks that jutted out of the sea near Star's home. David had seen them many times, and here, with her wonderful embroidery, Star had made them look almost like sea creatures rising out of the foam.

"I took pictures of the house and of her," Lena went on. "I was just thinking that we could do a brochure. You know, make it a little bit different from the way they sold them in the craft shop where I found them. It's very cute, the craft shop, actually. Lots of pottery, a few horrendous paintings, some nice watercolors, but nothing else we could use, nothing like this. These are the gems."

David nodded and pretended to look at the second tapestry, which showed a little house hidden in the woods; but all the while his eyes were drawn to the pictures Lena had laid down on the table. The pale blue shingle house he remembered so well and the picture of Star herself shook him. She looked as if she hadn't aged. There was still something very exotic about her, even though she was dressed in faded jeans and an old T-shirt—clearly what she'd happened to be wearing when Lena had called in.

"She didn't want to pose, I can tell you that," Lena said. "But I begged her. I said that at Kenny's, we believe art is about the artist, too."

"Absolutely," David said. "I like her work; I think it would be good to stock these tapestries. Can you talk to her about terms?"

"Don't you want to meet her yourself?" Lena asked, surprised.

"There's no need," David said. "You're a director now, Lena." Lena had just been appointed to the board, so he made it sound as if this was part of her new brief, rather than his trying to avoid meeting someone.

"Of course," Lena said, pleased.

When Lena had gone, David still felt unsettled.

It had been well over thirty years since he'd seen Star. So much had happened since. He'd taken over Kenny's; he'd married Ingrid and had two beautiful children. Molly was in her first year of college, Ethan was playing lots of sports at school and not doing much else, and Ingrid—well, Ingrid was one of the most recognized people in the country. So David had done well for himself.

But buried inside him was a sense of shame about the past, a feeling that he hadn't done the right thing by Star Bluestone.

He'd loved her, no doubt about that. Adored her. Back then, he used to write poetry, inspired by her beauty, her wisdom, her wild sexual energy.

But he'd known they were too young and too different. Their sort of love wouldn't have coped with being poor and struggling to pay a mortgage, waking in the night with a colicky baby. He couldn't imagine Star doing anything so mundane, even though she was pretty practical around the house and grounds that she and her mother owned. That was how he remembered her: hair flying as she helped her mother in the garden, the pair of them digging away at some plant, hatless no matter what the weather, laughing, rejoicing, even if it rained. While everyone else David knew hurried indoors as soon as the first drops began to fall, Star and her mother enjoyed rain the same way they enjoyed sun: as though it was a gift, a gift they had no control over but enjoyed all the same. *Elemental*, that was the word for them.

"She's a lovely girl, son, but she's different, isn't she?" his father had said all those years ago.

Andrew Kenny had a way of speaking without raising his voice or sounding angry, yet communicating his meaning just as strongly as if he'd yelled it from a megaphone.

Star was too different for their world. With Star, David would stay writing poetry in the moonlight and would never be the man to take over Kenny's. Not that he wasn't able, but Andrew Kenny had invested far too much of his life in the store to let anyone take over the running of it if his judgment wasn't true.

David understood the subtext of his father's remark: *Choose Star or choose Kenny's. You can't have both.*

Thirty-five years ago, he'd chosen Kenny's; but at least once a week for six months after he'd told Star it was over, he found himself driving along the sea road toward her home with the intention of telling her he'd made the wrong decision. His father could keep the store.

But each time, he had turned toward home before the cottage came into view.

It was a couple of years after the split with Star that he met Ingrid. Nobody had said, "This is the sort of girl you should marry; she's clever, ambitious, ethical, strong, and passionate"—all the things that Ingrid undoubtedly was. No, he'd fallen in love with her all by himself. With her passion, her energy, her beauty. It was a very different sort of beauty to Star's rather wild attractions. Ingrid was classy, and now that David was working at Kenny's, there was a part of him that appreciated her elegance, style, and charm.

His mother, Sarah, who was delicate and high-strung, had adored Ingrid from the start. She'd only met Star a few times and had liked her—everyone liked Star; that innate kindness meant you couldn't not like her—but David's mother saw in Ingrid the sort of woman she would have liked to have been.

Ingrid never flattered her or fawned, but nor did she discount Sarah Kenny, which other people were prone to do. Some women, knowing that she was what was euphemistically described at the time as "bad with her nerves," even flirted with Andrew Kenny in her presence. David had seen it happen many times.

He could remember Ingrid's outrage the first time she'd witnessed this, at a Christmas drinks party at the family's house outside Ardagh. Several women in gleaming cocktail gowns were crowded round charismatic Andrew Kenny as if poor Sarah, standing helplessly by with a tray of canapés, didn't exist.

"How dare they ignore her!" Ingrid had said, outraged. "What sort of female solidarity is that?"

David had been startled by her reaction. He'd never really

thought about the way people treated his mother before. His mother was his mother and he loved her, even though he'd had to get used to her taking to her bed when the stress got too much for her. Something that seemed to happen a lot.

"Well, you know, they're friends of Mum and Dad, it's harmless," David told Ingrid.

Ingrid had rounded on him. "It's anything but harmless," she said. "There is nothing harmless about flirting with another man when his wife is right there beside him. How appalling is that?"

It wasn't the first time David had seen this fiery side of Ingrid's nature, but it was the first time it had been directed at him.

"If you're not going to do anything about it," Ingrid said furiously, "I will."

She might have been only twenty-five, but she'd been vice president of the students' union and her thesis was on female equality. Ingrid had swept over to where his father stood with two women. They were giggling girlishly, hanging on his every word. One kept touching his arm, and he was clearly enjoying the attention. David followed at a safe distance, fascinated and slightly horrified at what was going to happen.

"Mr. Kenny," Ingrid said in her most charming voice, "Mrs. Kenny was just wondering if you'd speak to her a minute about the party." She stared pointedly at the other two women. "It's such hard work organizing a party like this, making sure everything runs smoothly."

"Yes, of course," said Andrew Kenny, and moved off. If he was surprised that his meek wife required his presence, he didn't show it.

Ingrid turned to the two women, both much older than she, matrons glittering with jewels. "We haven't been introduced," she said coolly. "Ingrid Fitzgerald. I think I've met both of your husbands, though. Have you finished with them, ladies? I'm assuming you must have, the way you're talking to Mr. Kenny." The women's jaws dropped.

"I should just tell you," Ingrid said, "I'm working on a paper on feminism, and I'd love to interview people who are interested in demolishing the archaic values of monogamy. For instance, latching on to a new man while you're still married to someone else—it's an absolutely fascinating notion. I didn't think it would catch on in Irish society, but I see it has."

Under their heavy layers of foundation, the women went pale.

"Excuse me, I don't know what you're talking about," snapped one.

Ingrid stared her down. "I think you do. And if you think it's good form to come into a woman's house and flirt with her husband, I can assure you, it isn't." And she looked them both up and down, then swept away to where David was watching, just as astonished as the two women.

"Was it a bit too much?" Ingrid murmured into his ear as they walked away.

"Well, I don't know," he said. "I mean, their husbands are very good friends of Dad's, and if they say anything—"

"And you really think they're going to go home and tell their husbands about this encounter, do you?" demanded Ingrid. "God, David, I can see I have a lot to teach you about people!" And she'd hugged him. "I couldn't let those women hurt your poor mum."

He'd loved her so much at that moment for her absolute fearlessness. There was nothing that would stop Ingrid fighting for something that she believed in. It was a heady feeling. It wasn't so easy when her fearlessness was trained on you, though.

"Your wife is on the line," said Stacey, dragging him back to the present.

Star's tapestry was still on the table in his office. Lovely Star. For a moment, he felt irritated by Ingrid. For all she stood for: security, the right person, someone with ambition. The sort of woman who made his father proud of him. He loved her absolutely, but she was the exact opposite of Star.

He picked up the phone, and she didn't say hello, just burst into conversation: "Sorry, David, but I'm delayed at work. An emergency. The Department of Health is having a press conference, and I have to cover it in the studio. I probably won't make the dinner party, I'm really sorry."

"Fine," he said. "Good luck, I'll see you later," and hung up. She was always too busy. Busy and fearless. Sometimes he got tired of it.

A few days after Star had come circuitously back into his life, Ingrid had to go to a ceremony to receive an award, the *Irish Tatler* Inspiring Woman of the Year. She'd been given quite a few awards over the years, but she was very excited about this one.

"I've never seen you like this before," David remarked as he lay in bed on Saturday morning watching Ingrid trawl through her wardrobe looking for a suitable evening dress for the event.

"What do you mean?" she said crossly.

Bloody menopause, he thought.

She hadn't gone for HRT, had ventured down the alternative route instead, using supplements like black cohosh and CoQ10. David, too, had been made to take supplements every day until he rattled. He didn't mind, really, though he used to tease her about it in front of Marcella.

"She's trying to turn me into a young fellow, Marcella," he'd say plaintively, and Marcella would laugh.

"Too late," she would say. "You're too far gone for that."

"You don't normally get this het-up about award ceremonies, that's all," David said mildly.

Ingrid murmured, "Don't I?" and went back to her trawling. "This is a big one," she said after a moment. "Sorry, I don't know what's wrong with me. I've been feeling a little off the last week." Nobody was better than Ingrid when it came to saying sorry. She readily admitted her faults. "I tried on that red beaded dress I love, and it's too tight. I'm not eating any more than usual and I'm going to the gym, but I still look like I've got a big wad of packing around my middle. It's so depressing," she added, more to herself than to him. "I'm just fed up with the feeling that I'm falling apart. When I deal with one problem, another bit of me falls apart."

Her joints were giving her trouble, he knew that, and her neck was sometimes painful because of a displaced cervical disc. That had been bad lately, which always made her cranky.

"Everything bulges," she said gloomily, and put her hand up to her neck. "And why is it that, without anything I've done, the muscles in my neck are taut and the muscles in my belly are flabby? I have a six-pack in my neck where I don't want it. Why can't you decide where you want the taut bits, and have them all nice and loose in your neck and taut in your belly?"

David laughed. "Ingrid, stop. You're beautiful."

She shot him a look filled with a regret that he'd never seen on her face before.

"You know," she said, "I never thought I was beautiful. I thought I was okay, ordinary; but when I look back at old pictures of me now, I see maybe I was a bit beautiful, and I didn't appreciate it. I had no idea of my beauty or its importance; and now, when it's gone, I recognize that I was beautiful, after all, but I was too busy worrying about my looks to appreciate them."

"Yeah," he said with a sigh, and got out of bed. There was no point trying to rest now.

Putting on his dressing gown, he went downstairs and turned on the sports channel. Moaning about bad backs was one thing, but moaning about getting old was something he hated. He feared aging. Marcella often joked that men didn't get older, they aged well, like fine wine; but she was wrong. Men got old too, and they hated it just as much as women did. If Ingrid—solid, reliable, loyal, wonderful Ingrid—thought she was getting old, then he was too. He didn't want to get old. There was so much he wanted to do, so much.

That night, Ingrid wore not the red dress but a silvery one, some sort of silk taffeta thing with a bit of a fishtail that made her look mermaidy. Her hair was all curled tenderly around her neck. She looked as lovely as ever, he thought.

The awards ceremony was being held in the Mansion House, the lord mayor's residence, and a car arrived to drive them there.

"Hello, Mrs. Fitzgerald," said the driver politely to Ingrid. "And Mr. Fitzgerald."

David felt his jaw tighten. He wasn't Fitzgerald, he was Kenny—Mr. Kenny. He wasn't some appendage of Ingrid's.

"Relax." In the car, he felt Ingrid's soft hand take his, and she whispered to him, "Relax, Mr. Fitzgerald."

She thought it was funny? He stared out the window moodily and wished he weren't going.

At the ceremony, a beautiful girl from the magazine welcomed them and led them to their table. There were place names and they hadn't been put beside each other.

To David's left was the wife of a well-known actor, as famous for his amours as he was for his films. But the wife, who had pretty, slightly glazed eyes, didn't seem to care. She watched her stunning husband, who was sitting beside Ingrid, flirt with other women at the table and yet seemed content. Perhaps she didn't mind sharing him, didn't mind being expected to walk three steps behind. David wouldn't really have wanted Ingrid to be like that, but the idea was still somehow appealing.

The woman perked up mildly when she heard that David owned Kenny's. "Oh, I love that place," she said. "The organic night cream is fabulous. I love it. I'm truly into organic stuff. I was thinking of starting my own line."

"Really," said David absently, watching Ingrid talking to the famous actor as his equal, which was more than the actor's wife set herself up to be.

The placement of the people around the table said so much. The guests of stellar importance were seated beside one another, because they were part of a special club. Even if they didn't know one another, they shared the experiences and problems of being famous—having complete strangers come up to them as if they knew them, having fans think they owned them. Of course, the famous actor faced this all over the world, while Ingrid was only known in Ireland; still, it was similar. David and the actor's wife, however, were demoted to the appendage, or consort, department. Suddenly it rankled so badly that he wanted to walk out, just to prove the point. He was an important person in his own right, not just Ingrid's significant other.

David had been to many events over the years with Ingrid, and he'd never felt like this before. Was this part of getting old, too, this dissatisfaction with everything, knowing that when he was gone, all that remained would be Kenny's? When Ingrid was gone, her name would be on this award, her face would be in photographs on the television station's wall and all the places where she had made her mark. Her job meant that she could leave some other sort of legacy, whereas his name would more quickly be forgotten.

Ingrid smiled at him many times across the table, giving him the *Are you all right, darling, I'm so sorry we're sitting apart from each other* look he recognized after so many years together. But he was angry with her. He knew it wasn't her fault, that it was unreasonable, but he was still angry.

When she went up to accept her award, she spoke strongly about women who had inspired her, and talked about her belief in the importance of women being kind to other women and mentoring them. "Men do it very successfully. So should we," she said.

Everyone laughed and cheered; and then at the end, she thanked her family and David, without whom none of this would be possible.

And David, who should have been happy and proud, still felt bitterly angry. He wished she'd left him out of the speech by mistake. He wanted to be angry with her for something. He didn't know why, but everything felt wrong, and he had no idea what would make it right.

The following Monday morning, a girl at the perfume counter smiled flirtatiously at David as he walked past. He smiled back. It was a reflex; he smiled at all the staff. But there was something about this girl, Rosemary. She didn't look like a Rosemary, which seemed to him a gentle, old-fashioned type of name. This girl was anything but old-fashioned. Hot stuff, as his father might have said.

Andrew Kenny had liked hot stuff, the sorts of girls who were the opposite of his own wife. There had been a Brazilian lady once, wife of a Latin American business associate. Chiara, she was called. Up to then, David hadn't thought of married women having affairs with their husbands' tacit approval, but Chiara changed that. She was free, easy, and her husband must have known what she was doing.

David found this incredible. He had no point of reference for it. His mother had never given his father a moment's doubt; it wasn't the sort of thing she did. When he thought about it, and that wasn't often, David was almost surprised he'd been born. He couldn't imagine his mother in the throes of passion.

Ingrid had certainly never given him a moment's doubt, for all that she was beautiful and much admired. But Ingrid's looks weren't the hot, flirtatious type that would lead a man on. Besides, Ingrid was a deeply moral woman and utterly loyal. She would die rather than be with another man, die rather than betray their family.

It was different for women, David reasoned; most women were driven by straightforward desires to keep their mates and protect their families. But men were driven by more complex evolutionary needs, and those didn't have to interfere with the family or the job of protecting the people they loved, did they?

He slowed down and smiled over his shoulder again at Rosemary. She was dark haired, with a lovely tan. That was what had reminded him of the long-ago Chiara; even wearing her black beautician's outfit, Rosemary looked amazing. The simple tunic top clung in all the right places. Yes, his father would have approved.

"Hello, Mr. Kenny," she said breathlessly. "Would you like to try our new fragrance?"

David stopped and shook his head. "No, thank you," he said. "My wife might wonder if I came home smelling of"—he looked at the bottle carefully—"Honeyz."

This time, he favored Rosemary with a more paternalistic smile. He could see her becoming flustered, as if she'd overstepped some invisible line. She hadn't really; but David knew better than to mess around on his own doorstep.

"Are you enjoying working here, Rosemary?" he asked.

"Oh yes, Mr. Kenny," she said.

"Good. I like the staff to feel happy," he said, and walked on.

No, his dad had taught him a lot of things about the business, and chief among them was never to dally with anyone who worked at Kenny's. "Don't dally with anyone" would have made more sense, but that was impossible.

He'd been scared out of his mind the year before when Ingrid, the whole office of *Politics Tonight,* and indeed the whole of the country had been agog over a murder case involving a married school headmaster and several teacher girlfriends. The headmaster was the accused, the murder victim was his alleged girlfriend and one of his staff, and his alibi centered upon another female staff member. Ingrid, who wasn't easily shocked, had been horrified, shocked on behalf of the dead woman and shocked on behalf of the headmaster's bewildered wife, who'd known nothing until the police came to arrest her husband.

It was the sort of case Ingrid disliked working on because she felt there was no way to report it except sensationally, and she loathed sensationalism.

"How could she not have known?" she said to David one evening as they sat at home over dinner. "She must have suspected; there had to be something. He'd need a motorbike with a jet engine attached to get round to them all."

She'd been so fired up about it, she put down her fork and stared at David across the table. "She must have known. *I'd* know," she added almost angrily, glaring at him.

For several terrible moments, David thought that she *did* know, and all the things he ought to say deserted him, leaving only clichés.

It wasn't anything, it didn't mean anything, Ingrid; it's you I love.

All he could think was that, if only he could turn the clock back, if only she didn't throw him out, he'd never do it again.

He loved her so much: loved her, loved the children, didn't want to destroy their lives. Even if the headmaster was innocent of murder, his whole life had been laid open; the whole world could see his infidelities. David felt sick to his stomach at the thought of the same thing happening to him. Not that he'd murder anyone,

God, but imagine it all coming out. And stranger things had happened. Ingrid was a public figure. Her picture was in the papers if they went to a film premiere or award ceremony.

"Sorry," Ingrid muttered. "I'm getting carried away. You poor love, having to deal with me coming home at night, fired up about other people's injustices. It's just this case is driving me nuts. So, tell me about your day."

And David let out a breath, gently, carefully, in case she realized he'd been holding it in.

"Oh, nothing much to tell," he said. Thank you, thank you, thank you, he whispered inside his head. That's it, never again, no quick flings on business trips abroad, nothing, ever. Look at all you've got, look at all you could lose, don't do it. "I love you, you know that," he said to Ingrid.

"You're so sweet," she said. "I'm being the crazy journalist wife, and you still love me. Thank you."

He hadn't meant to after that, really hadn't. It was just the opportunities had been there. A trip away, a hotel room, a woman who smiled admiringly at him. He recalled an Internet joke he'd received about the differences between men and women:

Why do women cheat? followed by a litany of convoluted reasons.

Why do men cheat? Because the opportunity presents itself occasionally.

Then he met Steffi. And after Steffi, everything was different.

It was lunchtime in the Hatbox Café, and David, who sometimes had an early sandwich there before the rush, was holding his tray and his newspaper, looking for somewhere to sit. He spied Claudia at a small table at the window.

"David, this is my sister, Steffi," Claudia said as David bent to put his tray on the table next to hers. When he straightened up, the girl sitting with Claudia put a hand forward to shake his, and he found himself staring into an exquisite little face with wide-spaced blue eyes and a smile just as bright as Claudia's. While Claudia was dark—he later found out that she took after their father—Steffi was a true blonde like their mother, with the most amazing hair, long and silky as a swedish model's. She was older than Claudia, probably midtwenties, but somehow looked younger. Like a fairy from the Tinker Bell products they sold at the till in the children's department, David thought admiringly.

"How lovely to meet you. I've heard so much about you. Claudia never stops talking about how wonderful you are," she said guilelessly, and David, used to people being pleased to see him because of some scheme they wanted to run by him, felt himself melt.

"I haven't heard anything about you," he said, and moved his tray from the table next door to theirs. "Which is a terrible state of affairs. Where have you been hiding her, Claudia? Kenny's needs gorgeous creatures like Steffi around."

Steffi laughed happily. She had a light, melodious laugh, not like Claudia's effervescent giggle. Definitely Tinker Bell, he decided.

"Steffi dropped by to show me her new car," Claudia said. "She just got it yesterday."

"It's ten years old and it's a lovely silvery blue," said Steffi excitedly. "But it makes a very strange noise when you go up hills. A sort of clanking. I don't know why. Do you think it's all right, or should I go back to the man I got it from? I haven't a clue about cars."

"I'll have a look at it for you," said David.

Steffi put her small hand on his arm, and he felt a frisson of excitement. "That would be so kind of you," she said.

And David, who'd been talking to a somber accountant all morning about cash-flow projections, felt ten feet tall.

He'd looked at the car that evening; and somehow, because Ingrid was going to be out late, it seemed natural to take Claudia and Steffi for a dish of pasta afterward. They all chatted and laughed, and it was all very innocent, David told himself.

He had several glasses of wine, and Steffi insisted on dropping him home because he shouldn't drive.

"Just drop me at a taxi stand," David said.

"Goodness no, you've been so kind to me, I'll take you right home," she said. "You can tell me how I'm driving. It's ages since I had a lesson, and I'm very bad on hill starts."

If only Claudia hadn't said she needed to grab a few groceries and would meet Steffi later at the flat they shared, it wouldn't have happened.

Sitting in her small car outside his house, a house he knew was empty, David planted a kiss on Steffi's soft cheek and found himself asking her out to dinner again, alone.

"I'd love that," she said, eyes wide like a fawn's.

There was nothing overtly sexy about Steffi. With her innocent blue eyes and curtain of blond hair, she was the maiden waiting for her champion to come, and David fell at her feet. Steffi never demanded anything of him, never.

She simply wanted to be with him. It was heady, exciting, and hugely sexually thrilling. It took so much longer to get aroused these days, and although he'd never said anything about it to Ingrid, it upset him. But with Steffi, he was ready in an instant.

It wasn't her youth, he told himself, particularly when he had nightmares about Ingrid finding out. It was her gentle compliance. She was naïve and charming, and perfectly willing to phone the flower shop where she worked and tell them she couldn't come in when David had to go away on business and asked her to accompany him.

When he was with her, he felt the power and energy he'd had when he was a young man. But as soon as he left her, the guilt would set in.

Ingrid would be devastated by his betrayal. His other amours had been short-lived, but this wasn't. Six months became a year and counting. He knew that no woman would want her husband to have an affair, but he imagined trying to explain this one to Ingrid and knew that, while he'd have had some hope of repairing their marriage after a short, purely sexual fling, his relationship with Steffi would mean the divorce courts. Two years with a very young woman who was the polar opposite of Ingrid was indefensible. It would destroy Ingrid and their marriage. Forever.

Twenty

Do what makes you happy. Tell the people you love that you love them. Forget about waiting for a rainy day. Do it now.

Ingrid's new hairstyle caused ructions in the press.

First, it made headlines: "Short Sharp Shock for Ireland's Queen of Politics."

Next came the feature pieces in which women with long, curling manes of hair were photographed—unflatteringly—beside women with coolly short styles like Ingrid.

"Women Who Mean Business," ran the headline, followed by: "How Ireland's Movers and Shakers Are Turning Their Backs on Girlie Curls."

"You've started something with your new haircut," said Gloria as they sat in Ingrid's office with the papers spread out in front of them.

"That wasn't the plan," said Ingrid, putting on her glasses to peer more closely at a photo of herself with her new hairstyle interviewing a politician.

Her hair was still blond; but instead of flowing gently around her shoulders, it was cropped close to her head, so her bone structure and intelligent eyes were what people noticed, not a mass of hair. It suited her incredibly well, she had to admit, although it worked better because of the weight she'd lost.

This had all come about after that night with Marcella, Carla, and Nikki, when seeing the older, skinny woman with the face-lift and the Barbie hair had made Ingrid shudder at the thought of aging badly.

Her hairdresser had refused to do it at first. "You'll sue me," he said, clutching his scissors close to his chest.

"I won't," said Ingrid, folding up the picture of Judi Dench she'd brought in as inspiration. "If you don't do it, I'll go home and hack it off myself, and then come back for you to fix it."

"You've lost it totally," he groaned. "C'mere. Let me at you— but don't say I didn't warn you. You could go shorter by degrees, not whack it all off in one go."

"I like the idea of whacking it all off in one go," she said. "Zero tolerance for hair."

"If this starts a trend, we're in trouble," he went on gloomily. "Just because you have decent bone structure doesn't mean everybody else has. The place will be jammed with moon-faced women wanting Ingrid Fitzgerald haircuts, and they'll look like the Teletubbies when they get them."

Despite herself, Ingrid laughed. "I've never started a trend in my life," she said. "And you're being very cruel to other women. Who cares what they look like with short hair as long as they like it themselves? Life isn't a catwalk, and real women aren't models."

"So says you," he replied.

Sure enough, a few days after Ingrid appeared on *Politics Tonight* with her new haircut, the papers were predicting a rush for short, sharp cuts.

"It's freeing," Ingrid said to Gloria, rubbing her hands through the sleek, spiky hair. "No effort at all—just wash, dry for five minutes, rub some wax into the ends, and I'm ready. Should have done it years ago."

They'd just come out of a meeting about the next day's program. It was going to be an important show because the Minister for Health, currently embroiled in a scandal about cancer facilities, had finally agreed to come on the show.

The mood in the editorial meeting was jubilant, except down at Joan's end of the table when the producer said that Joan would be doing a report on women who'd been misdiagnosed with cancer, while Ingrid would be conducting the studio interview with the minister.

Jeri, the production assistant, poked her head round Ingrid's office door. "Hate to tell you, but Joan is spitting that she's not getting the interview with the minister," she warned Ingrid. "She's just marched into Jack's office."

Ingrid felt tired in a way she hadn't all day. She could sense Joan's fury toward her, which was an entirely wasted emotion, given that Ingrid wasn't in competition with Joan. If only she would understand that Ingrid worked for her own self-worth and not solely to annoy Joan, then it would be so much easier.

But Joan didn't get that she and Ingrid could actually support each other. They were the only women in elevated positions in a male-dominated world. Men were the senior players, and men played them off against each other. Joan was too busy fighting for her perceived corner to understand this.

Six months ago, Ingrid would have let her be, but not anymore. She waited until Joan emerged from the head of current affairs' office, then intercepted her in the women's bathroom.

"Clever about the new haircut," Joan said sharply as Ingrid walked in.

"Do you think I did this to be clever?" said Ingrid. "I did it to stop looking like I was trying to be girlish as I got older."

Joan's blue eyes, beautifully made up with lashings of mascara, widened at such honesty.

"You've made it clear that we're never going to be able to work together well," Ingrid went on. "I must have been in fantasyland to think otherwise. But we don't need to be having catfights. That's what they want, you know, Jack and his pals."

Joan still looked wary.

"Why don't women work well together? Come on, Joan, you've a politics degree, you can work it out, can't you?" Ingrid asked. "Okay, I'll tell you: divide and conquer. They like us to think we're a threat to one another. Usually there aren't enough women in the top levels for us to have worked out a helping strategy. We're so rare, we tend to view one another as adversaries rather than sisters in arms."

Ingrid took out her lipstick and slicked some on. With her hair short, she could wear bright red gloss. It looked sharp and sexy; she loved it.

"How long do you think I've got in this job?" said Ingrid calmly. "Ten years? Not a hope, Joan. I've three at the most, and then I'm out. You can learn from me in those three years, or you can continue to treat me like the enemy."

"I don't treat you like the enemy," said Joan suddenly.

"No? You certainly seemed to when I came back after my husband died."

For the first time, the other woman's brittle exterior seemed to crack. "I thought you'd gone for good. I thought I had a shot at being the chief presenter."

"Joan, working here is what I know, what I am. I've been here for fifteen years," Ingrid said. "With my husband gone, this is my solace. It might be your solace one day. This job isn't kind to marriages or relationships, remember that."

"I'm sorry about David."

Ingrid cracked a polite acknowledging smile. "Thank you."

"I didn't mean to treat you like the enemy, but—"

"But Jack says that, when I'm gone, you'll be the number one presenter?" Ingrid said intuitively. "That's one of Jack's favorite ploys. Divide and conquer works so well with female employees because we're all so anxious and insecure."

Joan was blushing under her discreet coating of Mac foundation.

"Or else he said to wait until I have a bad day, then strike and get me out? That's his other favorite plan. Maybe he read it in *The Art of War*, although I doubt it; Sun Tzu was probably smarter than that. But if you conspire to get rid of everyone who might be a threat, then one day the same thing will be done to you."

Ingrid was getting angry now. Anger at the world, anger at David and his unknown lover was emerging as anger in general. "What exactly did I do to make you think I was your enemy? I helped you in the early days, that's what I do with all women who work here; and now, I'm simply trying to do my job well. There's room for us all. Women don't need to nudge one another off with their stilettos."

"I'm sorry," Joan said abruptly. "You were so kind to me when I started, and I feel ashamed now—"

"I'm glad you remember it; but, tell me, have *you* mentored anyone yet?"

Joan looked even more ashamed. She shook her head.

"There you go. Start paying it forward for other women. We shouldn't be our own worst enemies in business. Mind you, I clearly didn't do a very good job or you wouldn't be working out how to elbow me out of my job. I took my eye off the ball there." Ingrid paused. "Took my eye off a lot of balls," she murmured.

"I am sorry." Joan grabbed Ingrid's hands. "You always seem so poised and in control, it makes me feel inadequate beside you."

"That's you projecting how you feel onto me," said Ingrid. "Another lesson women need to learn—most of the time, it's not about you. For the past few weeks, I've been trying to hold myself together, not make you feel bad." She ran a hand through her hair.

"I'd love short hair," said Joan ruefully, "but if I got it cut, everyone would say I was only doing it to look like you."

Ingrid grinned, a genuine grin. "Screw them," she said. "Who cares what everyone says? You only get one chance at life, you may as well do it your way. Do you want the name of my hairdresser?"

Marcella couldn't concentrate. The office plumbing system had been fixed, the noise and the workmen were gone, and the office felt like a morgue. There was no chance of Lorcan dropping in to check something, no need for him to sprint up the back stairs and poke his head into her office to deliver a smile.

She'd felt devastated from love affairs ending before, but nothing like this. What made it worse was that nobody knew. She couldn't even sob on Ingrid's shoulder because she hadn't told her about the relationship in the first place.

Everything reminded her of him.

A red dress in a shop window made her think of the red dress she'd worn on their first date.

A pickup truck made her think of his pickup truck, with its giant tires and music blasting out from inside.

Her bed looked huge and lonely when she went into her bedroom at night; it was the bed of someone who'd never share it with a lover ever again.

She would never feel his arms around her, his lips moving slowly over her body—she'd told him it wouldn't work, that his mother was right and he was too young for her. Despite his protests, she'd said their relationship had to end. One day, she told him, he'd be grateful.

"Grateful?" he'd snapped, looking so angry she'd been taken aback. "Don't make decisions on my behalf on the grounds that one day I'll be *grateful*!"

They'd met for morning coffee in a café near her home. Once Marcella had decided it had to end, she wanted to do it instantly. Meeting him close to her office would be risky in case people saw them. She'd known he wouldn't take it well, but she hadn't expected him to be so furious. A guy like him must have broken up with women a million times, surely?

"I've never met a woman so obsessed with age. My age, your age, Uncle Tom Cobley's age. What does it matter?" he demanded, so loudly that the two baristas behind the counter looked around in alarm.

"It does matter," Marcella said, getting quite cross herself now. "Your mother read me the riot act about being too old for you—"

"My mother reads everyone the riot act," Lorcan said. "She's been doing it so long, she forgets we're all grown-ups and can make our own decisions."

"But she hates me," said Marcella, anger vanishing to be replaced by something close to tears. She hated feeling so disapproved of. And what made it worse was that Antoinette had hit the nail on the head: Marcella wouldn't be giving Lorcan adorable babies just like him. Her biological clock had ticked right down to zero. Even if she wanted ten little Lorcans, it would be impossible without the application of science.

"She's right, too. I can't give you babies." The old lady at the next table craned her head to listen, but Marcella didn't care. "I wish I could, but I can't. So let's call it a day, Lorcan. I'd love to have your babies, but it's not going to happen, and I'll spend the rest of my life if I stay with you thinking about that. Eventually, you would too. It'd destroy us. Good-bye, it was wonderful, but it's over."

Before he could open his mouth to reply, she got up and hurried out, and he let her. She so wanted him to run after her; but when he didn't, she knew he understood. A man with a big family like that would want children. He was right in one way—the age difference didn't matter that much in most respects, but when it came to women's fertility, it did.

That had been a week ago, and she was still grieving over him. She got herself a coffee and avoided the biscuits in the office kitchen—incredibly, she was off her food, which was great for her stomach but made her face look haggard—and went into her office with the newspaper. She shut the door, her keep-out signal, and flicked in a desultory manner through the papers.

Finally, she read her horoscope, which was a sign of total insanity, as she never read horoscopes.

> *Virgo. A problem shared is a problem halved. You've been worrying over something and keeping it from those closest to you. Stop right now. Share it and see what happens.*

Marcella picked up the phone. Blast it. If she didn't tell someone, she'd go insane.

Ingrid sounded remarkably upbeat when she answered her mobile. "You'll never believe it: I had a heart-to-heart with Joan, and I think we've sorted it out," Ingrid whispered. "Hold on, I'll just close my office door. We were in the loo, and I came out and said it. . . ."

Marcella listened. Being a friend meant you listened to the other person. Finally, Ingrid finished.

"Ingrid, I have to tell you this," blurted out Marcella. "I've met someone."

"*Now* she gets round to telling me," said Ingrid cheerfully, sounding like her old self.

"You knew?"

"You sort of gave it away that night we were out with Nikki and Carla, when you looked all moony and involved when Nikki introduced us to that handsome financier guy."

"But you never said anything."

"I knew you'd tell me when you were ready. Besides, I felt it was my fault in the first place," Ingrid admitted. "With all I was going through, it was obvious you felt you couldn't tell me."

"Well, who wants to hear about someone else's sex life?" sighed Marcella.

"Sex life? Spill," commanded Ingrid.

Marcella spilled.

"He sounds wonderful," Ingrid said at the end. "Why did you end it?"

"I've explained it to you," Marcella said wearily. "His age, my age . . . you know."

"I don't know," Ingrid said. "Don't you get it, Marcella? All that doesn't matter. David and I looked like we had it all, and we didn't, it was just appearances. So stop worrying about appearances—they can lie. If you care about this Lorcan guy, go for it. You're the one who's sleeping with him, not all the naysayers."

"Wow, I never thought you'd say that."

"I've changed," Ingrid said. "I loved David, loved him more than anything, and you know what?" She paused. "I can't stop thinking that if only I'd known about *her* at the time, I'd have forgiven him, and we'd have moved on with our lives."

Marcella couldn't hide her gasp.

"Yes," said Ingrid. "Life is short, Marcella. David's death showed me that we don't have that much time here, so we ought to enjoy it with the people we love. Go get your Lorcan. Who gives a damn about what anyone else thinks?"

"But you're missing one important point here, Ingrid—babies.

Children, offspring. Lorcan is a very macho sort of man and he's great with children. He's not going to want a woman who's too old to have them."

"Did you ask him?" asked Ingrid, as crisply as if she were interviewing on-camera.

"Well, no. . . ." She had done all the talking on that point, and no listening, she remembered now, guiltily.

"How about you ask him and then decide? Otherwise," Ingrid said, "you'll always be wondering. And, as I know, that's not a nice way to be. Now, do you want to hear my news? It's not as exciting as having a fabulous young man throwing himself at you, but it's pretty good all the same."

Marcella smiled. Ingrid wasn't entirely back to her old self, but she was getting there. "Tell me," she said.

"I may have found a wonderful investor for Kenny's. Coincidentally, that's another thing that came about after our night out with the girls. It's Eric Johannsen."

"Handsome Eric?"

"Marcella," chided Ingrid, "it'll be a long time, if ever, before I'm in the market for a man—"

"But he is rather gorgeous," Marcella said gently.

"He's rather clever, too. I can see why he's so successful. He knew who I was, knew all about Kenny's, and had clearly heard we were in some sort of trouble. He phoned me two days later to talk."

"That's wonderful," Marcella said. "As we say in my business: 'I never met a billionaire I didn't like.'"

His phone was off, so Marcella phoned Lorcan's office to see where he was.

Josie, who handled all the calls and had come to know Marcella, was delighted to hear from her.

"Thought you were off the scene," Josie said with her usual bluntness.

"I was a bit, but I'm back now," Marcella replied.

"Good on ya, girl. He's been like a bear with a sore head this past week. What can I do you for?"

"His phone is off. Where is he?"

"Down by the docks in the new apartment block," Josie said. "Don't know why he's bothering his backside. With the state of the economy, nobody'll buy them now, but you know Lorcan: when he says he's finishing a job, he finishes it."

Josie appeared to be right. Not only were there no people viewing the beautiful apartments, but there didn't appear to be any builders or plumbers working on them either. Lorcan's truck was the only one in the parking area. The door to the apartment complex was locked. Marcella considered her options for a moment, then stood beside his truck and gave it a huge kick. Instantly, the alarm went off.

She counted to thirty before Lorcan appeared, running. He stopped when he saw her, held out his key to flick the alarm off, then opened the door to the building to let her inside.

"I take it you didn't come here to look at the apartments?"

"I came here to say sorry and ask you out to dinner," Marcella said.

Lorcan looked stony-faced for all of two seconds. "I thought I was too young for you, you were too old for me, and my mother was a major stumbling block?"

"You are, I am, and she is," Marcella said honestly. "So we need to talk, but I can't let you out of my life without discussing the problems."

"My mother isn't that much of a problem," Lorcan said. "She's tough, but she doesn't run my life."

"That's not what I'm most anxious about."

She looked around. There wasn't much to sit on, so she went over to a low, dusty windowsill and sat on that. He joined her, close but not touching.

Marcella steeled herself. Being brutally honest in business was a piece of cake; being brutally honest in relationships was terrifying.

"I'd love to have your babies, I told you, but I can't. I'm too old. When you hit forty-nine, your time has run out in the baby-making department."

The slight joke was her way of coping with the harsh words.

Lorcan reached over and took her hands in his. "I'm sorry," he said. "I'd love you to have my babies, too, but I'd already figured out that wasn't on the menu. I'm not stupid."

She grinned weakly.

"I know all that, and I still want us to be together."

"You already thought about it?"

"How could I not with my mother mentioning it to me? But, like I told her, I want to be with you, and I can live without kids if you can."

"What if it's not enough?" Marcella asked anxiously. "What if, five years down the road, you change your mind and hate me for being old and not being able to give you babies?"

"Marcella . . ." He knelt in front of her on the marble floor. "Do you think anything in life has guarantees? It doesn't. We love each other now, and that has to be enough. You might want to dump me in five years to move on to a younger model."

"Cheeky!" she said, but she was smiling, even though she was starting to cry. "You really want to make a go of it?"

His answer was a kiss, and she felt herself melt. How could she ever have thrown this away?

Marcella leaned against the hardness of him and closed her eyes. The sense of him holding her close—that was her home, even in a half-finished apartment block.

"I've missed you, crazy woman," he murmured into the cloud of her hair.

"Missed you too," she said.

The Mariner Pub was where the majority of the television station employees went at lunchtime. Cheap sandwiches, large portions of dessert, and enough noise via the sound system to drown all the plots and gossip made it a honeypot for staff.

It was big enough for someone to be anonymous, and better than the station canteen because the higher-ups never went there.

The last person Ingrid expected to see in the Mariner was Jim Fitzgibbon, David's old friend, the one she'd only ever endured meeting.

"Ingrid—at last!" he said, as she stood in astonishment at the till paying for her soup and sandwich. "I went into the television canteen looking for you, and they said a load of youse from the *Politics Tonight* office had come here."

So much for privacy, Ingrid thought. Any mad stalker would be able to locate her within minutes. *You've a delivery of boiled bunny rabbit for Ms. Fitzgerald? No bother, she's just down the road.*

"Hello, Jim," she said, drawing on years of experience in appearing mildly pleased to see people she disliked.

She didn't have the heart to ask him how poor Fiona was. The last time she'd seen her was at David's funeral, when Fiona had come over to offer her sympathies. Alone. The separation was obviously final. Next up, divorce. Jim had shuffled across from the other side of the church accompanied by the hideous Carmel, replete in floor-length mink. In her wild grief, Ingrid had barely been able to look at Carmel, thinking of the last time she'd seen her, when David had been by her side, when life had been hers.

"I need to talk to you, Ingrid," Jim said now.

He always sounded as if he wanted to offload a shipment of fake handbags. Ingrid had never been able to gauge what David had seen in him; maybe it had just been a case of maintaining links with people he'd known at school. But Jim would never be her friend.

"What can I do for you, Jim?" she asked. He would want something from her, not the other way round.

"Isn't there a quiet spot where we can talk?" Jim asked.

The place was emptying out after the lunchtime rush and a small table in an alcove had just been vacated.

"Grab that one," she told Jim.

He sat and waited while Ingrid cleared away the previous occupants' empty cups and plates, then cleaned the table with a paper napkin. He was useless, she thought crossly, just watching her working.

Eventually, she was able to sit down and began to eat. It was mushroom soup, her favorite. If only Jim would ask for whatever he wanted and go, so she could read her paper and eat in peace. Her social skills were rusty; she didn't want to go through the motions of being polite.

"How have you been?" he asked.

"Fine," said Ingrid. "Coping."

"Is probate sorted out?"

She eyed him suspiciously. Probate was a long, drawn-out legal nightmare. "What's this about, Jim?"

"Nothing," he said, clearly uncomfortable. He fiddled with the knot of his tie. "I know what was worrying David," he blurted out suddenly. "I didn't have the courage to tell you before."

Ingrid instinctively looked around to see if anyone could overhear them.

"The business," she said with deliberate calm. "I know, Jim. As I'm the person with a controlling interest in the store, the auditors have me on speed-dial; I know the store is in trouble. We've been doing everything to try to save it. Is that what you wanted to tell me? That we should sell Kenny's if we've any sense?"

"No." He looked mightily affronted. "Not at all; I wouldn't wish that on you, Ingrid. Don't I know what Kenny's meant to David, to you all?" His red face was very earnest, and Ingrid knew she'd offended him. "It's worse than that. He was very worried."

Jim stopped looking at her and began to stare into her soup bowl.

"I won't lie to you, Ingrid. He was terrified what would happen if you found out. About her."

Ingrid's hand began to shake and she had to put her spoon down. She had been able to hold herself together in the editorial meetings and in her confrontation with Joan; but now, with her husband's oldest friend telling her he knew about David's darkest secret, she felt all her strength ebb away.

"As God is my judge, Ingrid, I can tell you he loved you. Loved you more than anything. He wanted to end it, honestly, no kidding." Jim chanced a look up at her face. "I thought that if the auditors did any of that, you know, forensic accounting, they might come up with credit-card statements and the like. . . ."

"I found them," she whispered.

"That can't have been a walk in the park, if I may say so. But I tell you, it was in the past. He was ending it, Ingrid, except these things take time. No offense."

"None taken," she murmured.

Jim's pudgy hand patted hers in comfort. He was kind—she could see this for the first time. Behind all the bluster, Jim was a kind man; and no matter how hard it had been to come here today, he'd done it because his friend would have wanted him to. Jim knew she'd find out about the other woman, and he wanted to reassure her.

"How do you know he was ending it?" she begged, dignity forgotten.

"He was trying to organize a job for her in London, away from here."

"Maybe he wanted to go with her?" Ingrid said, all manner of scenarios springing up in her head. She wanted so much to believe what Jim was telling her. She'd meant it when she told Marcella that she would have forgiven David if only she'd known.

"Oh no, he didn't. He wanted her gone, believe me. He wanted her gone. He wanted me to give her a hand finding a flat."

"That's what you were talking about that night at dinner."

"A little bit, that's all. He made a mistake, Ingrid, and he knew that. David wasn't like me. He appreciated you, and he told me I was an idiot for letting Fiona get away. He was terrified you'd find out and leave him. Now, that doesn't sound like a man who was setting up shop with another woman in London, does it?"

Ingrid shook her head.

"Oh, and don't forget the anniversary trip," he added, delighted to have thought of it. "You'd been talking about a short cruise, but he wanted to take you on one of those round-the-world ones—three weeks! He was like a kid about it. He'd hardly have been so excited if he wanted to head off with a young woman to London, now, would he?"

Jim beamed at her, and Ingrid thought of her David and a young wan, as Jim had put it. How young was young? And who was it? Babe had said it didn't matter, that the only important fact was that the woman wasn't someone in Ingrid's life. Yet she wanted to know, yearned to know. Who was she, what age was she—was she young and beautiful, with unlined skin and a body that hadn't lived through fifty-seven years?

"Who was it?" she asked.

"Nobody you knew, just a girl."

"A girl?" Hateful words.

"Nobody you knew, a girl he had a fling with." Jim was getting loud now. "He made a mistake, Ingrid. That's all you need to know. She's gone, she was gone, really. He'd told her, and he was trying to be kind to her by helping her with the job."

"Why did she need help with a job?"

Jim pulled at his tie again. "She wasn't like you. She wasn't clever or anything. I think it drove David mad, to be honest. There's only so much of that daft-girl thing a man can put up with. You know, the sort of girl who doesn't know how to change a tire. Fiona could change a tire," he added wistfully. "But she couldn't change me."

"And David didn't like this girlish behavior?"

"Ah, you know yourself, Ingrid, it's very wearing. She wasn't you, that's all I know. That was enough for him. It was you he loved. Men do stupid things," he added.

Men do stupid things, Ingrid repeated to herself. Yes, they did, and then they were sorry for them. David had been sorry. She could feel it.

She wasn't sure why, but this conversation with Jim had eased her in a way that nothing else had. Jim was incapable of telling a successful lie—not one that would convince her, anyway. He was telling the absolute truth. Whatever this girl/woman had been to David, it had been over. She had to believe that. It gave her hope and strength.

"Thank you, Jim," she said, smiling at him warmly. "Tell me, what about you and Fiona?"

"I've burned my bridges there." He shrugged.

Ingrid shook her head. "If David had come to me and told me the truth, I'd have given him a second chance," she said, matching his absolute truthfulness. "You can't throw away a good marriage over a combination of stupidity and what you were brought up to do. Talk to Fiona. She may have moved on, but you don't know. Give it a chance."

"You think?"

Once Ingrid had thought Jim's features porcine. Today they looked appealing, his warm little eyes eager in his face.

"I think."

Ingrid got up. There was somewhere she had to go, someone she had to see.

"You haven't finished your lunch—"

"Not hungry." She hugged him. "Thank you, Jim. You've given me great peace."

Ingrid almost ran out of the restaurant and back to her car. She had hope in her heart again. There was one more person she needed to see: Star Bluestone.

She wasn't sure why, but when Babe had told her about Star, Ingrid had known that Star had some of the missing pieces of the puzzle. Perhaps David had confided in this woman he'd known so many years before. Maybe they'd met and talked often. If David had hidden her existence from Ingrid, innocent though that might have been, perhaps she knew things about David that Ingrid didn't. The very idea upset her, but she shoved it to one side: she wanted to see Star and ask her.

Ingrid realized her knuckles were white. Driving while stressed— was that an offense? She loosened her grip on the steering wheel and tried to concentrate on what she'd say to Star Bluestone when she got there.

Star. What a strange name. It was, Ingrid thought, the name an aging hippie might go by, a hennaed former rock chick with trailing skirts, hair like straw from decades of dye, and makeup from the children's dressing-up box. All ghoulish eyeliner, smudges, and the scent of patchouli oil.

It was easier to think of Star that way. Easier, too, because Ingrid had had Star's tapestry hanging in her hall for at least three years, and not once had David said: "The artist was a woman I loved many years ago."

It was wild and remote out on this part of the coast.

Ingrid didn't like remote places, even on holidays. No, she'd always preferred soignée hotels in cities with culture close by. Museums, galleries, the whole nine yards. David had agreed. Or perhaps he hadn't. Perhaps he'd been lying then, too.

Not that they hadn't gone on holiday in remote places, but there had always been a bit of culture attached: the pyramids, the Grand Canyon, the Great Wall, the Library at Ephesus.

And Ingrid had liked it all, but there was a certain fear in seeing places so huge, so ancient. Beside them, Ingrid had felt that shiver of insignificance. No human could ever compete with this grand-ness of scale. She'd always been glad to get back to the hotel, to sit in a comfortable chair, sip tea from a china cup, turn on the television news, and banish the wildness of the ancient world to the back of her mind.

Star's house was set in the sort of landscape that tourists loved: wild, windswept, a jutting-out piece of land that seemed to hang over the sea. Ingrid knew she herself couldn't have lived out here along a tiny track of a road, with no visible neighbors and nothing but the roar of the sea and the sound of the wind racing through the trees for company.

Beautiful, yes, she'd give Star that. But a person might go mad out here.

Following Lena's instructions—Ingrid had had to pretend she wanted a special tapestry commissioned when she'd phoned Lena—Ingrid turned right after five miles and followed an even more hopeless road, a track that appeared to lead to the sea. On the right, she saw a wooden sign swinging from a pole with BLUE-STONE written in cursive script.

Ingrid swung her car in past the sign and bumped along a drive made entirely of sea pebbles. The house revealed itself when she reached a curve in the drive. It wasn't the begorrah-style Oirish cottage Ingrid had been expecting, but a graceful clapboard house that looked as if it had been built by a seafaring captain in the seventeenth century in between bouts of chasing pirates. *Charming* was the word to describe it, Ingrid decided, and this unknown Star went up in her estimation.

She parked and got out warily.

Anything could come to welcome her or scare her off; these crazy hippie types always had mad animals like ostriches, yaks, or maybe a pet goat with a jeweled collar. But no menagerie came to greet her. Instead, a tall woman emerged from one side of the house carrying a vegetable trug and a trowel. Apart from her Wellington boots—ordinary green, no zany flowery ones—she was dressed perfectly normally in jeans and a gray fleecy sweatshirt.

Her long white hair was coiled up in a knot at the back of her head, and her skin was the creamy, nourished consistency of a model's in a moisturizer ad.

If Ingrid hadn't known better, she'd have put this woman in her late forties; but she knew that this was Star and that Star must be older than she was.

"It's lovely to meet you finally," said Star, as easily as if Ingrid had phoned first instead of turning up uninvited. "Come on in."

Saying nothing, Ingrid followed her into the house.

Inside, it was all beautiful and evoked in Ingrid a type of envy. She'd never have been able to live in such elegant clutter. There were pictures, books, ornaments, orchids being nursed back to health, single flower heads sitting in teacups, floaty muslin curtains that would be a nightmare for dust; and although it was all pristine, not a speck of fluff anywhere, it was so very easy to settle in here.

She could imagine David lying on the bigger of the couches, the one upholstered in a smudgy olive velvet; could picture him holding the model of a ship, admiring it as Star relayed its history, his head supported by an old barrel-shaped cushion.

This was beyond her ken, this exquisitely personal house with its wonderful artifacts, like a living museum. Ingrid had never had the gift for making a house beautiful. She'd paid people to do it for her. Her home was the work of two designers who'd argued over flooring—"American oak is *over*. Walnut, wide boards, are where it's at"—cupboards, and precisely what sort of taps to put on the cloakroom basin: "If you go for anything other than Starck, I will *die*!"

This house was clearly all Star's taste.

And beside the fire—a working fire, not a gas imitation one— were two wooden sculptures that were the exact replicas of the figureheads beside the stairs in Kenny's.

Ingrid gasped. "They're—"

"Morrigan and Brighid," said Star, following her gaze.

"I was going to say, the statues David had made for the store. I was surprised when I saw them," Ingrid went on, suddenly bitter that this woman still had some link with David that Ingrid hadn't known about. It kept getting worse and worse. What other people had he known and talked to, people he'd kept from his wife? "Did you suggest he make them?"

"Oh no," Star said, "I hadn't met David in thirty-five years."

Ingrid was astonished. "But your tapestries are in the store."

"More or less on the agreement that I didn't have to meet him," Star said.

Ingrid finally allowed herself to sit down. Sitting, all the fire went out of her. "Why not?"

"We'd parted too long ago for that. I don't hold with the current belief that you can remain friends with people you've once loved. Been lovers with, yes. Goodness, I have many friends I've made love to. But actually loved, no. It doesn't work. I didn't need that in my life."

"Thank you," muttered Ingrid, relieved. She knew somehow that Star was being totally truthful. It was impossible to imagine Star lying about anything, actually. Honesty seemed to shine off her, the light of the truly good and kind. "Babe told me about you, and I came because I thought you'd had an affair with David," she said quietly.

"You poor love," Star said with infinite kindness.

"I want to find out who it was with, even though his friend said it was over, he'd ended it and was terrified I'd find out. That was probably what killed him, not worrying over the store, for all that it's in trouble. . . ." She knew she was babbling, but Star didn't look surprised. She seemed to be following this strange narrative perfectly.

"Does it matter now who she is?" Star asked.

Ingrid knew the pure rage had burned off her, but she still wanted to know. "Yes, I think so. . . ."

"Well, then, that's what you have to do."

Unusual, Ingrid thought. Most people—well, people like Marcella—would have a counterattack to explain why it wasn't a good idea, along the lines of "But what good will it do you?" Star let you think for yourself.

"Just one more thing before I make us tea. Did Babe tell you about my gift?"

Ingrid shook her head.

"It's a kind of magic in my hands. Let me try on you."

She sat beside Ingrid and took Ingrid's cold, tense hands in hers.

Star closed her eyes and let herself connect to Ingrid's heart and soul. Images rushed past her and, drawing on years of practice, she made herself slow them down so she could concentrate on each frame. A younger Ingrid cradling a baby in her arms, staring at the tiny being with such intensity and love that they made a little cosmos all by themselves. Complete. There was another child, and the cosmos was made up of three heartbeats: Ingrid and her two children.

There was no sign of David yet. Star wasn't surprised. She'd seen this many times in women's pasts, the women who were completed by their children, and the ones who weren't, the ones whose heartbeats were always twinned with their man's.

There was Ingrid holding David in a tangle of sheets, and Star was proud that she didn't feel jealousy at this. She had made her peace with that past many years ago.

Sometimes she saw unusual objects in the images, and now she

saw a crescent moon, druidic symbol of female strength. Ingrid
was strong, strong enough to stand at her husband's graveside and
know she had to keep going, strong enough to keep going no matter what she'd learned. A man was in the stream of pictures: short,
gray-haired, with a clunky gold watch he kept waving around on
his animated hands, and wearing a loud navy striped suit. He was
important to Ingrid, although Star couldn't see why. But he helped
her. He held Ingrid's hands and she was crying with relief, but they
weren't lovers; it was a strange, tenuous link, but important.

"Do you know a man who likes navy striped suits and has a
big gold watch? Short, not much hair?" Star said, still holding
Ingrid's hands.

Ingrid's voice revealed recognition. "That sounds like David's
old friend, Jim Fitzgibbon. He's the one who told me it was over
with this girl."

A woman came into view, young, with long fair hair and the
innocence of another age. The lover. She was in the picture and
then flitted out, far away. It was odd, but the woman appeared
beside the girl Lena had brought out here, Claudia. . . . Star fitted the pieces of the puzzle together in an instant. This was what
she'd felt the day she took Claudia's hand. Someone close to her,
her sister perhaps, who was connected to David. But it was only
a weak connection, like a faint silk thread that quickly dissolved.

Then David himself appeared, and Star could almost feel him
sigh with relief.

David. She'd loved him so much and, since he'd died, she
hadn't felt any peace from his spirit. But she felt it now. Peace
and calm. He was looking into her eyes, his spirit connecting with
hers. In the vision, his hands were reaching for Ingrid's. That's
where he was happy, with Ingrid. The girl with the pale hair
wasn't the one he loved; she was like a will-o'-the-wisp who appeared and then disappeared.

Star tried to let that knowledge flow back into Ingrid.

Sorry, my love.

On the seat, Ingrid felt the oddest sensation in her body, like a
melting calm of acceptance.

Star let go.

"How did you do that?" said Ingrid, sitting back against the cushions, exhausted.

"I let you access what's in you, Ingrid," Star said. "It's not hocus-pocus—it's what all people used to have. Our connection with the spirituality of the earth, whatever you want that spirituality to be. It's probably very strong in me today because of my connection with David, my old connection."

"I'm sorry I accused you of still seeing him," Ingrid said.

"It's all right. I loved him. I'll always love him."

Her words winded Ingrid.

"I don't say that to upset you, but it's how I've felt for years," Star said.

"But—" Ingrid couldn't get a handle on this. "Why didn't you do something about it?"

"David left me. He loved me too, and still he left me. You don't choose who you love—otherwise we'd all be mad about Nelson Mandela and nobody else."

They both laughed.

"It's strange, but I felt him saying sorry," Ingrid admitted.

Star thought about how to explain what she'd seen. *What would you say, Mama?* she silently asked Eliza.

That was more of the magic of Bluestone Cottage: the magic of *place*. Both the druids and the white witches understood the power of sites or ruins where great knowledge had lived; and in this cottage, where Bluestone women had used their wise, gentle magic to help the local people for three hundred years, there was huge, benevolent power.

Not the whole truth, Eliza Bluestone's spirit let Star know. *Enough to help her, because she needs to go away from here with her strength recovered.*

"I saw someone else," Star said slowly. "A woman, a young woman, and she was in the distance in my mind. David was beside you, holding on to you, telling you he loved you and only you."

Ingrid felt her eyes brimming with tears, but none fell. She wiped them with her sleeve. "He's sorry?"

Star nodded. "You felt it too. He loves you and he wanted to say sorry."

"This other woman," Ingrid began. "My friend is supposed to be finding out who she is, because I want to know."

"Seeing the woman won't bring you any more peace," Star stated. "I know that. It will only hurt. Your curiosity will hurt you far more. Leave it alone. He's at peace, and you can be, too."

Ingrid looked down at her hands, examining them. "I know you're right," she said. "I *felt* it, felt everything you described. How did you do that?"

"I don't like to pontificate, but modern religions take away our power over ourselves. We are divine creatures and we have our own power. I can harness it, that's all."

Ingrid wanted to ask more, but she had the feeling—a very strange feeling for a woman who made her living by asking the question "why"—that she shouldn't. This was about belief, and now, after what had happened, she believed.

Through some strange miracle, she'd felt David say he was sorry. She couldn't tell anyone about this; nobody would believe it. That Ingrid Fitzgerald, with her logical, precise mind, would let another woman hold her hands and help her *feel*, in a completely indescribable way, what had really happened in the past with David. Yet that was just what had happened.

The Ingrid of a year ago would have shrugged and disbelieved. Now, Ingrid felt grateful to Star for sharing her gift with her.

"Shall I make us tea?" Star asked.

"I'd love that," said Ingrid, getting to her feet. She began to walk around the room, touching some of the beautiful objects. "I want to know all about you and this place. There's such a wonderful *feel* to this house."

Star smiled. "There's three hundred years' worth of women's hearts beating here," she said. "That's the magic."

Epilogue

Ingrid walked through the store, breathing in the smells and seeing the sights that made it so magical. It was Halloween and, in honor of the day, orange and black decorations festooned the store, with bats and witches whirling up above and pumpkins sitting on many counters. Star would laugh when she saw it all, Ingrid knew.

Halloween was really Oíche Samhain, according to Star, a pre-Christian harvest festival during which the veil between the worlds lifted and spirits could roam as they pleased. Star often talked to her about the pre-Christian traditions, and Ingrid found it fascinating. She'd told Star she ought to write a book about what she knew.

"What I know has to be passed down person to person," Star said, and Ingrid had grown quiet.

She felt sad that Star had no beloved daughter to follow her, although Natalie Flynn went to see her a lot and seemed to be like a daughter to her. But perhaps the magic only came from a true genetic link.

Star had known Natalie's mother and had kept a lot of her things: books, clothes, jewelry. Natalie seemed to love going there and listening to stories about her mother. Molly had visited Star, too, with Natalie.

"You won't tell her, will you?" Ingrid had said on the phone after Molly mentioned she was visiting Star's house with her friend.

"Of course not," Star had said. "That's yours to tell, if you wish to."

Ingrid had no desire to. It was the last issue she'd worried over: whether to tell Molly or Ethan, who'd returned from his travels now, about what had really gone on in their father's last few months. She'd finally come to the conclusion that it wouldn't help them in any way to know about it. Why tarnish their image of David? It might be harder for them to forgive him than it had been for her. And she had forgiven him.

The peace she'd felt at Star's house had stayed with her. She didn't feel rage or anger, just a sadness that he'd died without him ever telling her. Love wasn't the cliché of never having to say you were sorry: it was compromise and moving on. She understood that now.

It was hard to believe that it was more than six months since David had died. In one way, it seemed longer. Yet in another, he felt only a heartbeat away.

She'd said so to Marcella on the phone that morning.

"He would be so proud of what you've managed to do," Marcella said.

"I hope so," Ingrid said. "Now, you. How's Italy?"

Marcella and Lorcan were on honeymoon in Italy after a small registry office wedding. The speed with which they'd gone from getting back together to getting married had stunned everyone, but Lorcan was firm that he wanted to be married. Ingrid thought he was gorgeous and exactly the sort of strong character that a woman like Marcella really needed.

"Fabulous. I want to move here, but Lorcan says their plumbing is totally different, so it's a no-go," Marcella had said.

"Are you ready?" said a voice behind Ingrid now.

It was Star, carrying a folded-up tapestry.

"I'm ready," said Ingrid, hugging her. "Is this it?"

"Yes."

The two women took the escalator up to the café, where Ingrid had arranged to talk to the entire staff of Kenny's at ten past six when the store had closed. It was six now, just enough time to look at the tapestry.

Molly, Ethan, and Natalie were already in the café, sitting at a table having lattes.

Star laid out the precious tapestry on the table beside them.

Ingrid had commissioned it: a picture of the front of the store with David just visible as a figure leaning out of his office window. Made in the warm golds and ochers of the shop front, it was a beautiful work of art.

"Fantastic," said Molly admiringly.

"It's beautiful, Star," said Ingrid. "You are a genius."

Charlie, walking by with Shotsy, who was carrying their tray of coffee for her and tea for Charlie, stopped to admire it too.

"How fabulous," she cried. "I love it."

Star smiled at her. "I know you, don't I? You're Charlotte, Kitty Nelson's daughter." Star had never seen Charlotte up close, although she'd recognized her with Kitty at David's funeral.

Charlie knew she had assumed the usual slightly wary look she wore when people mentioned Kitty to her. But she shook it off. Things were different now. She wasn't Number Two Daughter anymore—not in Kitty's mind and, more important, not in her own mind. "Yes," she said, smiling. "I'm Charlie Fallon."

"Star Bluestone," said Star, and grasped Charlie's outstretched hand.

Visions of sadness swept by in a rush to be replaced by such love, love for a tall man and love for a skinny teenager. And in the background, in Charlie's arms, was a baby girl with a shock of bright auburn hair.

Star's eyes instinctively went down to Charlie's flat stomach. Charlie saw it happen and paled, shaking her head to show that nobody knew. Nobody except Brendan, Mikey, and the doctor so far.

Star leaned forward to whisper, "Congratulations, my dear Charlie. True motherhood is a great gift. One of the best of all. You have that gift in abundance, lucky you. Not everyone"—she paused meaningfully—"has it. I haven't met your mother for years," she added. "Give her my best."

Charlie felt as if she were sleepwalking as she followed Shotsy to a vacant table. The woman had seen everything in an instant. And then the glimmer of a smile began on her face. She'd said Charlie had the gift of true motherhood. She did. Charlie knew that she did. And she appreciated that gift above all others.

"You're not going all healthy on me, are you?" asked Shotsy, putting Charlie's tea in front of her. "Drinking herbal tea instead of coffee?"

"If I tell you this, you're not to tell anyone, okay?" began Charlie.

As the café filled up, Star stood beside Natalie.

"Do you want to come to me for dinner later?" she asked.

"No, I'm meeting Rory. He's coming to pick me up," Natalie said, and she glowed. "We're going out with Anna and Gavin to the pasta place down the road."

"What about Lizzie?" asked Star. She knew how distressed Natalie felt over Lizzie's obvious drinking problem—Des had been anxious that when Natalie heard about her mother's alcoholism, she'd be devastated. But Natalie had handled it well. "Mum recovered," she'd said. "That took huge courage."

"Rory and I were at a party with her and the gang a week ago," Natalie said.

Lizzie had got terribly drunk at the party, and the next day Natalie had gone round to Steve and Lizzie's house, sat down on an armchair—with Lizzie lying, groaning with a hangover, on the couch—and said: "Lizzie, you're my dear friend and it breaks my heart to see you like this. You must be going through absolute hell, thinking nobody knows about your drinking and hating yourself."

Lizzie had gone white, and Steve was bent over with his head in his hands.

"She won't listen to me," he said.

Lizzie had said nothing, just sobbed.

"I don't want to tell you how to live your life, Lizzie, but I think you need help." Natalie had got up and put all the alcoholism and rehab literature she'd collected on the coffee table in front of Lizzie. "I'm going now, but if you ever want to talk about it, I've got a story about someone really special who was just like you, and recovered. My mum. I'm so proud of her and what she did; she showed you can leave rock bottom and find happiness." She'd bent down, kissed Lizzie, and left.

Star beamed as Natalie told her the story. "You sound just like your mother there," she said proudly. "Talking of which, I found this. It was on the floor of the attic. I didn't open it."

"This" was a dusty, yellowed notebook with an elastic band holding it shut. She handed it to Natalie, who took it reverently.

Natalie advice! was written on the outside.

Natalie stroked the notebook as if it were the Rosetta stone.

"I just have to look at this," she said to everyone, and rushed off to find a quiet place. Ingrid was about to speak, but Natalie needed to know what her mother had to say to her.

"It's been a tough six months for us all," Ingrid said, looking out at the sea of faces watching her. "We all miss David so very much."

Beside her, Ethan snuffled, and Ingrid saw Molly put a discreet arm around him. He was like his father, she thought fondly, hated anyone seeing him get upset.

"And we would miss Kenny's if anything happened to it."

The mood of the crowd changed subtly, and Ingrid could sense the tension.

"But we're not selling. I've brought you all here tonight to tell you that Kenny's is here to stay. We have a new investor."

At this, Eric Johannsen emerged from behind her, looking every inch the urbane financier. "Let me introduce you to Eric Johannsen, who is now a shareholder in the company and promises that Kenny's, far from being sold, will be the one doing the buying out of other stores!"

The crowd roared. Ingrid had seen the crowd dynamic in action before. It was like a wave, a wave that lifted the mood until everyone was shouting with delight.

"Your store, your jobs are safe," Ingrid said when the sound had died down. "I'll let Eric talk to you for a moment."

She moved aside and, while Eric spoke briefly about the great plans for Kenny's, went to stand behind Molly and Ethan to kiss both their heads.

"David would be proud," whispered Star.

"I think he would," Ingrid murmured, smiling.

She looked at the store, her store, and felt huge pride in it. Thanks to her, this place was still going, would still be a haven for both the customers and the people who worked there. David had created a big family, and he'd left it to her to take care of; and that, she could do.

In a small office on the fifth floor, Natalie found peace. She slammed the door shut, sank onto a chair and carefully opened the notebook.

Darling Natalie,

I'm not here for you and that's the worst thing ever. I would give up years of my life to be there for you, but I don't have any to give. It's scary, the things you don't have any choice about. You get to pick hair color or where your flat is and pointless things you think are important, and you have no choice in how long you live with your beloved baby and husband.

I haven't always got it right. Understatement! Star will tell you, if she's still doing magic for beginners when you're old enough to come looking for me. But I screwed it up plenty. So don't do what I did, right? She'll tell you. Your dad doesn't really know it all because it might have broken his heart more than all this is currently breaking his heart.

Okay, tears there. I'm sad, but I am coping. I am saying this more for you than for me, actually. Star helped. She did this thing where she held me and I felt peace. I know I'm dying, but I felt an amazing sense of calm. It was like this love rushing all over me, making me think there was love waiting for me. I'm not scared of dying. Really not scared. And, Natalie, I have been scared in my life, believe me! It's going to be okay. The only scary bit is leaving you. I don't know how I'm going to do that. They'll have to pry you out of my arms when I'm gone. You are why I want to stay forever. You, darling, you.

But I won't be alone when I go; I'll be with my own mum.

Hell, tears again. I grew up without a mother, and it was the last thing I wanted for you. The difference is, you got a great dad. That's all I'll say.

If I was there, I'd be teaching you some of the stuff I learned along the way. Not that I learned it quickly—Jesus, no. Nobody learns as slow as me. I mean, lettuce learns quicker. But when I've learned it, it stays learned. Just as well, 'cos if you had to learn all I have twice, you'd be dead—well, that's happening anyway.

I wish I could write it all down beautifully but I have to do it my way, the Dara way. So this is it, condensed.

- *Be true to yourself. Sounds mad, doesn't it? I mean, what's true? But you'll know when you get there, trust me on this.*

- *Trust your instincts. I didn't trust any part of me, so I discounted my instincts too. But when I thought about it, nine times out of ten my original instinct had been right. I just hadn't paid attention to it.*

- *Be kind to yourself. Love yourself. Nobody else is going to be able to if you don't first. It's a hard lesson, that one, but important. If you love yourself, you won't let anyone hurt you. Sounds so obvious, but you'd be amazed how long it took me to get that.*

  You're probably okay. Honestly. Despite your eyebrows/ short legs/(put in whatever's appropriate here). Because you will have something that gives you great mental anguish about not being right, and occasionally it will give your anxiety something to hold tightly on to— that if it weren't for the eyebrows/short legs/whatever, everything would be great. They have nothing to do with it all whatsoever. People need something to worry about, like the 1950s needed Communism and then it was the permissive society. And one day, you will look back at an old photo of you and wonder why you worried about your eyebrows when you had so much going for you. . . . When you do the looking back at the old photo, by the way, you'll probably be dying, and the great truth of life will be hitting you over the head like a sledgehammer that says the young and living don't appreciate it and only the old and about-to-die do. I'm trying to bypass all that for you.

- *Life is what happens when you're making other plans.*

- *Only one person can change your life, and that's you. Don't wait for anyone else to do it, Prince Charming or otherwise. Be your own prince.*

- *Fight for who you are. It takes a long time to find who you are, but when you do, take care of that person. She's one of the most precious friends you'll ever have.*

- *Learn how to tell men you like them but aren't interested sexually. So important, this one.*

- *Be kind to other women. It really works—most of the time. And even on those days when it doesn't, it'll make you feel better inside. And on the outside, actually! Because spite carves out things in your soul, and it carves out things on your face too, the sort of lines that dermatologists say are from the sun or smoking, and are really from spite.*

- *When you're annoyed, don't speak from that place inside yourself that nurtures all past hurts. That will just make it all worse. Speak out of love and a desire to make things better.*

- *Learn how to say no. Practice. Say it at least once every day, and you know what? You'll get better at it.*

- *Sometimes, you can't fix it. Other people, for example, you can't fix them. You just have to decide whether it's worth hanging around until they fix themselves—or if it's worth hanging around even though they may never decide to fix themselves. Your choice over the hanging around, but when it comes to the fixing, you have no power. There's times when you just have to let go. Letting go works for a lot of life, actually.*

- *What doesn't destroy you makes you stronger. I just hope you don't have to go through that process in the first place. But if you do, it's true. Trust me.*

- *Life seems so long when you're in the middle of it, but when you know it's going to end soon, you realize how little time we have on earth. Don't waste it. Live for now. Not for tomorrow or yesterday. Now. You don't know what will happen tomorrow, and yesterday is gone, so all you have is this moment. Enjoy it.*

- *Make your choices matter. Do what makes you happy. Tell the people you love that you love them. Forget about waiting for a rainy day. Do it now.*

- *Get down on your knees every day and say thank you. Even if you don't feel grateful all the time, practice it, and one day you will appreciate all the good things. And that's one of the greatest gifts of all.*

- *It's never too late to stop and change the way you're going.*
  Never. I did, and look what I got—you and your dad.
      Talking of your dad, when you find a love like that and
  it's a once-in-a-lifetime love, hold on to him.

    I'm crying now, Natalie, I better stop. Star wants me
  downstairs because you need me. Did I tell you that? You're
  downstairs with her and I'm upstairs trying not to cry
  writing this. I can't write it with your dad or he just breaks
  down. He's a wonderful dad, but I guess you know that.
  I hope I finish this later, but in case I don't get to it, I love
  you, Natalie. Always have, always will.

                                                          Mum

Natalie searched the notebook, but there was nothing else written there. Still, that was enough. Lessons for a lifetime. She held the notebook close to her chest. She'd cried as she read it, but now she didn't feel like crying. Tears were for sad things, and this was so full of life.

Natalie turned her face up to the ceiling.

"I don't know where you are, Mum, but I'm going to listen to every bit of that advice," she said. "I'm going to make you proud of me."

From outside, she could hear laughter and what sounded like champagne corks popping.

She put the book carefully into her handbag and followed the noise toward her friends. Rory would be coming soon, and she didn't want to miss any time with him.